A GEORGIAN HISTORICAL MYSTERY

LUCINDA BRANT BOOKS

## Roxton Family Saga

NOBLE SATYR
MIDNIGHT MARRIAGE
AUTUMN DUCHESS
DAIR DEVIL
PROUD MARY
SATYR'S SON
ETERNALLY YOURS: ROXTON LETTERS VOL. 1
FOREVER REMAIN: ROXTON LETTERS VOL. 2

## Salt Hendon Series

SALT BRIDE
SALT REDUX
SALT HENDON COLLECTION

## Alec Halsey Mysteries

DEADLY ENGAGEMENT
DEADLY AFFAIR
DEADLY PERIL
DEADLY KIN

*'Quizzing glass and quill, into my sedan chair and away —— the 1700s rock!'*

WHEN NOT BUMPING ABOUT GEORGIAN LONDON IN HER sedan chair or exchanging gossip with perfumed and patched courtiers in the gilded drawing rooms of Versailles, Lucinda writes award-winning Georgian historical romances and mysteries with lashings of romance. All her novels are set in mid-1700s Georgian England, with occasional crossings to the France of Louis XV. Lucinda pulls up the reins at the French Revolution where she lost a previous life at the guillotine for her unpardonably hedonistic lifestyle as a layabout aristo!

lucindabrant.com
lucindabrant@gmail.com
facebook.com/lucindabrantbooks
twitter.com/lucindabrant
pinterest.com/lucindabrant/

**A GEORGIAN HISTORICAL MYSTERY**

*Alec Halsey Mystery Series*
*Book 3*

# LUCINDA BRANT

A Sprigleaf Book
Published by Sprigleaf Pty Ltd
A.C.N. 166 446 153
www.sprigleaf.com
admin@sprigleaf.com

Editing: Martha Stites & Rob Van De Laak
Cover art and photography: Larry Rostant
Design and typography: Sprigleaf
Cover model: Dan Cook

Sprigleaf triple-leaf design is a trademark belonging to Sprigleaf Pty Ltd
Georgian couple silhouette is a trademark belonging to Lucinda Brant
Typeset in Garamond Premier Pro and Gill Sans
Eighteenth century handwriting based on Allegheny Regular

First print edition: January 2016
Also available in ebook, audiobook, and foreign language editions

Deadly Peril: A Georgian Historical Mystery / Brant, Lucinda — 2016 ed. ii

ISBN-13: 978-0987243072 (Sprigleaf)
ISBN-10: 0987243071

10 9 8 7 6 5 4 3 2 1

*for my brother*
Craig

# *One*

CASTLE HERZFELD
PRINCIPALITY OF MIDANICH (EAST FRISIA)
LATE AUTUMN, 1763

*T*HE BEDCHAMBER WAS DARK AND AIRLESS. THE ODOR of stale urine, bloody phlegm, and medicinal, pervasive. Only one branch of candles cast a yellowed haze across the heavily embroidered coverlet from the bedside table. The wicks needed trimming but no one had bothered to call a servant. Focus was on the occupant of the big state bed with its enormous carved headboard—where all Margraves of Midanich came to die.

Leopold Maxim Herzfeld was breathing his last. Shrunken and weak, he was propped up on soft feather pillows. A white linen nightshirt with fine lace at wrists and collar covered wasted flesh, the collapsed veins in both arms hidden from view. He had been bled so often the fat-bodied leeches could suck their fill no more. In and out of consciousness, he rasped and gurgled, head thrown back and mouth wide, straining to draw breath down a tinder-dry throat to watery lungs.

A devoted servant had removed his master's silk nightcap and in its place had arranged a magnificent wig, the flowing locks pomaded, powdered and curled, as befitted its royal wearer. In life, such an artifice to fashion complemented Margrave Leopold's strong fleshy features. In his dying hours, the wig was a gross conceit. It served to underscore the state to which his health had deteriorated since returning to Castle Herzfeld six months ago, and why the whisperings about poison remained persistent.

A thousand candles illuminated the castle's chapel, where prayers were said around the clock. Devout members of the court came and went, filling up the pews. Some stayed for hours, on their stockinged knees, praying for a miracle—that Margrave Leopold would recover. If he did not, civil war was likely, and this on the heels of a decade of war that had seen the country occupied first by an enemy and then by an ally, both wreaking havoc on the countryside and its people.

Other members of the court, who were not willing to leave the future in God's hands, thought it politically prudent to loiter in the magnificent gilt and marble anteroom off the state apartments. They huddled in their court factions, arguing in fierce whispers, deciding if they would support one prince or the other, or remain neutral when civil war came. None could afford to leave the anteroom, for not only did they fear being betrayed in their absence by their friends, their movements were being carefully monitored by the household guard who lined the walls of the long room, and stood to attention at the doors to the state bedchamber.

Many a nervous courtier bedded down on a makeshift cot, sent lackeys to and fro for food and drink and to empty chamber pots. They scrawled updates to wives, mistresses, and daughters alike, who paced in their apartments within the castle complex, ready to flee with their belongings to their country estate at a moment's notice. Some had decided to take the drastic step of crossing the border into Hanover—the only option left to them if they wished to keep their heads.

Foreign dignitaries and bureaucrats, too, shuffled in and out of the state anteroom, wanting news. No one could tell them anything, so they went away again, and sent their subordinates to rub shoulders with the bewigged throng while they wrote reports home to their masters for instructions—support Prince Ernst, make overtures to Prince Viktor, or get the hell out of there while the country's borders and ports remained open.

Death of the Margrave was a foregone conclusion. So, too, should have been his successor. Son followed father, and had done for thirteen generations. Prince Ernst was the Margrave's eldest son. Yet there were those who favored the more charismatic Prince Viktor taking his father's place. But the younger half brother of Prince Ernst was barred from the succession by virtue of his common birth. The Margrave's second marriage had been a morganatic one.

The Seven Years' War changed everything.

Midanich was overrun by the French and then occupied by the English. Everywhere was chaos, battle and bloodshed. The end of war brought relief from battle, but not from hardship for the Margrave's subjects. And further afield, across borders, political and economic alliances were being redefined and rewritten, and not to Midanich's benefit. Many at court wanted a complete break with the old order, to which Prince Ernst belonged, and staked their lives on change. From his palace in the south of the country, Margrave Leopold had listened to these voices for change, and also to those courtiers who recommended the *status quo*. He had then journeyed north to Castle Herzfeld where Prince Ernst was stationed as head of the Midanich army, crossing the drawbridge and entering the main square with his entourage to the rousing cheers of his war-weary people, the obsequious bows of his courtiers, and the welcoming open arms of his eldest son.

Prince Ernst, who had fought bravely in the war, was honored in a public ceremony with the country's highest military tribute, the

3

Midanich Minotaur, a star and garter rarely bestowed. It was the last occasion the Margrave was seen in public. He never set foot outside the castle's fortified walls again. Within months, the seventeenth Herzfeld to rule in an unbroken line from father to son lay dying.

The head physician had no idea what had caused the Margrave's illness, but he was certain it was fatal. Yet the Margrave clung obstinately to life, his intermittent terror-stricken outbursts indication his mind was grappling with an inner conflict known only to himself. His physician said he was delirious. His priest said he was purging his soul of guilt. His son agreed with both of them. But no one knew what tormented him.

When the Captain of the Household Guard reported the castle's inhabitants were becoming increasingly restless for news of their ruler, whispers of poison growing daily more confident, Prince Ernst ordered a second detachment of troops deployed throughout the castle. What happened beyond the thick walls of Castle Herzfeld was of no interest—for now.

The court chamberlain appealed to Prince Ernst to have a proclamation of some sort read out, at the very least to the courtiers in the anteroom, if only to quell disquiet amongst their number. Prince Ernst said the court could wait; death would come soon enough.

When the head physician declared death to be imminent, the prince had the bedchamber cleared of its occupants. The Margrave would spend his last earthly moments with only family present.

At the double doors the chamberlain glanced over his shoulder for one last look at the Margrave, whom he had faithfully served for three decades. What he saw made him turn and pause. It was not that his master was unrecognizable in his skeletal form covered in a thin jaundiced skin. It was that the Margrave Leopold had used what strength was left to him to lift an arm off the bedcovers and point a finger in his direction. Alarmed, the chamberlain scuttled back into the dim light, only for the Captain to hiss,

"Leave him, Herr Baron. He's not in his right mind."

The chamberlain ignored him. He went to the end of the bed, the Captain on his heels. The Margrave struggled to lift his head off the pillows, stare fixed, as if willing his faithful servant to read his thoughts. The chamberlain moved up the bed, even closer.

"I beg you..." the Margrave whimpered, looking past his son who had taken hold of his hand, to the chamberlain. "Don't—leave—me... Not—*with her.*"

"Your Highness, of course I will stay if that is your wish."

"He's delirious, Haderslev. He doesn't know what he's saying," Prince Ernst said wearily, then addressed the captain of the guard. "Westover! Get him out of here. He's only upsetting him."

"Of course, Highness," Captain Westover replied and clapped a hand to Baron Haderslev's shoulder. "Herr Baron, it is time to leave."

"His Highness wants me to stay," the chamberlain complained, and shrugged the Captain off to step closer. "So I will stay!"

"Do not worry, Papa. She's not here," was Prince Ernst's whispered reassurance to his father.

"I don't—" the Margrave muttered, agitated, and fell back amongst his pillows. "Ernst. Don't—let her..."

"I made you a promise."

The Margrave closed his eyes, but he was no less agitated. "That—won't stop—*her*... She—she *hates*—me. Hates Viktor—*all of us.*"

Prince Ernst sensed the chamberlain and the Captain hovered at his back and he swiftly glanced around. "My stepmother," he stated, as if they had asked the question. He looked at Captain Westover. "Countess Rosine is under house arrest, yes?"

"As you ordered, Highness," the Captain assured him. "She is not to have visitors, and no one gets in or out without your permission."

Prince Ernst nodded. "And my brother?"

Before the Captain could answer, the Margrave opened his eyes and turned his head on the pillow to stare wide-eyed at his son, and burst out,

"Control her, Ernst. Do not allow *her* to—to—rule *you*." He let out a frustrated groan of pain and shut tight his eyes again. "Oh God, let this torment end!"

"Be still, Papa," the Prince replied, giving his father's hand a squeeze. He again looked to the Captain and the chamberlain. There were tears in his eyes. "For pity's sake. Allow us these last few moments alone!"

Both men blanched white and bowed low. With a nod they backed away into the shadows to the double doors. The room was so dark it was only with the click of the latch that Prince Ernst knew both courtiers were gone. He also knew his twin sister was there, lurking in the blackness, biding her time, waiting for the others to leave before showing herself, showing who was the stronger of the two. Prince Ernst, the great military leader, fearless in combat, victorious in battle, was weak against the wiles of Joanna.

Princess Joanna appeared out of the blackness to peer down at the father who had banished her from court, banished her from society, and had kept her a virtual prisoner in this fortress for over a decade. She watched him tossing and turning in the big bed under the haze of yellowed candlelight and gently patted his thin hand.

"Papa, I'm here," she whispered, kissing his brow then running a cool hand across his damp hot forehead. "It's Joanna, Papa. Your darling little bird has flown her cage to save you. Papa...?"

The Margrave's eyes blinked wide and he looked for his son. But it was Joanna who stared down at him with a loving smile. He was so overcome he began to cry. And when Joanna kissed his forehead again, murmuring soothing sounds, his thin frail body shook all over with great aching sobs that omitted no sound. She went about tucking his arms back beneath the covers, and then gently removed one of the pillows out from under his head, making sure not to

6

disturb the elaborate full-bottomed wig, and so his head lay flat in the bed.

"It's time, Papa," she said.

The Margrave shook his head back and forth, but he was so weak and with his body now constrained under the bedclothes, he was powerless. What fight for life he had managed to muster in his plea to the chamberlain had vanished. Yet, he still had his voice, thin as it was.

"Ernst!" he pleaded, looking for his son in the shadows. "Are you there?" But when his son did not respond he appealed to his daughter, though he knew this to be futile. But he had to try to reach into her mind—to what was left of it. "Joanna. Listen to Pa—"

"I don't do this for myself, but for Ernst, dearest Papa," Princess Joanna said calmly, covering the Margrave's face with the pillow and holding it firmly in place until her father was utterly still. "You understand that, don't you, Papa? For Ernst."

It was Prince Ernst who gingerly removed the pillow, to the sight of his father, small and frail in the big bed, mouth open, and the magnificent powdered wig askew and covering one eye. He gasped in shock, disbelieving his father was no longer breathing. He put his ear to his mouth, touched his cheek and then his forehead. But he knew, he knew as soon as he had looked at him that he was dead.

The Margrave Leopold Maxim Herzfeld, who had ruled the small principality of Midanich for thirty-five years, was dead. Murdered in his final hour. Prince Ernst, the decorated military hero of the last war, governor of Herzfeld Castle, and Leopold Maxim's eldest son, would now succeed as Margrave and rule Midanich.

And his sister, the Princess Joanna, would rule him.

He burst into tears.

# Two

HE CAPTAIN OF THE HOUSEHOLD GUARD AND THE court chamberlain had followed the physicians from the dark bedchamber, to allow their ruler some privacy with his family, and stepped out into the light and claustrophobic atmosphere of the crowded ante-room. A cluster of nobles surged forward in hushed expectation of an announcement. But the wave subsided when, at a nod from their captain, the household guards positioned along the walls took a step forward, gloved hands to bayonets. The courtiers retreated to huddle in the middle of the room, now surrounded by their Margrave's personal bodyguard, and wondered with rising panic if they were to be massacred there and then.

Out from this huddle stepped the British consul, who confidently walked up to the court chamberlain, who had turned to speak to the three physicians hovering by the closed double doors, bowed and said in French, "Excuse me, M'sieur l'Baron, but I have something that will interest you."

"Not now, M'sieur Luytens," Captain Westover ordered. "All official appointments are suspended. Baron Haderslev has more important matters to deal with. Step away and go about your business!"

"Business?" The word hit a raw nerve with the British consul. "All that I had was taken from me when peace was declared. I have no *business*."

"Then you would do well to return to Emden to resurrect what you can, and get your house in order. Perhaps you need a change of scenery—England...?"

"Resurrect it with *what*?" Luytens huffed. "And I'm not an Englishman!" He threw up a hand in hopelessness.

The action caused several of the household guard take another step forward. Captain Westover gestured for his men to stand down. His gaze swept the room and locked for a moment on several prominent nobles who had been pointed out to him as supporters of Prince Viktor—they would be made to disappear once it was announced the Margrave was dead. A small detachment of his men awaited them in the passageway. But then, no one was leaving the fortress—well, not alive—without his say-so.

"His Highness promised restitution and I want—"

"Fool! Look around you," the Captain hissed. "Do you see normality? Be warned. You do not have diplomatic immunity or protection of any sort, so you will be fortunate indeed if you make it back to Emden at all."

"Look here, Luytens. This can wait," a male voice said mildly, and in English.

Captain Westover did not understand English, but he recognized at once the tone of easy command and the look of a foreigner, one who understood French and no doubt spoke it, too. The gentleman who pushed past one of his soldiers and walked up to join them did so with a nonchalant confidence only the wealthy and titled exhibited, and none was better at it than the English noble tourist. Under his fine woolen greatcoat, the foreigner was dressed in brocaded silks, his wig was freshly powdered, and Westover was certain the buckles in the tongues of the Englishman's black leather shoes were set with genuine diamonds. All in all there was a freshness about his handsome person that suggested he was not only traveling with his valet, but an entire retinue of servants. Westover wondered on what charge he could detain him and ransack his belongings. Civil war could not come soon enough.

"You were foolish to bring your English friend here, Herr Luytens," Westover continued in German, confident the English tourist would be ignorant of that language at least. "You have put him in grave danger."

"Sir Cosmo, this is Captain Westover, head of the household guard," Jacob Luytens said in French, ignoring the Captain's warning. "The gentleman you wish to speak with is standing off to our right. The short man with the gold brocade vestment over his frock coat. That is Baron Haderslev. He is the Margrave's chamberlain."

"Not the best timing to deliver a letter, is it?" Sir Cosmo Mahon replied, chin in his linen stock, a nod to the Captain. "Perhaps the good captain here will pass it on, and we can be on our way."

"You said Lord Cobham insisted the letter be hand-delivered to the Margrave," Jacob Luytens argued keeping to the French tongue. "As that is now unlikely, the next best person is the court chamberlain. He will see the letter is received by the Margrave-elect Prince Ernst. You can then write to his lordship with a clear conscience that you did as he requested."

"It's probably not that important," Sir Cosmo said, taking a sweeping look about the cavernous opulent room and the huddle of fleshy-faced gentlemen in sober attire under guard.

The consul said these men were this country's premier noblemen, but by their black and brown wool worsted coats and unadorned shoes, not to mention their dour expressions, they looked a bunch of shopkeepers at best. And not a very friendly lot of shopkeepers! They made Sir Cosmo feel overdressed, and the guards in their elaborate blue and yellow uniforms and shining brass helmets made him queasy. One wrong move by anyone in this room and he was sure they'd have their swords unsheathed, and bloody carnage would ensue. The sooner he handed over the diplomatic pouch, the sooner he could get back down to the harbor, to the schooner awaiting to take him and Emily to Copenhagen. Emily must be wondering where he was by now.

"Just a long-winded letter about trade terms, is my guess," he continued. "God knows what sort of trade we do with—"

"Troops." It was Captain Westover who interrupted.

"Troops? We get troops—*from here*?" It was news to Sir Cosmo. "For what? I mean—Are—are soldiers a-a commodity?"

The Captain thought Sir Cosmo a naïve fool, yet he kept his voice and manner neutral, though he couldn't stop the sardonic twitch to his mouth.

"England needs soldiers to fight its wars, and to keep our neighbor, your English king's electorate of Hanover, safe from its foes. That requires a lot of men. Midanich's army for hire is the best in the world. Margrave Leopold saw to that."

"Is that so?" Sir Cosmo responded, hoping he sounded suitably interested.

He wasn't. Not in soldiers, wars, or fighting. Possibly because he had never had to worry about invasion. The last battle on English soil was almost twenty years ago and against a retreating haphazard Jacobite force, if memory from his Eton days served him correctly. So the last place he wanted to be was in close proximity to a pack of well-trained professional foreign soldiers.

The way the Captain was looking at him was unnerving, and it wasn't only the Captain who was staring. He suddenly realized he had become the most interesting gentleman in the room, no doubt because he had the Captain's attention and nothing much else was happening to fill the time. He ran the crook of his pinky inside the fold of his stock, prickly heat under his wig to be so scrutinized. He cursed himself for believing Lord Cobham that Midanich was on the way to Denmark, as if it were no more trouble than popping into his local coffee house before going home. When he thought of the sea journey from Emden—the ship following the coast, but careful to avoid the string of islands, the choppy waves of the North Sea, and the continual rolling to and fro, it brought the bile back up into his throat.

"As I said, let's leave the letter with the good captain," Sir Cosmo suggested. "He'll know when it's best to pass it on to the chamberlain. After all—given the circumstances..."

"An excellent suggestion," Captain Westover agreed. "Allow me to make one of my own. Leave here as quickly as you are able. I do not mean the castle. The country. Get out before it's too late. I hope you came by ship."

Sir Cosmo nodded and swallowed. "Yes. We are on our way to Copenhagen."

Captain Westover smiled. It was not pleasant. "Then you are almost there." He stuck out his gloved hand, waiting for Sir Cosmo to give him the diplomatic pouch without further discussion.

Sir Cosmo was eager to do so and rummaged in a deep inner pocket of his greatcoat. But before he could hand over the red leather *portefuille*, Luytens snatched it from him, and with such ferocity Sir Cosmo's mouth dropped open and he instinctively shied away. The consul then took the Captain by the elbow, a wary eye on his soldiers, and walked with him a little way off so as not to be overheard—not by Sir Cosmo but by the Midanichian nobles, for he spoke in their native German.

"I didn't bring the Englishman all the way here so he could give your master this," Luytens confessed, handing him the *portefuille*. "Nothing but dull trade documents; Lord Cobham is an officious bore. This fellow," he added, a jerk of his head in Sir Cosmo's direction, "is worth a king's ransom, to you and to me. We can both profit from this, but he is worth more, much more to your master—"

"To Haderslev?"

"No, to our Margrave-in-waiting Prince Ernst."

Westover was surprised and shot a look at Sir Cosmo, who was staring up at the ornate plaster ceiling through his quizzing glass. He scoffed.

"Unless he's got a king's ransom aboard ship, you're wasting your breath and my time!"

"Do you remember the last ambassador from England? It was before the war. Snub-nosed fellow by the name of Parsons. Got himself expelled; his secretary stayed on."

"What's Parsons to His Highness?"

"Not Parsons. The secretary."

"Get to the point, Luytens!"

"The point is, the English ambassador's secretary became good friends with the Prince—*very* good friends. They were inseparable. Reason Parsons got expelled. The Prince didn't like sharing the secretary's time with him..."

Westover shrugged. "So? Parsons should think himself fortunate he got out of here at all. What of it?"

Jacob Luytens suppressed the desire to sigh his impatience and explained.

"It was the Prince who introduced the secretary to his sister, against the wishes of the Margrave, and by all accounts it was that perverted *ménage a trois* that led to the Princess and the English secretary—"

"Shut it! Not another word!" Westover growled, and pulled the consul by his upturned cuff further down the room. "His Highness is not cold in his bed; the Prince is within a breath of being declared Margrave in his place, and you have the-the *stupidity* to resurrect an episode that, were the Prince to come to hear what we were discussing, would cost us our lives!"

Luytens could not suppress his excitement. He almost hissed.

"Ah! So you *do* know all about the English secretary and the Princess!"

"I know enough not to talk about it openly! What's your game, Luytens? If you weren't married to my cousin, I'd have had you thrown off a parapet by now."

"Not so hasty with your condemnation, Westover. I've found a way for you to do something which will make the Prince forever grateful. We stand to gain much more than what was lost during the war. I promise you. But you have to act, and act quickly. You have to detain my English friend over there."

The Captain looked across at Sir Cosmo Mahon, who was now staring at the face of his pocket watch, as if he were late for a prior appointment, and pulled a face. The foreigner looked a fat-witted fool.

"Detain? For what?"

"Does it matter? Just detain him. Make up a reason." Luytens grinned. "Sir Cosmo Mahon just so happens to be the said English secretary's best friend. And there is a female traveling with him, a Miss St. Neots, who is presently awaiting him onboard ship. From what I can gather, she's the English secretary's sweetheart. So we have the means..."

Captain Westover's straight black brows drew across the bridge of his long nose. "The means...?"

"Sir Cosmo and Miss St. Neots. They are the means." When the Captain still looked puzzled, Luytens added as one enunciates to a child, "If you detain them, make them stay here—"

"Arrest them is what you mean!"

The British consul nodded. "Have it your way. If you arrest them then they will need rescuing, won't they? And who better to do that than the Englishman with whom the Princess became infatuated? I'll write to my masters in London seeking their help. A letter from Sir Cosmo will reinforce the need for his return."

A light came into the Captain's eyes. "Have the Englishman return to rescue Sir Cosmo?"

"Yes. He'll want to. And besides, he'll have no choice if his government says he must."

"And the Prince?"

"He'll be Margrave Ernst, and you'll be able to offer up this Englishman to him any way you please. His Highness will be eternally grateful to you, and in turn, you will owe me. I think it a fair trade, don't you?"

Westover threw back his head with a laugh and gave the British consul an affectionate punch on the arm. "You sly devil, Luytens! I like it. I like your plan very well indeed!"

"Westover! For God's sake! This is no time for levity." It was Baron Haderslev flanked by two soldiers. "Why are you standing around sharing a joke when something must be done? Prince Ernst has called for a priest! *A priest*. And the dear Margrave—he has finally breathed his last! God rest his soul. And this lot won't go until they've seen his body. *Do* something!"

The double doors to the bedchamber were flung wide and the crowd of nobles had lost all patience with waiting. They had broken the line of soldiers, who had not been ordered to draw their bayonets and so were doing their best to stem the tide with brute strength. But through sheer weight of numbers, the nobles pushed through the line, and forged *en masse* into the bedchamber, wanting to be the first to see with their own eyes their much loved ruler was indeed dead. And to save their own skins by offering up their undivided loyalty to the Margrave-elect. And while the curious and the loyal supporters of Prince Ernst rushed forward, those who were in two minds, and the nobles who had thrown their lot and their lives in with the fortunes of Prince Viktor, slowly backed out of the room in the hopes of being able to slink away unseen and forgotten in the melee. Once out of sight of the troops, they ran.

A few gestures from Westover and his men knew what to do. They scattered, some into the bedchamber to protect the Margrave's body and the Margrave-elect, others to round up those nobles who had chosen to flee. Another few went to inform their fellows, down in the barracks in the vaulted casements, and out along the parapets and at the gates, that the castle must be secured against egress.

In the midst of this turmoil, Sir Cosmo remained fixed to the parquetry, not knowing what to do or where to go. He looked to Luytens, as a ship does a lighthouse, to provide safe passage through this sea of chaos, oblivious that at that very moment he was being betrayed and cut adrift.

As Westover strode across the room to the bedchamber he barked orders to two of his men to arrest Sir Cosmo. This Englishman was now a prisoner, and to throw him in the cells.

Luytens followed him, saying at his back, "He's not a common criminal—"

"He's no longer your responsibility, Herr Luytens. I'll send some of my men to fetch the girl. There can't be too many Englishwomen at the docks." Westover looked over his shoulder. "And the other Englishman, the one who was secretary here? You're certain he'll come?"

"Yes. For them. I'd stake my life on it."

"Good. That's incentive enough for you to make certain he does."

Baron Haderslev, who had rushed on ahead of the Captain, now stopped in the doorway to wait for him. He had recognized the British consul and wondered what Luytens wanted. The man was untrustworthy. Despite his mother being a Midanichian and his father a Dutchman, he was neither, and he certainly wasn't an Englishman, which meant his loyalties were to no one but himself. A more treacherous individual the baron had yet to meet. His thoughts were interrupted when he was diverted by shouts in a foreign tongue. He heard the name Luytens but the rest of the tirade was impenetrable. It was a tall well-fed gentleman in a tailored coat and powdered wig calling out for the British consul as he was forcibly ejected from the room by two of Westover's soldiers.

"What's going on, Westover?" Haderslev demanded. "Who was that? Why is Herr Luytens here?"

"The gentleman under arrest is an English traveler. He is going to be very useful to us, and to our new Margrave."

Baron Haderslev was intrigued but skeptical. "To Prince Ernst? How so?"

"Because, my dear baron, he will bring us what the Prince and Princess have craved for a very long time."

"What's that?"

"Revenge on the Englishman Alec Halsey."

# *Three*

LONDON, ENGLAND
WINTER, 1763

ALEC HALSEY AND HIS UNCLE HAD RETURNED TO London from Bath to a note from Olivia, Duchess of Romney-St. Neots demanding they alert her the instant they set a foot inside Alec's St. James's Place townhouse. But both nephew and uncle agreed they should wait until morning. They were travel weary, covered in the grime of riding in inclement weather, and the hour was late. Both knew what drama awaited them the next day, so with a nod of understanding, one to the other, they went off to their respective apartments to bathe and sleep off their exhaustion.

However, the following morning as they ate a breakfast of soft-boiled eggs, bread and butter with marmalade, and sipped coffee, neither felt any more rejuvenated for a good night's sleep.

"It's the worry," Plantagenet Halsey offered, pushing aside his plate. "Can't sleep while m'mind is churnin' with all sorts of possibilities, real or imagined, of what's happenin' to those two young people and their entourage. We'll all feel better when we can *do* somethin' about it."

"Yes," Alec replied, preoccupied with his thoughts as he sliced up an apple. "What mystifies me is why Cosmo and Emily were in Midanich at all. It was not on their itinerary, and it's not the usual destination, even for those who travel to the northern kingdoms of Norway and Sweden, or even as far as St. Petersburg. In fact, it's a backwater in every sense. It has a bland, flat, featureless landscape which is constantly flooding because it is below sea level, and there's *always* a gale blowing in off the North Sea. As for the court politics—" Alec swallowed hard. "Suffice that since my return, and with the war, no Englishman has had to set foot across its borders. So it's not a place for the traveler. One must have a reason to go there."

"Your second or third posting was to Midanich, wasn't it?"

"Posting?" Alec huffed laughter at the word. He offered his uncle slices of the apple. "It was my second posting. But it's not where I requested I be sent. I was *relegated*. I asked for an Italian state, and Lord Cobham saw fit to send me to a Germanic principality, and as the secretary to Sir Gilbert Parsons, the most punctilious diplomat in the service. He never wrote or dictated a report or letter the entire time I was his junior that he then didn't have me rewrite at least twice!"

Plantagenet Halsey chomped on the slice of apple. "Perhaps Mahon and Miss St. Neots ended up in Midanich by mistake. You did say Mahon has no sense of direction."

Alec chuckled. "There might be something in that. After all, they were supposed to be traveling on to Berne, which is in the opposite direction. They would be in Switzerland now if Selina—if Mrs. Jamison-Lewis—if—" Alec met his uncle's steady gaze. "If she had not miscarried in Paris."

"You can't blame her for that," the old man replied quietly. "But—"

"Uncle, I—"

"—you do.

Alec put aside the ivory-handled paring knife. "I don't *blame* her. Miscarriages are a fact of life. It's just—"

19

"She did what she had to do to survive that hell of a marriage to a sadistic lunatic. As a consequence, she worries she can no longer bear children."

Alec was stunned. "She confided that to you?"

Plantagenet Halsey shrugged as he reached for a second slice of apple. "I just happened to be there when she let down her guard... Fell all to pieces upon seeing Miranda and her newborn. Holding an infant can do that to you." He gave a huff of laughter. "I remember holdin' you for the first time..."

"Uncle, it's not what Selina did in her marriage that concerns me. God knows I'd forgive her anything—murder—where that monster of a husband is concerned. It's just that she did not see fit to confide in me what happened in Paris. She miscarried our child. Not hers—*ours*. I had a right to know. As it was, I found out in the most public of settings. It was a shock. I was in shock. I think I still am."

"I dare say she was tryin' to spare you the—"

"—grief?"

"That, and other particulars..."

"Other particulars?"

"I've said too much already," the old man answered gruffly. "Not my place. What I do know is that she thinks you blame her."

"That's not what I think at all!" Alec said bluntly, frustration with his uncle's evasiveness making him sound harsh. "She should know me better!"

"Well, my boy, you have a strange way of showin' her differently. You left Bath without exchangin' a civil word with her. A'course she thinks you blame her."

Alec scraped back his chair and went to the sideboard to collect the silver coffee urn off its warming stand. It gave him a moment to collect himself, to cool his temper, and to turn his thoughts from Selina, if only momentarily. He poured into his uncle's porcelain dish then his own, before setting it back over the candle and returning to the table, adding coolly,

"I don't want to discuss this now. It's stupidly self-centered of me to be maudlin over something that could have been, and now won't be." He looked across at the old man, saying gently, "And, it seems, may never be. Though I think that an overly dramatic reaction on her part... Did I tell you Tam is spending a fortnight as guest of the Cleveleys?" he said, abruptly changing the subject because his uncle was regarding him with sadness. "They won't have anyone else attending on their newborn."

"Amazin' how the love of a good woman brings out the best in a man..."

"Yes. So you won't be amazed then when I tell you Cleveley has agreed to be Tam's sponsor for the final year of his apprenticeship."

"Ha! With the Duke's backin', I wouldn't be at all surprised if the Worshipful Company of Apothecaries just hands the lad his seal, no questions asked! So I take it Tam has reconciled himself to his profession and *not* being your valet?"

"Yes. I can't wait to share the news with Wantage that Mr. Thomas Fisher will be residing here as a member of our household. Jeffries will be accompanying me to Midanich."

The old man selected a sugar lump with the silver tongs and dropped it into his coffee, choosing his words carefully as he stirred the liquid. "As I remember it, you barely escaped that country with your life. And I've never been able to prise much out of you about your three years there, other than you were imprisoned, and it was through the personal intervention of Midanich's king—"

"Margrave Leopold."

"*Him*—that you were released and escaped across to Holland. At the time, you said nothin' and nobody would get you to set foot in that God-forsaken place again. So I'm guessin' returnin' will be damned dangerous for you."

"Yes. It will be."

"And you tell me that Midanich is now in the midst of a civil war?"

"Believe me, Uncle, civil war is the least of my worries about returning to Midanich."

The old man sat up. "And you're still not goin' to tell me what happened to you while you were there, are you?"

"Best you don't know," Alec replied. "It would only disturb you. Thankfully I can't tell you. I gave a verbal account upon my return, and not to Cobham, but to the Spymaster General Lord Shrewsbury. And then I didn't tell him absolutely everything. I couldn't. Parsons was also interviewed." Alec smiled crookedly over his coffee cup. "I dare say he was damning of me. After all, he blames me for his expulsion from the country. A great loss of face for an ambassador. Though... I'm not sure what rankled him most: The fact he was expelled, or that he was imprisoned for two nights in the castle's dungeons and thus kept from his dinner. At least he wasn't tortured."

"And you were?"

"Yes. I was given a—um—personal tour of Castle Herzfeld's subterranean vaulted casements. There is a torture chamber complete with medieval implements. Bone-chillingly fascinating..."

Plantagenet Halsey held his nephew's gaze. "Let someone else play the hero."

"You don't mean that. You know I must go."

The old man sighed and nodded. "Yes, of course you must."

A commotion beyond the dining room had uncle and nephew looking to the double doors. The next instant, the doors were thrown wide and two footmen stumbled to get out of the way of a determined little old lady in purple silks and strong perfume, her grey hair upswept and festooned with pearls and ribbons. It was Olivia, Duchess of Romney-St. Neots.

"YOUR GRACE, HOW LOVELY TO SEE YOU THIS FINE MORN," Plantagenet Halsey said jovially, rising to his feet, his arthritic knees making it slow going. "I just wish the occasion for your visit was a less worrisome one."

"Worrisome?" The Duchess pulled herself up short and glared at the old man, who had ended his salutation with a bow. "It's not—it's not—*worrisome*. It's a—it's a—*catastrophe*."

Alec stepped forward. "Of course it is," he agreed soothingly, and took the hand the Duchess held out to him, and drew her closer, to kiss first her hand, and then her rouged cheek. "I won't tell you not to worry. You must. But if it is any comfort, I have already begun preparations for my departure for Emden."

"Emden?"

"Midanich's largest port. I set sail at the end of the week."

"Oh, my dear boy, why is this happening?" the Duchess asked tearfully. "Why is my darling Emily in such a God-forsaken place? Why did Cosmo take her there? They were supposed to be going to Italy to see her mother! Do you think—I can hardly say it because it has kept me up every night since Cobham read me that horrid letter—But do you think—" Her voice dropped to a whisper. "Do you think they are still—*alive*?"

Alec squeezed her hand, saying confidently, because he believed this much was true, "Yes. Yes, I do. And I mean to do everything in my power to bring them home safe. That is a promise."

The Duchess blinked tears away as she looked up into his blue eyes, and for the first time in a sennight she allowed emotion to get the better of her. She let out a sigh of relief and nodded, wanting to believe him. But then she burst into tears, turned away, and allowed herself to be gathered up in the old man's embrace. It was some time before she was more herself. She apologized for falling apart, and was most embarrassed to discover she had wept all over the front of Plantagenet Halsey's fine red wool waistcoat. He told her gruffly not to worry herself over a trifle, pressed his clean white linen handkerchief into her hand, and took her through to the adjoining drawing room with its view of the Green Park. Here he sat with her on a silk striped settee while Alec poured her a cup of tea.

"I've re-read your note several times since receiving it in Bath," Alec told her conversationally as he handed her the teacup on its saucer, then perched on a wingchair opposite. From a deep frock coat pocket he produced a folded single sheet of paper and a green shagreen case that contained his wire-rimmed spectacles. "And I'm afraid it raises more questions than it answers, so I hope you won't mind if I ask you to explain a few puzzling details to me?"

"Oh dear, I can hardly remember what I wrote," the Duchess apologized, sipping at her tea. "I was in such a state of distress I fear I fainted when Cobham announced Emily was being held hostage. He told me—just like that! As if it were the most mundane thing in the world—"

"Insensitive blackguard!" Plantagenet Halsey interrupted, grinding his teeth.

"More fool than fiend in Cobham's case," Alec replied mildly. "Go on, Olivia."

The Duchess put her cup on its saucer and continued, saying with a sigh, "Yes, he is—both! So once Peeble had revived me, Cobham waved a letter practically under my nose, as if it, too, were hartshorn! I barely heard one word in five of what he was saying. Besides, what did I care about the politics of the place, or who was ruling, or who had started a civil war, or what our British consul has done to help— and on he went! You may smirk at my lack of interest in a country I know nothing about, my boy, but none of that matters, does it, when it is Emily's and Cosmo's lives that are at stake! All I wanted to know was if Emily and Cosmo were safe and well. And how does Cobham answer me? He shows me... He shows me—Forgive me, I am not being very strong, am I?"

She thrust the cup and saucer at Plantagenet Halsey and when he took it, rummaged through her velvet reticule for a handkerchief, until quietly reminded that in her fist she had the old man's. After dabbing at her eyes, then blowing her nose, she sniffed and continued.

"He showed me a snip of blonde curl, saying it was Emily's and sent as proof she was indeed being held hostage. And a ransom has been demanded. He said the sensible—if you can believe he had the audacity to use the word *sensible*—thing to do would be to prepare myself for the—for the—worst! Well, of course I fell all to pieces again! So you mustn't take as gospel the details in that letter I wrote you. All that I truly know is that my darling granddaughter and my nephew are prisoners in a far-off land that is at war, and here I sit, unable to do anything, powerless and frustrated, and-and *useless*. I knew you and Selina would return to London as soon as you were made privy to this shocking state of affairs. And here you are, my boy, and already making plans to effect a rescue. You cannot know how-how—*soothing* it is to have you sort through this mess; even Cobham says you are the only one who can help them."

At that, Alec looked up over his rims from skimming through the Duchess's note and frowned. "Cobham said that—about *me*? I wonder why?"

"The man's just statin' the obvious."

Alec grinned at his uncle's categorical affirmative. "Thank you. But why would Cobham say it?"

"I agree with your uncle," the Duchess said. "But as to why Cobham says the things he does is anyone's guess! Not even Selina can fathom him and she's his sister. He wouldn't even allow me to read the letter he'd received from Cosmo. He evoked some official edict about state secrets, and only those persons in confidence— *persons in confidence* indeed!—with a need to know are to have access to it. If he, too, weren't my nephew I'd complain about him to the Privy Council, have him removed from his position as Head of the Foreign Department." She sighed with annoyance. "It is too tedious being related to practically everybody!"

"Yes, it must be," Alec agreed with the twitch of a smile, a glance at his uncle, hoping he would refrain from launching into an inflammatory speech—as he had done many times in the Commons—on the vileness of nepotism within government, on what he called a corrupt system made up of unthinking relatives preferring blood over ability, to the great detriment of the country. Thankfully, his uncle kept his peace, so Alec added,

"Best to leave Cobham where he can do least harm, Olivia. He'd only apply for another position someplace else, and where he could actually cause a mischief. As it is, he can hardly take a step in the Foreign Department without Shrewsbury breathing down the back of his stock. And as very little of significance happens in the northern countries of the Continent to worry us—"

"Except for civil war, kidnappin', and ransom demands!" the old man stuck in with a snort of derision.

"Point taken, Uncle," Alec murmured and dropped his gaze through his lenses to the Duchess's letter. "You mention here Emily and Cosmo are prisoners of Prince Viktor and there has been a demand for money and jewels..." Again he looked up over his rims. "Quite frankly, I find this impossible to believe—"

"That they've been taken prisoner?" the Duchess interrupted swiftly, a catch to her voice; hope rising.

Alec shook his head. "No. Not that. That Prince Viktor would take hostages and make ransom demands. He just isn't the sort of fellow who would do that. I spent time with him on and off over the period of three years I was in Midanich, and such behavior is out of character. It just doesn't sit well with his nature. But, then, he was only a boy... As the son of a Margrave he is wealthy in his own right. So making ransom demands is uncharacteristic, and, to put it bluntly, beneath him."

"Perhaps he's run mad or run out of money?" Plantagenet Halsey suggested with a shrug. "The Continent has just had seven—or is it ten?—years of war. Can't be cheap equippin' an army to send 'em off across the border to run amok in your neighbor's garden."

"Will you be serious!" the Duchess demanded, though the old man's précis of the Seven Years' War had her smiling for the first time since entering Alec's townhouse.

"And there's the fact that most of 'em are inbred. Got to be. They can only marry each other. Insanity must be rife in their family history. So coupled with the lack of funds... Madness and poverty are a deadly combination. Nothin' to lose if your brain cracks. Oh, except y'life. But if you're insane, you'd not think of that, now would you?"

"For a man who abhors Lord Cobham's politics, your views certainly align with his bigoted thinking," Alec quipped, folding the letter and slipping it into a pocket, along with his spectacles in their case.

When the old man winked at him, he raised his black brows, realizing then that his uncle was doing his best to get a rise out of the Duchess; at the very least, distract her thoughts from her granddaughter's dire situation. So he fell in with these plans, adding dryly.

"But I suppose you must. You are, after all, one of them."

"Alec? Are you accusing your uncle of being an inbred madman?"

Alec bowed. "I am, Your Grace. And agreeing that Cobham must be one too."

"Your Grace must pardon my nephew for statin' the bleedin' obvious!"

"Stop it! Both of you!" she demanded and rapped the old man on the velvet knee with the closed sticks of her fan. "I know what you're about—both of you!"

"You do?" uncle and nephew said in unison.

"You're trying to divert me from the horrid fact Emily is in the clutches of a Continental lunatic! But I won't be diverted. Please! Don't apologize." She appealed to Alec. "Just be serious a moment, and tell me truthfully that you know, in your heart of hearts, this Prince Viktor isn't the sort of mad monster who would kidnap a sweet girl and a gentleman who couldn't hurt a fly and demand a treasure chest of gems and coin. Can you do that…?"

Alec did not hesitate. "Yes, I can do that, but—"

"Oh, thank God!" the Duchess said on a loud sigh and closed her eyes, a gloved hand pressed to the little silk bows of her heaving bodice. And then she caught the word *but* and opened her eyes wide. "There is a *but*?!"

"Yes. Viktor has two elder siblings. A half brother and sister—twins. Prince Ernst and Princess Joanna. Prince Ernst is the Margrave you mentioned in your letter who is holding firm in the north. Castle Herzfeld is located there, on the hill of the coastal port. It is an impregnable fortress. Enormous. Thick outer walls, an inner wall, and a deep moat between both. And in its center a magnificent castle, with turrets, towers, and a labyrinth of palace buildings."

The Duchess's shoulders slumped. "So you think it is this brother, this Prince Ernst, who is holding Emily and Cosmo prisoner?"

"Yes. In all probability," Alec said and huffed his exasperation. "But it's conjecture until I've spoken with Lord Cobham, and read the letter for myself. Only then can I make better sense of this imbroglio, and hopefully have a much clearer notion of Emily and Cosmo's situation, and what I must do to ensure I bring them safely home. What is it, Wantage?" he asked, as his butler trod lightly across the room.

"Lord Cobham and Sir Gilbert Parsons, my lord."

Alec had only time to raise his eyebrows in surprise when the Duchess burst out,

"Splendid! I demanded they come here first thing this morning. They're late. Now you will have your answers, my boy, and then we can finally *do* something!"

Alec refrained from commenting that he would have preferred to call on the head of the Foreign Department in his office, and said to his butler, "Thank you, Wantage. We will see his lordship and Sir Gilbert in here."

"Yes, my lord," the butler responded, and with a slight clearing of his throat added quietly, "Mr. Jeffries would like a word…"

"He will have to wait," Alec said, staring past his butler's shoulder and out the window at the blue sky above the Green Park. "And so will Cromwell and Mazarin…"

"If I could make a suggestion, my lord…?" Wantage asked, and continued when his master gave a nod of assent. "As Mr. Jeffries is now your lordship's valet, perhaps he could take the hounds for a run about the park?"

"Yes, perhaps he could," Alec responded placidly, ignoring his butler's self-satisfied smile.

He knew very well Wantage was pleased Hadrian Jeffries had replaced Tam as his lordship's gentleman's gentleman. His butler had never taken to Tam Fisher. But telling Wantage the good news that Tam was returning to St. James's Place as a member of the household and not a servant could wait until he had spoken with Jeffries. But Lord Cobham and Sir Gilbert could not wait. Though it did not mean his two faithful greyhounds should forego their morning exercise, however much he wished he could take them off their leads for a run about in the sunshine. Giving the task to Jeffries would certainly test that man's mettle—having his immaculate person pawed and nuzzled by a couple of friendly hounds. He might even get the chance to peer out the window to see how his new valet was faring, particularly when Cobham settled into one of his long-winded pompous speeches about upholding the good name of the department, *ad nauseam*.

"Thank you, Wantage. Oh, and we will need more tea. Best fill the large teapot."

When the butler announced Lord Cobham and Sir Gilbert Parsons, the head of the Foreign Department, to everyone's surprise but Alec's, wasted no time on small talk and got straight down to business.

"Well, Halsey, this is a fine bloody mess! What are we going to do about it, eh?"

# *Four*

TWENTY MINUTES EARLIER, LORD COBHAM HAD stepped from his carriage to the cobblestoned pavement of St. James's Place to meet a sedan chair carrying the rotund Sir Gilbert Parsons. The two Herculean-sized chairmen had transported the corpulent occupant from his coffee house around the corner, and were relieved when ordered to set down their passenger at the top of the short street. It meant they need not take him all the way to Number One St. James's Place, and up the steps and inside the luxurious townhouse. With a dismissive wave, Lord Cobham sent the chairmen back to the chair rank on busy St. James's Street, and turned to his departmental subordinate.

"You do appreciate what's at stake here, Parsons," Cobham said without preamble, anchoring the end of his ivory-topped walking stick between two filthy cobbles and leaning forward. He took a look up and down the deserted street before continuing in an under-voice. "My reputation and your sinecure, should anything go wrong. Understand?"

"Perfectly, my lord," Sir Gilbert replied in a monotone, adding without emotion, "You desire me to journey to Midanich to secure the release of the Duchess of Romney-St. Neot's granddaughter, and her nephew. Both are presently captives, as far as we can ascertain, in the Margrave's castle fortress in the town of—"

"I don't need to be told what I already bloody-well know!" Lord Cobham blustered. "And I don't want a geography lesson. I couldn't care less if they were being held captive on the moon. Damn it! If the moon is where I need you to go, then the moon is where you'll bloody-well go!"

His lordship pulled his receding chin into his stock and stuck out his bottom lip. To Sir Gilbert he immediately took on the appearance of a stunned cod, albeit one with bushy red eyebrows. In Sir Gilbert's opinion, Lord Cobham had the face and complexion not even a mother could love.

"Fact is: The Duchess is my aunt. Can't have relatives upset. Bad for the digestion," his lordship continued in a more subdued voice, and sniffed. "I'm sending you abroad so you can redeem yourself after the diplomatic debacle of '53. Need I remind you that because you were sent packing and Halsey got himself in a pickle, His Majesty lost the services of Midanich's troops-for-hire? It was only the recent war that reinstated that service. I'm sending you for two reasons: To show that trumped-up little country it can't trifle with England. And, more importantly, so you can keep an eye on Halsey. He's the one they want to negotiate the release of Miss St. Neots and Mahon." He sighed his frustration, gaze staring up at the milky gray clouds. "God knows why..." He brought his small eyes down from the clouds to stare hard at his subordinate. "Do you, Parsons?"

"No, my lord. It is as much a mystery to me as to you. Why the Margrave would request Alec Halsey, given it was his insufferable behavior that got me expelled and him incarcerated, is, frankly, baffling."

"A mystery indeed..." Lord Cobham murmured, then stated, staring his subordinate in the eye, "Halsey may be the one who's been requested, but I am putting you in charge of the legation, because I trust you to—"

"Thank you, my lord. I will endeavor—"

"—do as you're told. I don't trust Halsey! The man is a loose cannon and a law unto himself. He has—*scruples*." Lord Cobham pulled a face of disgust. "Sanctimonious piffle!" He jabbed a gloved finger in the air, close to Sir Gilbert's snub nose. "You will keep him in check, Parsons. And do a much better job of it than you did the last time, if you want to return to the comfort of your desk! Do you hear me?"

Sir Gilbert certainly did hear him. He wanted nothing more than to return to the security his deskbound employment afforded him. Since his expulsion from Midanich and being sent home in disgrace, he had not had another posting to the Continent. The past ten years had been spent slouching over other people's correspondence in the cipher department. Everyone, from Lord Cobham, to his dear wife on, down to his wigmaker, viewed his relegation with a mixture of embarrassment and pity. Publically, Sir Gilbert was suitably humbled. In truth he was happy to be home and in a position within the Foreign Department that bored him almost to incompetence. He loved his comforts, particularly his daily visits to his preferred coffee house in the morning and his favorite chop house in the evening. But as he owed his position and thus his living to Lord Cobham's good graces, he had no say in the matter of whether he stayed behind a desk or sailed off on a diplomatic rescue mission which had disaster inked all over it before the ship had the wind in its sails.

"Yes, my lord," he replied tonelessly. "Loud and as clear as a church bell."

Lord Cobham peered at his subordinate for signs the man was being sarcastic, but as Sir Gilbert held his gaze with a suitably neutral expression, he continued, and with a look over his shoulder, as if he half-expected to be overheard. But the cul-de-sac was empty of pedestrian and horse, so it was an unnecessary, and in Sir Gilbert's opinion, an overly-dramatic gesture.

"To be frank, Parsons, the reason we are having this discussion out here, before we call on Halsey, is that the release of Miss St. Neots and Sir Cosmo is not to be the primary goal of *your* mission. Leave that to Halsey. What you are to do is to identify, and make contact with, a member of Margrave Ernst's court—a traitor—"

"Traitor?"

"Not to us, Parsons. Not to England. A traitor to Margrave Ernst's cause. Someone who is working to further his brother Prince Viktor's claim to the throne."

"Who is this traitor, my lord?"

"If I bloody-well knew that, Parsons, would I be asking *you* to uncover his identity? Keep up! Keep up!"

His lordship threw a hand in the air and let it drop heavily to his side, saying with a crooked, conciliatory smile as if addressing a simpleton, "Look here. In the scheme of things, it doesn't matter which of the brothers—Margrave Ernst or Prince Viktor—triumphs. What is important is that their civil war ends, and soon. If they keep fighting each other there'll be no troops left, and where would that leave England, eh?" He paused long enough for Sir Gilbert to open his mouth to respond, then added with a grunt, "If anyone is going to kill off Midanich's troops, it's us, fighting for England, not over a brotherly squabble. And when that civil war ends, His Majesty's government must be seen to have supported the winning side from the very beginning of the conflict. Do you understand, Parsons?"

"And if it comes to light we were hedging our bets?" asked Sir Gilbert. "Both Margrave Ernst and Prince Viktor are unlikely to consider His Majesty's government a trustworthy ally then, are they, my lord? It could ruin relations with the country for the fut—"

"Damme! You're sounding like that sanctimonious Halsey, and I don't care for it, Parsons! Listen, man. His Majesty and His Majesty's government ministers will believe the head of the Foreign Department over the ravings of a bloody nobody ruler of an insignificant principality in the middle of God-knows-where in Europe. Understood?"

Sir Gilbert did not contradict his superior. He could see his point in wanting to ensure England backed the right horse, or in this case, the right brother. Who won the civil war was unimportant. But he wondered how he was to discover the identity of the traitor without he himself being discovered and getting himself expelled, and for a second time. Now, that would be a first!

"Not one bloody word of this to Halsey."

"Yes, my lord. You have my confidence."

"I'll be the first to pat you on the back with hearty congratulations when you've managed to kill two birds with one stone."

"Two birds, my lord? A stone?"

"Ernst and Viktor! Do use your brain, Parsons," Lord Cobham complained. "By *kill* I mean give both the hope that His Majesty supports them for the post of Margrave. But if you can't manage it, it will be cold suppers for you from here on in. Leave Halsey to sort out the mucky business of getting the hostages released. With any luck, he'll get himself locked up again, and for the greater good—that greater good being *my* reputation and *your* position."

*And Selina's good name*, he thought to himself, knowing his headstrong sister was on the cusp of accepting a marriage proposal from Alec Halsey. Despite being her elder brother and head of the family, he was excruciatingly aware that his position and his opinion held no sway over her. She would do as she pleased; which didn't please him.

"If, by some fortuitous happenstance, Halsey manages to secure a release," he continued, shaking his thoughts free of his recalcitrant sibling. "Then it will be a success for the department, and for me. And that's how it will be written up in your report, Parsons— Parsons?"

"Yes, my lord. I will write up a report."

"So you bloody-well will! And it'll be over my bloodied carcass before I allow m'sister to marry the likes of Halsey. She's a Vesey," he added, momentarily forgetting he was talking to an inferior in an open street, and not confiding in a member of his club. "The man murdered his brother—regardless of what a coroner has to say to it! Egad. I'll not have such blood polluting the Vesey line. Regardless of my aunt wanting him to rise to the dizzying heights of ambassador one day. Ha! That's not bloody likely either! But one can't say that to elderly aunts, Parsons. Mere females don't understand these things."

"Very true, my lord," Sir Gilbert said in the silence that dragged after his superior's diatribe. "I may not have seen Halsey in over a decade, but papers have crossed my desk in that time from his superiors in The Hague and at Paris about his unfortunate practice of being ruled by conscience. And then there is his predilection for engaging in bedroom politics. Pardon, my lord, but if Halsey had spent more time in his breeches than out of 'em we'd not have ended up in deep water—literally; the dungeon is below sea level. That's what got me expelled from Midanich."

"What got you expelled, Parsons, was your own stupidity. Demanding Halsey keep his breeches on when he was in the midst of a torrid affair with the Margrave's daughter was signing your own warrant for banishment. Halsey's salacious brand of diplomacy won out. See that house?" Lord Cobham asked, jabbing his walking stick in the direction of a free-standing double-fronted townhouse, the first in a well-appointed secluded row that all backed on to the Green Park. "That's where he lives now. Shares it with that obstinate uncle. Silly old windbag who pontificates in Parliament about ending slavery and universal education for brats. Ravings of a lunatic! The man's another loose cannon, and an explosive one. But no one can touch him because he's an MP. Yes. You may very well stare, Parsons. It's the sorry truth. And I'm afraid I have more startling news..." He shuddered and closed his eyes as if steeling himself for the announcement he knew would shock Sir Gilbert to the core. "His Majesty has seen fit to raise Halsey to a marquessate—"

"*What*?" Sir Gilbert staggered back as if struck by Lord Cobham's walking stick. "Plantagenet Halsey is a-a marquess? *Bloody hell*."

"No! No! Not the uncle! *Alec Halsey*, your departmental junior. He's now *Marquess* Halsey, and so I am forced—yes, *forced*—to swallow up my pride and do the right thing by his nobility, if not his person, and treat him as one of us. Can you believe it, Parsons?"

"I don't believe it!" Sir Gilbert stated. "My subordinate— *ennobled*?"

"Sticks in your gullet, too, eh," Lord Cobham said with a chuckle at the face Sir Gilbert showed him; as if a foul odor had assailed his nostrils. "I'll wager you never thought your secretary would now be a bloody lord, and living like one too!" He swished his walking stick around to point it at Sir Gilbert, adding with a frown and in a low voice, "But you're not to let his elevation dazzle you. You're head of the legation to Midanich. This is your second chance—your *only* chance. You're the senior diplomat. Don't let him forget who's in charge—that just because he's been ennobled doesn't mean he gets to run things *his* way. Understand?"

"Yes, my lord. Don't concern yourself. I've learned my lesson. I'll wave my credentials under his ennobled nose, when and if I need to," Sir Gilbert replied, sticking out his jaw.

"Good man!" Lord Cobham replied with a self-satisfied sniff. "I've told you what I consider is important on this mission. But what I say inside those four walls—" He swung his walking stick back around to point at Number One St. James's Place, "—will be what Halsey wants to hear. All to keep him off the scent. Understand?"

Sir Gilbert had no idea what scent his lordship was sniffing at, though he suspected it smelled of traitor and double dealing, so he nodded obediently and verbalized his agreement when Lord Cobham glared at him.

"So let's get this tedious meeting over with," Lord Cobham continued, turned on a heel and strode down the short street toward Alec's townhouse. He kept talking, expecting Sir Gilbert's short wide person to keep apace with him. "I'm due at White's for a hand of piquet before dinner. And you, Parsons, have portmanteaux to pack. Come along! Come along! Can't keep Lord Bloody-High-and-Mighty waiting!"

As Sir Gilbert scrambled to match Lord Cobham's stride, then follow him up the three shallow steps and into the wide expanse of a black-and-white tiled entrance foyer, he wondered if his now ennobled junior secretary cared to remember who he was. Sir Gilbert's question was answered almost immediately upon entering the Lord Halsey's morning drawing room.

"A CUP OF TEA, MY LORD, OR WOULD YOU PREFER COFFEE?" ALEC asked politely in answer to Lord Cobham's rude outburst upon entering his drawing room.

"Eh? *Tea?*" Lord Cobham responded, brought up short in the middle of the Aubusson rug by the mild question, as Alec knew he would be. Blinking, he lost his belligerent tone and responded in kind. "Tea. Yes. A cup of tea."

Alec nodded to Wantage, who stood to attention at the tea trolley with a liveried footman, before looking past Lord Cobham to the man at his back. Alec immediately recognized him and met him with hand outstretched.

"Sir Gilbert! What a pleasure to see you after all these years. I just wish it had been under happier circumstances. You are looking well, sir."

That Alec greeted him with genuine warmth, and had the good manners to refer to him as 'sir', lifted Sir Gilbert's mouth into a smile and he shook hands with the younger man as if it were only yesterday they had said their goodbyes on the steps of the Foreign Office building on the Strand. For an instant, he forgot everything

Lord Cobham had said, and the well-trained subordinate bowed to title without a second thought.

"Congratulations on your elevation, my lord," Sir Gilbert replied, and in answer to Alec's compliment he patted the front of his wool waistcoat which was buttoned tightly over his paunch. "Too many years stuck behind a desk will do this to a man. Whereas you, my lord, haven't changed a jot."

"Tea? Coffee?"

"Coffee, my lord. Thank you."

"And how is Lady Parsons? As I recall, she was partial to making fly fringe...?"

Sir Gilbert grinned, even more in charity with Alec for remembering his wife's little after-dinner occupation while the men played chess. "Ah, you recall that, do you? Maria will be flattered. Even more so when I tell her it was *Lord* Halsey asking after her fringes."

"For God's sake, Parsons," Lord Cobham hissed out of the side of his mouth, "pull yourself together!"

"As to that, Sir Gilbert," Alec continued smoothly as if Lord Cobham had not spoken, "you may tell Lady Parsons I was persuaded to accept the honor against my better judgment by those who presume to know my best interests better than I!" Adding before the Duchess could protest, "Allow me to make you known to Her Grace, and to my uncle..."

"Aunt Olivia?" Lord Cobham wondered aloud as he thrust his walking stick at the footman to take the cup of tea offered him by the butler. He blinked down at the Duchess as Sir Gilbert stepped away from bowing low over her outstretched hand. "Why are you here?"

"Y'look as if you've seen a ghost, Cobham!" Plantagenet Halsey declared pleasantly, sipping at his cup of tea. He had the Duchess's cup refilled and said to her in an undertone, "Here. Drink this. You'll need it now more than ever to get through this meetin'."

The Duchess glared at him, eager to tell him what she thought of his coddling ways, when she was diverted by Lord Cobham, who said, with a sniff and a significant look down his nose at the old man,

"Apologies, Aunt Olivia, but this matter can only be discussed between members of my department. The sensitive details in documents are not to be divulged to persons who do not have a right to know. If it was to get out and about, it would do irreparable damage to relations with a Continental court. What we say within these four walls must not reach the ears of our enemies. And our enemies are everywhere!" He looked at the old man. "I must insist, you, sir—"

"Don't be ridiculous, Clive!" the Duchess said dismissively. "We are talking about rescuing my granddaughter and my nephew, and you are talking pompous drivel. Where's Shrewsbury? Why isn't *he* here?"

"Otherwise detained," Lord Cobham replied in a much subdued voice. "Seems our Spymaster General is playing nursemaid to his ill granddaughter. Nothing serious, so I'm told. Thought nurses took care of that sort of thing. But what do I know? I don't have grandchildren—or children, for that matter. So he's left it in my hands to deal with the—"

"Did you bring that letter, the one addressed to Lord Halsey, or not?" the Duchess demanded. When he nodded over his teacup she straightened her back. "Well? Where is it? You might have the right to withhold it from me, but you cannot do so from him. If anyone can make sense of this travesty, Alec can—and get on with doing something about it! Which is more than your department is doing!"

Lord Cobham opened his mouth to refute such claims, but as it was his aunt making them, he knew when to bow to *force majeure*. With a surreptitious roll of his eyes at his subordinate, as if to say he was compelled to humor his elderly aunt's whims, he handed Alec a folded piece of paper with a broken seal, saying stiffly, "For your eyes only, Halsey."

Alec took the letter and retired to the window seat to read without distraction. He heard his uncle make an innocuous remark to Sir Gilbert, and the Duchess ask her nephew how preparation was progressing with the outfitting of a schooner, and then he was lost in Sir Cosmo Mahon's letter.

The more he read, the more understanding he had of the perilous situation in Midanich, and was able to unravel truth and fiction from the Duchess's panic-laced account. He was acutely aware of the danger Cosmo and Emily faced as prisoners in a war-torn country, but Cosmo's dictated letter made that realization much more urgent. He heartily wished he had the ability of flight, for to fly like a bird, and at speed, would enable him to rescue Cosmo and Emily within days, not weeks. Cosmo's letter had the effect of making him feel thoroughly impotent, and that every hour which passed until he could free them would be interminable.

He was eager to be off within the hour, but knew this to be an impossibility. So many things had yet to be arranged, not least the requisitioning of a suitable ship whose captain and crew were prepared to travel north in this weather and perilous situation. And this despite the danger that awaited him returning to a country he had successfully fled and vowed to never return. He knew precisely what awaited him at Castle Herzfeld. He'd been subjected to violence just short of torture, and witnessed the madness that lurked in the shadows inside those thick walls, escaping within an inch of losing his life. Now, ten years on, those traumatic events had lapsed into the stuff of nightmare. If not completely forgotten, then at least so successfully suppressed that he could rest his head lightly upon his pillow.

And yet here he was, preparing to travel to Midanich, and this time well aware of the evil that awaited him. He did not shirk from it; he could not. Two people very dear to his heart were in dire straits and needed his help. So be it. He must go. If it crossed his mind that he might have to sacrifice himself and change places with Cosmo to ensure his and Emily's safety and escape, such a circumstance was instantly dismissed as irrelevant. All that mattered was securing his friends' release. His dread was secondary. He would deal with the Margrave and his sister when the time came. For the time being, he needed to focus on the here and now. So he perched his spectacles on the bridge of his bony nose and lowered his eyes to Sir Cosmo Mahon's carefully scripted letter.

*Dear Alec* [he read]

*I am writing what is dictated to me by a court official. He does not understand English. I do not write in French, do I? So I will do my best to sprinkle this letter with a few sentences here and there to alert you of certain particulars. Our consul, Jacob Luytens, is to verify under oath that what I've written is a true and correct translation from the French spoken by the official, whose native tongue is German. And that everything I write is a true reflection of my situation. It is quite a language coil, you, my dear friend, would have no trouble unraveling. The sworn oath has put us all in danger, should this be seen by the wrong pair of eyes.*

*Mr. Luytens assures me he will get this letter to you. I must trust him.*

*I am treated well, though held against my will. I have been assigned a small room within the palace. My watch, clothes, portmanteaux—everything—has been confiscated. I scratch the days on the wooden floor of my room under the rug, when the sun rises. I am neither permitted quill and paper nor books. Once a day I am taken under escort to walk in the courtyard, or atop the inner wall where there are no grisly reminders of war, whichever takes my fancy. I am fed at breakfast and at dinner, and my chamber pot is emptied daily. While I wish I could bathe more often than once a fortnight, under the circumstances to soak in a hot bath is a small luxury I have come to cherish.*

*Matthias, my valet, is permitted to shave me every other day, and then is gone. We snatch conversation while we can. He tells me he is not mistreated, though I see he has a black eye and bruises. He says the heads on pike staffs along the parapets are of traitors or deserters—a warning to others who feel so inclined to speak out or flee. It is positively medieval. I feel I have walked into a scene from Hamlet, whose country is not so very far from here.*

*The court chamberlain, Herr Haderslev, has visited me upon two occasions. I am to be granted an audience to plead my case with the Margrave when he returns from engaging opposition forces in the south. I am told it will be the last battle before the winter weather sets in. I have requested an audience with the Margrave's sister Princess Joanna. But our consul says the princess lives in seclusion and is never seen during the daylight hours because of her delicate condition. He would not elaborate what that condition was.*

*I asked Matthias if he knew anything about this condition which keeps the Princess hidden. The next time he came to shave me, he told me that no one speaks of what is known as the "unspoken truth". It has a long, complicated German name, but this is the rough translation. I asked Mr. Luytens. He said writing it here would be enough to alert you—that you do, indeed, know more than Matthias can discover.*

*I live in hope the Princess will grant me an audience. My dearest Alec, hope is all I have left.*

*I have seen Mr. Luytens upon three occasions. It is all the contact I am permitted with our British consul, and this in a month. If it were my fate alone, I would consign myself to it, but it is the thought of Emily who keeps me awake at night.*

*The last time I saw Emily was when we said our farewells aboard ship in port, she to await my return the next day to set sail for Copenhagen. Our Consul assures me she is being accorded every civility as the granddaughter of an English duchess. But as he has not seen her, I fear what I am being told is not the truth. The look in his eyes tells me so. I do not know if it is to spare me or to torture me, because not knowing how she is, if she is alive or—no, I cannot write it here—is sending me mad. The only fact keeping me sane is that the estimable Mrs. Carlisle is with her.*

*I asked Matthias to find out what he could but when he attempted to make enquiries he came up empty-handed. Everyone lives in fear, not least the servants, who are a closemouthed lot who never lift their eyes above the stone flagging. And as my valet's movements are heavily restricted by the palace guard, and he cannot speak the local language, he is sadly deficient in his information.*

*Confined to my room and alone, my mind wanders to fearing the worst, and I do not mean death, dearest friend. Death would be preferable and a godsend for a beautiful young woman such as Emily. As you know, in a time of war atrocities are perpetrated on the defenseless, the weak, and particularly on females, all because they can.*

*Please, for the love of God, whatever you do, do not mention my fears to Aunt Olivia. Create whatever fiction you prefer, but keep her spirits buoyant. She must continue to hope, as I hope, that we will come through this, if not unscathed, at least alive and whole. So, please, Alec, do not breathe a word until you have seen our expired earthly forms for yourself. And then, again, do not convey the worst to her but some fiction which will allow her to sleep peacefully.*

*Margrave Ernst has declared his country to be in a state of civil war. Troops are everywhere. I hear them parading across the courtyard, and these are just the elite palace guard. I am to tell you that beyond the walls of this impenetrable fortress, war ravages the countryside. Prince Viktor is declared a traitor to his country for taking up arms against his brother and for calling the native Frisian troops to arms. Any Frisian found in Viktor's colors is immediately shot. No prisoners are taken. Thousands of people are displaced and ruined because of the merciless actions of Prince Viktor, who is controlled by his mother, the "she wolf"—the Countess Rosine. This is how she is described to me. Our consul Luytens nods his agreement with the official and makes no contradiction, so I am to assume he agrees with this assessment.*

*Herr Luytens has been back to Emden and returned at considerable personal risk. He says all ports are now controlled by the army, but that Emden remains open because it is through this port that all goods are channeled, and thus provides valuable income for the country, not least the Margrave's war effort. And so it is at Emden you are to disembark, and with the ransom, the details of which our consul is to send by separate cover. Whatever the amount—bring it!*

*To be frank, dear fellow, I hold grave fears Emily and I won't leave this place alive if you do not agree to Margrave Ernst's demand to present yourself at Castle Herzfeld to negotiate our release. No one and no other method is acceptable to him.*

*As a show of his resolve, and so that you know this letter is indeed genuine, I enclose a curl of Emily's hair given to me. It will be familiar to you, as it was at Christmastime.*

*Also enclosed is a safe conduct pass in the name of a Baron Aurich, signed by the Margrave, and with his seal. The pass allows you and members of your party to pass through all checkpoints unharmed, and to receive assistance from the Margrave's troops should you require it. He takes every precaution to ensure the safe arrival of this Baron Aurich, who I must assume is your good self, though why he addresses you as such and to what purpose, only you and he know.*

*My dear fellow, I am so very sorry to put your life in such danger, too. Forgive me, I have smudged the ink with my blubbering like a girl. God! To what levels have I descended in this hell!*

*Luytens will take this, my letter, the authorization and the ransom demand in the diplomatic portefuille as far as Emden and then send it on through Holland. Our consul will remain in Emden pending your arrival. You have forty days to comply and then Luytens, too, will be arrested. As he is a native of this country and not ours, he will not be accorded the same courtesy I have received, but find himself flung in the castle dungeon. He tells me only one man has escaped Herzfeld dungeon—your esteemed self. Even the official who dictates this letter to me speaks of that escapade with awe.*

*For God's sake, Alec, get here with all speed.*

*Cosmo Mahon*

# *Five*

LEC FOLDED THE LETTER AND SLOWLY REMOVED HIS eyeglasses. He did not immediately rejoin the others by the fireplace. He turned on the window seat cushion to look out on the expanse of the Green Park, but was oblivious to the view. He did not notice his greyhounds dashing about between the leafless trees, his valet in vain pursuit. His thoughts were miles away, across the North Sea with Cosmo and Emily, and their dire predicament. Then, in an instant, he suppressed his morbidity. He needed to be strong and optimistic, for them and for Olivia, and because he needed to get through the next several weeks of not knowing, until he was back at Herzfeld Castle, and could see them for himself.

There was so much to organize before he could even set sail. The journey from Harwich to Emden was a crossing of some four days, and that on calm seas, before he set a booted foot in Midanich again. Landing at the port of Emden was only the beginning, for then there was the journey overland to Herzfeld, with the chill winds blowing in off the North Sea, and the dragging slowness of travel over a swampy wasteland, first by canal boat and then astride a horse.

He had been given forty days. He had even less time now, because Cosmo's letter had arrived a sennight ago. There was not a day to waste. Which was just as well. The lack of time and the logistics of travel would now preoccupy his thoughts, and stop them wandering to futile probabilities until he was on his way. So he returned to the fireplace and poured out a second cup of coffee to give himself a few moments to clear his mind, while the others in the room made polite conversation awaiting his response to Cosmo's letter.

"I wish to keep this for a day or two, if I may," Alec said to Lord Cobham, indicating Cosmo's letter. "There is a lot to digest, and I want to be certain I've not missed any of Cosmo's messages to me."

"Messages? There are messages?" Lord Cobham was clearly surprised and he looked reproachfully at Sir Gilbert. "You told me the backroom fellows had been over every word of this letter and found nothing hidden to report."

"That is so, my lord," Sir Gilbert started to explain, when Alec stepped in.

"They wouldn't know what to look for. This is not written in any known code or cipher because Cosmo doesn't know such codes. Yet, he has done his best to alert me to certain particulars. For instance," he continued, looking to the Duchess, "he refers to the curl of Emily's hair as *given to me*. Not that it was snipped from her head there and then. And he adds *It will be familiar to you, as it was at Christmastime*. He is telling me that the curl of hair sent with this letter is not new. Two Christmases ago, Cosmo showed me a porcelain snuffbox—a gift. Framed in its lid was a curl of blonde hair." He smiled slightly. "I have no idea if it was Emily's hair, and I did not ask."

"So this curl might not belong to Emily?" the Duchess asked expectantly. "Those fiends might not have cut my darling's hair at all?" When Alec nodded, she closed her eyes on a sigh of relief. "Oh, thank God..." But in the next breath she was glaring at Lord Cobham, voice trembling with anger. "You told me it was Emily's! *You* said if they could cut off her hair what wouldn't they cut off next, perhaps a finger, if we didn't do as they demanded!"

"Well, Aunt, they could very well do that," Lord Cobham

protested. "These Continental types are barbarians at best, so I was just trying to—"

"What? Scare the poor woman witless? Insensitive muckworm!" Plantagenet Halsey growled. "I'd always thought you had as much brains as a sea sponge. This confirms it. And you've got zero feelin's to match!"

"Sir! You have no right to malign the head of the Foreign Department with such—"

"You shut your crumb hole! I've more right than you!" the old man interrupted Sir Gilbert, and so ferociously the rotund little man stumbled backwards, teacup rattling on its saucer.

"Oh hush! All of you!" the Duchess demanded and looked eagerly at Alec. "What else does Cosmo, say, my boy? Does he mention how they—how Emily is being treated? Her health? Are they being accorded every civility?"

"Cosmo is thankful Emily has the estimable Mrs. Carlisle as her companion, which should give us some comfort," Alec replied, indirectly answering her questions because he wasn't prepared to share the contents of the letter with her.

"Yes! Yes, Mrs. Carlisle is with her," the Duchess said with surprised relief, as if she had just remembered the woman's existence. "A most excellent woman; my second cousin. Poor as a churchmouse, but I've always done what I can for her. If there's one thing I know about Ellen Carlisle it's that she is not one to fold in a crisis, and she most definitely is not prone to hysterics."

"Then she's just the sort of female Emily needs with her at this time," Plantagenet Halsey said in a rallying tone.

"Yes. You are right," the Duchess agreed, and smiled for the first time since entering Alec's townhouse.

"So I may keep this letter for a day or two...?" Alec asked, repeating his request to Lord Cobham.

"It's most irregular," Sir Gilbert said with a frowning shake of his head, "and not Foreign Department policy to allow important documents to leave the department."

"But as it is now in my house," Alec enunciated patiently, "then surely that makes it outside the department?"

"I beg to differ, Hal—my lord," Sir Gilbert continued smoothly, and now in his element. "Lord Cobham is, for all intents and purposes, the department. Thus, wherever he is, so is the department. And so the letter, being here in your drawing room with his lordship present means the letter is in effect still in the department. Thus, once Lord Cobham leaves this room, and you retain the letter, it no longer remains in the department. Do I make myself clear?"

"As mud!" Plantagenet Halsey stated. He looked to his nephew, and said with heavy sarcasm, "And you survived three years as this punctilious pontificator's subordinate without poking him with your blade?" When Alec merely lifted his eyebrows by way of reply, he slowly shook his head. "I'm in awe of your self-possession, m'boy."

"Sir Gilbert is in the right. But you have my permission to keep the letter for as long as you need it, Halsey," Lord Cobham replied haughtily. He coughed into his fist and continued, gaze firmly on Alec, though he could not help a nervous glance at his aunt as he spoke. For all his self-deluded importance as Head of the Foreign Department, with dozens of men's livelihoods dependent on his favor, when it came to his female relatives, particularly this aunt who was a duchess, he was little more than a quivering blancmange in their presence. A prickle of heat spread across his scalp under his wig, and his cheeks flamed to match the color of his thick red eyebrows as her indignation grew in magnitude with every word of his explanation.

"I had hoped to inform you of the department's decision in private, but I am sure you—er—um—would prefer that I just get on with it so you can continue with the arrangements for the journey as expeditiously as possible. Sir Cosmo Mahon's letter requests your presence to negotiate his and Miss St. Neots' release, and makes no mention of anyone else. But, given the seriousness of the situation, I have decided Sir Gilbert will accompany you. Put more correctly, you will be accompanying *him*. He is—and I don't need to remind you of the facts, Halsey—the senior member within the department, with vastly more years of experience with Continental types. He was the Minister Plenipotentiary and you his subordinate as *chargé d'affaires* when you were both last in Midanich, so—"

"*Wh-What*? Clive? This is outrageous! *Outrageous.*"

The Duchess had jumped up on her two-inch heels, and so quickly she almost overbalanced. But as Plantagenet Halsey had reacted in a similar fashion and was now standing beside her, he was there to grab her elbow before she fell flat on her face. She hardly noticed, such was her fury.

"I understand you are upset, Aunt Olivia," Lord Cobham stuttered into pompous explanation, "but this is departmental business and not your concern—"

"Not my concern? So—you—think! It most certainly *is* my concern! And I will make it the concern of the Privy Council if you attempt to belittle my godson by this—"

"Your Grace—Olivia—if you will allow me to—" Alec began, but was just as rudely cut off.

"Alec Halsey is a marquess, a *marquess*, Cobham! Do you know what that is, Clive? Of course you do! One title below a duke. To point out fact, he's higher up the aristocratic precedence ladder than you'll ever be! And this, this *person*," she continued, rudely flapping her fan in Sir Gilbert's round face, "is-is a—*nobody* who has as much consequence as a-a—*flea*. Do you truly expect *me* to allow a nobody to rescue my granddaughter from a Continental maniac? Well, do you, Clive? *Do you?*"

While Lord Cobham's brain worked to find a suitable response that would placate his infuriated aunt—his lower lip wobbled uncontrollably—Alec stepped into the breach, and before his uncle could add fuel to the Duchess's fiery tirade. He said mildly, but not without a hint of exasperation at wanting this meeting concluded,

"Lord Cobham's decision is an astute one, Your Grace. Not withstanding Sir Gilbert's experience and intimate knowledge of the Midanich court, by sending him as minister shows the new Margrave that His Majesty's government bears Midanich no ill will. After all, Sir Gilbert departed the court under trying circumstances, and I—"

"*Trying circumstances*? I was tortured and humiliated!" Sir Gilbert blurted out.

Humiliated, yes, and Alec understood Sir Gilbert's humiliation. It was not every day the most senior ranking diplomat at a foreign court was expelled; a subordinate, yes, but never the minister. But torture? It was the first Alec had heard of this and he blinked in surprise.

"Tortured?" he asked, concerned, and waited for Sir Gilbert to elaborate.

With all eyes upon him, Sir Gilbert squirmed, cursing himself for his uncharacteristically belligerent outburst. He was suddenly sheepish.

"Two nights locked up without food and then unceremoniously bundled into a coach for the coast, and forcibly put on a boat! That's torture in my books."

Alec thought of his own harrowing experience, at the abuse he had endured at the hands of Prince Ernst and his sister, the Princess Joanna, and Sir Gilbert's assertion was so ludicrous by comparison he could think of nothing to say. So he inclined his head to Sir Gilbert's definition and suppressed a smile that it took the mention of food, or lack thereof, for the rotund little gentleman to be at his most animated since entering the drawing room. When his uncle rolled his eyes to the plastered ceiling, Alec's smile widened into a grin.

"You read some mighty tame books, if you think that's torture!"

Plantagenet Halsey huffed in dismissal, a pointed glare at the man's paunch.

"Listen here, Halsey—" Lord Cobham began, and was cut off before he could launch into a spirited defense of his subordinate

"And yet, despite such depravation, Sir Gilbert has elected to return to Midanich as His Majesty's representative," Alec said smoothly. "This will surely indicate to the new Margrave that past wrongs are forgotten by His Majesty. It also lets Margrave Ernst know that you, Sir Gilbert, and English sovereign interests, are not to be trifled with." Alec looked to Lord Cobham. "No doubt this was what you had in mind to tell Her Grace all along, was it not, my lord?"

"Had in mind...?" Lord Cobham repeated slowly, as if surfacing from a trance. He came to life when Alec continued to look at him expectantly. "Yes! Yes! Couldn't have said it better myself. That is precisely my reasoning!"

"Couldn't have said it at all," Plantagenet Halsey muttered within his nephew's hearing.

"No one is more in support of His Majesty showing this Margrave we English are not to be trifled with," the Duchess agreed, somewhat placated. "Sir Gilbert can throw his weight about wherever and at whomever he likes, but what does it matter who is minister of this or anything else when all that is truly important is rescuing Emily and Cosmo?"

Alec kissed the Duchess's hand and smiled down into her moist eyes.

"My pride is not the least injured Sir Gilbert heads the legation," he told her quietly. "He is an excellent choice for Minister Plenipotentiary. His appointment frees me up to concentrate exclusively on Emily and Cosmo's situation. No doubt Cobham and Sir Gilbert have worked out some plan with the help of the department, and His Majesty's blessing. Perhaps they are going to offer the Margrave favorable trade terms or ships, or whatever else he desires, to aid me in my endeavors? So in effect you have all of us working for the same goal, but coming at the problem from different corners of the room. Does that ease your mind just a little?"

"A little," the Duchess conceded with a pout, mollified by Alec's reassurances. She looked past his shoulder at her nephew, tongue firmly in cheek. "Of course that's precisely what you were also going to tell me, wasn't it, Clive?"

"To the word, too," the old man added, and for his cheekiness got a poke in the ribs from the Duchess's fan.

"Yes. Yes, precisely my thoughts, and what Sir Gilbert and I had discussed prior to coming here," Lord Cobham lied through his teeth. "Isn't that so, Parsons?"

"Was it? Ah! Yes!" agreed his minion, nodding vigorously. "Precisely my thoughts on how we should approach the problem upon reaching the Midanich Court. Halsey here—"

"*Lord* Halsey," Plantagenet Halsey cut in.

"Er, yes, forgive me. Lord Halsey and I will present our credentials and I will open trade negotiations with Margrave Ernst in the hopes that through these diplomatic efforts we shall secure the release of those two good people," Sir Gilbert explained. "And while I am in these negotiations, Lord Halsey is free to pursue alternative avenues that may need to be applied to free His Majesty's subjects from a foreign prison, should dialogue between our nations prove less than satisfactory."

"You are a diplomat after all, Parsons!" Plantagenet Halsey declared, but it was not meant as a compliment. "What you mean is, while you sit on your rump sipping coffee and offering your respects to a Continental tyrant, my nephew will be riskin' life and limb by breakin' in to a dank dark dungeon?"

"Oh, it's not that dark, Uncle," Alec quipped. "But it is dank. But you needn't worry I am required to storm a dungeon. Cosmo has been accorded a room in the palace complex. So at the very most I may have to bust down a door!"

"And Emily, where is her room? Is it near Cosmo's?" the Duchess asked anxiously. "Does Mrs. Carlisle have a separate room, or is she quartered with Emily?"

"What of this ransom?" Alec asked, again ignoring the Duchess' direct question and hoping to divert her before he would be forced to lie to her outright. He asked after the British Consul's ransom demand. "What does Mr. Luytens' letter command as a ransom?"

"No need for you to concern yourself with that for the time being, my boy," the Duchess told him, suddenly making movements to leave, flouncing out her silk petticoats and letting her fan dangle on its silken cord about her wrist so she could draw on her kid gloves. "Cobham and I are putting our heads together to sort out what is needed. You have a great deal of preparation to do before we leave for Midanich, and this is at least one matter I can take care of and not bother you with the minor details." She put out her crooked arm to Lord Cobham. "Come along, Clive. Your dear wife is waiting for us to dine and—"

"But I'm expected at my club. I have to—"

"That can wait. This cannot."

Lord Cobham instantly capitulated. The only sign of his frustration was in the way he snatched his walking stick from the footman with a loud sniff. He obediently gave the crook of his arm to his aunt, bowed silently to the room and escorted her to the waiting carriage. Sir Gilbert was left to wait in the vestibule while a junior footman ran to the top of the street to secure him a sedan chair.

Alec had not insisted he be shown Luytens' letter, though he found it odd in the extreme that the Duchess did not want to discuss the ransom with him, least of all show him the letter. He was just glad to see his godmother finally take her leave so that he need not deflect more questions regarding Emily, and because he was eager to get on with the hundred and one matters which required his attention before setting sail. But just as he was about to excuse himself and go in search of his valet, his godmother's words struck him and he regarded his uncle with a puzzled frown.

"What did Olivia mean *we*?" he asked. "Just now she said I had a great deal of preparation to do before *we* leave for Midanich."

"We do," his uncle said matter-of-factly. "So much so I wish Tam were here to help me, or at the very least mix up some more of that lotion he concocts to help m'arthritis, so I can take it with me."

Alec was not to be diverted. "What did she mean?"

"Just what she said. We do have a lot to do before the ship sails."

"You keep using the word *we*, too. Why?"

Plantagenet Halsey clapped his nephew on the shoulder. "Because, my boy, *we* are coming with you."

# Six

"IDON'T KNOW HOW MANY WAYS TO SAY IT. MIDANICH is in the midst of a bloody civil war. And I'm not swearing at you when I use the word bloody, though I could very well do so, such is my frustration in not being able to convince you of what awaits us—no, *me*. There is no *us* or *we*, just *me*. Do you understand?"

"Yes. Yes. Understand completely," Plantagenet Halsey muttered, attention on a long checklist of items considered necessary for travel to foreign winter climes. He looked about at Hadrian Jeffries, who was in his master's spacious dressing closet, the doors wide on several mahogany clothes presses, and arms full of white linen shirts. "When did you say m'tailor would be here to deliver those fur-lined breeches?"

"Later this afternoon, sir."

"How many pairs did you order for his lordship?"

The valet glanced at Alec but answered the old man. "Four pairs, sir. Three are fur-lined. The fourth pair is of a heavy twill cord, which his lordship says affords enough warmth within doors at those places where there are Dutch stoves installed to heat the rooms."

"Got y'self a pair of fur-lined breeches, too, I hope?" Plantagenet Halsey asked the valet.

"Yes, sir. His lordship was very generous in having me fitted for a suit, and an all-weather cloak."

"Good. You'll need 'em. His lordship is intimate with the weather in that part of northern Europe, and he says it's damnably freezing and blowing gales off the North Sea all of the time. And there ain't nothin' to stop the winds blowing far inland because the landscape is so flat and featureless. Sounds damnably inhospitable, wouldn't you say?"

"I would, sir," Hadrian Jeffries responded with a rare smile, which disappeared the instant his master spoke.

"I am still in the room," Alec stated flatly.

"Ah, and so you are!" Plantagenet Halsey winked and smiled lovingly at his nephew. "And we'll talk when you stop haranguing me about our upcoming journey, which you've been doin' since yesterday mornin'. Olivia St. Neots and I are comin' with you and that's that."

Alec nodded to his valet to get on with what he was doing and went through to his dressing room, the old man following. He tried to temper his annoyance and worry and be conciliatory.

"Even if I were to sanction you both being part of the legation, you must see that permitting Olivia to do so is foolhardy at best, and shows a wanton disregard on my part for your safety. If something were to happen to her—or to you..."

"I won't change my mind, and you have as much chance of convincin' Her Grace to stay at home as you do of findin' a kernel of wheat with your name etched upon it. Don't you see, she needs somethin' to occupy her mind, just as you do—as do we all. All she thinks about is what that lovely young girl and that fine young man are being subjected to, imprisoned in a hostile country that, yes, is at war. When she first told me her plan, well, I reacted the way you have. But the more I thought on it, the more I could see it will be a good thing, for her and for me. We can't stay here pacing the leather soles off our shoes while you go off into God-knows-what danger. Besides, you've not given me a chance to explain what we intend to—"

"I'm sorry, but I can't allow it," Alec interrupted bluntly as he perched on the edge of the window seat. He continued before his uncle could interrupt him. "I've never mentioned what happened to me while I was in Midanich...why I was imprisoned... how I managed to escape a prison fortress... why I vowed I would never return..."

"You said you weren't permitted to tell me. Somethin' to do with Foreign Department regulations and official secrets." Plantagenet Halsey shook his head and chuckled. "That Sir Gilbert Parsons, he's up on all the do's and don't's, ain't he? Officious little turnip! You must've snapped a few quills in frustration in your time, workin' for him!"

The old man was trying to lighten the mood, but one look at Alec and he knew he'd taken the wrong tack altogether. It was obvious that even after all these years, his nephew's experience on that particular diplomatic posting still affected him greatly. He could see it in the way his arms in their white linen shirt sleeves were stiff at his sides, with his long fingers curled about the polished edge of the window seat frame, and so tightly the whites of his knuckles were visible. It was as if he was forcing himself to remain seated and calm when he felt anything but composed. And most telling of all, his nephew could not look him in the eye.

Plantagenet Halsey instantly tempered his cheerfulness. He sat beside Alec and said in an altogether different tone, "You know you can tell me anythin'. I'll listen. I'll never judge."

Alec took a few moments to steel himself before he spoke. Thinking back on events within Herzfeld Castle still had the power to make him nauseated. Since his escape he had done his utmost to consign the ordeal to the far reaches of his memory, and with every intention of it remaining there. Reading Olivia St. Neots' note at Bath about Cosmo and Emily's plight had brought the harrowing experience hurtling out of oblivion to again take center stage. What was worse, what paralyzed him with dread, was that he knew precisely what awaited him in Midanich, and if he hoped to save Cosmo and Emily he would have to succumb; there was nothing he could do to extricate himself from the inevitable.

And if what had happened in the final weeks of his time at the castle was personally traumatic, the months preceding his imprisonment haunted him. He had become too close to the Margrave's heir, Prince Ernst, and matters had escalated to a point where he had not only put his life, but also the lives of a countess and her young son in peril. He had been so naïve and trusting, so arrogantly self-assured, he had not foreseen the dangers of what was to come, firstly from his friendship with Prince Ernst and his sister the Princess Joanna, and then from his affair with the Countess. Then again, he doubted anyone could have done so, so complete was the sinister subterfuge. That, of course, was of no comfort to him.

"Yes, I do know that," he finally replied to his uncle's assurances. "Thank you. I wish—I wish I could confide in you. But you do not need to be burdened with this. And, selfishly, I don't want your high opinion of me to change."

"That will never happen!"

Alec grinned at the fierceness in his uncle's instant reply and he relaxed.

"Do you know, while I was in that fortress prison, it was thoughts of coming home to you that kept me resolved? That, and not wanting to disappoint you."

"You've never disappointed me, m'boy, and that's the truth. I should've added that you can *not* tell me, if you so wish. It is entirely at your discretion." The old man's brow furrowed for a moment. "Are those two young people in for the same ordeal you experienced?"

"Dear God, no!" Alec assured him quickly. "That's not to say what they are experiencing isn't an ordeal, but I am hopeful—and I must remain so—that they will be treated as political prisoners, and be accorded every civility. They are merely the bait. I am the one the old Margrave's children want."

"Children?"

"Prince Ernst and his sister, Princess Joanna. Ernst is the newly-elevated Margrave. But it is his sister who rules, through him."

"I guess they didn't like you runnin' off like that, eh? Not used to being defied, is my guess."

When Alec showed surprise, Plantagenet Halsey explained.

"You've been asked for specifically by name. That's not the usual way of negotiatin' the release of prisoners between kingdoms, is it? A sovereign usually decides who to send to bargain for his subjects with a foreign power. In this case it is the foreign power who has requested you. That's either because that foreign power has a special cordial relationship with you, or—and I fear this is the case—this new Margrave has gone to all this trouble because he thinks you've wronged him, or someone close to him, and he's seized upon a unique opportunity to lure you back. As you were imprisoned and managed to escape, I'd say it's the latter."

"Not the Margrave—his sister," Alec said abruptly. "The Princess Joanna."

"That don't surprise me."

The old man's smile only deepened the furrow between Alec's black brows. "Doesn't it? It should. It's much more complicated than you can ever imagine."

"I'm not makin' excuses for you. I don't know the circumstances. But if you engage in bedroom politics, then there're bound to be miscalculations from time to time."

"Miscalculations!? Ha!"

"I ain't just sayin' this because I'm your doting old uncle... I might look as if I date from Biblical times, but I was a young male in my prime once, and I did my fair share of bed-hopping. Ask Olivia St. Neots—"

"Good God, *you* and Olivia?"

The old man sat tall, hands to his boney knees. "I don't see why not!" he answered belligerently. "But no," he added quickly. "She was a good girl and I was a Corinthian of the first order. When we were both much younger, she'd put her little nose in the air and refuse to even acknowledge I was in the same room. And it had nothin' to do with my politics. She was wise to stay well clear of me *then.*"

"What changed her mind?"

Plantagenet Halsey gave a bark of laughter. "You think she's changed her mind? Still calls me *caitiff* when she thinks no one is listenin'! Baggage!"

Alec hid his smile at this level of intimacy between his republican uncle and a duchess steeped in aristocratic privilege, and repeated his question.

The old man shrugged and said simply, "You. More correctly, you changed my life. I couldn't raise a cub and carry on with my wicked ways, now could I? That ain't bein' a responsible parent, or much of a role model. But it's taken how many years for Olivia St. Neots to change her opinion of me? How old are you? So, you see, I had a reputation once, and I wasn't backward in braggin' about it, too—arrogant idiot that I was!"

Alec gave a huff of embarrassment, a hand to his black curls and a look up to the plaster ceiling, before dropping his gaze to the wooden floor. He regarded his uncle with a grim smile.

"If only it were a case of a satisfied pleasurable romp in a few beds, jealous stares from ineffectual husbands, and me swaggering about, the English diplomat lover! The only part you did describe correctly was the latter. I let hubris get the better of me and allowed myself to be flattered. And then I overstepped the boundaries of good manners. What happened after that I can blame on no one but myself. In my defense, there were sinister forces at work that I had no control over. Had I been less of a smug lothario and not allowed myself to be flattered I'd not have ended up in a predicament from which there was no escape—Damn! I've told you more than I intended."

"Don't upset yourself. You've told me enough for now. At the very least, upon this return visit, your eyes will be wide open to any mischief, sinister or otherwise. That must be small compensation."

"There is that..."

Plantagenet Halsey patted Alec's shoulder and slowly got to his feet. Hadrian Jeffries had twice come through the doorway only to turn on a heel and retreat into the closet. He couldn't let the valet do so a third time, so he returned the checklist to Alec's dressing table and said in the doorway,

"I'd best see how m'packing is coming along, and before m'tailor arrives with those breeches. Which is warmest—beaver or bear? No matter. I'll trust to his judgment."

"Uncle! You can't—You can't come with me—to Herzfeld. You simply cannot."

"Don't worry yourself, m'boy. Her Grace and I are only sailin' with you as far as the Dutch seaport of Delf—Delfzijl," Plantagenet Halsey told him. "It's on the left bank of the river Ems estuary, across from Emden. But you'd know that."

"Yes, and I'm impressed you do."

"Courtesy of your godmother, who gave me a geography lesson on the area when she and Cobham were arguing over where to drop anchor. Her Grace was all for sailing into Emden's harbor, but Cobham won't loan her his schooner without her promisin' to steer clear of Midanich altogether. So Holland and Delfzijl is as close as the captain is permitted to take us."

"I'd assumed we'd be sailing on the Harwich to Helvoetsluys packet. Going by private schooner will be positively hedonistic in comparison, and save us at least a day's sailing, weather permitting. Sir Gilbert will be pleased."

"Mere mortals might sail by packet, but not Olivia St. Neots. You think your checklist is as long as your arm! Hers stretches the length of Pall Mall! Amongst her necessary items, she's takin' along her sedan chair. Have you ever heard the like of her?"

Alec chuckled. "Is she? I wonder if she is aware that the principal means of getting about in Holland, and Midanich, is by canal boat? But if it makes her more comfortable to have her chair aboard, then so be it. It could be a nice private place to be ill, if she's prone to sea sickness." He became serious. "If you stay put in Delfzijl, then I welcome your company on the journey. But you must promise not to allow Olivia to convince you to cross over to Emden. I'll be three days' travel away, so can't help you. I don't need the worry of you and Olivia, too."

"You just concentrate on what you have to do, and I'll take care of Her Grace."

Alec squeezed his uncle's upper arm affectionately. "Thank you." He then turned to his valet, who now stood in the doorway with a pair of knitted breeches over his arm and holding a pair of soft kid fencing shoes. "M'sieur Poisson arrived?"

"Yes, sir. Mr. Wantage had him shown up to the Gallery, and I had your swords fetched and sent up, too."

"An hour of hard physical exercise will help clear your mind of worry for a while, and rid your brow of that furrow," Plantagenet Halsey said. "Nothin' better to relax the limbs and clear the head than vigorous swordplay—Well, there is one other thing," he added quietly and with a wink as the valet retreated back into the closet, before he sauntered off.

ALEC REFRAINED FROM COMMENTING ON HIS UNCLE'S WICKED aside and went to change into his fencing clothes. And when he returned to his dressing room, tired and sweaty, after an hour's fencing practice, his thoughts were surprisingly free of Midanich,

Cosmo and Emily, and even Selina. But one glance into the closet, at the leather portmanteaux all lined up in a neat row, lids thrown open, and full of clothes and personal accoutrements for travel, and his peace of mind evaporated.

Such was his preoccupation with what was ahead of him that he stood in the middle of the room as if made of stone, unaware his bathwater was ready, or that his valet waited to help him undress. But a footman accidently hit the side of the door with an empty copper as he exited down the servant stairs, swore under his breath, and brought Alec out of his private reverie. He quickly unbuttoned his linen waistcoat with a muttered apology.

"Excuse me, Jeffries. Thoughts miles away..."

Hadrian Jeffries silently took the waistcoat, then the unraveled stock, and finally his master's linen shirt. He returned for breeches, smalls, and stockings once Alec was soaking in his bath. He then busied himself in the closet with the last of the packing of Alec's clothes—the fur-lined breeches and waistcoats delivered that morning—until he was called through to the dressing room. He found his lordship with a silk banyan thrown over his breeches and open-necked white linen shirt, searching through the grooming implements on the marble top of his dressing table.

Alec picked up a crystal bottle here, a tortoiseshell-backed boar-bristle brush there, before fiddling with the silver grooming implements from his filigreed etui. When he accidentally spilled its contents amongst the clutter, it was too much for Hadrian Jeffries, who stepped forward.

"Sir, I'm sure I can find what it is you're looking for."

"Mr. Halsey dropped the travel list here... No matter. Without my eyeglasses, I can't read it anyway... I thought I'd left a small box and a set of rims..."

"No need to find the list, sir. I can tell you precisely what's on it. And your spectacles and the ring are in the middle top drawer,"

Hadrian Jeffries stated, wondering why Alec wanted the travel list, why he had suddenly forgotten where his eyeglasses were kept, and why he had mentioned the ring box. He itched to lean across and scoop up the scatter of little silver implements from the etui. Instead he rearranged the hairbrush and crystal jar to where he had first placed them. "I'll tidy this immediately, sir. If you'll just let me—"

"Leave it," Alec commanded softly. He put a hand to the back of the Chippendale dressing chair beside his dressing table. "Sit."

Hadrian Jeffries instantly stepped away from the dressing table and did as he was ordered, cleft chin up and balled fists on his knees. He watched Alec sit on the dressing stool opposite and shove his hands in the pockets of his silk banyan.

"Firstly, allow me to apologize for not having this conversation with you earlier," Alec said, aware of the guarded look in his valet's eyes, as if he were expecting a berating. "I had hoped to put your mind at rest in Bath, and then circumstances dictated otherwise. And in the coming weeks there will be little time for either of us to think beyond surviving. You do realize there will be danger, on many fronts? And I don't just mean from soldiers. Travel to the Continent always presents a myriad of difficulties. Everything from dealing with corrupt customs officers who want their cut, to intolerable food, and then there are the appalling roads. Though where we're headed, thankfully most of the journey cross-country is by canal..."

When Alec paused, Hadrian Jeffries realized it was an opportunity for him offer up a reply.

"Yes, sir. I do know that. I have some little experience of going abroad, particularly of travel by canal. I spent two years in Utrecht."

"Did you?" Alec was genuinely surprised. He had not been expecting that revelation. "So you speak the language?"

"Dutch? Yes, sir. A little. Enough to be understood, and then some."

"Good. Excellent. That will come in useful. Dutch is the language spoken by the inhabitants of Emden, Midanich's busiest port, and our first destination."

Alec paused again, but when the valet offered up nothing further about his time in Holland, he continued, saying apologetically, "Since Tam was otherwise engaged in his studies you stepped up admirably to take on his duties. But you were here, employed in this house, before Tam became my valet, when John held the position...?"

"Yes, sir."

"Wantage tells me John took you under his wing, and that he was training you to be a gentleman's gentleman at the time he up and left?"

"Yes, sir, but please excuse me when I tell you that Mr. Wantage hasn't got it quite right," Jeffries said, and continued when Alec put up his brows. "I was a gentleman's gentleman before I came here to be an under-footman."

"I presume Wantage is unaware of this, but that John knew?"

"Yes, sir. John got me through your door, and as an under-footman. We were introduced at the Stock and Buckle—"

"The coffee house on King Street where upper servants meet?"

"That's correct, sir. Once I'd shown John my reference for Mr. Halsey, he vouched for me with Mr. Wantage."

At this, Alec took his hands out of his pockets and sat up, puzzled. "A reference for my uncle? Has he seen it?"

"No, sir. I felt there was no need, once I got the job—er—position as under-footman."

"You still have this letter?"

"Yes, sir."

"Where are you from, Hadrian? What are your family connections?"

At these questions, Hadrian Jeffries vacillated. He expected Alec to ask him who had written him the reference. At the very least, where he had been employed and by whom as a gentleman's gentleman. So he was unprepared for such a personal question. Not even Mr. Wantage had asked about his family. And if he'd been content to remain an under-footman this question may never have been put to him. But when John had left Alec's employ he had jumped at the chance to take his place, and put himself forward. Mr. Wantage was all for it, particularly as John said he should be given the post, even if temporarily to show him, and of course the master, of what he was capable. And then his chance was gone all because of that upstart Thomas Fisher, who, it was obvious to everyone downstairs, had never been an upper servant, least of all valet to a nobleman. Yet, not a year into his post and Tam Fisher was no longer valet, and he, Hadrian Jeffries, had the post... Well, almost...

Of course he should have expected such a question from Lord Halsey; the nobleman was anything but conventional. He also knew not to be evasive or lie to him; the man was too keen of brain to be fobbed off with a pat response. So Hadrian told the truth.

"Edinburgh, sir. My family is still there. All of them. I'm the only one to come south."

Alec hid his surprise and said evenly, "You've lost your Scots brogue. Deliberately?"

"Yes, sir. I worked hard at it. But not for the reason you think."

"I don't know what to think, Hadrian. Your reasons are your own, but I am interested to know why. But only if you wish to tell me."

Hadrian Jeffries nodded, mollified by Alec's moderate tone.

"Apologies, sir. I just want you to know it wasn't out of any sort of deception. My father believed that a man could only better himself through honest hard work and speaking well—as well as our betters south of the border. So we were given lessons in elocution so we wouldn't sound Scots." For a moment Hadrian Jeffries permitted himself to smile. "My elder brother Trajan refused to lose his Scot's tongue. No matter that he was beaten every time he opened his mouth. Trajan's a Scotsman through and through, and no amount of voice training was going to take that from him!"

"There is nothing wrong with being proud of your heritage, Hadrian—or of your name. I take it Jeffries is a surname you gave yourself?"

"Yes, sir," the valet answered stiffly. Adding in a rush, "But Hadrian *is* my Christian name."

Alec smiled. "With a brother named Trajan, of that I had no doubts. Do you also have brothers so named Nerva, Antony, and Marcus, by any chance?"

"Nerva, sir? No, sir. There's only Trajan and me."

"Ah. What a pity your father did not have five sons to name after the five good emperors. No matter. Any sisters?"

Hadrian Jeffries had no idea who or what were the five good emperors but he could answer the latter question. "Yes, sir. One sister—Marcia."

"Of course. Marcia was mother of Trajan, and wife of Trajanius Pater. Your father has a partiality for the history of the later Roman emperors."

It was a statement but the valet answered Alec anyway.

"Yes, sir. He does. He was a Latin scholar. He went to university on a scholarship."

When Hadrian Jeffries did not offer up anything further about his family or his name, Alec let it rest and moved time on, saying quietly, "Am I to presume then you are not from a family in service?"

"If by service you mean servants of a great household, then no, I'm not, sir. My father is in service of a different kind. He is the chief advocate's head clerk in stables. Stables are called chambers here in London, so he's head of chambers in Edinburgh, if that makes sense?" he explained to clear Alec's furrowed brow. "I'm the only family member to go into household service."

Alec mentally sighed. How had he ended up with two valets in the space of nine months who were both not as they first appeared. They might be poles apart in temperament and yet their circumstances were similar, in that neither had been born into service or was trained to do the job specifically required of them. Although, he had to admit, Jeffries was an excellent gentleman's gentleman. He asked the same question he had asked Tam.

"Are you a runaway, Hadrian? Are you in trouble with the law?"

"Me, sir?" The valet was offended, but he evaded answering the question nonetheless. "Begging your pardon, but why would you think so?"

"You are not using the family name you were given at birth. You have suppressed your accent. And, you just told me you come from a good family, with a father who holds a well-respected position amongst the judiciary in Scotland. Thus it is simple to assume you came to London to hide...?"

"Not to hide. I came to London in disgrace," the valet stated simply. "My father and brother know where I am. Trajan occasionally writes. Father does not. My sister has been forbidden from contacting me, though she does send the odd letter. Her husband is a well-respected advocate and can't afford to have the likes of me for a brother-in-law. More so because I'm a valet, than what I did."

"What you did...?"

Hadrian Jeffries gulped. He had walked into his own verbal trap, and by the way his lordship was regarding him, the only way out of it was to tell the truth.

"Those two years I spent in Utrecht, it was as valet to the son of a knighted advocate. He wasn't particularly interested in study, and spent his time in more pleasurable pursuits, if you get my meaning."

"I do."

"To cut the story short: He cheated on an exam. He was given a second chance. With that second chance he sent me to sit the examination for him. I got for him a distinction, and that got him noticed by the examiners. He wasn't up to passing an exam, least of all getting the best mark in the year! So the second cheat was discovered and he was thrown out of university in disgrace. For my efforts I was dismissed from his service. That's when I came to London."

"You did not consider studying for the bar yourself?" Alec asked. "You obviously have an aptitude for it."

The valet took a moment to reply, and when he breathed in deeply then slowly exhaled into his fist, Alec got the impression Hadrian Jeffries had made up his mind to confide in him. So he remained suitably grave and prepared himself not to be surprised by anything the younger man told him.

"What I have, my lord, is a picture memory," Hadrian Jeffries confessed flatly. "If I read something I want or need to remember, then I do. Word for word. If I see something I want to remember, then I can, as a picture in my mind's eye, and relate all the details of that scene back to you as if I am once again in that room, or that setting. Marcia says it's a gift from God. My father thinks I'm a freak. That's how I managed to get that distinction on that paper. But I could no more get up and argue a point of law as fly! And an advocate is not what I ever wanted to be. You believe me, don't you, about my picture memory?"

"Yes, I do. I suspected something of the sort when you never took the travel list with you when you went on errands to the various merchants. Nor did you have it on you when ferreting out my collapsible travel furniture up in the attic. It remained on my dressing table the entire time. That is, until you moved it. Perhaps after my uncle picked it up to peruse?" Alec smiled thinly. "Not that you forgot the list's existence, but once you had committed the inventory to memory it was superfluous to your requirements, was it not?"

"Yes, sir. I did not see any reason to carry it about once I'd stored it in here," he said with a tap at his temple.

"You will forgive me if I tell you I had Wantage double check the inventory as it was loaded onto the wagons."

"It was all there, wasn't it?" the valet asked, somewhat offended. "The two folding chairs, the collapsible camp bed, the *nécessaire de voyage*, travelling kettle, four bundles of beeswax candles, the three *billets doux*, ten sacks of coal, the four brass foot warmers—"

Alec put up a hand "Yes. Yes. All fifty-eight items—"

"Sixty-two. There are sixty-two items on that travel list. I trust Mr. Wantage didn't miscount—"

"No. I'm certain the entire inventory is now on its way to Harwich, including the brass foot warmers and sacks of coal." Alec smiled. "And I agree with your sister. Your extraordinary memory is a gift, and one that could come in useful—But we'll discuss that later," he added, rallying from thoughts of how he could best use such a skill while in Midanich. "What I need to talk about is your present position as my valet. Is your chosen employment something you want to do, or something you see as a temporary position until you find a more suitable vocation?"

"I'm not about to run off and be a-an apothecary or a-a physician or such, if that's what worries you, sir," Hadrian Jeffries stated with uncharacteristic harshness. "I'm no Tam Fisher!"

"No, you are not. Thomas Fisher is an apothecary, not a valet," Alec replied calmly, ignoring the younger man's derisiveness. "I will tell you now, so that you can rest easy, or you can make up your mind to do something other than remain in this house. When Tam returns from Somerset, it will not be as my valet, but as my ward. He will no longer be a member of the household but a member of the family. Do you foresee a problem with that, Mr. Jeffries?"

Hadrian Jeffries did not hesitate. "No, my lord. I do not."

"Good. So tell me: What are your expectations for the future?"

"Expectations? Future?"

The valet blinked and hesitated. Not because he did not have an answer, but because no one had ever asked him, not even his father, who had assumed he would do as his elder brother had done before him, as had his grandfather and great uncle before that. But since his earliest memory, Hadrian Jeffries had only ever wanted an uncomplicated life, surrounded by wealth, privilege and beautiful things. But for one with his humble origins, such a life was the stuff of dreams. Yet, he dared to continue to dream until a solution presented itself. There was only one vocation for him—valet to a wealthy gentleman, preferably a nobleman. And once his mind was fixed, he went about achieving his dream. Never indolent, he spent years working his way up the servant ladder. So he was justly proud and entitled to expect nothing less than the position he was now in: Valet to a peer of the realm.

When Alec repeated his question, adding with a wry smile, "I am genuinely interested, Mr. Jeffries." Hadrian Jeffries believed him and was eager to share his philosophy.

"My expectations have always been single-minded, sir: To serve. To excel at being a gentleman's gentleman. That's the simple answer. I like the work. I like the living. And I like the routine. If I may be so bold as to say that I do excel at anticipating my master's wants and needs, and to seeing that other servants do the same. I like order. The maxim—everything has a place and there is a place for everything—is very true. And I enjoy what others consider mundane. I like the sorting, the putting away, and the taking care of well-tailored beautiful clothing. I enjoy shining shoes and buckles, and nothing gives me greater satisfaction than to know my master is well cared for and his fellows consider him well-dressed." The valet gave Alec a quaint little nod and a smile. "I like being *your* valet in particular, my lord."

"Good. I am just as pleased to have you as my valet, Jeffries," Alec replied with a smile, and stood; the valet did likewise. "And so the post is yours for as long as you want it—"

"Thank you, my lord! Thank you. You won't regret your decision!"

"But you may just regret yours," Alec said with a laugh. "Routine it may be here in St. James's Place, but when I travel it is anything but ordinary. Though..." he added with a sigh of regret. "This trip you won't have the looking after of my hounds. Mazarin and Cromwell will remain here with Mr. Fisher."

"You can be assured I'll be vigilant in making certain order is maintained, sir; even more so in foreign climes. You need not worry about your household arrangements. And I am competent enough in a number of foreign tongues to be able to carry on a rudimentary conversation. At the very least, make myself understood."

"Yes. So you can. That is a very useful skill to have. But," Alec added on a sudden thought, "let's keep your language skills between us for now. It may be to our advantage if it is thought you are ignorant of all but the English tongue. And best not to mention your exceptional memory, either. We'll keep that between us, too. Does Wantage know?"

"No, my lord. I've not shared my—*ability* with anyone but you. It's nobody's business but mine—and now, yours."

"Thank you for taking me into your confidence. I should warn you—though I am sure you have gathered as much from my conversations with Mr. Halsey—that we are setting sail for a dangerous place. With Midanich at war we are particularly vulnerable to both sides in the conflict. We'll need to keep our wits about us."

"Yes, sir. I understand. I am not easily daunted."

Alec smiled. "I'm pleased we had this conversation, Hadrian."

"As am I, my lord," Hadrian Jeffries replied with a quaint little bow. He glanced at the timepiece on the mantel. "Shouldn't we be getting ready for dinner now, my lord? It's gone the hour..."

Alec mentally smiled at the use of the first person plural but said blandly, as he removed the little ring box from the middle drawer, "Yes, we should. We must not keep Mr. Halsey waiting. But before I do so, tell me: You looked inside this box, didn't you?"

The valet blushed. "Yes, sir. I did."

"Thank you for being truthful. Though I expect nothing less than the truth—always."

"I only did so because I'd never seen the box amongst your things, sir, and so I wondered if it might belong to Mr. Halsey. But—"

"—he would not own, nor wear, such an ostentatious piece of jewelry, would he?" Alec interrupted, prising open the lid so his valet could take another look at the heavy gold ring on its bed of velvet—a carnelian intaglio armorial seal mounted on a thick gold band. "I want you to commit this coat of arms to memory, Hadrian. And when we are in Midanich, if this ring is not on my finger, you are to know where it is at all times, and to guard it with your life."

Hadrian Jeffries took the little box and studied the carnelian intaglio, running a finger delicately over the design cut into the precious orange stone. He then closed the lid and handed it back to Alec with a nod. "Yes, sir. With my life. You can depend on me."

"Thank you. And thank you for not asking me about it," Alec said, leaving the box on the dressing table to shrug off his banyan. He picked up his linen stock off the back of the chair and stood before the long looking glass to tie it. "It is a long and involved story that does not bear repeating. But the significance of that ring will become immediately apparent once we step foot in the principality... Oh, and before I forget," he added after a moment of staring at his reflection; Hadrian Jeffries suspected his master's thoughts were miles away. "Would you be so good as to give Mr. Halsey that written reference? I'm sure he would like the opportunity to offer a reply to—to...?"

"Mr. Cale, sir. Mr. Joseph Cale. Chief Advocate recently retired.

He was kind enough to write a letter of good character for me, when others would not. I suspect my sister—Marcia's influence. She's married to Mr. Cale's son, and is on very good terms with her husband's parents. Mr. Cale fairly dotes on her."

Alec paused in the act of tying his stock. Joseph Cale. Now there was a name and a man he had not heard spoken of in his presence in almost a year. Salacious slander linked Cale forevermore with the Countess of Delvin, Alec's mother. Cale was not only rumored to have been his mother's lover but as a consequence of their torrid affair while she was newly married to the Earl of Delvin came the birth of a child. Alec was that child, and his Uncle Plantagenet believed Joseph Cale to be Alec's true father. Alec did not believe it. He could not. He wanted nothing to do with Mr. Joseph Cale.

He made no comment, but it was obvious to Hadrian Jeffries in the way Alec roughly handled his stock that he was angry.

"Shall I fetch your frock, sir? I chose the midnight blue—"

"Whichever! It doesn't matter!" Alec snapped, but was instantly repentant. "Sorry. Yes, of course the midnight blue coat will suit. Jeffries. A moment! There is one circumstance I did forget to mention." When the valet turned at the door and waited, banyan now folded and over an arm, Alec felt awkwardly foolish. It was because thoughts of his mother's affair and its consequences made him instantly and inexplicably think of Selina, and the consequences of their affair—that she had recently miscarried their child. He could not live through another such heartbreaking event, not unmarried. He needed to be at Selina's side as her husband not her lover. Only as husband and wife could they openly support each other in their grief, as parents, and in good conscience. There was only one solution—well, there were two, but he did not want to live his life without Selina, and he could never live as a monk. So marriage it was, and the sooner the better.

Alec turned away from his reflection and lost his scowl.

"When I return from Midanich, I am getting married. That will bring its own set of unique requirements, not only for you as my valet, but to the rest of my household. I thought you should be the first to know. Please keep it to yourself until I have had a chance to speak with Mr. Wantage."

"Yes, sir. Of course." Hadrian Jeffries made Alec a charming bow. "May I be the first to wish you joy, my lord."

"You may, Hadrian. Thank you."

As Alec watched his valet turn and almost skip into the dressing closet, his thoughts were full of Selina—where she was, what she was up to, and when he might see her next. Little could he have known that at that precise moment Selina Jamison-Lewis was just a street away in St. James's Square, and she was not only thinking about him, she was discussing him with her aunt, the Duchess of Romney-St. Neots.

# Seven

"HE'LL NEVER AGREE TO IT." SELINA WAS ADAMANT.

"He doesn't have to if he doesn't know about it, does he?" the Duchess of Romney-St. Neots countered loudly. She was standing close to the other side of the tapestry dressing screen, in the hopes of being heard over the activity of the *corsetière* and her assistant who were assisting her niece with the fit of a pair of jumps—stays without buckram and which closed across the breasts with hook and eye.

"He won't be poking his head into the carriage on the trip to Harwich, and once we're on our way, there is little he can do about it. If I want my niece to accompany me, that's that."

There was a long silence punctuated by murmurings and the rustle of fabric, and then a yelp when the *corsetière*'s assistant unintentionally pricked Selina's arm with her tacking needle. Selina could take no more fussing and so she shooed the three women aside and stepped out from behind the screen for a breath of air.

"Let me take a look," the Duchess stated, and turned Selina this way then that, critically inspecting the half-finished undergarment as the *corsetière* explained what had been done, and what still needed doing to fulfill the Duchess's unusual request.

Madame *Corsetière* began in her halting English but when the

78

Duchess asked her a question about the quilting of the fabric in French, Madame continued in her native tongue. She explained that the two front halves of the jumps would secure over Selina's breasts using metal hook and eye closures. An extra layer of quilting had been placed between the cotton lining and the chinchilla fur, and it was here, just as the Duchess had requested, small pockets had been sewn and were concealed so that only Selina would be aware of their existence. Madame did not have the bad manners to ask what these hidden pockets were to contain, but stressed that the comfortableness of the undergarment would be determined by the weight of the pockets' contents.

The Duchess was delighted with Madame's work but brushed aside her difficulties in having the garment finished in two days' time by doubling Madame's fee. With Selina divested of the garment, the *corsetière* and her assistant departed, breathless at the sum they were to be paid and the task ahead.

"I wonder if they know you mean to stuff those little pockets with jewelry?" Selina asked, slipping a silk banyan over her chemise and petticoats with the help of Peeble, her aunt's lady's maid.

"It matters not. What matters is if you are perfectly reconciled to my request," said the Duchess, a jerk of her powdered hair towards the sitting room door—signal for Peeble to leave them alone. "I've no idea how many days you'll have to wear those stays, but I foresee at least three weeks. That's a long time to be burdened with such a responsibility. You won't be able to take them off, only to bathe, and you can never let them out of your sight even then."

"I'll wear them for ten months if it will help free Cosmo and Emily. Though I don't understand why you want to keep this a secret from Alec. Concealing jewelry in this way is inspired."

"Thank you, my dear. I do have the odd moment of brilliance," the Duchess replied with a quick smile and then was serious. "I don't want him to know for the same reasons I don't want him to know you're traveling with me until we reach Harwich. You are the most precious thing in the world to him. So do you think him likely to sanction you carrying a king's ransom concealed in your bodice, at any time, least of all in a foreign country at war? Never! Nor would I, under any circumstances except these. It weighs heavily on my conscience to have to use you in this way, but if there was an alternative to securing Emily's release, I would gladly use it. You do understand that, do you not, my child?"

"Of course, Aunt," Selina instantly reassured her with a smile. "I fully expect Alec to be displeased when he realizes I am accompanying you and Mr. Halsey to Holland. But he won't blink an eye in opposition because he will see that it is the right thing to do. You cannot go alone, even if you have Mr. Halsey for support. But once we reach Dutch waters, how are we to persuade Alec to agree to taking me with him, and not to leave me behind with you?"

"He won't have a choice. Your name is inked on the letters of introduction. Thus you are an official member of the English legation."

Selina was unable to hide her amazement. "How did you manage to get Cobham to agree to it?"

The Duchess's eyes lit up and her smile was conspiratorial.

"I didn't," she cooed. "I summonsed the chief clerk of the Northern Department, a Mr. Larpent, to visit me. I told him a fib. I said this silly old woman had spilled her coffee across the original document, and that I would be forever obliged to him if he would write up a separate letter of introduction. And to please not tell Cobham of my mishap. That we would keep it between the two of us, and Cobham not be the wiser, or he would be very angry with me! Of course a toady such as Larpent could not whip out his quill and ink fast enough to oblige me. I then had a Privy Councilor put his signature to the document. The Earl of Salt Hendon to be precise. His grandmother and my mother were first cousins. What? Surely you cannot be shocked by my tactics," she retorted when Selina gasped and then giggled behind her fan. She shrugged and pouted. "There isn't a level low enough to which I will not stoop to secure Emily's freedom. And Cobham and I are in accord on one thing at least. That the Margrave will be sympathetic to a kinswoman being given access to Emily. Of course, your brother had no idea that I would choose you as that kinswoman, or he quite rightly would have refused. Your safety—"

"Oh, it's not my safety he cares about," Selina interrupted flippantly. "Though, that is not strictly true. What I should have said is that he cares more for the Vesey name than he does my personal safety, or my happiness. But I am not afraid," she assured the Duchess, took the hand held out to her, and sat beside her aunt on the chaise longue. "Once I am reunited with Emily I am determined we will not be parted. They'll have to wrench me from her!"

The Duchess teared up at such ardent sincerity and gently brushed a stray sprung curl from Selina's flushed cheek. Her niece had all the appearance of a fragile ethereal beauty with her delicate cheekbones, white skin and apricot-red hair. But beneath the waiflike exterior she knew her to possess a natural resilience for survival, born of an arranged marriage to a violent brute. She also knew that at her core Selina was an unashamed romantic who was fiercely loyal to those she loved.

"Thank you, dearest. I do feel better knowing you are going to her," the Duchess said. "And I care very much for your safety, so it is imperative you tell no one about the jewelry. The British consul's letter may demand a ransom, but it does not stipulate its kind, and my jewels are only to be used as a final recourse. Cobham has suggested, and I agree with him, that the Margrave be offered a goodwill gesture from one monarch to another. So I am sending my most prized possession: The mechanical gaming table by the Roentgen brothers."

"The one where the leaves turn like the pages of a book?" Selina asked, and when the Duchess nodded, recalled, "I teased Cosmo for using that wondrous table as a lure to attract females. He had discovered the hidden latch that allowed for the box containing the backgammon board to spring up from table's center as if by magic. He publically challenged anyone to discover its whereabouts. And do you know, not fifteen minutes later and completely unaware of his challenge, Alec strolled up with Emily and not only demonstrated the mechanism, but showed her where to find the latch. The look of defeat on poor Cosmo's face had us in stitches of laughter!"

"Yes, I remember it well," the Duchess said with sigh. "I've never seen Alec with a bigger grin, and Cosmo so dog-faced!"

"Forgive me. I did not mean to upset you," Selina apologized, as the Duchess quickly dabbed her eyes dry with the corner of a lace handkerchief. "Offering the table as a goodwill gesture is an excellent notion. Even if soldiers ransack the baggage looking for jewels and coin, they won't be interested in a table, no matter how inventive, or dare take it, if it's for their ruler." She turned at the sound of porcelain cups and plates rattling and watched Peeble cross the room with a tray.

"Put the tea things here, and then you may ready my gown for dinner. And send word to Evans to have Mrs. Jamison-Lewis's gown readied, too. You don't mind staying here with me, do you?" the Duchess continued, as she made them both a cup of tea, Peeble gone on a curtsy.

"Not at all. In fact, it gives me a place to live until we are off on our nautical adventure."

The Duchess passed her niece a cup of milky tea. "So you have finally decided to sell the house you shared with J-L?"

Selina shook her head. "Not sell. Lease it out. Alec wants me to sell Hanover Square but Cleveley advised against it. He says I need to keep some form of independence. Then again, he also advised me not to marry Alec."

"What?" The Duchess was so dismayed she almost overset her teacup. "He gave no such advice!" When Selina nodded, she sat up tall and said, "How dare he! Hypocrite. Fatherhood should've mellowed him, particularly at his age, or at the very least, marriage to Miranda should've done so. He has no right interfering in your happiness."

"Oh, he has mellowed. Do not think otherwise. He's besotted with her, and his newborn son."

"Is the baby—*well looking*?"

Selina smiled. "By that do you mean does he look more like his beautiful mamma than his papa? You may rest easy. Baby Thomas does have a great look of Miranda. Which surprises me."

"That he should look like his mother?"

"No. That I could see that he does. I've never held a newborn before... They are so tiny... I see now why parents fall instantly in love with their offspring..."

The Duchess caught the note of wistfulness and tried to keep her voice neutral. "I would have thought the fact Alec is now a marquess reason enough for Cleveley to give you his blessing."

"Yes. But he says as Alec is now a peer he must marry a female who can give him a son; an heir. Everyone knows I was unable to give J-L a child, and we were married for six years."

The Duchess snorted her contempt.

"What utter porridge! What would Cleveley—a male, and who is not your physician—know about your fecundity? Arrogant presumption! To be truthful—and I can say this now without fear of upsetting you—I was relieved your marriage remained childless." She shuddered. "J-L was a monster. That you had to endure such violence was appalling enough! To bring a child into that household... For him to witness his father mistreat his mother—*never*."

Selina swallowed and said quietly, "May I confide in you, something I have never told another? Of course, Evans knows—no one else."

"My dear, you may tell me anything and it will go no further; that I promise."

Selina nodded. "Yes. I know that. I'm just afraid—afraid you will think less of me for what I—"

"Now it is you who are talking porridge! Tell me or no, but let me be the judge."

"Very well... I realize I must forever live with the consequences, but I am reconciled to it, and for the reasons you stated. I did not want to bring a child into such a horrible world, so I used a number of-of—*methods*—to ensure conception did not occur."

"But I thought... Didn't you suffer several miscarriages whilst married to J-L?" the Duchess blurted out in surprise, then added quickly, because she had broken the confidence of another, "Your sister-in-law told me in the strictest of confidences."

Selina shook her head. Try as she might she could not stop the tears from spilling down her cheeks.

"I lied to J-L, and to others, and more than once, that I was pregnant. In truth I was not. I needed the-the *respite* from his loathsome attentions. I'm not proud of myself, but nor am I sorry my hateful marriage remained childless." She quickly dabbed at her cheeks, sniffed, stole a glance up at her aunt through her lashes, and confessed all. "It was only a little over a month after J-L's death that Alec and I were—*reconciled*. That we—that he and I—"

"Reconciled is one way of putting it," the Duchess interrupted flatly. "Go on."

"And then, just after Emily, Cosmo and I arrived in Paris I discovered I *was* pregnant. To tell you a truth, I was terrified the baby might be J-L's. And so when I miscarried, my overriding emotion was one of relief—that I was rid of that monster's child. And then I was overcome with the most appalling thought: What if I had not lost J-L's child at all, but Alec's? And then the physician who attended on me gave it as his professional opinion that because

I used methods of prevention during my marriage, I may now never carry a baby to term. So you see now why I can't marry Alec, and why I am—I am so *utterly* miserable!"

At that confession, Selina fell all to pieces. With a trembling hand she shoved her teacup onto the low table to be gathered up by the Duchess and held until the sobs subsided. When she was finally quiet and still, the Duchess sat her up, brushed the silken red locks from Selina's flushed face, gently kissed her forehead, and finally held her face between her hands and looked into her niece's dark eyes.

"Oh, my dear sweet girl, you are to stop punishing yourself this instant," the Duchess stated. "I don't give the snap of two fingers for a Parisian physician's opinion! You will have children, of that I am convinced." She sat back and clasped her hands in the lap of her petticoats. "And if you want the truth, you will be plagued by more miscarriages. It is a sad fact of life which we females must accept. Why I had three miscarriages before I gave Romney his firstborn son. And we went on to have ten live children as you know. Not that I wish a cricket team on you, my darling, but it does underscore that what you suffered in Paris is nothing unique and should be put behind you."

"But what if—"

"No! I won't allow you to wallow in what-ifs! Nor will Alec, when he knows your ridiculous reason for having refused to marry him. You finally have a chance for a good life, a happy life, and with Alec, and you will not refuse him a second time. Do you hear me?"

Selina nodded obediently but she was anything but optimistic. She sighed forlornly. "He may not ask me again. I tried to speak with him at Bath, to explain why I could not bring myself to tell him about the miscarriage I had in Paris, but he would not listen. If you had but seen the anguish in his eyes, you'd know he—"

"—was upset *for* you," the Duchess reasoned. "No doubt that was the first he'd heard you were pregnant..." When Selina bit her lower lip and confirmed her statement with a nod, she smiled in understanding. "Don't you see? He discovered all in the same breath, and in public, you were pregnant, then miscarried, and that you had kept both from him. And you wonder why he is upset?"

"I should have told him when—"

"—you spent that week together in Paris in *reconciliation*?" When Selina dropped her gaze to the wet handkerchief scrunched in her lap the Duchess smiled crookedly, and said, tongue firmly in cheek, "When your physician prescribed you keep to your bed after your miscarriage, I'm sure he meant bed *rest*."

"I did have a month of complete bed rest," Selina said in a small voice. "Before Alec—"

"No more *reconciliations*, Selina. Do you understand me? I won't have you and Alec sharing a bed outside of wedlock, again. That not only results in-in—*consequences*, it invites scandal. Particularly when you are both less than discreet."

"But... We were discreet," Selina contradicted. "We rarely left the apartment. We—"

"You were seen at the Louvre by Lady Russell—*kissing*. That woman is an inveterate gossip. Naturally, now everyone knows what is going on between the two of you!" The Duchess sniffed loudly when Selina dared to bite back a guilty smile. "No more vulgar public displays! It is beneath you—*both*."

Selina lowered her lashes. "Yes, Your Grace."

"With his brother barely cold in his grave, and rumors Alec had a hand in Delvin's murder, he can't afford to have society whispering about him—or you! If it weren't Emily's and Cosmo's lives that are in the balance, I would dare suggest this mercy dash to Midanich a godsend for the two of you, to at least calm the gossips, for them to focus on someone or something else while we are abroad. Do you understand me, Selina?"

"Yes, Your Grace."

"Good. I am most serious. You may think me a prudish old lady, but if I do know one thing about vigorous males it's that they are potent. I wouldn't be at all surprised if after your cavort in Paris you're breeding again, and you don't even know it yet!"

Selina gasped. "Aunt Olivia! I assure you—"

"Can you?" The Duchess looked her up and down and raised her arched brows. "Can you truly assure me you are not breeding, my dear?"

Selina took a moment to contemplate her answer, and shocked herself with her response. "No. No, I cannot."

"There, then! So perhaps you will now accord my advice the seriousness it deserves."

"You have every right to your anger, Aunt," Selina responded despondently. "If I had not invited Alec to Paris... if I'd hurried to Berne to meet Emily and Cosmo instead of remaining with Alec, they would not now be locked up!"

"I will not allow you to blame yourself. That is a wasteful exercise. Truth be told," the Duchess added as she stood and shook out her quilted petticoats, Selina doing likewise, "had you rushed to meet them you too, would now be locked up with them." She linked arms with her niece and walked through to her sitting room. "Come. Let us do something useful. We may just have time before dinner to start sorting through my jewelry collection for pieces to put in those little concealed pockets. The first will be a ruby necklace that once belonged to my mother-in-law. It's a gaudy piece and I never wore it. But I could not in good conscience rid myself of it without cause." She gave a trill of laughter edged with hysteria, then became instantly somber. "I can think of no better cause than offering it as part of the ransom, can you?"

"I cannot," Selina agreed with an understanding smile.

"I only pray that the ransom will satisfy their captors. God help them if it does not! I hate to think... Oh, my dear girl, why is this happening?" the Duchess demanded, her façade of strength slipping away. "My head—my head is full of all sorts of terrible imaginings!"

Selina put her arms around her.

"Please, Aunt, we cannot begin to imagine what has happened. If we do, we will surely go mad. We must simply play our part to make certain Emily and Cosmo are released. I have every confidence in Alec making it so. We must be steadfast in that belief."

"Yes. Yes, of course. You are the voice of reason, and I—I am being a wet goose! I will be good and not let my mind wander."

Selina kissed her cheek.

"We shall both be good."

They said no more. Yet, contrary to their confident smiles and their determination not to fill their thoughts with all sorts of alarming notions, their inconsequential conversation, while they pawed over the Duchess's considerable collection of jewels and rare gems, blanketed their thoughts—thoughts that were all for Emily and Cosmo, and how they were being treated. It was easy to delude themselves, sitting as they were in a pretty sitting room in St. James's Square, London, that Emily, as granddaughter of a duchess, and Cosmo, as nephew of one, were being accorded every civility at a foreign court. Self delusion was all the hope left to them, the reality in Midanich, quite beyond their comprehension.

# Eight

HERZFELD CASTLE, MIDANICH

IR COSMO MAHON HAD BEEN HELD CAPTIVE LONG
enough to know every inch of his cell—he refused to call
it a room. Every crack in the white-washed wood paneling;
how many strips of wood made up the polished parquetry flooring;
the number of knots to the fringe of the small rug in front of his
bed set into the wall. Counting was all that was left to him, that
and his memories of home. But he tried not to think of his beloved
England. What he wouldn't give to see the dome of St. Paul's rising
into a soft blue sky. He vowed never again to take for granted such
a majestic sight, or to complain about the recklessness of chairmen
dashing in and out of London traffic endangering the lives of their
passengers, or bemoan that the parks, particularly the Mall, were
being frequented more and more by all sorts of riffraff. And if his
valet wanted a full day off every fortnight to visit his ailing mother
in Hoxton, he could have it. He was such a sentimentalist and so
much affected by thinking of family and friends that more than
once, at night, under cover of darkness, he curled up in a ball on his
bed and sobbed like a child.

During the day, he forced himself to count his blessings. They were small, but blessings nonetheless. A blue-and-white tiled Dutch masonry heater in the corner kept him warm, and so warm that sometimes he opened out the small mullioned window, despite the icy winds that forever whipped about outside. And he was thankful for that window, for it allowed him to see the passing of day into night, to see the winter sky, the stars, and the falling snow. It provided normality to his lonely days. He watched the castle's inhabitants going about their daily lives: Servants scurrying across the courtyard between different wings of the palace, soldiers marching in formation, the same ginger cat in pursuit of a mouse. Sometimes, if he kept his attention on the bank of windows directly opposite, he would see movement; once a window opened and a face appeared. But instead of calling out or trying to catch the attention of the person who peered out, he shied away, as if not wanting to be seen. It was an instinctive reaction and it made him question if isolation was sending him mad.

Snow was a blessing. When he was escorted on his walk along the parapets, he no longer had to avert his gaze from the decaying heads stuck on pikes, a grotesque reminder to all what happened to deserters and traitors. The snow blanketed this macabre warning in white. But perhaps he was becoming immune to such grisly sights? Though there had not been a new head added to the pikes in a month. He counted that as blessing, too.

His Irish valet Matthias was not a blessing—he was a godsend. He had no idea how Matthias kept up his optimism but he did, and having a visit from him did wonders for morale. He looked forward to seeing him, and for the rest of the day after he'd been shaved, he was pulled out of his melancholy, convinced he would be rescued—that Alec was on his way.

And then, a month into his captivity, he made a thoroughly reckless decision, one born of his frustration at the situation in which he found himself. Once made, he could not back down. It was to have far-reaching consequences he could never have imagined.

He learned from Matthias that all males at court were barred from wearing facial hair of any kind. The decree dated back to the Margrave's grandfather, Margrave Maxim, at the turn of the century. Maxim had made the decision after learning the Russian Emperor Peter, styled "the Great", had brought in such a decree in St. Petersburg, not only amongst the nobles, but every male serf within the new Russian capital.

"It's an odd thing to do, ban beards and mustaches, wouldn't you say, sir?" Matthias asked in his lilting English, and in a low voice, one eye on the guard who stood to attention by the door. He was deliberately being slow to set out his shaving implements next to the bowl of warm soapy water so there was time for conversation, his master seated close by, holding the blue and white patterned shaving bowl under his chin in readiness, "I know it ain't the fashion to wear a beard or mustaches, but if a gent left the hair on his face, who's to tell him he can't? Not his king, that's certain. It wouldn't pass our Parliament, would it, sir?"

"It certainly would not," Sir Cosmo agreed. "If such a ludicrous bill ever made it to the Commons, the chap who proposed it would not only be laughed at, he would also be carted off to Bedlam as a lunatic!"

"That's what I said to the lads below stairs. I said we *English*men have freedoms and rights. As well as freedom of speech, we can read what we please, and write it too! And we have the freedom to grow our hair on our heads as well as our faces, as long as we pleased, if we pleased. And no one could take that right from us!"

Sir Cosmo chuckled. Not least because Matthias always made a point of stressing his Englishness and in his sing-song Irish lilt. Yet did not consider this at all incongruous, given most of his countrymen considered English occupation of Ireland as an invasion they could well do without.

"Hear! Hear!" agreed Sir Cosmo. "But you had best temper your enthusiasm and your tongue or you'll be accused of inciting riot amongst your fellow servants. They might throw up their hands and make for the border and a ship to England to see these liberties for themselves."

"They aren't employed, and they can't do as they please. They're slaves—serfs—who have no rights at all."

"Indeed? Then that's even more reason to keep them in ignorance. Poor sots. And I don't want their disaffection coming back on you."

"Don't you worry about that, sir. They wouldn't think of raising riot against their betters. There's no fight in 'em. They'd no more take up arms as grow a beard. If you get my meaning."

"I do. But to ban facial hair seems rather specific, and odd, don't you agree? I can think of a hundred and one other things worth banning if I was a despot. Stopping a fellow from wearing a beard wouldn't be on the list, you can be sure of that!"

"Me too, sir. If you'd just hold that bowl a bit firmer under your chin. That's the way," Matthias said as he proceeded to make a lather with soap ball and bristle brush. "According to Kurt—he's a second footman—it has to do with that business regarding the 'unspoken truth'."

"Does it?... Interesting... Have you managed to discover what that is—this *unspoken truth*?"

"No, sir. No one can tell me, but I did find out it has to do with the ban on beards and mustaches. And that it has everything to do with their ruler."

Matthias did not use the word Margrave. Master and servant had agreed that even though they conversed in English any word that might alert the guard—who only spoke the local German dialect—as to the content of their conversation, should be substituted for another.

"But as I only rub shoulders with serfs," Matthias continued, "I couldn't tell you what that *everything* is. Not one of 'em has ever been in their ruler's presence or his sister's, to point out fact. Their personal servants are in a different wing, and keep to themselves. Now if you'll just lower your chin, sir, I'll get to work on that stubble."

Instead of doing as his valet asked, Sir Cosmo removed the bowl and sat up, leaving Matthias with a bristle brush dripping soap lather onto the floor. The valet's surprise, then gasp and quick movement to get the lathered brush back to the bowl of soapy water, had the yawning guard standing to attention, suddenly interested in what the fuss was about.

Sir Cosmo shoved the shaving bowl at his valet, snatched the towel from the front of his waistcoat and got up out of the chair.

"No more shaves, Matthias. I have decided to grow a beard!"

Matthias blinked at his master and wondered if imprisonment was finally wearing him thin. After all, while he mingled and talked to people, and roamed most of the servant passages of the palace at will, his master did not. But Matthias was not a thick-head. He realized he was given such freedom to see if he was up to anything untoward for his master, like passing secret notes, or dispatching secret letters, or making contact with secret individuals. All of which he was not. He knew his every move was shadowed by men in the Captain's pay, paid to report back every word and deed. But Matthias also knew his dear master had no such freedoms, and while he was not mistreated, his master certainly was. Locking him up in a small bedchamber with a view of an inner courtyard many floors below, and with nothing to occupy his mind was tantamount to sticking a monkey in a cage with no mates and nothing to do, not even a branch to swing from! The boredom alone would send any sane creature mad. And this sudden pronouncement was surely proof of that.

Sir Cosmo walked to the window, the guard one step behind, as if he expected his prisoner to squeeze through the small narrow opening and fling himself to his death. Sir Cosmo had certainly lost some fat, but he would need to lose half his height as well to fit through that opening.

"Come sit down, sir," Matthias coaxed, doing his best to keep his voice neutral so as not to further alarm the guard. "It won't do to make any grand gestures, not with this lot."

Sir Cosmo sat on the hard window seat and faced his valet, a quick scowling glance at the guard, who retreated once more to the door now his prisoner was seated.

"Matthias, allow me this one tiny rebellion against my incarceration. I have no say over any aspect of my life, but this—this will suffice to keep my spirits up. I shall cultivate facial hair until such time as I am rescued." He dared to smile. "If nothing else, it will surely infuriate those who are holding me here. It may even come to the attention of their ruler, and then I may get my wish granted for an audience."

It took Matthias less than a minute to think it over. He then nodded, returned the sharpened razor, whetstone, scissors, and damp lather brush to the tortoiseshell toiletries box. He bowed.

"Very good, sir. I just hope it does you more good than harm. I'll see you in two days' time. They can at least let me comb and trim the hair on your head."

That was the last Sir Cosmo saw of his faithful valet. By the tally under his bed, that was thirty five days ago; the full beard on his face, which he could not see because he had no access to a looking glass, also told him so. And for his recalcitrance in not allowing himself to be shaved (despite threats he would be held down and the deed done regardless of his wishes), not only was he refused permission to see Matthias, but he was also denied his weekly bath and put on a ration of one meal a day. All he had to do to have his privileges restored was to allow himself to be shaved. He would then see Matthias, have his clothes laundered, be given two meals a day, and his bathing privileges would be returned.

Sir Cosmo held out, and this despite an even greater melancholy descending upon him. It was just as well he was separated from Emily, for he would hate for her to see him in such a deplorable state, he who had always been immaculately groomed. What must he look like, with his hair matted (he had long ago given up wearing his tired wig), an ill-kept beard, and his person reeking of bodily odors that were akin to that of a barn animal?

For the first time in a long while he allowed himself to cry in daylight, and he did not care whether the guard looked on. He crawled up into his bed niche, pulled the filthy sheets up over his head, and cursed his vanity. Equal doses of self-pity and self-loathing mixed with a weariness of spirit turned his crying into quiet, aching sobs. Mind fatigued with turmoil, he fell into a deep sleep.

He was shaken awake two hours later. He had guests. The Court Chamberlain, the Captain of the Guard, and three beefy soldiers.

~ ~ ~

"ARE YOU LISTENING, M'SIEUR? M'SIEUR MAHON?" CAPTAIN Westover demanded in French. "It is imperative you know how to conduct yourself in the presence of His Highness. You are not to make eye contact. You are to keep your eyes lowered at all times. You are not to speak unless directly addressed. You will—M'sieur Mahon? Are you listening? Lift his head! Lift it! I want to see his face!"

A tuft of Sir Cosmo's matted hair was grabbed and his head jerked up for the Captain's inspection. Sir Cosmo's eyes rolled in their sockets and his jaw fell open. Baron Haderslev, who stood at the Captain's shoulder, took a step closer. The stench of the prisoner's breath knocked him back and he pinched his nostrils shut before he caught sight of the foaming spittle oozing from the corner of the man's cracked lips.

Captain Westover snapped his gloved fingers to the guard standing to attention in the doorway and beckoned him.

"A bucket of icy water! Now!" he barked in his native German.

The Baron remained incredulous that this bedraggled and hirsute prisoner was one and the same as the debonair Englishman pointed out to him in the anteroom the day Margrave Leopold had died. He glanced at Captain Westover to see his reaction, but the Captain had turned a shoulder to have words with one of his soldiers, leaving the Baron to stare at Sir Cosmo, face flooding with shame.

In truth he had forgotten the Englishman's existence, and thus that he was a prisoner. So caught up had he been, firstly in the funeral arrangements for Margrave Leopold's interment, and then the elaborate investiture for his successor. The day after the ceremony, Margrave Ernst had gone off at the head of his army to engage Prince Viktor's rebel troops in battle, the Baron and the court waving him off across the drawbridge.

Margrave Ernst in full armor, breastplate painted a glossy black and emblazoned in gold with the Herzfeld coat of arms. A luxuriant full-bottom wig of elaborate curls, made from the long hair of twenty blonde virgins, covered his bald pate under a tricorne hat edged in ermine. His leather gloves were studded with precious stones, and the cape pinned across his shoulders was of ermine lined with chinchilla. Such an elaborate suit of clothing only heightened the glaringly obvious. The Margrave was as fine-boned and petite as his twin sister. No amount of manly attire could transform him from appearing the *petit-maître*. He would always be one of Plato's moon people, neither male or female in appearance.

Sir Cosmo's existence was only remembered by the Baron when Ernst returned from battle, a month after setting out, with only half his troops, and one victory from three battles. The final engagement had seen him flee, the severe weather aiding escape to the safety of his castle. Prince Viktor encamped for the winter at Friedeburg

Palace in the south with his ever-growing number of supporters and troops. The only factors stopping Prince Viktor from pressing his advantage were the weather and Castle Herzfeld's impenetrable defenses.

After a meeting of ministers, the Margrave had detained the Baron, wanting news of any correspondence from the British consul regarding the return of Alec Halsey. Haderslev had prevaricated and immediately sought out Captain Westover. And now, here they were, standing over the prisoner, and the Baron feeling oddly ashamed. After all, the Englishman had done nothing wrong. His only crime was being the best friend of Alec Halsey. He was also a gentleman, a member of the ruling class in his own country and should have been treated accordingly, if not for the fact that the Margrave had decided to hate all Englishmen since Alec Halsey's escape.

The Baron's shame did not stop him watching on impassively as the Captain brutalized the Englishman, ordering Sir Cosmo's head be shoved into the bucket of icy water.

This served the dual purpose of cleaning the prisoner's face and bringing him fully awake. And to ensure he was attentive, the Captain told Sir Cosmo that if he did not supply immediate responses to his questions, he would find not only his nose but his lungs full of water. Did M'sieur Mahon understand? And before Sir Cosmo could respond, the Captain made a gesture and Sir Cosmo's head was thrust under water a second time, and long enough for him to start struggling for breath.

The Baron saved the prisoner taking in water when he laid a gloved hand on the Captain's sleeve. "No more. Give him something to dry himself."

The Captain nodded to one of his men who threw a towel on the floor at the prisoner's knees.

Sir Cosmo was now sitting on his haunches unassisted, taking deep breaths to fill his deprived lungs. Finally, he wiped his face and beard dry then rubbed his matted hair. He remained where he was, eyes lowered, but did not heed the Captain's warning to remain silent until spoken to.

"Is Emily—Is Miss St. Neots well?"

"She is not your concern, M'sieur—"

"She is my *only* concern!"

"You will speak when spoken—"

"I demand you take me to her! Until I see her with my own eyes I won't believe you—"

"Enough of your demands!" Captain Westover growled, and cuffed Sir Cosmo hard across the ear for his insolence. "Another word and I'll have your eyes put out, and then what will you see, eh, Englishman?"

Sir Cosmo fell, chin hitting the parquetry hard, teeth cutting into his lower lip and drawing blood. He remained sprawled on the floor, whatever fight left in him draining away with the blood that dripped into his beard.

"I said, no more!" the Baron growled in German. He hurried forward and took Sir Cosmo by the elbow and helped him to his knees. "Be obedient, or I cannot help you or your female companion," he hissed in his ear in French, before stepping away.

"Where's his valet?" the Captain demanded of one of his guards.

"The valet will not be joining us," the Baron replied. "His Highness wants the Englishman as you see him."

"What?" The Captain was so shocked his mouth dropped open. "With that hair grown on his face?" he finally said in a thin voice. "But—no one is permitted into the presence of His Highness like that! To grow facial hair is against the law. I will not break the law, and I will not allow you to—"

"You forget yourself, Captain," Baron Haderslev replied curtly. "It is only breaking the law if *we* do it. The law was instituted by the Margrave's grandfather. Our Margrave, his grandson, can break the law—change it—do whatever he likes. Understand me?"

Westover stared at the Baron in mutinous silence then nodded.

"Very well, Herr Baron," he conceded. "But the prisoner should at least be bathed and put into a change of clothes before he is taken into the presence of His Highness."

There were voices in the corridor beyond the small room. The soldiers at either side of the doorway came to attention, chins up and eyes straight. Captain Westover's voice trailed off. He beckoned the two soldiers standing over Sir Cosmo to come closer; they knew what to do if the prisoner moved even a facial muscle.

"No time," Baron Haderslev hissed over his shoulder, then stepped forward to greet his sovereign.

THE SMALL CHAMBER WAS SUDDENLY CROWDED WITH GEN-tlemen. Sir Cosmo peered through the tangle of hair that fell into his eyes at the cluster of boots and heeled shoes; the fabric-covered shoes better befitting a woman, or a nobleman when the short-statured Louis XIV ruled France. One pair of boots stood out. They were of highly-polished black leather, molded to the wearer's feet, with square toes and gold spurs to the heels. They stretched up over the calves and ended just above the knees in a large cuff, folded over to show the leopard skin lining. A row of silver buckles up the outer side secured the leather to the leg. Sir Cosmo countered thirteen buckles. He was good at counting these days. It kept him calm. He rightly presumed such luxuriant boots belonged to the Margrave, all other footwear remaining two steps behind. Sir Cosmo dared not lift his chin, keeping his gaze on those pair of boots. He remained on his knees, head lowered, and hands clasped in front of him, suitably supplicant. Yet, he was unable to stop his shoulders from shaking with private humor. He chuckled to himself at the grave absurdity of his situation and how, even in solitary confinement and treated with violence, he still had it in him to covet a fine pair of boots.

99

"Lift his head. Show me his face."

At Margrave Ernst's commands, Westover nodded to a guard who once again grabbed a handful of Sir Cosmo's hair and jerked his head up, but this time until his nose pointed at the ceiling. There was a collective gasp from the knot of courtiers. None had ever seen a full beard before. It not only covered the prisoner's cheeks and chin but his throat as well.

The Margrave held a perfumed handkerchief to his nostrils and gingerly stepped closer, captivated. The courtiers stayed where they were but unconsciously leaned forward, just as fascinated.

"And he's a nobleman, you say?"

"Yes, Highness," replied Baron Haderslev.

The Margrave continued to peer down at Sir Cosmo, intrigued. When he spoke he briefly removed the handkerchief from under his nose, then replaced it, sniffing each time he did so.

"It's a different color to the hair on his head…"

Haderslev and Westover exchanged a wary glance, neither knowing how to respond.

"Does he understand what I'm saying?"

"No, Highness. He speaks French and English but no German."

The Margrave shook his head, disappointed, and with a limp movement of a bejeweled finger indicated the guard could let go of the prisoner's hair.

"And he's a nobleman, you say?" repeated the Margrave. "Halsey spoke all three, and Italian, Spanish, *and* Dutch, too." He gave a huff of annoyance, then sniffed deeply of the bergamot scent sprinkled on his lace handkerchief. "And this is *his* best friend? Are you certain?"

"According to the British consul, yes, Highness."

"Has he told you anything I don't already know about Halsey?" the Margrave asked his Captain of the Guard.

"No, Highness. That is, I don't know what you know about Herr Halsey."

The Margrave looked to his chamberlain.

"And you? Has he told you anything worth repeating?"

In spite of himself the baron blushed guiltily because he did not want to reveal he had forgotten all about this Englishman's existence. So he lied. "Nothing, Highness."

"Then I must see what I can do to get the ape to talk. Though I have never heard an ape speak, in any language…"

When the Margrave looked over his shoulder at the huddle of courtiers, to a one they tittered. Haderslev and Westover exchanged a wary glance, communicating the same thought—*mindless sycophants*.

"Forgive me, Highness, but I—" began the chamberlain and was cut off.

"Is Halsey on his way?" asked the Margrave. "Can you at least tell me *that*?"

Haderslev looked to Captain Westover, who said without hesitation, "Yes, Highness. I had a report from my agent in Emden yesterday. A scout sent word that when Halsey's ship entered the Ems estuary it was met by one of ours, and boarded. As you know, we have a flotilla patrolling the estuary, picking off ships with cargo—mostly Dutch heading for Delfzijl—and taking them under escort to Emden, where their goods are confiscated."

"And our Dutch neighbors? Have they challenged our sovereignty of the Ems?"

"Not to my knowledge, Highness. The ships in Delfzijl's harbor remain at anchor. But I am yet to receive word from our spies in Amsterdam as to whether our neighbor is preparing to send ships to defend their claims to the Ems."

"And Halsey? Did his ship come alone, or was he escorted by his arrogant English navy?"

"His ship entered the estuary alone, and from the scout's report, crossed from England without escort."

LUCINDA BRANT

"Good. As soon as you get word he's is on dry land, tell me. The Princess Joanna is very desirous of being kept abreast of news of her—of our friend."

"Yes, Highness," Westover replied. "I have soldiers quartered at every village along the canal, to keep the peace, and to watch for traitors. Prince Viktor's troops may have bedded down for the winter, but they are not far from—"

"I don't care about *him* or his Frisians!" the Margrave spat out with annoyance. "I'll have them wiped off the map come spring. Now I must prepare for the arrival of our guest. My sister will want to know..."

When the Margrave let the sentence hang and the silence stretched, the Baron felt compelled to move time on.

"Highness, with your permission, the prisoner must be shaved, it is the law, and perhaps he should be bathed and put into a new suit of clothes as befits his rank."

"By all means clean him up," the Margrave replied with a dismissive wave. "But leave the beard—for now. It will afford the Princess some amusement—"

"The Princess?" The Baron was appalled. He spoke without thinking. "Surely Your Highness cannot mean to subject *Her Highness* to such barbarism?"

The Margrave lifted his chin. "Herr Baron. Do I know my sister better than you?"

"Yes, Highness," Baron Haderslev replied meekly. "Forgive me. Of course. I was only thinking of her—"

"Thinking of her?" the Margrave snapped. "Why were you thinking of her? You should not be thinking of my sister at all!"

The Baron shrugged and tried to appease his master. "I was not thinking of her in that way or any way. It was a figure of speech, Highness. I only meant—"

"Get out! Go! Leave us!" the Margrave screeched, not at the

102

Baron, but at his entourage, who were restless and tittering amongst themselves, some were even daring to point a finger at the bearded prisoner who remained on his knees with his gaze fixed to the floor. "Go away! Now! Not you, Herr Baron," he added when Haderslev made motions to follow the courtiers, who were now scrambling to all try to fit through the doorway at once. "What is so amusing, eh?" he demanded of his Captain of the Guard.

"Nothing at all, Highness," Westover answered soberly, the antics of the Margrave's group of painted and patched friends wiping the smile from his face.

"Is he dangerous?" the Margrave asked, waving his handkerchief in Sir Cosmo's direction, as if he just remembered the prisoner was still in the room. "Will he go—*wild*?"

Westover thought it odd a general who had commanded an army in the field would ask such a question, particularly as the prisoner remained passive with head bowed, but he did not hesitate to answer. "I do not believe so, Highness."

"Then you leave, too. Haderslev and those two standing over there may remain."

Captain Westover hesitated, a swift look at the Baron to see if he also thought this request an odd one. After all, as captain of the Margrave's personal bodyguard, it behooved him to remain with his sovereign lord and master at all times. But when Haderslev did not make eye contact or object to the request, he did as he was told. With a curt bow he left the room. But he did not go very far. He waited and listened on the other side of the door.

"So, Englishman," Margrave Ernst said, addressing Sir Cosmo in perfect English. "Tell me everything you know about your good friend Alec Halsey."

# Nine

EMDEN, MIDANICH

ALEC STOOD ON THE DECK OF THE SCHOONER *THE Caroline*, chinchilla-lined wool cloak buttoned up to his chin and felt tricorne pulled low on his black curls. A fine mist of water droplets—a mixture of drizzle from the heavens and sea spray which slapped hard up against the hull—covered him from hat to polished jockey boots. But he was oblivious to the weather. His gaze was on the town emerging out of the fog as the captain skillfully maneuvered the two-masted sailing ship to dock in Emden's harbor.

The schooner was being escorted off the starboard bow by a naval sloop of French origin, commandeered by Midanich as a spoil of the most recent conflict. Two merchant frigates remained out in the deeper waters of the estuary, having helped the sloop bring the schooner into the harbor, to stop *The Caroline* making an attempt to run for the safe haven of Dutch waters, and a shoreline which was within swimming distance. Alec suspected the frigates had also been confiscated and overrun by pirates in the pay of the Margrave.

More than two dozen fishing boats bobbed up and down in the freezing waters, sails and flags flapping wildly in the unrelenting gusts that whipped up the brackish waters into waves and drenched their hardy occupants. In this weather, and in this season, these herring luggers were usually moored, the fishermen shore-bound and bedded down for the winter. Alec presumed they had been forced to take up sail, as another deterrent to *The Caroline* making for Holland. Again, Alec's suspicions were confirmed when one of the pirates laughingly pointed out through the rigging to the flotilla of watercraft and made a derogatory remark about such a pointless gesture.

But the schooner which had transported Alec and his party from Harwich across the North Sea had no plans to flee.

*The Caroline* had been met by the French naval sloop as it sailed in through the narrow channel south of Borkum Island at the mouth of the Ems river. Resident whalers on the island had watched with interest as the naval sloop fired a shot across the bow of the English schooner. *The Caroline* acknowledged the warning by hoisting a civil ensign, signal that the craft was not military so meant no harm, and thus should be allowed to continue on its way. But the naval sloop stayed between the English schooner and the Dutch coast, coming alongside and boarding her when she was within sight of Emden. The French sloop's crew were little better than pirates, privateers at best. And despite the captain giving his word that *The Caroline* would not make for Dutch waters—the town of Delfzijl had been their original destination—the pirates wanted guarantees, and so six of their number remained onboard while three crew from *The Caroline* were taken hostage on the sloop.

The Duchess of Romney-St. Neots, Selina Jamison-Lewis, Sir Gilbert Parsons, and their respective servants, were all ordered back below deck, and to remain there. Incredulous and angry, all had suffered varying degrees of sea-sickness on the three-day journey and were keen to see land, and thus were reluctant to return to their cabins, whatever the threat to their mortality.

The Duchess collapsed in the arms of her niece at the thought of having to return below. She had been the most ill, and her pallid cheeks still carried a green tinge. The pirates threatened to manhandle her, and the other women with her, if she and her companions did not do as she was ordered. Incredulous and vehement in his denunciation of the outrageous behavior of a bunch of ruffians, Plantagenet Halsey strode forward to offer the Duchess assistance. Instantly pistols and cutlasses appeared and were waved menacingly in the old man's face.

Alec stepped in and the impasse was peacefully resolved. And this without the need to draw his sword, which, for a reason known only to the pirates, they had not confiscated upon boarding. The passengers reluctantly returned below at his calm insistence they would be more comfortable out of the icy wind and sleet. He, however, was ordered to remain topside, because he spoke Dutch and could translate the pirates' demands to the captain of *The Caroline*, who knew only English.

To his surprise, Plantagenet Halsey was permitted to remain, and was motioned to stand by his nephew on the quarterdeck. The flame of possibility that the pirates might be reasonable men after all was extinguished when Alec revealed to his uncle he was only there to guarantee Alec's cooperation. If he proved recalcitrant, the old man was to be tossed overboard.

"Let 'em try!" Plantagenet Halsey growled low, but there was no fight in his tone. He pulled his woolen cloak tighter about his shoulders and held it firm at his throat. "It would take at least three of those crusty beggars to lift my scrawny carcass, least of all heave me overboard. Fools."

Alec gave a huff of laughter at his uncle's bravado but made no immediate comment, gaze remaining firmly on the view. So his uncle silently joined him at the port side railing, the biting wind flecked with ice that snapped at their flushed cheeks ignored, as was the bosun's whistle and the activity at their backs, crew scurrying to prepare the rigging for docking.

Alec ruminated on their situation, and what he intended to do about it once they disembarked and the passengers of *The Caroline* were safe and warm.

He had not anticipated a flotilla would be awaiting their arrival, or that his travelling companions would be forced to travel on to Emden. He could have kicked himself for not thinking such a scenario a possibility, because it made perfect sense. With Midanich at war, any vessel sailing the Ems estuary with a cargo worth having was fair game. The usual supply lines had been cut off, and resorting to piracy was one way of making up the deficiency. His only hope was that their ship had not been targeted specifically because he was on board, but that they were like any other ship commandeered by pirates in the pay of the Margrave. He was certain agents of Midanich's ruler had been ordered to take prisoner any person traveling with him, all to ensure his compliance was absolute. As if Emily and Cosmo's incarceration was not enough to obtain unconditional obedience!

His gloved hands gripped the railing a little too hard and he squinted as the port town of Emden emerged from the mist. This medieval township was so familiar to him: The huddle of terracotta roofs; the imposing walls of the star fortress which enclosed and protected the city on three sides; and the nine towering brick and earth windmills—one to each triangular bastion that projected outwards from the high city ramparts. Stretching into the wintery sky like protective giants, tall and proud, the windmills' long canvas sails turned with monotonous yet comforting regularity. Driven by the incessant wind that blew in off the North Sea, they were majestic symbols of the town's prosperity, the wealth and independence of its merchant inhabitants, and could be seen for miles, out across a windswept plane of swamps and marshes. Such was their powerful symbolism that they not only appeared on the town's coat of arms, but on the Margrave's armorial.

Upon seeing these beacons of prosperity and free will some eleven years ago, Alec had been filled with a sense of adventure. Emden was his first look at Midanich, and the seaport's quaint architecture and orderliness surprised and delighted him. Heavily influenced by its Dutch inhabitants, Emden's red brick and sandstone townhouses rose four and five stories high, and were neatly squeezed together along the numerous canals that crisscrossed the city. These waterways were the roads, and the low-roofed boats—called trekschuiten—were the vehicles by which people and goods were moved throughout this orderly town. Aside from the enormous windmills, the only other buildings of significance which had been proudly pointed out to him upon his arrival were the Calvinist church, with its imposing spire, and the Customs House at the dock. The church had stood for over a hundred years. And if it was the town's symbol of religious tolerance for those Dutchmen who had fled their homeland to escape persecution by the invading Spanish, the Customs House, with its copper roofing and distinctive dovecote under the roofline, was the symbol of its wealth—wealth either brought with them by the Dutch-speaking settlers, or accumulated through hard work upon resettlement.

And yet, in the past decade, Emden had been invaded, first by the French, and then occupied by the English during the Seven Years' War. While Alec was hard-pressed to see any outward signs of the tumult of invasion—all the windmills still stood, and the townhouses and public buildings showed no outward signs of violence—he wondered how it had affected its populace.

The last invasion and threat to England's sovereignty had been almost twenty years ago, with the Young Pretender's failed march on London. He remembered how panic had seized London, everywhere was talk of bloody massacre. Ordinary citizens were seized with terror and went to extraordinary lengths to secure and defend property and family. Emden's citizens must have gone through something similar and worse, because the enemy had succeeded in taking over the town and much of the rest of the country. And to add to their woes, Emden's citizenry was now caught up in an internal struggle.

It left Alec speculating, not for the first time, to which brother the town had pledged its allegiance—the new Margrave Ernst, or his half-brother Prince Viktor. And to whom the soldiers quartered at Emden, and the pirates who had commandeered *The Caroline*, owed their allegiance. He supposed he would not have long to wait to find that out. Just as he would soon discover if his letters to Jacob Luytens, the British Consul resident in Emden whom he also considered a friend, had been received. His most recent one was sent as soon as he knew he would be returning to Midanich. He had hoped such news would be enough to prompt the British Consul to send a reply, but again, this correspondence was met with silence.

It was Jacob Luytens who had helped him escape the country ten years ago, stowing him away on a cousin's herring lugger. Alec had remained under the weight of the fishing nets until the boat was well out into the estuary and heading northwest. He had wanted to catch a last glimpse of the town, and watched it disappear over the horizon, the slowly moving sails of the towering windmills his last best memory. Filled with relief, his legs had then collapsed under him.

Now, as *The Caroline* was slowly being warped to the pier, watched on by its pirate escort and flotilla of luggers, it was not excitement or relief that made his knees weak, it was dread. It was the sort of sickening anxiety that came with the certainty of knowing the time was almost upon him to have to account for the consequences of his impetuous actions of a decade ago. His life would once again be turned inside out, and he knew with absolute certainty that the Margrave Ernst and his sister Joanna intended he should pay, and pay dearly, for his disloyalty.

What he had not anticipated was his uncle, his godmother, and Selina bearing witness to his return, and all that that entailed. They were supposed to be on the other side of the estuary, in Holland, safe from harm and ignorant of events unfolding in Midanich. More to the point, ignorant of those events concerning him. While he had every confidence in keeping from them the most repellent of his transgressions, there were some factors about his time in Midanich that were on the public record and thus revelation was unavoidable.

He took a deep breath. So be it. He could not, and now would not, hide from his past.

Forcing himself not to betray his inner emotional turmoil, he turned to the old man.

"Uncle! I need you to listen carefully."

"Fascinatin'!" Plantagenet Halsey exclaimed, attention elsewhere.

He was peering down at the wharf, at the strong-armed men winding the thick rope from the schooner around several large capstans affixed to the pier, pushing the capstan bars with all their might in a circle, which wound the rope tighter, and this in turn pulled the ship to the pier. Plantagenet Halsey was all admiration for the ingenuity in bringing a ship mechanically alongside a pier without the use of wind and sail.

"And here I'd been thinkin' we'd need to drop anchor out in the channel and be tossed into boats and made to row." He turned to look at Alec, and rubbed his gloved hands together; the action had nothing to do with warming his hands. "Can't wait to see how they manage to off load Her Grace's sedan chair," he added gleefully. "Mayhap she can be taken up in it and walked down the gangway. She's been ill enough to warrant it. Eh?"

"Perhaps. Though I doubt she would feel any better being bumped about in a chair," Alec said with great patience. "I need you to listen to me—"

"A'course, my boy."

"Whatever happens once we set foot on solid ground, please remember: I am still me—Alec—your nephew."

"Yes. Of course you are," the old man replied. Though it was obvious from his accompanying weak smile he had no idea what Alec was talking about. "You always will be."

"I'm not expressing myself at all well," Alec apologized self-consciously. "But it is important I have your assurance that whatever happens, whatever you witness or hear about me, you will keep your surprise and your shock—yes, you will be shocked—to yourself. I will confide in you—eventually. But, for now, in the next little while, I need you not to react, but to take everything I say and do in your stride—as if these matters concerning me were always known to you."

"You want me to lie?"

"Of course not!" Alec retorted. He moved closer, a gloved hand to the railing, so as to be heard over the barks of command and attendant commotion that comes with disembarkation. "What I am asking is for you not to show surprise, because if you do, if you question anything that happens from now on, it will greatly unsettle Olivia and Selina. I don't want either of them upset, nor do I need them or Sir Gilbert asking questions—questions I'm not prepared to answer, not until Emily and Cosmo are removed from danger. So I need you to be at your confident best."

"Ha! So my lack of reaction will express confidence, while I remain in ignorance?"

Alec smiled. "Something like that, yes."

Plantagenet Halsey patted his nephew's shoulder. "It's as well I do have confidence in you. Whatever you want. I'll not ask, and I won't flinch. On my honor. You can count on me."

Alec's smile widened and he squeezed his uncle's hand that touched his shoulder. "Thank you."

"Besides, the last thing I want is Her Grace and your apricot beauty in any distress. Though—and this will be the last time I ask—why are you keepin' your distance from Mrs. J-L? You've not said more than two words to her since Harwich."

"She shouldn't be here!" Alec replied harshly, adding before turning to address his valet, who had emerged from the hold with a pirate at his back and a pistol to his ribs, "And you just broke your promise. No questions! What is it, Jeffries?"

"Sir Gilbert, my lord, is causing a—um—*disturbance*," Hadrian Jeffries reported tonelessly in English. "I've been sent to fetch you to communicate this individual's wishes to him."

Alec suppressed a heavy sigh. He waved to the pirate to lead the way.

"Sir—!"

Alec stopped from brushing past his valet, looked him in the eye and waited.

"This individual has permission to slit Sir Gilbert's throat if he doesn't instantly comply," Hadrian Jeffries said under his breath. "Regardless of your efforts to make him see reason."

"What you say? Tell!" the pirate demanded, poking the barrel of his pistol deeper into the valet's ribs.

"My servant says you have greatly upset the kobold that possesses my friend," Alec said smoothly in Dutch, and in such a bland voice that it took all Jeffries' self-control not to laugh out loud at his master's outrageous assertion that the head of the English legation was inhabited by a sea sprite. "Now I must calm him before he curses you all. And do put away your pistol."

"That barrel of a man he is possessed of a-a *spirit*?" the pirate asked fearfully, carrying out Alec's command without hesitation, a look over his shoulder as if he expected the kobold to be hovering at his back.

"Yes. And if you and your fellow seamen do not wish to be cursed into eternity, you'd best pray I can calm Meneer Klabautermann. Now take me to him."

The pirate's eyes widened with terror.

"*Klabautermann*? His name it is Klabautermann?"

"Yes. Is something the matter?" Alec asked evenly, knowing very well he was preying on the superstitious nature of all sailors.

He had remembered a story told him by the captain of the herring lugger while taking him to safety all those years ago, about a sea sprite which fishermen and sailors alike welcomed and feared in equal measure. This sea sprite was believed to assist them with their seafaring duties. But as well as having the ability to rescue those washed overboard, the sprite could turn nasty when required. As it was never seen in its true form, it was not a stretch to convince this pirate and his fellows that Sir Gilbert was possessed. Giving him the sprite's Germanic name was a stroke of comic genius, and so thought Hadrian Jeffries, a chuckle bubbling up in his throat and inexpertly suppressed.

In the pirate's panic to appease the kobold-possessed Sir Gilbert, he rushed after Alec, who strode across the deck, calling out to his fellows to stay well back and not enter the hold. There were magical forces at work below that needed to be appeased.

Hadrian Jeffries was forgotten, left on the deck beside Plantagenet Halsey.

"I don't know what my nephew said, but he's certainly put fear into that salty blackguard and his friends," the old man commented.

"His lordship's quick thinking has saved Sir Gilbert from being turned into fish bait," Hadrian Jeffries said with satisfaction.

"And so it begins..." Plantagenet Halsey muttered, and with that cryptic remark, he pulled his damp tricorne hat down over his grizzled hair and crossed the deck to join the rest of his party, who were emerging out of the darkness of their tiny cabins into a cold and blustery winter's day.

THE PIRATES HERDED THEIR ENGLISH CAPTIVES TO THE
narrow gangplank, cutlasses drawn but no longer waved menacingly.
All but two of their number stayed well back, word having gone
round that the Englishman who resembled a beer barrel may or may
not be possessed of a sea sprite.

"I knew these cutthroats would finally come to their senses once
you had the good sense to inform them exactly who I represent," Sir
Gilbert commented to Alec with a self-satisfied smile as he joined
him on deck. "His Majesty's subjects are not to be trifled with."

Alec mentally rolled his eyes at Sir Gilbert's self-delusion and
new-found bravery, but made no comment, turning away to ensure
everyone was accounted for while they waited for the gangplank to
be set in place. He then briefly and quietly told them of his plan, to
be carried out once they were on dry land, to which everyone readily
agreed, except Sir Gilbert who remarked pompously,

"You did not add, but I am certain it was a momentary lapse,
that as head of the legation I will lead this formation; I have in
my possession the necessary certified documents to present to the
officials. Once they, too, realize who I am and why I have come, I
am confident of receiving the full cooperation of these foreigners."
He smiled thinly at Alec, adding, "I may not be able to speak the
language of pirates, but my French linguistic skills, as you are well
aware, my lord, are not to be sneezed at."

"They will serve you very well indeed once we reach Herzfeld
Castle and the court, Sir Gilbert," Alec responded patiently. "But here
in Emden the citizenry speak Dutch—the language of merchants.
And the career soldiers, German. So if I can be of any assistance...?"

Sir Gilbert was momentarily flustered. "As my subordinate, of
course you can be of assistance, my lord! Now let us get off this
vessel at once!"

Despite being weak and still green, the Duchess was determined
Alec should realize once and for all time that as a marquess he had

precedence over everyone on board, herself included. And she said as much to Sir Gilbert, who listened in silence, though his expression told her he was merely assuaging her because her rank and his good manners demanded it.

But when Plantagenet Halsey touched her arm, a finger to his lips for her to desist, it was the meaningful look in his eye that made her press her lips together and say no more.

And so down the gangplank they went, one at a time, all eager to get ashore despite the constant drizzle and incessant windy weather. The ladies with their red wool cloaks and hoods pulled close about their quilted petticoats and capped coiffures, the gentlemen with their fur hats or tricornes down low over windswept hair, grey wool cloaks covering fur-lined great coats that were buttoned from boots to stubbled chins, gloved hands deep inside large fur muffs, which Alec had presented to each English passenger, male and female, knowing that such a winter accoutrement was essential in this part of the Continent, to ward off the bone-deep ache only a North Sea winter wind was capable of producing.

The group then proceeded along the overcrowded and noisy pier as directed by the patrolling armed soldiers, who were sending a multitude of passengers from a number of seized ships along a narrow pedestrian thoroughfare. The English passengers huddled together in the formation agreed to on board, so that the Duchess, Selina, and their respective lady's maids would be most protected, not only from the foul weather, but also from any jostling and unpleasantness from strangers, military and civilian.

Sir Gilbert Parsons headed the group, a step ahead of Alec and Hadrian Jeffries. Plantagenet Halsey with the Duchess of Romney-St. Neots on his arm was next. Then came Selina Jamison-Lewis and her lady's maid. Behind them the Duchess's lady's maid and Sir Gilbert's man, and at the rear two of the Duchess's most beefy and burly upper footmen brought along on the journey, because they could lift any portmanteau or trunk required, and were able to carry their mistress in her sedan chair. Most importantly, the Duchess had confided to Plantagenet Halsey with a smug smile, the huge size of their fists and the muscles in their calves would be enough to ward off the legions of thieves and pickpockets known to roam the Continent. The old man had chuckled at her contingencies, pointing out there were just as many, if not more, such petty criminals in London alone, and she had never worried about *them*. But now, looking about the pier at the swarm of bedraggled strangers as well as the dozens of soldiers, two gorilla-sized footmen might come in very useful indeed.

The pier was barely wide enough for a single horse-drawn town carriage or wagon, but such land vehicles were unnecessary. In this remote corner of the Continent, everything, from people to goods, traveled by way of the many canals built for the purpose. The cargo offloaded from the ships come into the harbor or brought in by rowboat from those frigates anchored out in deeper water, was no different, and heavy horses under the supervision of their handlers trudged up and down the pier pulling barge after barge laden with confiscated cargo to the Customs House.

Alongside the path used by the heavy horses was the narrow pedestrian walkway to which all the passengers were being directed. Canal and walkway ran the length of eight four-story red brick townhouses, the steep mansard roofs and plaster embellishments proclaiming their singularly Dutch character. And at the end of this row stood an imposing red brick building with a green copper roof and a clock tower bearing the coat of arms of Midanich. This was the Customs House, and dividing one wing from the other was a majestic arch under which ran the canal to a central depot. Here the barges were emptied and their loads sorted for inspection.

Bales of cotton, wool, and ready-painted textiles were indiscriminately slit open; wooden crates, their lids splintered, the straw stuffing tugged and pulled apart to reveal their contents;

personal luggage sorted and tossed onto ever-growing piles—many of the portmanteaux and wooden trunks with their locks broken off, the clothing and personal items considered worthless discarded in the filth and grime underfoot by workers searching for anything of value. Sacks of maize, flour, and dried pulses, crates of cheese wheels, and barrels of small beer and wine were more carefully inspected. Food and drink were most precious commodities to a fortress town during a siege, and even more so in the barren winter months when fishermen were confined to shore and the citizenry relied on stores, stores which now had to be shared with the hundreds of soldiers occupying the town.

Overseeing these customs inspections were officious men in drab greatcoats and plain black tricornes, the round brass insignia Alec knew very well pinned to their hats, indicating their status as officials employed by the city. And overseeing the overseers were soldiers with bayoneted muskets in blue wool and shiny brass-buttoned uniforms, and imposing mitre caps of red wool with a front plate of intricately beaten brass. They were professional soldiers, grenadiers in fact, and their fighting skills in times of siege were highly prized, and along with their brother soldiers, the fusiliers, were a source of revenue for their Margrave. They were exported, just like any other commodity, to countries such as England, which had no standing army and were in need of professional soldiers. Alec also knew the grenadiers, as experts in siege warfare, were usually garrisoned at Castle Herzfeld, and that Prince Ernst, now the new Margrave, was their Officer-in-Chief, and as such, they were fiercely loyal to His Highness.

So it was the Margrave's grenadiers who had managed to occupy and hold Midanich's wealthiest town and largest port, and now they would do so until the spring thaw, when Prince Viktor would aim to take Emden. Whoever controlled Emden controlled Midanich, and for Alec, at this moment in time, having troops loyal to the

Margrave in control of Emden and overseeing the Customs House would play to his advantage in ensuring the safety of those he loved and needed to protect.

And that moment might come sooner than he had anticipated, as he took in the serpentine line of cold and weary passengers that stretched the length of the pier, under the arch and into the Customs House to a central processing depot. Crushed together and only able to move as fast as the person in front of them, the passengers were nonetheless prodded, poked, and shouted at by soldiers who had nothing better to do with their time than harass these glum civilians. No adult dared protest, and all conversation was kept to a minimum, the only sounds of complaint coming from cold and hungry children and babes in arms who were oblivious to the frightening situation in which their parents found themselves.

Joining this queue of harassed humanity were the English passengers from *The Caroline*, who remained, as Alec had counseled them aboard ship, quiet and as inconspicuous as possible. It being winter was to their advantage in one singular way. Cloaks and long coats concealed the luxurious cloth and embroidery detailing of their clothes, though nothing could hide the expensive tailoring and fit of their outerwear and boots, and the ladies' leather and fabric shoes, protected from street grime by matching pattens.

It was a matter of proceeding to the front of the line without attracting the attention and ire of the military. People of wealth and status were particularly preyed upon in times of conflict because they had the most to offer and the most to lose. They could be stripped of their clothes and their possessions, and many would do and say anything not to be stripped of their dignity. With this town, indeed with the entire country, in upheaval, Alec warned that the normal rules of civility and status did not apply. Anything was possible. The military was in charge. Their loyalty was to no one but the Margrave and his family.

Just as Alec was reminding his party to not say or do anything that might bring them unwanted attention, a scuffle broke out a few feet ahead. A customs official singled out a passenger in an overlarge cloak who was acting suspiciously. The man was ordered to step forward to be searched. The wife would not let go of her husband's arm. Two small children clinging to her skirts began to wail. More soldiers arrived on the scene. The woman was shoved violently aside. There were screams and shouts as she fell hard to the pavement, her sobbing children going down with her. The man in the over-large cloak pulled a knife and lunged for the closest soldier, only to be hit hard on the back of the head with a musket butt before being dragged away between two soldiers into the dark reaches of the depot.

Those around the fallen woman and her children helped her up, their protestations muted for fear of being dragged away, too. One of the men dared to stick his face in that of a soldier's and for his insolence was hit across the face. As he staggered and was pulled back into line by his fellows, blood pouring from a cut to his brow, more soldiers arrived, bayonets at the ready. Just then a shot echoed deep within the depot and the line of passengers went quiet and still. One of the soldiers who had dragged away the man in the overlarge cloak returned, said a few words to his captain and was dismissed. The captain then turned on a heel and strolled down to the head of the line, not a word or a look at the man's wife, who had just been made a widow. It was left to her friends to give her the heart wrenching news. Her howl of misery could be heard all along the pier.

"They shot the fellow," Hadrian Jeffries said in wonderment, a look at Alec to see if he had understood correctly. "My lord...? They-they shot him for concealing a sack of coal. *A sack of coal...*"

"Yes," Alec stated, the coldness in his voice masking his anger. He turned to his uncle and the Duchess, eyes troubled. "I know I apologized on the schooner, but I can't tell you enough how sorry I am you are being put through this. I didn't anticipate we'd be boarded by pirates, and in hindsight I should've insisted you both travel via Amsterdam. But this—" He waved a gloved hand in the general direction of the shuffling line of passengers and patrolling soldiers, "—is no surprise to me, and I am well equipped to deal with it. You are not. Nor should you need be. But once we pass through the Customs House, you will have a warm house where you will be safe until my return. That I promise you."

"Think nothin' of it," Plantagenet Halsey said dismissively to mask his concern. "Her Grace and I would sleep in a barn if it'd help your cause to free Emily and Cosmo. Wouldn't we, Your Grace, eh?"

"A barn, yes. But with you...?" quipped the Duchess with a snort of derision, which considerably lightened the mood. Before the old man could find a suitable retort, she leaned in to Alec to say seriously, "My boy, do not worry about us. This is as nothing to what my granddaughter and Cosmo must be suffering. When I think of them in that castle all alone, and look at these soldiers, these *brutes*—At least I—*we*—have you to protect us, while they—they—Oh damn!" she added, eyes filling with tears when Alec drew her to him and kissed her forehead. "I promised myself I wouldn't cry, and I won't! I won't fall all to bits! Not here! Not ever. Not until you have them safely returned... Did I hear correctly?" she added, changing the subject; anything was better than allowing her thoughts to dwell on her granddaughter, particularly now she was in this wretchedly drab foreign town crawling with foreign soldiers, and none of them able to speak a civilized tongue. "Did I hear Jeffries say that fellow who was dragged away was killed for hiding a bag of coal?"

"And that surprises you?" Plantagenet Halsey scoffed. And to take the Duchess's mind off her granddaughter and their present dire predicament, if only for a few minutes, he said to goad her, "Our justice system ain't any better. We hang people for less!"

"But we don't shoot them just like that!" she argued, her shoulders snapping back with indignation, swallowing the old man's bait whole. "Not without a trial. We have due process of law—"

"Due process of law? Ha! A street urchin steals bread because he's hungry, not because he's a thief! And what does our due process of law do? Takes the child from his parents and transports it across the Atlantic. Or if he's a pickpocket who absconds with some daydreamer's pocket watch, it's because he needs to pawn the thing for food, not because he wants to know the damn time of day! And what's the outcome? He's strung up! So don't tell me about due process of law, Your Grace."

"What utter drivel!" The Duchess seethed. "How can you compare a soldier shooting a man in cold blood to a court of law deliberating upon the actions of a thief!? Property must be secured, and thieves made an example of, or our country will descend into anarchy. You've made some idiotic remarks in the past, Plantagenet, but this is utter flimflam. It is beyond anything! All that salt water has addled your brain!"

"Now, Your Grace, let's agree to disagree," the old man replied soothingly, a lift of his brow with a look of apology at his nephew, realizing his ploy was far more successful than he had planned. "And even you have to admit, he drew a knife on the military. Only a Bedlamite would do such a thing. *And* he was concealin' coal under his coat. And coal must be in high demand at this time of year, so worth a pretty penny, is my guess—"

"At least *we* give thieves a chance to explain their actions. This poor fellow was given none at all, and he has a wife and two small children and a-a family—Oh God..."

"Yes, he does. Most thieves do too..." Plantagenet Halsey muttered, and took the Duchess in a comforting embrace when she turned into his shoulder and fell against his coat, crying. "Anythin' we can do for that widow and her brats?" he asked his nephew quietly.

"Already considered and will be dealt with," Alec responded, and was distracted when a hand tapped his shoulder.

It was a customs official. At his shoulder were two soldiers. Everyone in Alec's group breathed in and waited. Sir Gilbert, Hadrian Jeffries, and Plantagenet Halsey were the only ones not to be filled with dread. Sir Gilbert, because he had his nose in a sheaf of documents, and was thus preoccupied. The valet, because he understood most of what was being said, even if it was heavy with dialect. And Plantagenet Halsey, because during the course of the conversation there was an exchange of gestures, the last one, by his nephew, making the customs official laugh and shake his head. Not understanding Dutch, the soldiers took the laughter and smiles as a sign there was little for them to do, so they walked away, the customs official soon following. Alec's party breathed easy.

Plantagenet Halsey might not understand what was being said, but some gestures were surprisingly universal; such as making a continual circular motion with a finger up to one ear.

"So you told 'em my brains were scrambled, eh?" the old man stated, shuffling forward with the rest of the group, when the line of humanity lurched forward several paces bringing them ever closer to the customs checkpoint. He wasn't offended in the least. "If it helps get us through this ordeal the quicker and before a nice warm fire, I'll act the Bedlamite."

Alec waited until the line came to a halt once more before facing his uncle.

"Better to be thought a lunatic than a spy. You'll at least be left alone, now—possibly given a wider berth." He looked at the Duchess and added apologetically, "Both of you will. I let it be known that as my mad uncle's wife you are the only one who has the power to control his—um—fits of distemper."

"Ain't that the truth," the old man muttered, with a chuckle into his upturned collar.

The Duchess was too shocked to make a suitable retort. But it wasn't Alec's lie to the customs official which stopped her tongue, it was the sudden heat she felt in her face. She was blushing like a schoolroom miss, and at her age, and over an old republican rake. Sea sickness must have affected her brain too! It was not the old man who was the lunatic, it was she!

"Peeble! My fan! And salts!" she demanded of her lady's maid.

"Don't you worry," Plantagenet Halsey said, not to the Duchess, but to Peeble, who was at their back. "Her Grace won't be fallin' any further than into my arms! Now I think the boy has somethin' else that needs sayin', so you, Madam wife, must be quiet."

The Duchess shut her eyes on a shudder. "Good—God!"

Alec allowed himself to smile at the light comic relief his uncle and godmother's dramatic interactions were providing in an otherwise tense situation. He knew his uncle's behavior was calculating and that he had successfully diverted the Duchess and the rest of the group away from their predicament, if for the briefest of moments. His gaze swept over the group, faces pinched with cold, yet there were smiles, and they were a little less wary. Yet their anxiety returned when a group of soldiers marched past and were soon heard terrorizing newly-arrived passengers further down the line.

If his uncle could divert their attention with his silliness, then he could do likewise by boring them all with the petty details of what they could expect once they arrived at the Customs checkpoint. It was a ploy he had learned from the very man standing in front of him. Sir Gilbert was a master at spouting administrative balderdash, and on too many occasions to mention had bored Alec to stupefaction. He could but try...

"When we arrive at the checkpoint just up ahead, you'll be asked if you have anything of value to declare. To which Sir Gilbert—"

"Eh? What?" Sir Gilbert muttered, bringing his nose out of a sheaf of documents he had taken from the *portefuille* he held close to his chest now that the rain had stopped. "What? Yes! Yes. Carry on! Good to see you are fulfilling your duties as my junior minister in explaining the procedures required to ensure we are able to complete the necessary formalities to successfully transition to the official point of egress. We must be prepared. Prepared for all contingencies. These are trying times. Trying times indeed!"

"To which," Alec continued as if Parsons had not spoken, "Sir Gilbert will respond to the customs officials that we do not have anything to declare or—"

"—he'll be taken away and shot!" Plantagenet Halsey interrupted gleefully. "Quite a responsibility for you, hey, Sir Gilbert, bein' head of a legation."

"I beg your pardon, sir! But I do not find your humor at all—"

"—humorous...?"

"Stop it!" the Duchess hissed. "Both of you!"

"Just actin' the part I was given to play," the old man muttered lightly. "As I see you are, too. Well done."

"It has always been the usual practice amongst countries who have signed accords," Alec explained with extreme patience, "to permit their diplomatic legations to enter and exit their respective countries with their luggage untouched and thus not inspected. It is also usual to allow members of a legation to be waved through customs without being searched—"

"So they could be carryin' an entire Sevres dinner service under their frocks or petticoats and the officials will turn a blind eye to it all?"

"Precisely," Alec replied to his uncle's question. "And as often happens with all sorts of commodities, particularly textiles and lace, and spirits which are contraband. We have similar procedures at our ports. But what happens in peace time is often vastly different to what can be expected in times of war, when anything and everything is possible."

"Just so," Sir Gilbert agreed. "I'm surprised and annoyed that our Mr. Luytens has not seen fit to be here to greet us. It's his job to get us through this tiresome business, and unharmed."

"The British consul." Alec explained to the others, "Yes. Jacob Luytens should be here. He may have been held up for any number of reasons, or perhaps his informants have yet to realize the English legation has arrived, and not sent him word. Though I'd have thought with *The Caroline* in port, that sufficient fanfare of our arrival..."

His voice trailed off on a sudden thought. Talk of customs procedures made him remember the ransom note, to which he had not given much consideration since the interview at his townhouse with Lord Cobham. And that was because his godmother had dismissed the need for him to read it. If he were inclined to be cynical, he would think that deliberate on her part. But why?

"Your Grace. Mrs. Jamison-Lewis," he said abruptly, looking at both. "If you have anything to declare, such as jewelry or coin, you would be wise to hand it to me now."

"Jewelry? Coin? Why should you think we would?" the Duchess replied a little too quickly and vehemently. "You specifically warned us before we left London that we must leave any valuable trinkets at home. What you see here on my ears are paste. So too, my necklace and ring. We don't have a diamond hairclip between us. Do we, Selina—*Selina*?"

"Yes, Your Grace," Selina replied steadily, not a look at Alec, and her gloved hands within her muff tightly intertwined and pressed protectively against her velvet bodice. A bodice that had under it the pair of jumps with the secret pockets full of enough jewelry and jewels between the quilted cotton layers to purchase a German baronial manor, if not a *schloss*. "Not one diamond hairclip between us." That much was true.

Something in the Duchess's tone, and Selina's mannered reply, made Alec instantly suspicious. But he was not given the opportunity to interrogate them further because Sir Gilbert was demanding his attention. They had finally come to the head of the line. Alec reluctantly turned away to act as interpreter, and thus failed to notice the two women grab at each other's gloved hands for mutual support of their lie.

But Plantagenet Halsey saw the gesture, and made a mental note to find out exactly what was meant by it. Now was not the time. Now he just wanted this interminable wait to be over with, and to be out of the freezing weather and into a warm room with a cup of hot tea. He was very sure everyone else around him felt the same. And then something happened that would have far reaching consequences for all of them, and answered why his nephew had forced that promise out of him aboard ship. Still, the shock of discovering the truth behind that promise could not have been more startling. Cup of tea be damned. He needed brandy, and a good lie-down!

# Ten

As Sir Gilbert waited to present his red leather wallet full of documentation, he droned on at Alec that he wanted every word interpreted, not just a précis. But Alec was listening with only one ear, a technique he had perfected while Sir Gilbert's junior all those years ago. His blue eyes searched for Jacob Luytens amongst the crowd beyond the Customs barrier where sat two officials at a long low mahogany table, with an elderly secretary and his assistant inking into pages of thick ledgers.

The Customs officials were perusing the identity papers of three men ahead of them in the queue. All were of middling years, merchants by the look of their somber clothes and boots, and most likely residents, as they were conversing fluently in Dutch. This allowed the official to get away with telling them more than the German-speaking soldiers would have permitted, and been very surprised to hear. The official gave what sounded like a rehearsed speech, warning them that the entire town was under martial law, and that every citizen was required to comply and show instant obedience. But then he added a statement that Alec found most interesting indeed: That if the men wanted to know the true state of affairs in Emden, they were to seek out their kinsman who worked for the English and was a regular at *The Golden Swan* inn. There was a meeting after dark, which at this time of year meant no later than four in the afternoon.

Alec knew only one man in Emden who worked for the English: Jacob Luytens.

The three men then had their identity papers stamped, folded, and returned, before being escorted by two soldiers to collect their belongings from the designated piles down by the canal, less than fifty paces away. Here citizens of the town, wealthy travelers who could pay the duties imposed, and the very poor who owned little of worth to the state but were healthy enough to be put to work, were collecting up their personal belongings. They were not, however, permitted to take everything they owned. Those items designated for the war effort were duly confiscated.

Alec cast his gaze over the steadily increasing piles of seized goods being offloaded from the tugboats which continued to come and go, hoping to recognize the cargo from *The Caroline*—his bags, trunks, crates, and belongings, and the belongings of his fellow passengers. But they had yet to arrive. So he was about to give his full attention to Sir Gilbert, who had slapped down his documents before the Customs officials, when there was a loud splash, as something or someone fell or was thrown into the canal.

A shout for help went up. It was definitely a someone. Wharf laborers threw down what they were sorting and rushed to the water's edge. One of the jagers who handled the horses pulling the tugs along the canal had been knocked into the icy water. He had disappeared below the surface. A wharf laborer grabbed a coil of rope from a bollard. Another jumped up onto one of the boats, then up on to its low roof, and scampered across to disappear down the other side. The man with the rope slung the coil over his head and followed.

The long line of passengers rippled forward, eager for a look, some from macabre interest but most because it was a welcome diversion from the boredom of waiting to be processed. There was a good deal of splashing and cries for help out of their line of sight because of the horses and tugboats blocking their view. This made the crowd even more curious to catch a glimpse of the action, and they surged closer.

The soldiers were forgotten as passengers broke ranks and scurried to the water's edge. The captain sent a sergeant with a squad, not to assist in the rescue of the poor unfortunate drowning, or his fellows trying to fish him out before he froze to death, but to aid their comrades in forcing the crowd back from the canal to the walkway. The sight of more soldiers marching up and down the line was enough for most to obey, but there were those too caught up in the dramatic rescue who either did not hear or ignored the command. And it was only when they were shoved back or had the butt of a musket slammed hard into a rib, and men began collapsing to the cobblestones, that the rest of the passengers quickly complied, the corporal bellowing at them in his mangled Dutch mixed with his native German, as to what happens to those who do not do as ordered.

But a girl in a plain woolen cloak and worn half boots ignored the directive and remained riveted, mesmerized by the rescue of the jager. Before her grandfather could pull her back beside him, a soldier had her by the arm. He did not push her towards the crowd, but dragged her away, two grinning soldiers eagerly following.

Watching the girl being manhandled decided Selina. She could no longer be a bystander; she was beyond patience; something had to be done, and at once. She glanced at Alec, to see his reaction, but he was preoccupied, his back to the group and deep in conversation, interpreting for Sir Gilbert with the Emden Customs officials. So she took matters in hand. Later she was to wonder at her impetuosity, but it was an instinctive reaction, one which stemmed from her own experience at the hands of a violent husband. No longer would she or other females with whom she came into contact suffer male abuse.

She gave no thought that her foolhardy actions would jeopardize all that Alec had striven to achieve to keep the English legation from being targeted by the military. Nor did she give a care to her personal safety, forgetting she had a treasure chest of jewels and coin hidden in her stays. Out of a sense of natural justice—the vulnerable and weak must always be protected—all she cared about at that moment was restoring the girl to her grandfather.

Selina broke from the orderly line. The Duchess gave an involuntary gasp. Plantagenet Halsey called out to her. Her lady's maid grabbed for her cloak. Hadrian Jeffries took a step out of the line to see what Mrs. Jamison-Lewis meant to do, saw her approach the soldiers who had a girl in custody and immediately interrupted Lord Halsey in mid sentence, thrusting himself between Sir Gilbert and his master.

Several passengers behind the English legation turned as one sending the queue whiplashing all the way to the back of the line. The girl's distraught grandfather saw Selina sweep up to the soldiers, and followed on her cloak hem.

Everyone who was witness to this extraordinary scene had the same thoughts: What did this woman mean to do? What could she possibly say to these soldiers? Was she insane? Perhaps that was it. She must not be in her right mind.

Selina wasn't precisely sure what she was going to do either, and in hindsight would agree her actions appeared the act of a madwoman. But that did not deter her. She tugged her gloved hands out of her warm fur muff and let it fall on its riband about her waist, to grab at her hood, holding it close under her chin, to keep it over her hair, and the cold out. With a fistful of quilted petticoats in her free hand to stop the hems from trailing in the muck, she bustled along the canal edge as fast as her pattens would allow, intercepting the soldiers with the girl between them before they disappeared into the Customs House.

Half a dozen bored soldiers guarding the customs checkpoint, stamping their boots to ward off the bitter cold, watched with veiled interest as a female in a red cloak and an old man tripping on her hem confronted a corporal and two of their fellows, who had between them a plump little bird. The girl would do nicely to alleviate their frustrations, and without the fear of catching the pox, as was likely to happen with the whores on offer in this rat-infested backwater. Perhaps the female in the red cloak could be coerced to join her. Their chilled bones were momentarily forgotten as they nudged each other with bawdy insinuations and eagerly watched the little drama unfold.

"Unhand her!" Selina ordered, pointing to the girl; as if this was enough to bring instant obedience. She repeated her command in French, hoping they might at least understand the universal language of travelers. They did not.

Her audacity so surprised the soldiers that they came to an abrupt halt, but they did not let go of the girl. They had no idea what Selina had demanded but by her tone of command and expression they knew she was outraged. Far from becoming angry, they laughed.

Selina ignored them and addressed the frightened girl.

"*Aucun mal ne viendra à vous. Je promets. Comprenez vous?*" (No harm will come to you. I promise. Do you understand?)

"Madame, Sophie is deaf," the girl's grandfather replied at her shoulder. "The reason she did not hear the order to get back in line."

"You are not French or German—" Selina stated, momentarily diverted by the old man's cadence.

"Yorkshire in England, Madame. The Reverend Shrivington Shirley, at your service, and this is my granddaughter Sophie—

"How do you communicate?" Selina interrupted; she had no time for introductions, however arresting she might consider the Reverend's story or his name.

"I speak to her with my fingers, Madame."

"Then tell her to remain calm, and that I will not allow her to be harmed."

"Thank you, Madame. She is only fourteen and—"

The Reverend was struck hard in the kidney with a musket butt and fell to his knees, eyes watering with the pain. His granddaughter thrust out a hand and tried to pull away. Selina turned and helped the reverend to his feet, growling at the soldier who remained over him with musket raised.

"Leave him be! He can do you no harm! Get up, M'sieur," she added in a fierce whisper to the old man. "Get up—for her! Be stronger than you are!"

No sooner had Selina helped the girl's grandfather to his feet than she was grabbed. She struggled, and with an arm free of the folds of her cloak, struck out wildly, knocking the soldier's tall mitre cap to the ground with a clatter, which sent his comrades into appreciative whoops of laughter.

But with the hood of her cloak falling to her shoulders, the soldiers' laughter died and Selina was instantly let go. There was a loud collective gasp from the crowd, from fear—wondering what the soldiers meant to do to her for striking out at one of their own—and in admiration of Selina's beauty, her fair face framed by a cloud of apricot curls which flashed bright in the grey winter light like a fiery beacon suddenly ablaze against a night sky.

The corporal, who held the girl, shoved her at his subordinate and made Selina a magnificent bow, slightly mocking in its execution. He recognized in her delicate features, the luxurious fur-lining of her red cloak, and the richness of her soft velvet gown beneath, that here was a lady of wealth and possibly rank, who must be accorded respect. But something else sparked in his eyes as he raked her over from pattens to upswept red-golden hair—lust. Selina saw it and blushed in spite of herself. But she kept her chin up and did not take her dark eyes from the corporal. Secretly, she was relieved he had the intelligence and innate good manners not to touch her. Still, she did not trust him or his fellows to remain well-mannered for long, and her dark eyes followed the corporal warily as he slowly circled her, speaking in a tongue she did not understand.

"Here's true beauty! A wondrous prize indeed!" declared the corporal in German to his comrades. "What say we have a little fun with her ladyship. Eh?"

"Yes! Fun! Let's have some fun!" sniggered his two companions.

"Do you know," the corporal said with exaggeration, "I suspect her ladyship of hiding contraband under her petticoats. Why else would she be so brazen as to attack us in so unladylike a manner, unless she were hiding something, eh?"

"But if she were a lady she'd have no need to hide anythin' under her hoops," reasoned the soldier with his arm about the girl's waist. He jerked his head at the Customs officials. "Those Dutch dullards over there will just let her pass, as they have every other person of rank and fortune, as long as they pay the duty owed, get to tick off their wretched column work, *and* hand over what they owe us."

"God have mercy! Claus, I wonder if there's anything between those big jug ears sometimes!" the corporal complained wearily. He spelled it out. "If we suspect citizens of concealing goods, what did the captain tell us we are duty bound to do?"

"We are duty bound to search them, sir!" answered Claus's comrade.

"Precisely! All sorts of contraband can fit under a fine lady's hoops. Why only last week two of our lads found three linen bags full of precious tea strapped to the thighs of a merchant's wife. And she wasn't half as pretty as this porcelain-faced princess! And in the name of our Margrave, everyone must make their contribution to the war effort, wealthy sots and poor; but particularly the wealthy ones! It wouldn't surprise me if this girl and the old man belong to this fine lady," the corporal continued, more to convince himself that what he was about to do was justified. "No doubt they were to provide a diversion so that her ladyship could sneak through Customs without any of us being the wiser to her concealed goods!"

The soldier named Claus and his comrade shared a wide-eyed look. They stifled giggles like two naughty schoolboys. Claus's comrade snorted. "Concealed goods! Ha! Ha! Now *that* is funny, sir!"

The corporal's pun was unintentional but he smiled and swaggered as if he'd meant it. He became serious, and waved a gloved hand at the subordinate who held onto the girl.

"Put her in a holding cell. She'll make for good after-dinner pudding. Then send two men to escort her ladyship indoors. The least we can do is offer her privacy from these *schmutzigen bauern*," he added with a contemptuous tilt of his heavy chin to the line of weary passengers who were furtively watching proceedings. "Well? What are you waiting for?" he growled at his subordinates. "Kick the old man's backside back to the queue! And take the girl away!"

"Madam! For pity's sake! They mean to rape my granddaughter!" the Reverend Shirley blurted out in English as he was taken by the scruff of the neck. "And to search under your petticoats! Madame! You must help—"

Claus punched the Reverend in the gut, winding him so he could not complete his sentence.

Selina's face went white, and she winced at the use of such gratuitous violence, watching the Reverend Shirley be dragged away. She glanced at the girl, who was struggling to be free of the soldier's hold, and wished she could offer her comfort, to assure her she would not allow harm to come to her. But it was pointless to speak up because the girl would not understand her, and could not hear. And nor would the soldier, who did not speak a civilized tongue. And if she tried to go to the girl, to embrace her, the corporal was standing so close to her he would grab her in an instant. So she maintained her silence and waited her opportunity.

She was not so worried for herself. An innate sense of her place in the world, of her lineage and noble family connections meant she had a misplaced confidence that the soldier's threat was an idle one. And if they were idiotic enough to try and search her, well, she was certain Alec would stop them.

And then he did.

The corporal dared to caress a fat curl of bright hair that fell forward over Selina's shoulder, and breathed near her ear; she smelled onions and was nauseous.

"So, *liebling*," he murmured in German, confident she could not understand him, yet just as thrilled by this, "do you have the same pretty colored hair between your legs? We shall soon find out..."

Selina slapped his hand away. Far from taking offence the corporal laughed.

"You're a feisty one! Isn't she, lads?"

But the two soldiers were not laughing. They weren't even looking at him, their attention had been diverted over the corporal's right shoulder. The corporal was about to ask what was wrong with them when he felt something cold and sharp tickle the back of his ear. But it was the calm measured voice of command that garnered his instant cooperation.

"Move away. Slowly. Hands raised. Do not go for your sword or I will cut your throat. Stand with your fellows. You two! Let the girl go. Bayonets to the ground!"

The corporal and his two subordinates did not hesitate to obey. Released, the girl stood there, wondering if her rescuer was friend or foe. But when he inclined his head to her with a smile and pointed his rapier to the crowd and back she knew she was free. She smiled at Selina, bobbed a quick curtsey to her rescuer, then scampered away to find her grandfather.

All the while, Selina had remained facing the two soldiers, the corporal at her back, knowing she had been rescued, but not understanding the German spoken by her liberator. With the girl swallowed up by the onlookers, and the corporal moving to stand with his subordinates, she turned to thank their rescuer, hoping he might at least understand by her smile if not her French, that she was grateful to him.

And there was Alec, sword drawn and gaze on the soldiers. Selina blinked her confusion. Hearing him speak in German altered his mellow voice so completely that it took her a few moments to reconcile the man she knew and loved with this stranger. She just stood there, unable to move. But he did not ask her to. In fact, he was not looking at her at all.

SELINA'S CONFRONTATION WITH THE SOLDIERS HAD LASTED a matter of minutes, but to those involved and to the onlookers, time had slowed a minute to an hour. Time then sped up again when a tall, darkly handsome gentleman in tricorne and long fur-lined cape appeared, as if from nowhere. His sword was drawn and such was the purpose in his stride and the look in his eye that the crowd once again held its collective breath in expectation.

No sooner had this gentleman disarmed the corporal and his comrades, sent the girl back to her grandfather, and rescued the beauty—to the appreciative smiles of the crowd—than two dozen grenadiers burst out of the Customs House and spread over the dock like a great blue wave splashed up over the canal. They charged with bayonets drawn. Seeing this wave rush towards them, terrified passengers tripped over themselves to back out of harm's way. The soldiers stopped a mere bayonet's length from them, turned their backs, and stood shoulder to shoulder, forming an impenetrable barrier between them and their commander. Half a dozen of their number had already surrounded Alec and Selina.

Everyone waited for the commander.

The dock secure, the Colonel took his time to walk its length.

His uniform was crisp, the gold facings to his blue frock coat bright. A polished silver gorget, white silk sash with over-large tassel tied about his waist, matching white-cuffed gloves, and gold-trimmed tricorne proclaimed his rank. Well-polished black boots were encased in appliquéd splatterdashes which buckled from the bridge of his foot and up over his knees. He strode with the confidence of command, and the knowledge that everyone's life was at his whim. As such, his sword remained in its scabbard, and in his gloved hand he held a gold-topped baton.

"Lower your sword!" he demanded of Alec, pointing the baton threateningly. He repeated his command in French, adding, "By order of His Highness the Margrave, I, Colonel Henrik Müller, order you to lower your sword!"

Alec replied in German. "Willingly, Herr Colonel. First you must do likewise—and order your men to stand down."

The Colonel was taken aback, not only by Alec's impeccable German but also by his bravado. He covered his amazement with a smug smile. It was this he showed to his men, as he looked about to ensure the queue of passengers were secured. This gentleman was either a reckless hero or an heroic idiot. Either way, he had a death wish. He appealed to Selina.

"Fraulein, tell your friend to put away his sword or—"

"Herr Colonel, does the House of Herzfeld have your complete loyalty?" Alec interrupted.

Again the Colonel was incredulous. But he did not hesitate to answer. "Of course!"

"And your men? They are all loyal to their Margrave?"

"To a man!"

"Very well then. I order you, in the name of His Highness, to have your men stand down, and to allow this lady to return to her party—"

"You? You order *me* in the name of—in the name of *my* Margrave?"

"Do as you are told or face the consequences for disobeying a direct order, Herr Colonel!"

Colonel Müller could hardly believe his ears. Nor could his men. They all waited with expectation as to what he would do. The captain decided this gentleman was the latter—an heroic idiot. He lost his patience.

"Listen, fool!" he hissed, stepping up to Alec. "I am the one giving the orders! If you do not sheathe your sword, I will have my men cut you down! Understand? Now I will escort this lady to—"

"No, Herr Colonel."

Alec's sword was under the captain's heavy chin before the man could blink. The tip caressed the bare throat, just above the folds of his linen stock. All eyes remained riveted on them; the soldiers' senses heightened, muscles tensed but unmoving; the crowd swaying as one; Selina as rigid as a statue.

The Colonel's startled gaze followed the length of the blade up into Alec's unblinking blue eyes. His voice was reed-thin. "I raise my hand and you are dead."

"As are you, Herr Colonel."

With his right hand engaged in keeping the sword point steady under the captain's chin, Alec used his teeth to loosen the soft kid glove from the fingers of his left hand, eyes unwavering on his quarry. With the glove loosened, he gave the soft leather tip of his gloved ring finger a small tug, then let the glove drop at his feet.

"Stay still, Herr Colonel," he ordered softly when the grenadier dropped his chin. "I do not want to spill your blood, but I will, if you force me to it."

The Colonel's gaze was on Alec's ungloved hand, which had disappeared inside the folds of his clothing. But the warning brought his gaze up, not to Alec's face, but to a wad of parchment, tied with black ribbon, produced from an inner chest pocket of Alec's wool frock coat. Yet it was not the folded parchment that held the

Colonel's gaze but the large armorial intaglio ring on the long ring finger of Alec's left hand.

The Colonel squinted at the intaglio, trying to decipher the simple motif. In his abstraction he was unaware that Alec had withdrawn the point of his sword from his throat, thus allowing him to step close enough to see the detail carved into the carnelian. Three five pointed stars, one of which was within the walls of a triangular parapet, all on a simple shield, and above the shield a coronet from which sprouted the head of a ram. The engraving was unmistakable: The imperial coat of arms of the House of Herzfeld. As was the soft orange gemstone. Carnelian was native to the country, hence its adoption by the Margraves of Midanich as their official gemstone. Only the nobility were permitted to wear jewelry made from carnelian, and only members of the House of Herzfeld an armorial intaglio.

Again the Colonel squinted, as if by doing so somehow the official seal would transform into something else entirely. But it was still there when he opened his eyes wide and refocused. The significance of the armorial ring was immediate, yet seeing it on the finger of a stranger come off one of the ships was so wholly unexpected that it took the Colonel a few moments to process. What he did know was that this gentleman, whoever he was, was no ordinary man. He belonged to the House of Herzfeld. What his relationship was to the Margrave was of no matter, and was not a question the Colonel could put to him. But why hadn't this *edler herr*—nobleman—made himself known immediately he set foot on terra firma? Why arrive incognito into Emden? Had the crew of his ship been sworn to secrecy? Had his entourage also? Again, the Colonel knew he could not ask any of these questions of a member of the House of Herzfeld, but such a circumstance was odd, and with the country at civil war...

Of course! It suddenly made perfect sense. A family representative of the Margrave would not travel openly, and not across country, not with the traitorous Prince Viktor's men prowling the marshes on the other side of the high walls, not until he could ascertain the loyalty of the troops who held the town secure. It would be necessary for him and those in his party to travel by sea and around the archipelago, and thus remain under cover until he knew if the city and its officials were loyal to Margrave Ernst. Reason his loyalty had been questioned. Reason he had been shown the ring, rather than this nobleman state the obvious. It was a test, for him and his men. The Colonel knew what he must do.

ALEC WATCHED THE COLONEL'S WRINKLED BROW CLEAR, AND when the man's gaze flew up from the intaglio ring to his face, he knew he had the soldier's unquestioning loyalty. He mentally sighed with relief that his ruse had worked. Slowly, he sheathed his sword. It only remained to reinforce the complex subterfuge. So he held out the parchment.

"I think you'll find my papers are self-explanatory, Colonel—?"

"Müller! Colonel Henrik Müller," the Colonel stated, coming to attention and saluting. "My apologies for my earlier insolence, and for not recognizing—"

"How could you do so, Herr Colonel? The country is at war. These are trying times. We must all be ever vigilant. It is not unproblematic knowing who is our friend and—who is our enemy. Please," Alec added smoothly, though his heartbeat thudded in his ears as the Colonel finally and gingerly took the parchment, "take your time. Verify the documents, if need be."

He waited and watched as Colonel Müller untied the black silk ribbon and carefully unfolded the soft vellum. There were two documents. The first was the safe conduct pass signed by Margrave Ernst which had been sent with Cosmo's letter of entreaty. The second was an older document whose existence he had shared with only one other—Lord Shrewsbury, England's Spymaster

General—and one he had hoped to consign to his private history and a locked lower drawer of his writing bureau, along with the intaglio, both never again to see the light of day. Cosmo and Emily's incarceration changed all that. This second document was signed by Margrave Leopold. It bestowed upon Alec the title of baron with all the inherent privileges such a noble title conferred, and this along with the intaglio, had been instrumental in aiding his escape from Midanich ten years earlier. Alec hoped it would do so again, but this time he needed it and the intaglio to do much more; this time it was not only his life which was at stake.

While the Colonel read, Alec cast an eye over the half-dozen soldiers close by who had followed their Colonel's lead and instantly come to attention, bayonet muskets over a shoulder. He then looked further afield, to the long row of somber-faced soldiers standing shoulder to shoulder, acting as an insurmountable barrier between their Colonel and the disembarked passengers. He saw that they, too, had come to attention, bayonet muskets at their sides and chins up, as if about to be inspected. He did not look at Selina, though he was keenly aware she was staring at his profile in mute astonishment, no doubt with a hundred—or perhaps just one—questions on her tongue. He wanted to smile, to find some light relief in the situation in which he now found himself. But just the thought of confessing past events of this diplomatic posting made him sick to his stomach, even after all these years, and instantly sobered his mood.

His gaze returned to Colonel Müller. The soldier's thin upper lip was beaded with sweat despite the bitter cold. Alec guessed that underneath the man's military frock coat and regulation issue shirt his body was a lather of perspiration. It wasn't every day an ordinary soldier handled documents personally signed by not one ruler, but two; Margrave Leopold had been particularly revered by his subjects. Alec had some sympathy for the poor Colonel's state of shock and did not wait for him to find further words of apology.

"Now that you are aware of the situation, Colonel Müller, I am confident of your cooperation, and your—loyalty."

"Yes, *Herr Freiherr*! Of course *Herr Freiherr*!"

"Herr Baron will do."

"Yes, Herr Baron! Of course, Herr Baron!"

"Good. You will have my party escorted out of this weather," Alec commanded. "I require fitting accommodation—a house, not an inn. The British Consul, Herr Luytens, he was to have arranged this, and may already have done so. Find out. Our luggage from *The Caroline* is to be waved through Customs, and delivered as soon as possible. I do not want my guests inconvenienced more than they already are. Sir Gilbert Parsons, head of the English legation, is my guest and is to be given every courtesy. And you, Colonel Müller, will personally see to the needs of the elderly couple." He permitted himself to smile. "She is an English duchess; he has arthritis and a bad temper if riled. You may have a sack of coal for your efforts—"

"Herr Baron, I hardly deserve—"

"—if the luggage is delivered undamaged and unopened. You will assist my majordomo, Herr Jeffries, who will oversee this process. Should he not be given your full cooperation, and he discover any item omitted, I will hold you personally responsible, Colonel Müller. Is that understood?"

"Perfectly, Herr Baron!" the Colonel replied. He quickly folded the two documents and retied the black ribbon. He held them out with a slight bow. "I will see to it all, at once. Herr—Jeffries will be given every courtesy, as will every member of your party. Herr Luytens will be found, as will the direction of the house he has arranged. Your luggage will not be touched—by anyone. Whatever you want, it is yours. Whatever you need, it is yours, Herr Baron! My men and I are at your disposal."

Alec waved a hand in dismissal, eager to end the interview, and went to scoop up the glove he had dropped, but the Colonel was there before him. And when Alec put out a hand to take it from him, the Colonel saw it as a signal to pay homage to the House of Herzfeld. He caught at Alec's fingers and pressed his lips reverentially to the intaglio of the Herzfeld family ring. To a man, the soldiers came to attention and saluted, the clack and stamp of their boots coming together on the cobbles, the only sound along the entire length of the canal.

It was with this salute that Alec realized that silence could be deafening. The Dutch-speaking officials inside the Customs House had been urged away from the warmth of the ovens to brave the icy winds to see what the fuss was about, and huddled together by the Customs checkpoint. Jagers stood immobile at the heads of their heavy horses come to a stop along the well-worn path beside the canal. Brawny stevedores, silent and watchful, sat atop cargo still to be offloaded from the gently rocking tugboats. And even above his head, high up in the spider web of complicated rigging of the tall ships, sailors dangled their legs from masts, precariously surveying proceedings with the seagulls for company. In fact, every man, woman, and child was silently fixed on this little drama unfolding before them. It was as if the Margrave himself had come amongst them. For the majority of the soldiers, a representative of the House of Herzfeld was being in the presence of their ruler, and as close as they would ever get to the Margrave. Everyone, civil and military, hung upon Alec's every word.

It should not have surprised him, but it did. It also made him exceedingly uncomfortable. But he knew the choice to leave his past buried for as long as possible, and remain incognito until he arrived on the other side of the country at Herzfeld Castle, had been taken out of his control the moment Selina had recklessly confronted three soldiers over a girl in their custody, and an old man being abused. All he had wanted to do was to avert a catastrophe. The arrival of a regiment had put paid to plans of a swift and surreptitious end to a dangerous situation. He then had no option but to reveal his identity to the Colonel. So much for entering Emden by stealth!

He wanted to blame Selina and her foolishness in interfering in what was not her business, and for endangering her life, but that would be petty. It was not her fault. The choice to remain incognito had been taken from him the moment *The Caroline* was boarded by pirates, and he learned the town was under martial law. But to be unmasked so publically, and with Selina as witness, had stripped him of every vestige of self-respect. He had been living with this black cloud from his past for a decade, and had successfully (or so he thought) managed to live with it if not completely put it behind him. Now that it had burst over his head there was no going back. But how to explain this episode in his past, in all its incredulous detail, and to the woman he loved, without being branded a liar and a fraud? That would take all his diplomatic dexterity. The outcome was entirely in her hands.

Thank God Selina did not understand a word of German, though that seemed a moot point. There had been enough in the gestures and expressions, not to mention homage paid by the military, for anyone but the blind and deaf to know something of great significance had just occurred, and he the center of it all. But now was not the time nor place to account for his sins, so he snatched back his hand, face brick red to be so revered, and roughly pulled on his glove to cover the ring and warm his cold fingers. He wanted to turn heel and stride away, instead he calmly offered his arm to Selina, saying blandly,

"You'll freeze if I don't get you within doors this instant. You've not experienced winter until you've spent it here, in this marshy wasteland of a country!"

Selina pulled the hood back up over her coiffure and put her gloved hand in the crook of his arm. She did not know what to say in response to what she had just witnessed, so quipped,

"Do you know, that's the first two full sentences you've spoken to me since Harwich. No! I lie. Since Bath. Since you refused to speak to me on the stair at Barr's of Trim Street." Adding with a wry smile when he remained mute, "Perhaps after this little affecting display, I, too, should offer to kiss that most interesting intaglio you're wearing? Or are the military the only ones required to pay you homage—whoever *you* are—*Herr Baron*."

"Don't add to the absurdity!" Alec snapped. "You don't know the first thing about—about—any of it!"

Startled by his uncharacteristic harsh tone, Selina swallowed down her hurt and pulled free her gloved hand. "No. No. I do not. I—"

"Forgive me," he interrupted with quiet apology. "I—I'm not myself..."

"Now there's an understatement if ever I heard one!"

"Selina! I will—I will tell you—*everything*—but not *now*. Not *here*."

"I wonder...," she said, regarding him impassively. "Would you have felt the need to confess *everything* had you not been forced to it?"

A huff of laughter escaped him, but Alec did not hesitate in his response. He offered her his arm again and was relieved when she took it. They continued on toward the Customs House, soldiers at their back, and to the sounds of the dock coming to life again.

"Yes. Yes, I had every intention of confessing my sins—*to you*," he stated. "But not until *after* we were married. And I would have told you as an aside; just one story of many adventures as a conceited junior diplomat; nothing of significance; nothing worth your worry." He smiled down at her. "And all of it occurring before I had made your acquaintance—"

"When I was Selina Vesey—before my horrid marriage?"

"Yes. You were still in the schoolroom when I was posted here as Sir Gilbert's secretary."

They walked on in silence, Selina's gaze on the Customs officials going about their business, but seeing none of it. She'd had a flash of insight.

"It was Cosmo and Emily's kidnapping which changed all that for you, wasn't it?"

"Yes."

"What—what *happened*—to you? What is happening—to *us*?"

"It's—difficult."

"*Difficult?*" She stopped and faced him, dark eyes full of concern. "Of course I cannot begin to imagine what-what—*difficulties* you faced on your posting here, but I have a great foreboding that in this wretchedly bleak place you are not the Alec Halsey I know and love—"

"Selina! I-I—Yes! No! You're right," he confessed. "I'm not *your* Alec; not here. Not until I accomplish what I'm here for—to free Cosmo and Emily. Foolishly, I'd hoped to spare you—Olivia—my uncle—and myself, the wretchedness of a confession. I now realize that for wishful thinking. That was never going to happen. *Please.* Let me get you out of this miserable cold, to somewhere where we can talk in comfort."

She nodded but stood there a moment longer, ignoring the activity all around them, and Sir Gilbert making a scene with the Customs Officials demanding to know in French what the devil was going on. She looked up into his eyes and held his gaze.

"I believe I can manage any confession you care to make to me. God knows, I have one of my own for you, which you did not permit me in Bath, and which should have been made well before, when you came to Paris—"

"Selina, there is no need for—"

"Yes! Yes, there is! But, you're right. Now is not the time for that, either. But..." She swallowed and pressed a gloved palm to his chest, over his heart. "Can you assure me that the Alec I love will return to me?"

146

"Yes," he said with a smile, resisting the urge to caress her cheek. He could not afford to be open with his feelings in this place; the Margrave's—and Luyten's—spies were everywhere. "That's a promise. When I have Cosmo and Emily safe." He did not add, "*Because if I cannot save them, I cannot save myself.*"

# *Eleven*

$S$ IR COSMO WAS ABOUT TO STEP OUTSIDE HIS LITTLE
room for the first time in over two months. Yet he hesitated.
He wondered if he was about to be tricked—so his captors
had an excuse to punish him. No sooner would he be in the
passageway than he'd be set upon, accused of trying to escape, and
he'd be dragged to the dungeons and there he'd be tortured and
left to rot.

Despite the cold dank air in the corridor, a trickle of perspiration
slid between Sir Cosmo's shoulder blades. His hands were tied and
he was surrounded by a swarm of soldiers, which gave him every
reason to believe his fear justified. Perhaps he was being escorted
to the dungeons, and not, as he was led to believe, to dine with the
Margrave. Giving him hope would subdue him enough until it was
too late to shout for help.

But even if he did shout, who would hear him? And who would
care? The very idea he was off to dine with anyone, least of all the
ruler of this God-forsaken place, set his back to stoop and a prickly
heat to break out across his forehead. For all that, he began to
shake, not with despair but with silent laughter, the sort of laughter
madmen and hermits indulge in, and which is incomprehensible
to others. And the more he thought about what his valet had just

confided in him, the more hysterical with fear he became, convinced he would never leave Castle Herzfeld alive.

EARLIER THAT AFTERNOON, SIR COSMO WAS PERMITTED TO bathe, and not just with a jug of water and a basin. It was his first bath in a month. A copper was brought up, and a procession of sour-faced servants came and went with hot water. Soap and a washcloth were provided, and for his mattered hair he was given a comb and a spicy-scented herbal wash. But he was not allowed to shave. So he washed his full beard with the remainder of the herbal wash.

The Margrave wanted to talk to him about their mutual friend Alec Halsey, but said he could not do so while Cosmo stank like a latrine. Hence the bath. And once he was presentable he would join the Margrave for dinner. Cosmo could hardly believe it possible. He had not left his little room in two months. As he soaked in the scented water a dread came over him. Perhaps this was a ruse for a more sinister purpose?

But then Matthias appeared in the doorway, hugging a bundle of clothes to his chest.

Sir Cosmo leapt from the bath, taking half the bathwater with him, hastily wrapped the bath sheet about his narrow hips, and greeted his valet with open arms and a beard dripping water. Dear sweet Matthias, with his long nose and even longer face, was such a welcome sight his eyes filled with tears. More than once, when curled in a ball on his narrow bed in utter despair, he was convinced he'd never see his devoted servant again.

Matthias was just as happy and tearful. He quickly dumped the bundle of clothes on the unmade bed, hiding his astonishment that with a full beard his master was barely recognizable. But it was not only the beard... Sir Cosmo had lost all his fat. He was thin and wiry, his face gaunt and his sunken eyes held a haunted expression. It was a look Matthias recognized in the gaze of mistreated animals who feared approach because it was usually accompanied by pain and suffering.

All this the valet kept to himself. He quickly washed his hands in the soapy bathwater, which gave him time to master his emotions, and caught sight of his ragged nails and scuffed knuckles. He who prided himself on his appearance and cleanliness as a gentleman's gentleman had not had access to his grooming implements in so long he'd stopped looking at his hands. But what was this small upset compared to what his master was being put through? The sad state of Sir Cosmo made him want to sob.

"You are a sight for these sore eyes, my dear Matthias!" Sir Cosmo said with forced cheeriness, and stepped back to look his valet from head to toe. "Still feeding you I see. And treating you well, are they?"

"Yes, sir. And I, you—overjoyed to see you, that is. And you're lookin' mighty fine indeed, all things considered," Matthias said buoyantly, trying to match his master's cheeriness. But he failed miserably and turned away, forcing the lump of sentiment back down his throat as he busied himself shaking out then arranging on the bed frock coat, breeches, clean shirt, cravat, drawers and stockings. "Here, sir, let me help you on with this shirt. A fresh set of clothes will make you feel more the thing. Though I'd wished they'd let me shave you."

"Ah! Yes, well, I wish *now* I'd let you shave me too, all those weeks ago," Sir Cosmo confessed with a heavy sigh, but quickly followed this with a smile, as if this would lift the depression from his shoulders. "Still, if it wasn't for this beard, I might not have had a visit from the Margrave. Did they tell you he came to visit me? Yes! I was being questioned and having my head plunged into a pail full of ice. I said to myself: *This is it! I'm not going to see tomorrow, or Emily, or Alec, or you, dear Matthias, ever again.* And then the Margrave arrives with an entourage. Imagine! My little room full of people..."

When Sir Cosmo's voice trailed off, Matthias handed him a pair of linen drawers, asking quietly, "Why had the Margrave come to see you, sir?"

"No idea. To invite me to dinner I suspect," Sir Cosmo said matter-of-factly, then gave a little nervous laugh. "Did you know he speaks English? Yes. *English*, Matthias. Surprised me so much I almost forgot to keep my eyes lowered. One minute everyone around me is speaking in German—which might as well be utter gibberish, for I can't make it out at all—the next I hear my mother tongue, and spoken very well indeed. I almost went to pieces there and then. Not a sweeter sound have I heard in such a long time, until you, just now, dear Matthias..."

"The Margrave speaks English? That is a surprise."

"Yes! Astounding, isn't it? But that isn't the most surprising thing about his visit," Sir Cosmo continued as he tied the strings of his linen drawers. "I still don't know what he looks like. I was ordered to keep my gaze on the floorboards at all times. On the floor! Odd sort of demand—not to be permitted to look at him. What is the point of wearing ermine and gold crowns, if the great unwashed, of which I was one until just now, can't get to fawn and gawp at you? Makes me wonder if there's something wrong with the chap. Is he horribly scarred from the pox or from battle? Perhaps he has only one eye or is his nose as bulbous as a gourd that one can only stare open-mouthed at the poor fellow? Do you have any idea as to his countenance?"

"No, sir. I suspect I'll never have the privilege of seeing him, even from a distance," Matthias told him evenly, unbuttoning the falls of a pair of velvet breeches before handing them over. "I'm now *quartered*—if you can call a cot in the corner behind the pots and pans that—in the scullery, where you're blessed if you see daylight from one day to the next. But don't you worry about me. I keep to myself and spend m'time polishin' whatever needs polishin'." He lowered his voice. "Which ain't much these days on account of the

silver being gathered up and melted down for the war, so it's said."
He raised his voice again, adding with a sniff, "At least I don't have
to spend m'days like the rest of the poor sots, who are up to their
elbows washing the grease off mountains of plates and bowls—it's
a stinking business, and brutal."

Sir Cosmo looked up from tucking the billowing folds of his
shirt into his breeches. His voice held a note of trepidation.

"You've not been-been—*mistreated*, have you?"

Matthias had not, but a beating was not the worst punishment
meted out below stairs. He well remembered his first day in the
kitchens, a stiflingly hot place with the temperature and humidity of
a Caribbean island. An under-cook, a short bow-legged Frenchman,
a deserter of the Seven Years' War who now could never go home,
gave him a simple warning—to keep his head down and stay well
out of the way, and if given a command, obey it without question.
He had then pointed out one of the cauldron stirrers, an old man
with a crippling stoop. The under-cook told him the stoop was from
the many beatings that had broken bones over the years. But still
the pot stirrer couldn't keep his opinions to himself and was forever
cursing his lot in life. Finally, they cut out his tongue.

But the Frenchman told Matthias not to worry. Serfs weren't
killed. They just had a toe or a finger hacked off, or if they were
particularly recalcitrant, like the cauldron stirrer, their tongues
removed—nothing too drastic, nothing that could impede them
getting on with their daily drudgery. So Matthias just needed to
keep his mouth shut and his tongue would stay between his teeth!

"Matthias?" Sir Cosmo repeated his question, more anxious than
before. "Have you been beaten?"

The valet shook his head free of grisly images.

"No, sir. Just put to work. I'm useful. And I do as I'm told. Which
is the best way of keeping my head on my shoulders, and my tongue
between my teeth."

"Good. I would hate to think—I couldn't go on if I knew you were being maltreated. I'm determined we will leave this castle alive, Matthias."

"Yes, sir. We will. *All four* of us will. I have every confidence in Lord Halsey comin' to our rescue, as you must, too."

Sir Cosmo nodded, and let his chin drop, to concentrate on buttoning the six horn buttons of his falls, and so his valet would not see his ready tears. Incarceration had turned him as soft as runny egg. Oh, what he wouldn't give for a nice soft-boiled hen's egg and a slice of bread and butter! He knew mention of the number four was Matthias's tactful way of referring to Emily and her companion Mrs. Carlisle. And he knew himself for a coward for not asking after them when Matthias had first arrived. But he could not bring himself to talk of Emily, because that led to wondering about how she was being treated. That Matthias had not mentioned the two women until now could only mean bad news, and so he was greatly relieved when his valet ended his anxiety.

"Sir, I have nothing to report about Miss St. Neots or Mrs. Carlisle. And as they say: *No news is good news*, isn't it? Perhaps you'll have an opportunity to enquire about them at dinner? They may very well be there, too. Mightn't they, sir?"

"Yes. Yes. They might well be..." Sir Cosmo replied, wanting to believe this with all his heart, but knowing it for wishful thinking. He fidgeted with the waistband of his breeches, muttering to hide his embarrassment at the tears in his eyes, "These need better tailoring. A button or two moved..."

"Yes, sir. They do," Matthias agreed. "The band was always a bit loose. I should've mentioned it at the time we took collection of the ensemble."

It was a lie. The breeches had fitted perfectly upon first wearing. Usually the bulk of the shirt tucked in at the waist made for a snug fit, but not today. It was one thing for a shirt to hang more loosely than usual, that could be overlooked, but the breeches were so loose they looked to be made for another man. And they had been, the man his master had been before they'd set a foot in this bleak God-awful place. Matthias knew the waistcoat and frock coat would also be too large for his master's emaciated frame, but it did not stop him holding wide the silk waistcoat with a cheerful smile. He next offered Sir Cosmo the cravat. But as there was no looking glass to aid in the tying of this article of fashion his master just stood there, staring at the strip of fine linen between his shaking fingers.

Matthias gently took the cravat from him, placed it about his neck and set to tying it. The tremor in his master's hand would have put paid to tying the strip of linen with any expertise, so it was as well there was no glass.

"I did discover something that will be of interest to you, sir," he said, to divert Sir Cosmo from his sartorial woes.

Matthias's conspiratorial tone snapped Sir Cosmo out of his melancholia. He was suddenly all ears and eyes for his valet's revelations. He glanced over at the guards—who were both dozing in a corner—then returned his attention to Matthias, who was carefully knotting the cravat under his hirsute chin.

"Yes? What?" Sir Cosmo hissed.

"You asked that I find out what I could about the *unspoken truth*," Matthias said. "But as most of the fellows around me don't see light, least of all know much at all, and none understand English, I thought I'd be having a spider's chance in bathwater of finding out anythin'! But then, one day, one of the guards from the Margrave's household regiment comes up to me. I thought I was done for. But no. He wasn't there to beat me or arrest me. He'd heard I was an Englishman. A'course I didn't correct his assumption. To these foreigners an Irishman and an Englishman, and for that matter a Scotsman, be one and the same. So this palace guard he takes me aside and tells me he was in a unit that fought with the British army in Flanders

during the war just past... How does that feel, sir? Nice and snug?"
he added, running a finger lightly along the edge of the folds of the
cravat he'd tied under Sir Cosmo's chin. "Not too snug, is it? Beggin'
your pardon, but it be rather more difficult to arrange the folds what
with you having a beard—a very nice beard it is too, sir!"

Sir Cosmo smiled as he stretched his neck. "Thank you for saying
so, but as soon as we are out of here, one of your first tasks will be
to get rid of this unfashionable mange! You were saying about this
palace guard who fought with us in Flanders... What did he want?"

"Nothing more than to spend time in m'company speaking
English. I was relieved to hear him say so, and more than a little
surprised he wanted conversational practice. He has dreams of
running away to England. He's heard so much about the place. Who
wouldn't want to run off home—our home—after living in this
barbaric wasteland, is what I say."

"Just so, Matthias," Sir Cosmo agreed. "I have dreams of never
leaving England again. And I won't, once I get out of here. *Ever.*"
He shook his head. "And if your friend manages to escape across
the Channel, he'll be mistaken for an Irishman, spending his time
listening to you! No. Don't move. Stay where you are. I think the
knot still needs your attention." Adding in a whisper as he fiddled
with the lace of his cravat nestled in the ruffles of his shirt, "If you
move away, and those two wake up, we might not have another
chance to speak candidly. Your guard who speaks English—You
asked him about this *unspoken truth?*"

"I did. But it's not only what he knows, but how he knows it. He
did something brave in the war, and for his heroism, Hansen—that's
his name—was promoted to the Margrave's personal bodyguard. To
cut the story short, one day I asked Hansen as casually as I could
about this *unspoken truth.* And he told me—just like that—as if
it was commonplace. I did wonder if that was because we spoke
about it in English, so it wasn't quite so shocking a transgression

as if he'd told me in his native tongue. Oh, and there is the fact he said if I mentioned it to anyone, or blabbed it about it was him as what told me, he'd cut m'tongue out. And as that happens quite regularly around here, I knew his threat weren't an idle one. Anyway, I thought it a fair deal, and shook hands on it."

Sir Cosmo let out a bark of laughter at Matthias's blasé attitude to such a threat, and instantly clapped a hand to his mouth to stop himself from laughing further, a furtive glance over at the guards, one opening an eye then instantly closing it and settling back to sleep, before saying in a much subdued tone,

"Well, that's enough of an incentive to keep quiet, isn't it?"

"Yes. Except I made no promise not to tell *you*. Hansen says the *unspoken truth* has been known to exist within the House of Herzfeld—that's the Margrave's family—for years. But it's never spoken about openly—"

"Hence it's known as the *unspoken truth*?"

Matthias grinned. "Just so, sir! Hansen says there's bad blood in the House of Herzfeld. And those family members who have it in their veins can't hide it."

"Margrave Ernst—?"

"Yes, sir."

Sir Cosmo frowned. "But how does it manifest itself? I mean, how does one know who has this bad blood and who does not?"

"His hair—"

"His—*hair*?" Sir Cosmo pulled in his chin. "What about his *hair*?"

"Sorry, sir. I meant his *lack of* hair. He—the Margrave—he doesn't have any—hair—*anywhere*."

"No hair?" Sir Cosmo was incredulous. "What do you mean: He doesn't have any *hair*—*any*where?"

"Yes, sir. No hair. None on his head. None on his body. No eyelashes or eyebrows. None. He and his sister the Princess were born that way."

Sir Cosmo slumped down on the small stool in the pool of light under the window. "Good—Lord... I've never—I've never heard anything like it. Have you?"

"No. But what with the fashion for wigs, it's difficult to know who has real hair and who be bald. You could be hairless, sir, and who'd know, except those who attended on you at your toilette. Certainly the ordinary man would be clueless."

"There is that I suppose..." Sir Cosmo conceded, unconsciously stroking his beard. "Still, even if a man shaves his head, or his wife doesn't have but two hairs to hers, and both of 'em wear wigs, you'd still jolly-well know if they were without eyebrows and eyelashes!" Sir Cosmo gave a shudder and pulled a face. "Ghastly. Positively ghastly."

"But at least the Margrave ain't horribly scarred or got a bulbous nose the size of a gourd, as far as we know, which was your first fears, weren't they, sir?"

"Yes. They were...."

"And it does explain one thing," added Matthias. "Why there's a law forbidding courtiers from growing beards and mustaches, if their ruler can't grow one himself. No small wonder why he came to gawp at your beard, sir."

"No small wonder, indeed! I'd wager none of those fellows had ever seen a full beard before. Well! I'd never have thought of myself as a zoo exhibit, or a rabble-rouser for that matter. But this beard has certainly turned me into one. And I'll wager that if the rebel Prince Viktor is triumphant he'll repeal the law banning beards, and every man and his widowed mother will grow one!"

Matthias grinned. It was so satisfying to see his master sounding like his old self. But the grin soon fell into a frown recalling the rest of what Hansen had confided about the *unspoken truth*. He believed him because he had overheard a most interesting conversation between the Court Chamberlain and a foreign diplomat who had missed his opportunity to flee to his homeland while the borders were still open. They conversed in the language of diplomacy— French. And as it so happened that was one language Matthias did understand. And so he lingered longer than was necessary in the state antechamber, eavesdropping while slowly clearing away the platters piled with food scraps. The two men were discussing the *unspoken truth* and the Margrave's sister, the Princess Joanna, in the same breath.

Since her father's death, the Princess was determined to regain her rightful place at court. She would not be silenced. She wanted her liberty. Her screaming tantrums with her brother resonated beyond the bolted doors of her apartment out into the passageways. And her wails of torment echoed through the turret's windows. As her twin was now Margrave, he had it within his power to rescind their father's edict that she never be released. She had expected this revocation to be her brother's first action. But he continued to keep her locked up because the unspoken truth had manifested itself in a most distressing manner in the Princess—her mind was unbalanced.

The diplomat tempered his surprise, and Matthias found himself inching closer, when the Court Chamberlain revealed he believed the Princess's instability of mind could be controlled. The diplomat asked to know the medicinal used in the treatment of lunatics. This had made Chamberlain smiled broadly. It was not a medication, but a person who could soothe the Princess's black moods. He named that person, and while the diplomat did not register recognition, Matthias knew at once. That name was the last two words he heard of that conversation. His eavesdropping was abruptly terminated when he was cuffed hard across the ear by a liveried footman and told to get on with his job.

"Here, let me finish dressing you, sir," the valet said, gathering his thoughts to reveal all to his master. "They might come for me at any moment, and you need to be ready for when you're fetched, too."

Sir Cosmo complied and shrugged his shoulders into the frock coat. He allowed Matthias to fuss over him, and wished he not taken such niceties for granted, particularly the services of his valet. He vowed never to do so again.

"Thank you, Matthias. And thank Heaven for small mercies," he said with another sigh, this one with relief. "If the worst of it all is that the Margrave has no eyebrows and eyelashes—one assumes he wears a wig—then so be it. I will look him in the eye, if and when the time comes, and with confidence." He forced himself to smile. "Who knows. Perhaps he'll invite his sister to dine, just to see my beard, which will afford her some amusement in her seclusion."

"About the sister, sir... There's more to this *unspoken truth* where she's concerned. She's not in seclusion because she *chooses* to be, but because she *has* to be. If you understand my meaning..."

Sir Cosmo completely misinterpreted what his valet was hinting at, saying with annoyance, "Just because she doesn't have a full head of hair, perfectly arched eyebrows and a row of dark lashes, shouldn't mean she's shut away—"

"No, sir. I mean... I don't think she's locked away because of *that*."

"Then if not that then what?" When his valet moved from foot to foot, hesitating, he added patiently, "Matthias, what is it you're *not* telling me? Better I know as not. As the Romans were used to saying: *Praemonitus praemunitus*."

"Pardon, sir?"

"To be forewarned is to be forearmed," Sir Cosmo stated, translating the Latin. "I don't want to make a fool of myself at dinner; say something out of turn; mention his sister; ask about— about Miss St. Neots, if it will prejudice our cause, and hers."

"Yes, sir. I understand. And you're right, it would be best if you did none of those things—mention the Princess or Miss St. Neots, because..." And in a few halting sentences he recalled the conversation overheard between the Court Chamberlain and the diplomat, omitting nothing, not even the wailing and the screaming, adding hopefully when he saw his master had blanched as white as a clean sheet,

"But the Chamberlain believes the Princess's madness can be brought under control," Matthias replied.

He crossed to the bed recessed in the wall, to give Sir Cosmo time to digest what he'd just been told, and because watching his master turn as white as a sheet made him think of sheets in general. He set to stripping the mattress of the tumble of filthy bedclothes and flat feather pillows. He next scooped up his master's discarded smalls, shirt and breeches and wrapped these up in the filthy sheet, reasoning he might be able to salvage at least the shirt with good laundering, and the stripped bed would give him the excuse to return with clean sheets.

"Under control?" Sir Cosmo said at last, and was skeptical. "What type of medicinal are we talking about? Laudanum? Or some derivative of such to keep her constantly sedated? Poor wretch! At least we now know why this *unspoken truth* is never talked about, and if it is, only in whispers..."

"It's not a medicinal, sir," the valet cut into the silence, hugging the ball of dirty laundry. "But a man—a nobleman. It's Lord Halsey, sir—"

"*Alec*—Alec *Halsey*?"

"Yes, sir. I didn't mishear the name. The Court Chamberlain and the Margrave are convinced Lord Halsey is just the man to control the Princess's broken mind."

Sir Cosmo had suffered a monumental shock. Yet he believed every word Matthias told him. The revelation answered the question as to why Alec, and not any other diplomatic functionary of His Majesty's government, had been requested specifically to negotiate the terms of his friends' release. It was a way of getting him to Midanich, his friends' lives the lure to make certain he returned. But while that answer closed the door on that question, which had baffled Sir Cosmo since he was first locked up, a whole host of other question-doors opened.

Why were the Baron and the Margrave investing all their hopes in Alec? He knew Alec had spent time as a Foreign Office flunkey here at the court. But that was a long time ago. What was Alec to this Princess? Had the Princess been waiting for Alec's return for ten long years? Was she the reason he'd ended up in the castle's dungeon, only to make a daring escape from a prison said to be impossible to break out of, and thus was still talked about today? And most baffling of all: Once Alec did return, how precisely was he going to control the Princess's madness?

And then it came to him, as if he'd struck over the head by a blunt object and the answer pounded into his brain. For added effect, at the same time, there was a short sharp rap on the door. The sleepy guards were immediately awake and stumbling about in response. Into the room marched four soldiers of the Margrave's household guard, and behind them, their captain holding in his gloved hand a coil of silken rope. It was time for Sir Cosmo to join the Margrave for dinner.

Matthias dropped the laundry bundle and fell to his knees before his master.

"Sir," he pleaded, wanting to be seen to be doing something, anything, so he wouldn't receive another cuffing for lingering. "Stick out your foot! I got to adjust y'buckles."

Mechanically, Sir Cosmo did as he was told, coming out of his reverie with dawning wonder. He knew why the Court Chamberlain and the Margrave wanted Alec in Midanich. The answer should have presented itself to him immediately when Matthias relayed the conversation between the Court Chamberlain and the foreign diplomat. After all, no one knew Alec better than he—they'd been the closest of friends since their teens at Oxford. He looked down at his valet.

"That poor creature's mind isn't the only thing that's broken about her. It's her heart, Matthias. The Princess suffers from a broken heart."

# Twelve

"REMIND ME: HOW MANY MILES FROM HERE TO AURICH?" Alec asked, studying the map of Midanich spread across the surface of a long table that held the remnants of a late dinner. When an answer was not immediately forthcoming, he glanced up over his rims, first at Colonel Müller and then at Jacob Luytens, both of whom sat opposite. "Is it twelve or fourteen?"

"Fourteen miles," Jacob Luytens responded.

Alec's gaze returned to the ordnance survey, provided on request and without question by Colonel Müller. He pointed to markings on the map just west of a church spire. "It's not shown here as complete, but can I assume the canal and its towpath now run the entire fourteen miles between here and Aurich?"

"It does. It was completed as far as Aurich just last summer, in time for the season's peat harvest," Jacob Luytens replied. He pointed to areas on the map. "This indicates the peat fields north and south of the township. There are more fields further northeast, here, near Eversmeer. There were plans to extend the main canal beyond Aurich come the spring thaw. If Midanich wants to pull itself out of the Middle Ages, then we need waterways. Without them we can't hope to get the peat sods here to Emden, and then shipped to market." He sat back in his chair and sighed, a resentful glance at Colonel Müller who was nursing a dry mug which had earlier been full of hot tea, and who was also closely studying the map. He was unable to keep the sourness from his tone. "But I doubt it'll be the weather that impedes progress, but this conflict—if it lasts beyond spring into summer. And even if it doesn't, there might not be the manpower needed to dig the trenches, or the peat fields, come to think on it. The war put paid to the last peat shipment being sent on to Holland, our biggest market, which means the consortia of investors, of which I am one, remain out of pock—"

"That's unfortunate, and not my concern for the moment," Alec interrupted curtly.

He was tired, physically and emotionally, and he itched to remove his eyeglasses. He wanted a bath—to wash off the day's grime, and the metaphorical dirt of his deception in not disabusing Colonel Müller and the town's representatives that he was there as the representative of Margrave Ernst. He had spent the day inspecting troops, the cannon and men positioned out along the star parapets, and talking with worried town officials about their concerns for the future. Such deception did not sit well with him, but he had to constantly remind himself that it was not only Emily's and Cosmo's lives that were now his concern if he did not pull off this ruse, but the entire party come over with him from England.

A warm bath and bed would have to wait. There was still much to do if he hoped to set off across country early the next morning. He could not delay beyond that. Every day which passed increased his anxiety for his friends' safety, and that, too, gave his normally placid voice a harsh edge.

"With respect, Herr Baron, it's not your concern, it's mine," Jacob Luytens stated, and muttered to himself, "Waste of good fuel to have it stockpiled in a warehouse..."

This bitter and thoroughly selfish remark was enough to momentarily divert Alec's thoughts from his upcoming journey.

He studied his merchant host over the rims of his spectacles.

"Correct the assumption, but surely having a stockpile of turf this side of the Ems is a godsend to Emden's citizens this winter? With the town suffering siege conditions, and very little in supplies getting in, other than what is confiscated off the ships waylaid in the estuary, turf for their heaters is some small consolation...?"

Alec let the sentence hang, a significant glance at the kachelofen—the tall masonry heater covered in pretty blue-and-white ceramic tiles. Dutch in origin, such heaters were widespread throughout northern Europe. It stood in the corner of the long narrow room and almost reached the ceiling. It radiated constant warmth much more efficiently than any English fireplace, not only for the men seated about the table, but through a system of pipes, it ingeniously provided warmth to the rest of this four-story house.

Situated on the best canal in Emden, this substantial residence of colored sandstone with a red-tiled roof, belonged to the merchant, and England's consular official, Jacob Luytens. It was to Luytens' house Alec and his party had been brought when the British consul had finally arrived at the Customs House to greet his English masters, with no explanation as to his tardiness. And as his visitors were too tired to be bothered to ask for one, Luytens blithely offered rooms in his fine establishment until a suitable house, just a few doors up from this one, could be made ready for the Duchess of Romney-St. Neots, Plantagenet Halsey, and their servants. Its masonry heater requiring a full day of constant fuel before it reached an ambient temperature that would remove the winter chill from all the rooms and warm them sufficiently for habitation.

"The distribution of heating supplies is a matter for Emden's council," Jacob Luytens stated evenly, keeping his anger in check for the benefit of Colonel Müller. But he could not help adding in a rush, in his native Dutch, when Alec remained impassive, "With respect, you know I'm a merchant first and foremost. I must make a profit. As it is, I've still much to recoup since the English occupation during the last war. And now this—a bloody civil war! The last thing any of us was expecting—or wanting. If this lot get wind of a stockpile, I stand to lose my entire investment."

Alec remained unmoved. There was something about the British Consul that put him on his guard. He could not place precisely what that was; that Luytens could barely meet his gaze certainly made matters awkward between them. They had parted as friends ten years ago, and Alec had assumed the friendship remained unchanged, despite distance and time. But when Alec had stuck out his hand in greeting, Luytens had taken it reluctantly, and with none of the enthusiasm associated with the meeting of long-lost friends. And not five minutes into their conversation, the merchant was making enquiries about the requested ransom in jewels and coin, a ransom of which Alec remained ignorant, though Luytens' persistent enquiry confirmed his suspicion that Sir Gilbert, with Olivia's blessing, had brokered a deal behind his back (and that was something else for him to deal with).

But what surprised and disappointed him most was that Luytens could not provide any assurances that Cosmo and Emily were safe and being treated well. Alec had had to ask. Luytens' reply was perfunctory at best, which only increased Alec's anxiety—either Luytens did not know, or his friends were not being accorded every courtesy as political prisoners. Alec had not insisted on a report, not with his uncle, godmother, and Selina within earshot. And now the merchant was willing to let his fellow citizens freeze to death for the sake of his profit margin?! What had happened to the man who had risked his own neck to save Alec's all those years ago? Had the Seven Years' War and now this civil unrest turned him into a mercenary?

"You know better than anyone at this table," Alec said quietly, "that in times of war sacrifices must be made—"

"Sacrifices? What would you know of sacrifice, Herr Baron?" Luytens demanded, fists pounding the table, clattering the crockery and causing the black-and-white house cat curled up on the rug in front of the kachelofen, to wake in fright and dash out into the corridor as the door opened. "When was the last time England was occupied by a foreign power and its subjects terrorized? When did an Englishman—you—last have to defend home and hearth from his neighbors?"

"I'm not here to debate history with you, Jacob," Alec replied calmly.

Colonel Müller rose off his chair the instant Luytens pounded the table, a hand to his sword hilt, but Alec shook his head, and he sank back down. The Colonel did not understand Dutch. Neither did Plantagenet Halsey or Sir Gilbert Parsons. But all three recognized disrespect in tone and action.

"It's late and we would all like to go to our beds. But first we must finalize the details of this journey. If you feel you've been inadequately compensated by His Majesty's government," Alec continued in English, for the benefit of Sir Gilbert and his uncle, who had been patiently silent throughout most of dinner and a discussion which had been conducted in German, and when remembered, sprinkled with French to try and include the two older gentlemen, "I suggest you take up your grievance with Sir Gilbert later tonight, or very early tomorrow morning, before I head off. But at this very minute, I need your advice for the journey to Castle Herzfeld." He glanced significantly at Colonel Müller, who was ignorant of the conversation, and back at Luytens. "I don't need to remind you why I am here."

He let the sentence fall away, to give Jacob Luytens time to find his equilibrium, and to allow Sir Gilbert to add to the conversation if he wished to. But neither Sir Gilbert nor his uncle said a word. In fact they had said very little since the incident on the jetty, which was most uncharacteristic, particularly for Sir Gilbert, who had spent the entire sea voyage pontificating. A glance at both and he suspected their silence was due more to continued shock than good manners; they were still coming to terms with the revelation that the title Baron of Aurich had been personally bestowed upon him by Margrave Leopold. He politely declined to reveal the why, the what, and the wherefores of such an honor, though he had reluctantly shown them upon request his baronial ring, and the documents attached to his elevation.

Earlier that day, his uncle had told him as an aside that at the docks Sir Gilbert had removed his nose from between his diplomatic documents just in time to witness Colonel Müller grab Alec's hand to kiss the intaglio. That, and watching the soldiers along the jetty salute him had sent the diplomat reeling, the documents dropped from his hand to the filthy wet cobbles without a thought. The old man had chuckled and shook his head, but Alec derived no amusement from his deception, and could not apologize enough for not being able to take him into his confidence; he still could not. To which Plantagenet Halsey had patted his shoulder and told him not to worry: He had every confidence in him. Far from clearing Alec's conscience, it made him more wretched. And that in turn, made him want to set matters to rights with all speed.

Perhaps more tea would help keep them awake, and put everyone in a better mood. So he lifted his mug with a smile, a signal to the housekeeper who sat on a bench by the heater, knitting, to bring more tea. With a shy smile and a quick curtsey, she came forward to collect the teapot so she could refill it with hot water from the brewing kettle in the adjoining kitchen.

"Aye, you've been generous to a fault with your coin for the upkeep of your guests while they'll be staying here in Emden," Jacob Luytens begrudgingly conceded, reverting to the German language to include Colonel Müller. "I daily count my blessings that my wife and four of my children are out of harm's way in Holland. They were visiting Elsa's mother when the borders were closed. But I have my eldest, Hilda, with me," he added, a nod to the girl who had come to fetch the teapot. He watched her clear away the used bowls and cutlery, and deftly handle a stack of plates. "Hilda's a good girl, an excellent housekeeper and cook. She'll keep the house clean and warm, and her old father fed, until her mother and brothers return."

The girl smiled, dropped another quick curtsey and scuttled from the room, returning several times to collect up the remainder of the dinner dishes, and finally to set a heavy teapot full of freshly-brewed tea and a plate of aromatic ginger biscuits, baked that afternoon, on the table. She then retreated to her seat by the kachelofen and took up her knitting. Her father handled the large teapot and refilled everyone's mugs, then set the milk jug and bowl of candied rock, used in lieu of sugar, in the center of the table with the biscuits. He took one from the plate and held it up as he offered the plate to Plantagenet Halsey, saying in halting English, "Ginger. Is very good. Take two."

"As you are fortunate, Jacob, you cannot surely wish to begrudge your fellow citizens, and the Margrave's militia, some good fortune, also?" Alec said smoothly in German for the benefit of the Colonel, and so Luytens could not renege on an offer about to be forced upon him. "Colonel Müller will be most grateful to have access to the stockpile of turf. In giving it freely, the Colonel will ensure it is evenly distributed. Is that not so, Colonel?"

The ginger biscuit suddenly lost its flavor. The merchant did not like having his hand forced. But he was not surprised. His English friend had a smooth tongue and a handsome smile that meant people went out of their way to help him. He'd saved his life years ago, and in return for what? In the decade since he had aided Alec Halsey's escape from Midanich, the man had gone on to inherit title, wealth, and a life of leisure while he, Luytens, the British Consul of Midanich, had lost everything to wars and ill-timed investments. Life had been unfair, and it was not his fault. Well, that was about to change. He'd been promised a King's ransom if he could entice Halsey to leave England and travel to Midanich; Baron Haderslev said that in itself would be a miracle. Well, he'd performed that miracle, because here was Halsey sitting at his table in Emden. He had managed to get the nobleman this far; he could certainly perform another miracle and have him return to Castle Herzfeld; that was but one small step further to him, Luytens, being richly rewarded for his part in the capture and incarceration of Alec Halsey.

So while he had no wish to waste good turf on an occupying force—Emden's stores of grain and other essentials were already dangerously depleted with the need to house and feed the grenadiers—a moment's reflection was enough for Luytens to realize that if the Colonel thought the offer of turf was freely made, it could play to his advantage when he required a favor in return.

"Of course I wish every one of our citizens—and the militia—to be warm this winter, Herr Baron," Luytens replied, tempering his anger and giving Alec a curt nod. He looked to the Colonel. "I will inform the City Council that it would be in their best interests—and the collective good of the entire community—for the stockpile of turf to be handed over to you and your men for distribution amongst all the residences within the town's walls."

Colonel Müller looked to Alec. "If I may be permitted to comment...?" When Alec nodded, the Colonel's mouth twisted into an unpleasant smile as he addressed Jacob Luytens. "You were wise to offer up the turf freely, Herr Luytens. Now knowing about the stockpile, I would have been obligated to tear every warehouse apart in search of such a precious resource. In winter, turf is more precious than gold. But of course, you know that. But perhaps you did not know that withholding resources from the Margrave's army, particularly in time of war, is a treasonable offence? The Baron has saved you and your people unnecessary expense and suffering. Herr Baron," he added, addressing Alec in an entirely different voice. "I give you my solemn word that this—gift—will be distributed first to those in need, particularly to the hospital, the orphanages, and the churches, then amongst the townspeople and my men. I cannot thank you enough. You, and through you His Highness, will save many from freezing this winter."

"Please, Colonel, no thanks are necessary," Alec stated, cutting him off, a heightened color to his cheeks at such effuse gratitude. "That you will take the right and decent action and see that those in most need are provided for is all the thanks I—and His Highness the Margrave—require."

Alec believed the Colonel would do right by the people of Emden because he was fundamentally a good and decent man. He wished his uncle was able to understand the German language; the two men would have found much in common to discuss, regardless of their opposing political sentiments.

"Now, if we could return to the map," he continued, not a glance at Jacob Luytens, who he was certain was simmering away with resentment and embarrassment at being called to account; the Colonel's threat would only add to his bitterness. "Let's go over the logistics of the journey one last time. Colonel, you have been able to fulfill my requirements?"

"Yes, Herr Baron." Colonel Müller showed Alec the pages of a small leather-bound ledger, which had scrawled in it a long and detailed list. "Four trekschuiten—barges—have been outfitted: Two for yourself and your traveling companions, another loaded up with luggage and stores, and a fourth—a cargo barge—has the five sledges, requisitioned from members of the town."

"Sledges?"

"Yes, Herr Baron. The canal terminates at Aurich, so from there the journey is overland. And at this time of year, the marshlands might not be entirely frozen, but the road will be sufficiently icy to carry the sledges, and at speed."

"And the horses and drivers needed...?"

"Aurich has horses, but I do not hold out much hope of its citizens being able to supply you with the type of animal which has the speed and endurance you require. The town was badly treated by the occupying French force; anything of value was pillaged. Hence, livestock was taken, or eaten, and any horse worth its shoes, confiscated. It will take many years for that town—many towns—and our people to recover from such an occupation. But," the Colonel added with a shrug of acceptance, "war is war, and we are no longer occupied by a foreign power."

"No. Now we are at war with ourselves!" Jacob Luytens stuck in, raising his mug with mock congratulation. "After all those years of occupation by French pigs, and then snot-nosed Englishmen—no offence to present company—you'd think we'd have the brains to want peace at any cost. But not Prince Viktor—traitorous bastard."

Alec let Luytens have his moment, and then repeated his question with great patience, as if his host had not spoken at all, "And the horses and drivers, Colonel Müller?"

"Allow me to supply you with both. The regiment has the necessary horses—Frisians, the best there are. Two for each sledge. I also have drivers skilled in handling such apparatus in this weather. I am also assigning a company to protect you and your party and the trekschuiten. They will follow the towpath on foot, ahead and behind the jagers."

A company was between a hundred to a hundred fifty men, and the need for so many soldiers surprised Alec. "You expect to encounter Prince Viktor's forces at this time of year? Didn't you tell me the rebels had retreated as far south as Leerhafe for the winter?"

"That is correct, Herr Baron. The last communiqué reported a battalion of rebels marching from here—" The Colonel pointed to a spot on the map on the outskirts of the town of Wittmund and traced a line south to Leerhafe. "We can deduce from that, the Prince has indeed retreated south for the winter. But we must also assume he has left behind troops—perhaps a company—at Aurich, which he managed to overrun and occupy a month ago. That town is the largest and the best fortified, and it is strategically necessary, if he hopes to march on Emden in the spring. And so with Aurich in the hands of the rebels, it is not safe for you to leave the protection of the trekschuiten and the canal, without troops loyal to the Margrave to protect you and your party. I do not foresee the rebels leaving the safety of the town to engage a company of my men in combat. If I was in command of Viktor's troops, I would advise a strategy of containment—hold on to Aurich at all costs. Allowing a small party of travelers to move freely on to Wittmund is not so important that they would risk losing their hold on the town. But—" The Colonel gave a lop-sided smile. "—they would risk such an encounter and loss if they knew you were one of the party, Herr Baron. It is vital then that your identity be kept secret so that you are not taken prisoner by rebels, and become a hostage of Prince Viktor. You were wise to remain incognito on the sea voyage here."

"Do you suggest then that we move on at night while Aurich sleeps?" asked Luytens.

"No. That is not possible. The night must be spent on the canal at the lock." The Colonel smiled apologetically at Alec. "Even if it were possible to spend it at one of Aurich's inns, I would counsel against it. Your trekschuit, Herr Baron, will be more comfortable, warm, and of a higher standard than any inn."

"I do not doubt that, Colonel. Do you know which town Prince Viktor is using as his headquarters?"

"Friedeburg Palace. It was from its steps, and before a cheering crowd, that His Highness declared he, and not Prince Ernst, was the fourteenth Margrave of our country."

"Friedeburg? I know it well," Alec stated, ignoring for the moment the Colonel's passing reference to Prince Viktor as 'His Highness', the first and only time he had done so. But he was unaware he had punctuated his statement with a tired sigh, as his mind's eye flooded with memories long since suppressed.

If there were any happy memories from his time in Midanich, they were to be found at Friedeburg, the Margrave's summer palace, and the cultural and artistic heart of the principality. Its ornate audience chambers and salons teemed with scholars, artisans, courtiers, artists, and musicians, all vying for patronage. And of course, diplomats from foreign courts roamed the corridors, paying court to the Margrave and his family, and also spending inordinate hours gaining the trust and ears of government flunkeys who ran the state bureaucracy with precision, if not panache.

The collection of buildings was of pink and cream sandstone and whitewashed brick, with copper roofing, fanciful turrets, and gilded molding reminiscent of Versailles. It was at Friedeburg Margrave Leopold had resided with his second wife, Helena, the Countess Rosine, and where she had given birth to their son Prince Viktor, raised at the palace, far from Herzfeld Castle, the official state residence of the Margrave. So it was no surprise to Alec why the young prince had chosen Friedeburg to make his declaration, and as his headquarters for his war against his half-brother.

It was in the gardens of Friedeburg, with its numerous ponds sprouting fountains, and around every corner a secluded grotto, that Alec chose to spend most of his time one particular summer, and at the expense of his duties as a junior secretary for the British embassy. At the time such was his youthful over-confidence in his abilities that he was able to convince himself that time spent fornicating in grottoes with a foreign princess was, in a way, taking diplomacy to its natural conclusion of satisfying both parties to the agreement. What he had failed to understand because he'd been an arrogant idiot was that even before the illicit affair had begun, it was doomed to failure—uncovered and condemned, like all furtive agreements between foreign powers—because of its underhanded and thoroughly immoral nature.

How had he dared to presume he could get away with conducting an illicit affair under the nose of Margrave Leopold? To his shame he knew the answer: If he'd been thinking with his brain and not with what was in his breeches he would not have embarked on the torrid liaison in the first place. He managed to endanger not only his life, but the lives of others. That affair and its consequences were why he now found himself back in a country to which he vowed never to return, and why Cosmo's and Emily's lives were in danger.

"Herr Baron," Colonel Müller said, looking his way and clearing his throat to bring Alec out of his self-castigating reverie. "While Prince Viktor and most of his force are presumed to be spending the winter at Friedeburg, it would be remiss of me not to mention that there remain fierce pockets of resistance in the north amongst the villagers. They do not care if it is winter or not, nor do they follow the rules of engagement."

Alec forced his thoughts back to the present and tried to sound disinterested. He hoped, too, that by having his mug refilled with tea it would help to deflect his curiosity as to how Prince Viktor and his supporters were faring in the civil war. And in doing so, perhaps he could trip up Colonel Müller, or Jacob Luytens, into revealing where their real loyalties lay—with the newly-declared Margrave Ernst, or did they secretly support the rebel prince? As for his own hopes, they were invested in Prince Viktor. If Midanich was to prosper into the next century, then its only hope was with Ernst's half-brother. The country needed Viktor. The Margravate would not survive beyond Ernst without him. Alec knew better than any man living that Ernst and Joanna would ruin all that their father Leopold had managed to achieve for this small country which bordered Hanover. Because, when all was said and done, Ernst and his sister were little better than scheming lunatics.

"It must be a constant annoyance to the professional soldier to have to deal with ignorant peasants who do not understand such rules of engagement," Alec remarked, hoping to provoke either man into an unguarded response. "Such unthinking zeal sees them aid the rebel's cause by mounting raids and skirmishes. Yet by their very amateur nature, they are bound to fail from the outset."

"Ha! Fail?" It was Jacob Luytens. "If they do fail, it won't be through lack of trying! Most of the ignorant yokels who eke out an existence as subsistence sheep farmers at best are betting their best new season's lambs on Viktor overcoming all opposition. Optimistic rot! Everyone knows, whoever controls this port—the merchant jewel in the Midanich crown—controls the country. And with loyal commanders such as Colonel Müller and his grenadiers, we'll see this winter through, and the rebellion will be quashed come spring. Isn't that so, Colonel?"

"That is the wished-for outcome, Herr Luytens. But with most of the Margrave's soldiers wintering at Castle Herzfeld or at this port, the waterways and surrounding countryside are not safe, Herr Baron."

"Then the soldiers you have assigned to the journey will be most welcome, and necessary," Alec replied, noting how deftly the Colonel turned the subject back to Alec's trek across country, and without adding fuel to Jacob Luytens tirade about the rebels and their leader.

"The journey from here to Aurich...?" Alec enquired, sipping at his tea, and returning his attention to the map. "How long is that expected to take?"

"A day—"

"A day?" Alec was incredulous. "To travel fourteen miles by barge will take an entire day?"

"Yes, Herr Baron. You must remember there are four barges, with heavy cargo. And they all must remain together as one unit, or my men cannot possibly hope to defend them. But the journey by sledge from Aurich to Wittmund should progress much faster," Colonel Müller continued, drawing an imaginary line on the map. "Here the country is extremely flat, and thus should be easy to traverse, but it is also a great swamp land and pitted with treacherous waterholes."

He glanced up at Jacob Luytens and tried to keep the disapproval from his tone. "Digging out the peat has only made this situation worse. Removal of the sods has caused great bodies of water to rise up, making the land useless. I know this because I was once an engineer, and saw it firsthand in Holland. The Dutch have scoured their landscape of all the peat and created useless lakes where there was once good farming land. And now that country requires the peat from our land. It is ironic, is it not? Besides," he added with a shrug, "here it is so flat that any taper lit at night is seen for miles, and your enemy would see you coming and be prepared many hours before you arrived."

Jacob Luytens opened his mouth to make comment about peat production, thought better of it, mainly because the Colonel was right, so added with a grin, "We have a saying about the land being so flat you can already see on Wednesday who will come to visit next Sunday."

Colonel Müller nodded, not seeing the humor. "Regretfully, that is very true, Herr Luytens."

"And the time needed to reach Wittmund by sledge?" asked Alec, sitting back and finally removing his eyeglasses.

"Half a day, Herr Baron," the Colonel apologized. "That is, if the weather holds, and we do not encounter any—resistance. The greatest pockets of rebellion in the north are to be found between Aurich and Wittmund. The road is not safe and has rarely been travelled since the outbreak of the war. Thus this journey will allow for the gathering of much needed intelligence for the Margrave's generals."

"You say 'we', Colonel. Are you volunteering to lead this little expedition, and gather the needed information?"

The Colonel nodded. "I am not so much volunteering as assigning myself to your welfare, Herr Baron. And yes, it will allow me the opportunity to present a report in person to the Margrave." He addressed Jacob Luytens. "I will be leaving Emden's defense in the capable hands of Captain Rall during my absence. And this arrangement was made known to the town's councillors this afternoon."

"Then I welcome your presence, Colonel," said Alec. "And after we reach Wittmund, how do we proceed to Herzfeld?"

"All going well, and we reach Wittmund without incident, then the rest of the journey will also be by sledge. It is by far the fastest method of travel."

"Half a day's travel?"

"Yes, Herr Baron."

Alec suppressed an impatient sigh. Two days of travel for what would normally take a day at most, had it been summer not winter, and had the country not been at war with itself. Two days to keep the members of his travelling party safe, and before he could confront Ernst to bargain for Cosmo's and Emily's release. Bargain? He laughed at himself. He wished it were that simple.

"Time I retired for the evenin'," Plantagenet Halsey announced, slowly straightening his arthritic knees, a hand to his nephew's shoulder. "Comin', Parsons? I don't understand a bloody word they're sayin', so you mustn't either!"

When Sir Gilbert nodded and started stuffing his papers into his satchel, the old man turned to Alec, who had risen also, and squeezed his arm, saying in an undervoice, "You need to get some sleep if you're off in the morning, m'boy. But before you do that, there's someone who wishes speech with you..." He gave a jerk of his head at the doorway, and when Alec's gaze darted that way and his brow furrowed seeing Selina, the old man added with whispered annoyance, "I don't doubt that baronial ring has some magical power over this lot, what with them hangin' on your every word, and 'em all bowin' and scrapin' before you as if you're the Sun King come amongst them. So it's just as well you have me—and her—to keep your boots on the ground and your fine nose out of the air! I'm tired. You're tired. But we're both not so tired that I can't give you advice, and you'll take it. Now, for God's sake, go and make your peace with her! And don't expect any help from that damned ring!"

# Thirteen

LEC MANAGED TO TAKE A STRIDE TOWARD SELINA
when the skirt of his woolen frock coat was rudely tugged
by Sir Gilbert, who waylaid him with the demand that he,
as His Majesty's representative and head of the legation, was entitled
to a complete précis of the conversation with these *foreign types*.

"I'm not your lackey this time, Parsons!" Alec hissed through
gritted teeth and pulled his frock coat free.

But he instantly regretted his outburst. He was over-tired, and
he'd spent too many hours playing at Herr Baron he was forgetting
it was not who he really was, or wanted to be. Perhaps his uncle was
right—the Herzfeld baronial ring possessed some sort of magical
power over him and the inhabitants of Midanich. The ring had
helped him to escape Midanich ten years ago, and it was helping
him now to get to Cosmo and Emily. But whatever its supernatural
powers, real or imagined, he couldn't wait to be well rid of it—and
this time forever. But for now he had to keep up the pretense; too
many lives now depended upon it.

So when Colonel Müller came to life, taking an angry stride
forward, affronted that the fat little Englishman had dared to lay a
hand on a member of the House of Herzfeld, Alec stopped him with
a word. He made Sir Gilbert a short bow of apology and mustered

all his patience to say diplomatically,

"I will be only too happy to give you this précis tomorrow, when the journey by barge will give us all the time in the world. But for now you must excuse me." He had a sudden idea, gaze flickering to the satchel Sir Gilbert held possessively to his barrel chest, and extended his hand, saying with a considered frown, "And to facilitate our discussions, it would be beneficial if I was fully acquainted with His Majesty's business. If you wouldn't mind handing over the diplomatic pouch, Sir Gilbert."

The pouch was held more tightly to the diplomat's chest. "I would mind, sir! I mind very much indeed. There are documents—sensitive letters, memoranda—"

"All the more reason for me, as your subordinate, to have access to them, so that I am fully cognizant of His Majesty's wishes. And as you are retiring for the evening, you can hardly object...?"

He let the sentence hang and kept his hand extended, but Sir Gilbert would not be swayed until Colonel Müller took a step closer at Alec's back, and Plantagenet Halsey hissed at his ear,

"Don't be a bigger fool than you already are, Parsons! That soldier at my nephew's shoulder could not care less about you. He has no understandin' of your position, or of the English tongue, but I'll tell you one thing he does understand, and that's fealty. He'd have no hesitation in skewerin' you for not doin' as you're ordered."

"But I am His Majesty's representative! I have rights and obligations. I—"

"Not here you don't! No one cares a fig for you or, for that matter, His Majesty," the old man said with a huff, a roll of his eyes at his nephew, and patted Sir Gilbert's shoulder when the round little man reluctantly handed over the satchel. "There, now, that wasn't too painful, was it?"

"I must tell you, sir, I truly do not understand what is happening in this place," Sir Gilbert was heard to complain to the old man, who was shepherding him from the room with a hand lightly to the small of his back.

"Ha! You and me both, Parsons! You and me both."

IN THE INTERVENING FEW MINUTES SINCE SELINA HAD APPEARED in the doorway and Alec had taken possession of the diplomatic pouch, she had come further into the room and was now in quiet communication with Luyten's daughter Hilda. And from her smiles and gesturing, trying to make herself understood to a girl who possibly spoke three languages, but English was not amongst them. So he resumed his seat and waited, the diplomatic pouch on his lap forgotten, grateful for the respite and content to watch Selina. He could watch her all day. He was unaware that while he watched her, he was being watched.

Jacob Luytens sat forgotten at the table, dunking a ginger biscuit in his tea, a silent observer to the exchange between Sir Gilbert and Alec Halsey, and understanding it all. As he understood now, without the need for translation into any language, the universal look of love... of being in love. He watched with great interest the light that came into Alec's blue eyes, the softening to his lean face, and the small smile that played upon his mouth as he gazed upon the fine-featured English beauty with the porcelain skin and flaming red hair. And while his first thought was the correct one—Alec Halsey was deeply in love with Selina Jamison-Lewis—his second thought was predatory: How to use to his advantage this most interesting revelation.

Luytens was unaware half his biscuit had plopped into the milky depths of his tea.

ALEC HAD NOT SEEN SELINA OR HIS GODMOTHER AND THEIR ladies in waiting since the day before, when they had been escorted to the British Consul's house by Colonel Müller and his men. Olivia had continued to be unwell, and Selina had stayed by her aunt's side, taking their meals in an upstairs parlor, where it was quiet and uneventful. The Duchess needed time to recover, not only from the sea journey, *The Caroline* being boarded by pirates, and the ordeal at the docks, but the realization she was in a foreign country at war, never mind the bitterly cold weather—any one of which would have been enough to send even the most stoic of elderly aristocratic matriarchs to bed with a megrim.

It was the first and only time Alec was pleased Selina had accompanied Olivia to Midanich. That she was to travel to Herzfeld Castle with him had come as a momentous shock, when Sir Gilbert had shoved letters of introduction signed by Lord Salt under his nose, citing His Majesty's wishes. Papers he now had in his possession in the diplomatic pouch, and which he could very easily put to the flame as if they did not exist. Without papers, he could then refuse her travel beyond the fortress walls of Emden. That had been his first reaction to the news, such was his fury. But a sleepless night's reflection, and considering the matter dispassionately, he saw the need to have a female along to tend to Emily, in her incarceration and later, when released. He just wished with all his heart that female was not Selina.

WITH A SMILE, A NOD AND A BOBBED CURTSEY, HILDA WAS able to make Selina aware that she understood what she wanted and went off to do her bidding. It was signal enough for Alec to excuse himself to the Colonel, who was busy collating the maps on the table, and Jacob Luytens, who sipped his tea in contemplative silence, to approach the love of his life. But the couple had time only for an exchange of smiles, when Hadrian Jeffries materialized in the doorway. Alec knew that the moment for a private word with Selina must again be postponed; he needed to speak to his valet about his day.

Jeffries had spent the afternoon at the docks, overseeing the soldiers loading the trekschuiten for the journey east to Aurich, and by the look on his usually impassive features, he wanted an urgent word with his master then and there. But what intrigued Alec more was that Jeffries had not divested himself of his greatcoat, gloves, and muffler, and over his arm he had Alec's chinchilla-lined cape and black tricorne hat, as if he were in expectation of his master going out into the chill night air.

"If you would excuse me for a few moments, Mrs. Jamison-Lewis," Alec apologized.

"I will be with Her Grace," Selina stated, adding with a thin smile of regret, "Aunt Olivia asked that I fetch you. She needs a word, and tonight would suit her better than tomorrow morning, when I assume we will be setting off at dawn."

With that, she went back up the narrow staircase to the bedchamber she was sharing with the Duchess of Romney-St. Neots, leaving Alec to peer after her, the unsettling dread in the pit of his stomach returning, knowing her use of the plural of the personal pronoun was deliberate.

"Have you eaten at all today?" he asked his valet, finally tearing his gaze from the now empty stairwell. Hadrian Jeffries looked worn out.

"With the soldiers, sir. At the docks. Some sort of cabbage stew sopped up with day-old bread, but I was hungry."

"All go smoothly?" Alec asked quietly, drawing his valet down the corridor to the front of the house, so they could speak freely. They might be conversing in English, but he knew Jacob Luytens understood the language well, even if he could not speak it fluently,

"Smooth enough, sir. That is, I accounted for all our portmanteaux, trunks and crates, and they were loaded up without a fuss. And the cabin—called a deckhouse on a barge, so I'm told— has been fitted out with all manner of the comforts brought with us—carpets, bearskin rugs, coal heaters, and furniture. It looks as if the journey is to be a long one, sir?"

"A slow one is more apt. And we will all be grateful for the warmth. There is little protection between us and the North Sea; the land north of here is all marshes and peat bog. I trust the trekschuiten are being guarded?"

"Yes, sir, guarded with their lives, so their commander told his men. So no opportunity for anyone to do any sneaking about."

Alec thought of the ransom Luytens had mentioned earlier, and asked, "So someone has been sneaking about—looking for anything in particular?"

"Yes, sir. There was. An *associate* of the consul was skulking about the docks while the barges—sorry, *trekschuiten*—were being loaded up and fitted out. He made enquiries of the dock workers, and those soldiers overseeing the loading, about what was in the crates in particular. And as they could not tell him, he started poking about, as if he had a right to be there. When he was confronted, he said he was acting in an official capacity as the consul's representative. The soldiers found this surprising, and the dock workers could not care less who he was, and he was ordered away or face a firing squad."

"You are certain he is in Luytens' pay?"

"Yes, sir. I saw him here at the house at first light. I don't forget a face or—"

"Thank you, Jeffries. I know that," Alec said with a smile at his valet's taking offence. "And the other matter I asked you to take care of...?"

"The woman made a widow at the docks, and her two children? They are with her dead husband's sister. What I gathered from their conversation, the new widow had warned her husband time and again no good would come of his smuggling activities. I pretended to know only German, and thus they were free and easy with their speech in Dutch before me. And in this way I learned that the widow was more upset that her children had lost their father, and a provider, than any feelings of a tender nature she may have had towards him. Her husband's sister was more forthright. She said her dead brother was a *vrouwenklopper*—"

"Wife beater?"

"Yes, sir. In fact, the dead man's sister was blunter than his wife, and said the soldiers had done them all a favor, to quote her, sir— and I do beg your pardon—*by putting a lead ball in that klootzak.*"

"If our coal smuggler was indeed a wife beater, then she is well rid of him, though I do not agree with the methods used of disposing of him! You gave her the coins and the sack of coal?"

"Yes, sir. The tears shed upon that occasion were genuine, and they could not thank you enough for your generosity. As the house had as much warmth as an iceberg, at that precise moment the sack of coal was worth ten times what you gave them in gold coin."

"No doubt when their house is warm again, they will turn their attention to their good fortune. Thank you, Jeffries. You've done very well."

"Thank you, sir."

Alec's gaze flickered over the cape draped over his valet's arm and the hat in his gloved hand, and he asked the inevitable. "I was about to dismiss you for the evening, and take care of myself. But I fear you have more to tell me, or more for me to do tonight...?"

Hadrian Jeffries saw the tiredness in his master's eyes and heard it in his voice too, and he dearly wished he could draw him a bath and send him off to bed. But he knew Alec would not thank him if he kept him in ignorance of what was going on outside this very house. He also knew Alec would want to do something about it, and before the soldiers took matters into their own hands, as they had done at the docks—before more innocent lives were lost, however worthless they were considered by relatives and friends alike.

"Yes, I do, sir," Jeffries apologized as he shook out the cape. He held it open and put it across his master's shoulders when Alec turned his back for him to do so. "I apologize, but there are two matters that will not wait until morning, particularly as we are setting off at dawn."

"I suppose I can always sleep aboard the trekschuit..." Alec muttered, chin up to allow his valet to button the cape across the front of his cravat. He forced himself to be more alert than he felt, pushed the diplomatic satchel on Jeffries in exchange for the knitted muffler held out to him, and this he tied about his neck. "What cannot wait until morning?"

Jeffries next handed Alec a pair of fur-lined gloves.

"You remember the old man and his granddaughter you saved at the docks?" When Alec nodded, he continued. "Well, sir, the servants here tell me he's been to the house a couple of times today, and turned away each time without any of his messages being passed on. And this he told me himself when he spoke to me just now."

Alec looked up from smoothing the leather glove over the intaglio ring. "I had no idea he'd called. He's here—*now?*"

"Yes, sir. He and his granddaughter both. They've been here since dusk."

"Since dusk? What does he want?"

"To put his case like everyone else, is my guess, sir," explained Hadrian Jeffries. "He's an Englishman—a reverend—and he and his granddaughter were on their way from England to Hanover via Holland when their ship was boarded just like ours and brought across the estuary here. He showed me his documents—one was a communiqué from the Right Reverend Richard Osbaldeston, Lord Bishop of London, and from a cursory glance at his other papers, he is who he says he is, and he is telling the truth—"

"As a reverend, I should hope so! Why the Bishop of London particularly?"

"The letter from the Lord Bishop gives the Reverend Shirley— Samuel Shrivington Shirley to be precise—the authority to marry English people abroad—"

"Any English couple?" Alec interrupted, and cursed tiredness

186

for speaking his wishful thinking aloud—his immediate thought that the reverend could marry him to Selina tonight, before he set out. Such a notion was not only absurdly romantic, he doubted the excuse of being in a war-torn country would be enough for Selina to agree, particularly with him in his role of Herr Baron. She would rightly make some flippant remark about just who was she marrying—the baron or the marquess? The baronial ring would not act in his favor this time. And because he felt the heat rush up into his face at his impetuous remark, and his valet was regarding him curiously, he waved a hand for him to continue.

"Yes, sir. Any couple who are in the Church of England," Hadrian Jeffries replied. "Such marriages as the Reverend performs abroad are recognized in England as legitimate, as if the bride and groom had indeed been married in an English church on English soil. And as the Reverend Shirley stuck this letter under my nose, I read it, and can verify that it is indeed what it says; it has the Lord Bishop's signature and seal. According to the Reverend Shirley, he has married hundreds of couples in this manner, from Verona to Paris, The Hague to St. Petersburg. And now, it seems, his services are wanted in Hanover."

"Why the urgency?"

"He says that if he does not arrive in Hanover within the next month, he may find his license revoked, because there is a couple there—not noble, but related to the Lord Bishop—who require his services post haste. The Reverend did not say so, possibly because his granddaughter was present, but it would seem the young bride-to-be is—" Jeffries dropped his voice and over-enunciated, "—already in the family way."

Alec closed his eyes for the briefest of moments to stop them rolling to the ceiling, and said with extreme patience,

"The Reverend Shirley must be aware that he is in a country at war with itself? That Emden is under siege conditions, and that no one gets in or out without fear of being killed, if not by rebels scouting for a way in, then by the grenadiers guarding this fort town? And that's not counting the fact that it is winter, which would see him and his granddaughter freeze to death within a mile of here!"

"Yes, sir. I did point these facts out to him. But he is adamant. Which is why he has requested that he and his granddaughter be given safe passage as part of your traveling party. And why he is still here after dark, waiting to put his case to you personally."

"Where precisely is *here*?"

"Outside the front door—"

"*Outside*? He and his granddaughter are waiting outside in this cold?"

"Yes, sir," Hadrian Jeffries replied. "They have nowhere else to go. All the inns are full—well, all the respectable ones are, and he can't take his granddaughter to the other kind on account of—"

"Yes. Yes. All right," Alec replied with an impatient sigh. He frowned. "But why have me dressed for the weather? Surely he and the girl can come within doors to speak with me?"

"Yes, they could, sir, but it's the other petitioners. There's too many of them." Jeffries pulled a face. "You wouldn't want to invite them indoors even if you could."

"*Petitioners*?"

"Yes, sir. They've been lining up since before dusk, now that they know where you're residing. The line extends for about half a mile, possibly longer, because I walked from the Customs House, and while it does not go all the way back to there, it does snake over three canal bridges, and from two directions."

When Alec stared at his valet as if he was speaking in riddles, wondering if in his tiredness his hearing was affected as well as his eyesight, Jeffries added with apology,

"I fear that if you—if the-the *Herr Baron*—does not give these people a moment of his time, or at least put in an appearance, mayhem may ensue."

"*Mayhem*?"

"They are orderly at the present moment, and it would seem all they want is for their grievances to be heard, but as I came indoors, I saw a patrol cross the bridge marching in this direction. After what happened at the docks yesterday—"

"Yes. Yes, I understand. You were right to fetch me." He stuck out his gloved hand for his hat and settled it over his thick black hair. "Lock that satchel away in my *nécessaire de secrétaire*, then fetch Colonel Müller. Tell him he's needed outside. The last thing this Herr Baron wants on his conscience," he added, mumbling to himself as he went briskly down stairs, "are more deaths!"

He nodded for the sleepy porter to open the front door, and in anticipation of the cold, squared his shoulders and settled his chin deeper into the soft woolen muffler snug about his throat. As expected, stepping out on to the top step he was met by a blast of icy air that snapped at his lean cheeks and sent his hot breath into the black night. What was wholly unexpected was the reception that awaited him. As his eyes adjusted to the glare of a multitude of flaming tapers held up into the night sky to bathe him in a golden glow, a rousing cheer of welcome went up amongst the crowd that left his ears ringing and his mind reeling.

Staring out across the sea of upturned expectant faces huddled together and pinched with cold, he was overwhelmed. "Dear God," he muttered. "What have I done..."

～　　～　　～

As Alec went out Jacob Luytens' front door, the associate of the British Consul, whom Hadrian Jeffries had correctly identified at the docks earlier that day, came inside via the servant entrance and immediately demanded a bowl of soup and some bread.

He then sat himself uninvited on a stool by the open kitchen fire and ate in silence; word sent upstairs that the master was wanted on a matter of urgency below stairs.

Jacob Luytens came fifteen minutes later, having waited until Colonel Müller went off with Alec Halsey's valet to quell a disturbance in the street by the canal. He was not surprised to see his associate, and he poured them both a cup of tea from the kettle on the hob, a jerk of his head to the cook to take herself off.

"Well?" Jacob Luytens demanded when his associate was unforthcoming and continued to slurp his tea in silence. "You have the ransom?"

"It's there all right."

"What? You don't have it with you?"

The associate eyed the consul as if he were brainless. "It's in a crate," he enunciated. "How was I to steal a crate out from under the noses of a dozen soldiers, the customs officials, and the Herr Baron's manservant, who was sniffing about, watching my every move."

"Was he? Then we'll have to steal it out from under their noses on the journey east." Luytens ground his teeth. "And if we're lucky we'll be ambushed and the Herr Baron and his sneaky-eyed manservant will get their comeuppance sooner rather than later! If not, he'll be incarcerated at Herzfeld Castle soon enough."

The associate's eyebrows shot up. "I don't know the Englishman, and can't say I care to, after what the English put us through in the war. I'm with you there. But you're about to betray a man you once called friend. Who sat at your table and broke bread with your family. And his country trusts you enough to make you its consul…"

"What are you? My confessor?"

"No. I'm your brother-in-law Horst Visser, and that gives me the right to say what I do. Elsa wouldn't want you to do this." He stuck out his bottom lip. "Steal from the English—yes. But betray a friend? No."

Luytens tossed the drip of tea left in the bottom of his mug on the fire and kept his gaze on the flames. His tone was flat. "Elsa and the boys are safe in Amsterdam. That's all that matters. And what I do—what I've done—I do for them." He looked at his brother-in-law. "Which isn't nearly enough, now the Herr Baron has seen fit to deprive me of my peat profit. Can you believe it? He's offered the entire peat stockpile to Müller to distribute amongst the needy! *The needy.* Damn him! So it's imperative we get our hands on that crate. Look at it as compensation for lost profit."

Horst Visser raised his mug of hot tea, as if in salute.

"You'll not hear a word of complaint from me."

"You can identify which crate?"

Horst Visser nodded. "Lost peat profit aside, why have you taken the Englishman in dislike, Jacob?"

Jacob Luytens threw up a hand as if it was not worth his energy to repeat, but he knew his brother-in-law would not let it go until he had an answer, so he said quietly, "It's got to do with Elsa. She told me just like that—threw it in my face like a slap—while we were arguing. I don't even remember what we were arguing over. But I do remember very clearly what she said. It was about her second youngest boy—"

"Peter?"

"Yes, of course Peter! I know his name!"

"Then why not call him by his name? You've always done that. Called him "her son", as if he's not yours at all. The boy knows it too. So does Elsa."

"Because he's not mine. He's *his*—he's Halsey's son!"

There was a moment of absolute calm, when all both men heard was the spit of the fire and a distant roar, like thunder, of shouting, or was it cheering? There could have been all out war in the streets for all these two cared.

Then Horst Visser shot up off the stool and grabbed his brother-in-law about the throat. He pushed him backwards, through the curtain of heavy pots and pans dangling from iron hooks around the rim of the enormous flue, and now disrupted, swung back and forth and hit both men about the ears; Horst not feeling a thing, while Jacob yelped to be assaulted by a heavy cast iron pan smacking him across the forehead. But Horst did not stop. He pushed his brother-in-law until there was nowhere else for them to go, Jacob's shoulders slammed up against the ceramic tiles decorating the fire surround, and with his shoes inches from hot ash.

"Take that back, liar! Take it back! Elsa would never break her marriage vows! Never! You're wrong!"

Luytens stared into Horst's blood-red face and his first thought was: Why was he the one being punished when it was Alec Halsey who had a case to answer? As ever, the man was touched by fairy dust! But by the savage look in the eye of his brute of a brother-in-law he'd be pummeled to pulp if he didn't tell him the whole sordid story. So he nodded and was reluctantly let go.

Horst stepped back, but his hands were still balled into fists. So Luytens took a moment to adjust his neck cloth and straighten the front of his plain woolen waistcoat, hoping to give his brother-in-law time to calm himself. He was sure he now carried a lump to his forehead and by tomorrow there would be a bruise. Still, it was better than Horst's fist in his face and a couple of his good teeth knocked out. Finally, he thrust his hands into his frock coat pockets and let out a sigh.

"That's what Elsa told me, Horst. As God is my witness—"

"Leave Him out of this!"

"She told me her boy—Peter—was his. That they had an affair. So what was I to do? Disbelieve her?"

"Yes! She must have said it in response to something you said or did. Elsa is a good girl. Always has been. And for some reason only known to her, she's always loved you."

"Calm down! Calm down! I know that—*now*." He gingerly put

a hand to his forehead and winced. A lump was already forming. "She found out about Berta and me, and so she thought she'd have her revenge—and it worked... for a time."

"Ugh! You and your whoring ways. I should beat you just for that alone!" Horst lifted his chin. "Go on. Tell me the rest. Tell me your wife is a faithful wife, or I'll—"

"Keep your fists down! She's chaste."

"Ha! So she *didn't* let this Englishman between her thighs, and Peter is *your* son, not *his.*"

"Yes. But it doesn't change the fact Elsa wanted the Englishman to rut her! The only reason she didn't was because *he* rejected *her.* Now that *is* the truth! She told me she tried to seduce him, but he said that as much as he'd like to take up her offer and bed her, she was my wife and we—he and I—were friends, so he politely declined." Luytens spat into the fire. "Politely! Pah! I've no doubt he was polite!"

"So you have accused your wife of infidelity, your son of being a bastard, and this Englishman of seducing your wife, and none of it is true? And you said all this to me, her brother? You're not only a bloody liar, Jacob, but a bloody fool! I should smash in your face regardless." Horst Visser kicked out at the stool hard and it ended in the fire. "Damn the ransom! I hope Elsa stays in Holland and leaves you to rot!"

When he turned to leave, Luytens grabbed his arm.

"Stay! I am a bloody fool, Horst. You can't walk out! By this time next week we'll be rich men! *Rich*, Horst!"

Horst eyed him with resentment as he retrieved the stool from the pile of ash and set it to rights. He had never warmed to Jacob Luytens. His parents thought the sun shone out of his arse. He strutted about as if he was hard-working and full of plans for the future. But Horst knew he lived off his parents' wealth, and his plans were schemes. Horst and Elsa came from a strict Calvinist family. Hard work, clean living and thrift repaid you, not schemes, stealing, and betraying friends. However, war and hard times had made Horst a pragmatist. He'd convinced himself that stealing from foreigners was just a way of taking back what they had stripped from Midanich and its people in the first place. No. He had no conscience about taking the English ransom. But he did about being party to betraying the Englishman and his friends.

"Just find a way of getting our hands on that ransom without getting us shot," Horst finally said. "I don't know what's planned for your English friend at the castle, but I pray you have nothing to do with it, and if you do, that you're not caught out! My sister and her children still need a provider."

Jacob Luytens shrugged his unconcern. "Don't you worry. I'll be careful. And what happens to Halsey won't be anyone's fault but his own. He's brought it on himself." He then slapped his brother-in-law's back as he showed him to the side door. "Who knows! The Herr Baron might come through it all, just as he did the last time... He has the Devil's own luck. I hope some of that luck rubs off on us. We'll need it to grab ourselves a king's ransom. Eh, Horst? By this time next week we'll be rich men!"

Horst Visser wanted to believe his brother-in-law. He didn't. He had nothing to lose, and everything to gain. Next week couldn't come quick enough.

# Fourteen

"I S HE ALL RIGHT? HE'S NOT BEEN ATTACKED AND INJURED, has he? Selina? Selina, what's going on down there? Tell me!"

It was the Duchess of Romney-St. Neots, and she was propped up against a bank of down pillows in the big plain wooden bed that was central to the room, a woolen shawl edged in ermine across her shoulders and a pretty night cap with puffed ribbon and trimmed with ruched lace covering her coiffure. She had been unwell most of the day, and so had stayed in bed, feeling green and sipping weak tea between spoonfuls of syrup of ginger and a decoction of ingredients only known to her apothecary, fed to her by her long-suffering lady's maid, Peeble. She was unsure if such remedies were helping or hindering her restoration to full health, but Peeble insisted she take her medicine, and she was too ill to argue. "Is he all right? He's not been attacked and injured, has he? Selina? Selina, what's going on down there? Tell me!"

It was the Duchess of Romney-St. Neots, and she was propped up against a bank of down pillows in the big plain wooden bed that was central to the room, a woolen shawl edged in ermine across her shoulders and a pretty night cap with puffed ribbon and trimmed with ruched lace covering her coiffure. She had been unwell most of the day, and so had stayed in bed, feeling green and sipping weak tea between spoonfuls of syrup of ginger and a decoction of ingredients only known to her apothecary, fed to her by her long-suffering lady's maid, Peeble. She was unsure if such remedies were helping or hindering her restoration to full health, but Peeble insisted she take her medicine, and she was too ill to argue.

The Duchess hated being ill. She hated being ineffectual even more. And she hated being cooped up in a foreign country, in a town overrun with foreign troops who spoke in a language that grated on the ear and made no sense to her at all. She had prepared herself to endure ignorance of the English tongue, but to discover that very few, if anyone, spoke the universal language of French positively scandalized her. She was in a land of ignorant oafs! She wanted to be home. She wanted her own bed and her own food, and the sounds of London outside her window. She was sure she was going to die in this place. And then she thought of Emily and Cosmo and mentally castigated herself for her selfishness. But thoughts of Emily, and what she must be enduring in an even bleaker place than this, brought tears and worry, and her heart would begin to race, and the cycle of sickness, apprehension and feeling sorry for herself started all over again.

Thus anything that provided a diversion was worthy of all her attention. And what was going on outside her window, down in the street that ran parallel to the canal, was vastly diverting. Yet it made her just as anxious because there was a lot of shouting and her godson was down there in amongst a crowd of cutthroats, thieves, and soldiers run amok, if what she had witnessed at the docks while waiting to clear customs was any indication of the rough types inhabiting this uncivilized fortress town.

"Selina! Put me out of my misery! Is he all right? Tell me he is all right!"

Selina reluctantly turned away from the window and let the curtain fall. She was suddenly cold, despite the wearing of a pair of padded jumps heavy with jewelry and coin. But the icy winter night air had seeped through the sill and had chilled her bones. So she bustled over to the masonry heater and spread her fingers to the radiant warmth. It helped, but there was something unsatisfactory about not being able to see a crackling fire, which would have made her feel as if her hands were warmer, even though she knew this for fanciful nonsense.

"Yes, he's all right, Aunt," she reassured the Duchess with a tired smile. "He's doing rather well, considering there's a great crowd of people all talking at him at once, and waving papers in his face. His valet already has his arms full of what must be petitions, and so a soldier is now following behind him, too, collecting up all manner of written scraps. God knows what they think he can do for them!"

"A great deal, if that display at the docks is anything to go by," the Duchess grumbled. "That soldier did kiss that intaglio he's wearing, didn't he? I didn't imagine it all?"

Selina laughed and shook her head. "No, you did not imagine it. Though I suspect Alec wishes it all a bad dream from which he could awake. You know he isn't one for grand displays of entitlement. Though he would be the first to uphold the tenets of *noblesse oblige*."

"He had the impudence to refuse an English marquessate when it was first offered, and yet here, in this wretched place, I'm told he's a baron of the royal household of Herzfeld!"

"I'm sure being Baron Aurich isn't a patch on being Marquess Halsey," commented Selina, tongue firmly in cheek, knowing Alec tolerated title and ceremony with reluctance.

"Well of course it isn't, Selina!" replied the Duchess, not hearing the ironic note in her niece's tone. "The very idea is absurd. An English marquessate outranks a foreign baronetcy in every respect, which would not hold much water at the Court of St. James's. And this despite the King's Germanic heritage. Still," she continued with a pout, settling her shoulders on the pillows and smoothing away a crease in the embroidered coverlet, "I am vastly annoyed he did not confide in me—confide in any of us—he was so honored when he was posted here all those years ago."

Selina left the warmth of the heater to sit on the edge of the mattress, and faced her aunt.

"It seems to be something of which he is not proud, and would keep to himself if he had the choice. But here, strutting about as Herr Baron is working to his advantage, and ours. No doubt he hopes, as we do, that the Herr Baron is better able to help free Cosmo and Emily.

"Yes, I'm sure you are right. And at least he seems to have the soldiery on his side—Oh! What has happened now? Go see! Go see!" The Duchess shooed Selina back to the window as a second deafening cheer went up.

Peering down into the street, Selina's interest was further piqued to find Alec standing by the canal edge, a little way off from the crowd in conversation with the old man and his granddaughter from the docks. She was so relieved to see them safe and well after their ordeal, and pleased they had sought out Alec, and that he was giving them his time. She hoped he could do something for them. A minute passed, perhaps two, and then a soldier ushered the couple into the house. Alec followed them, but he did not immediately go inside. He paused on the top step and turned on a boot heel to face the crowd. And when he put up a gloved hand to the multitudes swarming in front of him they cheered as one. The mob—what else could she call a hundred or more men crammed together along a narrow street under the glow of tapers waved aloft—then fell silent and surged forward, held in check by a line of soldiers using their bayonets as a barrier.

Alec addressed the crowd with Colonel Müller by his side. The colonel also said a few words at Alec's invitation. Alec then spoke again. Selina was unable to hear what was said because the window was closed. Not that she would have understood a word, because she was sure he was speaking in German or Dutch, or perhaps both. His facility for foreign languages never ceased to astonish her. A final cheer went up as Alec again raised his gloved hand, and he and the Colonel disappeared back within doors, Hadrian Jeffries and a soldier following, juggling armfuls of papers and scrolls between them.

She stayed watching a little longer as the soldiers dispersed the mob, who were at first reluctant to go, but soon realized nothing more could be accomplished tonight; with the temperature rapidly dropping, it was imperative to be indoors as soon as possible or face the very real possibility of freezing to death.

It was the soft knock on the outer door, not the Duchess demanding to know what was happening under her window, that made Selina turn into the room. Peeble appeared as if from nowhere in answer to it, and let the visitor in with a quickly bobbed curtsey before disappearing back into the cramped closet she was sharing with Selina's lady-in-waiting, Evans.

"You should both be asleep," Alec commented mildly as he closed the door and came further into the room. He was divested of cloak, muffler, and hat, and was stripping off his kid gloves. "But I'm glad you're awake. I can take my farewells now, as I would not want to wake you tomorrow before the sun is up." He glanced over at Selina as he slipped his gloves in a frock coat pocket, and held her gaze with one raised eyebrow, saying teasingly in something of his old manner, "I hope you won't mind this intrusion into your bedchamber, Mrs. Jamison-Lewis?"

Selina pressed her lips together to suppress a smile and failed miserably, felt her cheeks ripen, and lowered her lashes. Dear me! So all it took these days was a raise of his eyebrow in her direction to turn her into a giddy schoolroom miss?! She was missing their intimacy more than she realized. But that was only part of the equation. The soft timbre in his voice and that raised eyebrow was an invitation to reconciliation, and she couldn't be happier he had finally acknowledged her without the usual frowning glance, which had been her lot since Harwich, even if he still teased her by placing undue emphasis on her hateful married name. Before she could think of a suitable playful retort, the Duchess, who was too wrapped up in herself to notice the exchange between the couple, said into the silence,

"Don't talk rot, my boy! It's not Selina's bedchamber. It's mine—*ours*—until something more suitable than this hat box is got ready for us. Of course you're welcome in this old lady's chamber. Now do come here and let me look at you!" she demanded, sitting up and patting the space on the coverlet beside her. When he did as ordered, and kissed her forehead before propping a buttock on an edge of the mattress, she covered his ungloved hand with hers and peered closely at him. "Selina says you've been outside *talking* to a mob. At this late hour! And in this cold? I was in ready expectation of you being set upon, if not by them, then the soldiers turning on you or them, or both! After that dreadful episode at the docks, at the very least, shots to be fired."

"It wasn't so much a mob as a delegation."

"All with petitions for the Herr Baron?" asked Selina, sitting uninvited on the other side of the bed opposite Alec.

Alec nodded. "Yes. My long-suffering valet—well, he will be long-suffering after this night's work. Poor Jeffries! I've set him the task of reading through them all, and compiling a list with the help of one of the Colonel's men. I mean to look over the list and one or two of the petitions once I've said my goodnights and farewells."

"But—There must be dozens of them, if not a hundred?" Selina asked with alarm.

"Yes. I dare say there are. Though I'd rather not know the exact number or I might fall asleep before I begin."

"What can you possibly hope to gain by reading them tonight?"

the Duchess asked crossly, unconsciously squeezing his hand a little too hard. "You're worn thin. What you need is sleep."

"Yes. I shall sleep. Tomorrow. On the trekschuit. It will pass the time more agreeably than staring out at a flat landscape, waiting for the next windmill or church spire to appear out of the fog."

The Duchess was not to be placated, and said sullenly, "You've taken to this role as Herr Baron with such enthusiasm, I'm sure you can use the experience when we return to England and you finally take up your place in the Lords as Marquess Halsey." She sniffed and added archly, "I'll even have an intaglio fashioned of the Halsey coat of arms, if that's what it takes...?"

Alec suppressed a sigh of annoyance at his godmother's grumble of jealousy. It was not unexpected, given the English—from barrow boy to duchess—had an innate sense of superiority over their European neighbors, this despite the fact the vast majority of persons had never travelled beyond their own village. As an island nation, water provided a barrier that allowed for isolation and fear of the unfamiliar. And there was no greater barrier than language. He was acutely aware that his godmother had never travelled beyond England's shores, and thus was so far removed from her milieu that she might as well have taken up residence on an island in the Atlantic! He did not doubt that she was as frightened as she was baffled. So he tempered his response, particularly as he had no wish to answer questions about how he had acquired the title of baron, not before he had the opportunity to explain himself to Selina first, and in private—something he could not put off forever.

"No doubt I will take a kernel of experience back with me to England, but you and I both know that I don't require title to prop up my self-esteem, or an intaglio for that matter," he responded mildly. "What I also know, and you do too, my dear Olivia, is that here, in this place, my English marquessate is of no use to Emily and Cosmo. Yet if being the Herr Baron can aid in setting them free, then I will exploit my position far and wide."

The Duchess instantly teared up and felt miserable for her pettishness.

"Forgive me. Of course you must. I'm being a tedious old woman, and I had not meant to be," she replied remorsefully and quickly dabbed at her ready tears with the handkerchief Selina pressed on her. "Naturally you must do whatever it takes, be whomever you need to be, to rescue my granddaughter and nephew from this wretched place! That is all I wish for, have ever wished for." She sniffed and forced a smile. "'Tis a pity the Herr Baron cannot grant my wish, and get *me* out of here!"

"Oh? Before you've seen what Emden has to offer?" he teased. "What a pity I must leave in the morning, for I had hoped to take you for a stroll along the ramparts to show you the desolate landscape. Not a hill in sight, and marsh as far as the eye can see. But the windmills are truly magnificent. A true engineering marvel, and something of which the townspeople are inordinately proud. Yet I'm certain you won't be disappointed to forego such an excursion to have your wish granted," he added, and kissed her hand, keeping her fingers in a comforting hold, another glance at Selina. "Because tomorrow you will be leaving here. Not the house. The country."

The Duchess sat up with a sharp intake of breath. She could not contain her joyful surprise. "Tomorrow? Leaving the country? Truly? But where to—?"

"To Holland as first planned. I'm afraid it does mean another short voyage on *The Caroline*," Alec apologized. "Just to the other side of the Ems, to Delfzijl which should take no more than an hour once you've set sail. My uncle, the servants, and all your luggage will be going with you."

The Duchess leaned back on the bank of pillows with a sigh of relief, a hand to her bosom. "Oh, thank God."

"And short of having him arrested and bundled aboard, so will

Sir Gilbert," Alec added. "It's far too dangerous for him to remain in Midanich. Colonel Müller made that perfectly clear. He tells me that all foreign legations have closed their doors. Ambassadors and their retinues loaded up what they could into their carriages and fled across the border into Hanover, or took the last ship to Copenhagen, as soon as civil war broke out. Those few diplomats who remained were caught up in the fighting and captured, either by the Margrave, or by his brother Viktor. They remain prisoners of war. So now is not the time for Parsons to be making diplomatic overtures of any kind."

"I'll wager you'd made up your mind well before we left England to relieve Sir Gilbert of his authority and leave him in Holland, had we not been boarded by pirates," Selina said to Alec with undisguised relish. "Cobham's directives could go hang!"

At this Alec turned to regard her, and said bluntly, a pointed glance directed at his godmother to include her in his assessment, "Just as the two of you conspired behind Cobham's back to have yourself included in the legation to Herzfeld Castle. It is Lord Salt's signature on your safe conduct papers not Cobham's. So, yes, his lordship's directives can go hang. And so, it would seem, can mine, and all concern for your personal safety."

"My lord—Alec!" Selina stuttered to be so bluntly addressed. "You cannot blame Aunt Olivia because I—"

"The decision was entirely mine," the Duchess interrupted. "And Selina—"

"Please, Olivia. The time for excuses has long passed. I won't discuss this now," he stated bluntly, gaze still on Selina, who continued to regard him in the same manner, yet with a little defiant lift of her chin, though the ready blush to her throat spoke volumes about her feelings of guilt in deceiving him. "I merely want to make the point that you—both of you—must not keep anything from me in this dangerous place. The stakes are too high. So if there is anything else you wish to share with me, such as the ransom—"

"There is the Roentgen mechanical gaming table being offered as a gift to the Margrave as a goodwill gesture from one monarch to another," the Duchess said. "That is far more precious than coin and jewels, you must agree."

"I do. But the gaming table was not what Luytens mentioned when he broached the subject of a ransom with me. He specifically said, as you just did now, coin and jewels..." When his godmother shifted uneasily on her pillows and could not meet his gaze, he added quietly, "If you do have such a ransom, it would be best that I keep it safe. You should not have it anywhere near your person. I cannot stress enough that we are in a country at war. The normal rules of civility do not apply. You saw what happened at the docks. A man was shot for concealing a bag of coal." Alec leaned in to peer closely at the Duchess. "Olivia..."

"Oh, very well!" the Duchess confessed with a guilty grumble. "I did bring jewelry and gold coin with me."

"Thank you for *finally* telling me," Alec replied with the ghost of a laugh.

"You know I have no defense against you when you look at me like that!" the Duchess continued, still out of sorts. "I only did what was asked of me. And we—Cobham and I—did not want to take the risk of not bringing such a ransom, in case the gaming table was considered an unacceptable gift. Selina will bring the jewelry with her tomorrow—"

"Aunt. Your Grace. I thought we had agreed—" Selina interjected, but was ignored.

"And you will stop casting blame her way," the Duchess continued as if her niece had not spoken. "The idea of her traveling with you to help rescue Emily was mine entirely. I forbade her to tell you and Cobham. He would have been tiresome and trotted out all sorts of sensible reasons why she should not leave England. Not least of all she being his sister! A ridiculous excuse. And you would have done likewise. But for Emily—"

"Yes, for Emily, I agree with you," Alec replied, cutting her off. "We must think of what is best for her. And having Selina for support when we reach the castle will be just what she needs. But that won't stop me taking up my displeasure with you, my dear Mrs. Jamison-Lewis," he said addressing Selina directly, "tomorrow aboard the trekschuit."

"Good. I'm glad that's settled," the Duchess declared buoyantly.

She had no intention of allowing Selina to reveal where the ransom was hidden, because she held to the belief that her jewelry and coins might not yet be needed. Thus, what was the point of revealing something that was unnecessary, and would only add to Alec's burden of worry? She also knew she was being selfish. She would be out of the country and thus far away from his displeasure if there ever came a time for him to discover the truth. For now, she was just pleased to have suitably diverted him from asking anything further. She hoped to continue this diversion, and so said with practiced enquiry,

"So how did you manage to persuade the Colonel to allow us to leave tomorrow? Did the Herr Baron threaten him with his sword again to do his bidding?"

The corner of Alec's mouth twitched. "Nothing so heroic, or idiotic. Though it was quite dramatic, what with well over two hundred men converging on this house waving paper and demanding to have their grievances addressed by the Herr Baron."

"What did those fools think you could do for them that their own leaders, civil and military, could not? Dolts!" The Duchess scoffed. She gave a little shiver of displeasure and squared her shoulders. "I'm not surprised this place is at war with itself if it allows a mob recourse; it is the beginning of the end. Selina said the soldiers finally sent them on their way. But only after you addressed them. I trust you gave them a stern talking-to and told them to go back to their beds."

This elicited a reluctant laugh from Alec. He knew what his uncle would have to say about the Duchess's aristocratic distrust and fear when members of the lower orders congregated in numbers greater than three. Not to mention speaking of them as if they were children in need of correction, and not beings with genuine grievances. But he kept Plantagenet Halsey's censure to himself and said with a grin,

"Yes, I did give them a—um—*talking-to*, but it was not stern. I told them what they wanted to hear."

"Which is why they cheered you and went peaceably away again," stated Selina, and gingerly stretched out her hand across the coverlet.

"Yes," Alec stated, taking hold of her hand with a smile. "But they were not cheering me, but the Herr Baron."

Selina smiled in understanding. She smiled more because he was holding her hand. "Of course. But while we are in Midanich you are one and the same, are you not?"

"Yes, I suppose I am..."

"What did they want? What did you tell them?" asked the Duchess, and in her eagerness to find out the answers to these questions was oblivious to the fact the couple were holding hands, which surely meant a reconciliation, and should have been more momentous news to her than a mob outside her window. "Why did they cheer the Herr Baron?"

"I ordered the port opened so they can leave and return to their homes and their families."

"You can do that?"

"Baron Aurich can. He is a personal representative of the Margrave, and thus has jurisdiction over the councillors, and the military commander, and in the absence of his noble kinsmen, is de facto head of the military here. Thus Colonel Müller and his men owe him their allegiance."

"Good Grief! Are you? Do they?" The Duchess was astounded.

"Can you?"

"That mob, as you called them, my dear Olivia, are not the faceless masses. They are merchants, bankers, businessmen, travelers, and journeymen, caught up in this conflict without wishing to be. They are displaced, victims of this civil war. When the Margrave ordered the borders closed to stop men fleeing, and hostile forces from entering, these men became trapped. Some were visiting Emden on business, others to see family. Most were minding their own affairs aboard ships in the estuary or further afield, near the islands off the coast, and were boarded by pirates and privateers, just as we were. They and their ships were brought here. All they want is what you want: To leave here to return home to their families."

"And their petitions?" asked Selina.

"Demands for compensation, requests of one sort or another to see them safely home. Information about where they live. All of which I'm having Jeffries and Müller's secretary read through and compile into lists, in the hopes of making it easier for the customs officials and officers to process these men tomorrow with the minimum of fuss. Which reminds me," he added, suppressing a yawn behind his fist before addressing Olivia. "As *The Caroline* is the largest vessel docked in the harbor, I've given permission for it to ferry passengers to Delfzijl. And I am told there are people—family members—who have been stuck in that port waiting permission to cross to Emden, to be reunited with family here. So there will be an exchange of passengers."

"Oh, how marvelous that you've allowed for these families to be reunited for Christmastime!" said Selina, giving his fingers a little squeeze so that he looked at her. "I saw the old man and his granddaughter from the docks amongst the mob. Is the Herr Baron helping them, too?"

"Yes. The Reverend Shirley and his granddaughter will be accompanying me—*us*—as far as the east coast, and then travelling on to Hanover. It is the least I could do for them." He smiled crookedly. "Particularly as he is only too happy to grant me my wish."

Selina was about to ask him the nature of his wish, particularly as he was regarding her with a look in his lovely blue eyes that made her suspicious that she was somehow involved, when there was a soft scratching on the outer door. And again, as if able to anticipate visitors to her mistress' bedchamber, Peeble materialized in answer to it. On the threshold was a tired-looking Hadrian Jeffries, not come about the petitions or anything else requiring his master's attention, but with the welcome announcement a bath had been prepared for his lordship which was now full of hot fragrant water. Thus Selina was unable to ask her question until the following day, and then she was given the answer in the most surprising of ways.

# Fifteen

THE FOLLOWING MORNING, JUST ON DAWN, WITH THE
night sky turning from black to grey, and a blanket of fog
in Emden's clean cobbled streets, a military detachment
came for Selina Jamison-Lewis and her lady's maid. Wrapped head
to toe in furs, their gloved hands deep in large fur muffs and their
stockinged toes wrapped in fur-lined ankle boots, the two women
and their portmanteaux were taken by carriage under escort to a
waiting barge. The canal ride took them under several low bridges,
and away from the tall houses squeezed up against each other in
the town on one side of the main canal, and on the other past the
market gardens under intense cultivation for most of the year, but
now lying fallow for the winter.

When the barge docked, it was at the far end of a long wharf at
the mouth of the widest canal, which gave access to the Ems estuary
and the sea beyond. Here *The Caroline* and other smaller vessels were
being made ready for sail. Already passengers were waiting to board.
Some had been out all night, and all were now huddled around
makeshift campfires, luggage at their feet. Wharf workers scurried to
and fro from onboard these seafaring vessels, juggling supplies and
equipage for travel. Emden's port was once again opened to traffic,
to and from the harbor, allowing those who had been trapped for

many months to return home, and those forced to remain in Emden to finally leave.

And while such activity continued on at the east end of the wharf, Selina and Evans were set down away from the clamor, by a line of trekschuiten, also being made ready for a journey, but by a different route, not by sea but cross-country. Here, too, wharf workers were busy, crawling all over the barges, seeing to last-minute adjustments to the webbing of ropes that kept luggage secure, while jagers in heavy coats and nailed boots and smoking from long clay pipes checked the tack and leading ropes of their heavy horses. Boys ran around with flambeaux wherever light was demanded. Soldiers in their distinct blue wool coats and mitre hats, white splatterdashers over their shiny black boots, bayoneted muskets over a shoulder, and packs strapped to their backs, stood to attention listening to their commander bellow orders over the din.

Emerging from the barge to solid ground, Selina took in all this activity with a sweeping glance, and tried to fix beyond the tall ships to the wider body of water of the estuary. But the thick fog made that impossible. So she turned away from the noise coming from further down the dock with a pang of sadness, knowing the Duchess of Romney-St. Neots, Plantagenet Halsey, Sir Gilbert Parsons, and their servants would soon be making their way to *The Caroline* for the journey west, to Holland and freedom. She, on the other hand, would be traveling east into territory unknown to her, but in the knowledge she was helping aid in the rescue of Emily and Cosmo. And she was taking this journey with the love of her life, which made it more than bearable. She could hardly wait to spend time with him, and to be properly reconciled. She was ever hopeful and just that little bit excited at the prospect, which made the parting from her aunt and Alec's uncle that much more bittersweet.

She nodded to the captain who was patiently waiting to escort her and Evans to the head of a procession of five large trekschuiten.

Each barge was tethered by two heavy horses in control of jagers, who doffed their hats in deference to Selina as she swept past. The first trekschuit Selina passed was laden with four—or was it five?—sledges and their equipages. The horses needed to pull these sledges were rugged up and being walked in pairs up and down the wharf by their handlers, who Selina rightly assumed were also the drivers for the sledges, to be used on the second leg of their journey east from Aurich. The next two barges were loaded down with cargo under tarpaulins secured with rope, while the fourth and fifth barges were passenger trekschuiten. She knew this because they were different in build to the previous three vessels. They had a longer hull, and were fitted with a long, low wooden deckhouse with a curved roof, that had curtained windows along the starboard and port sides, and a set of shallow steps at either end leading down into the cabin from the deck.

The occupants of these vessels had yet to board, and were blowing their breath into gloved hands as they stamped their feet, warming themselves by a fire blazing in a large drum. She did not recognize any of these men and correctly assumed they were the personal servants and lackeys of the occupants of the first barge. She was to learn later, amongst their number were a cook and his assistant. This second trekschuit was equipped with a small kitchen to provide meals for passengers and the officers of the soldiers charged with guarding the convoy of barges, and the life of the Herr Baron and his party of travelers.

Standing by a second fire in a half barrel in front of the leading trekschuit was the British consul Jacob Luytens, and beside him a large man with heavy jowls whom Selina had seen at the consul's house. With them was the Reverend Shrivington Shirley and his granddaughter Sophie, and behind them, a little way up the dock, a second contingent of smartly turned-out soldiers, also wearing the tall mitre of the grenadier, who were being issued with last-minute orders by their commander. Watching over the proceedings, the collar of his blue wool military coat pulled up over his ears and his black felt tricorne lowered over his brow, was Colonel Müller.

The captain escorting Selina made her a quaint bow before marching up to the Colonel and saluting. The Colonel looked up just as the Reverend's granddaughter saw Selina, eyes widening, and smiling with genuine happiness to see her. A tug on her grandfather's sleeve had him looking her way, and she pointed in Selina's direction then skipped up to her and dropped a curtsey. And when Selina removed a gloved hand from within her muff and extended it to the girl in greeting, Sophie took this as an open invitation to throw her arms around her.

Selina gave a little laugh at the girl's enthusiastic welcome. But Evans was unamused at such forwardness from one who was not her mistress's social equal.

"I suspect she has no idea as to my consequence, Evans," Selina quipped, and stepped back with a smile. Yet she kept a light hold on the girl's arm and maintained eye contact as she pointed her muff over the girl's shoulder so she would not be startled, and would notice the Colonel before he was upon her, given she was unable to hear his approach. "She meant nothing by her embrace, M'sieur Colonel," she assured him in French, thinking he meant to chastise Sophie for her forwardness.

If she had learned anything about the dour Midanichians, it was their strict adherence to social rank and protocol. This circumstance she had remarked on to Plantagenet Halsey, saying that the English by comparison were practically republicans, which should make him happy. To which he had told her that she was a blessed troublemaker and if she could name one member of her family, or his, other than himself, with a republican bone in their body he would eat his sealskin coat!

"She is young, and her deafness may preclude her from expressing her happiness in the usual manner."

"Yes, Madame. You may well be right," Colonel Müller stated with a formal bow. "Please come with me. The Herr Baron wishes a few words before our departure. Do not worry about your lady's maid," he added when Selina instinctively glanced over her shoulder, then passed her large fur muff to Evans. "She will not be inconvenienced for long. We will be boarding in the next quarter hour."

"Thank you, Colonel," Selina replied, offering him her gloved hand when he stepped onto the barge first and held out his hand to her so she could step down from the wharf onto the boat without incident.

He continued to hold her fingers until she was steady and had a hand to the brass rail of the steps that led down into the cabin. He then went before her towards a curtain at the far end of the deckhouse, and here he waited, silent and as dour as ever, thought Selina with a small sigh. She wondered if he ever smiled, as his was not an unfriendly face, and his eyes held a hint of something more than an occupation with military drills and giving orders. But she recognized that the life of a soldier was not an easy one, so perhaps his war-time experiences, and this recent civil war, which must be upsetting for any soldier, was weighing on his mind. Whatever his disposition, she was just glad to have him and his men guarding them on this journey into open territory which was said to be plagued with rebels and inhabitants hostile to the country's new Margrave. But what she was most particularly glad about was the esteem in which the Colonel held Alec as the Herr Baron. She did not doubt the man would lay down his life in Alec's service, and that made her like him regardless of his disposition, dour or otherwise.

She took her time to join him, surprised by this trekschuit's interior, which was deceptively spacious and opulent, and not what she was expecting of a barge in the austere environment of Emden, where the interiors of the houses had more in common with the practical merchant Dutchmen than they did the baroque excesses of the Austrian and French royal courts. But not this trekschuit.

With a wide, low, and slightly convex roofline, from the towpath she had assumed the space within to be cramped. But she was able to stand to her full height with the calash hood of her cape back off her hair. And while the deckhouse was not excessively wide, there was sufficient room for a wooden bench either side, running under the length of the windows, and near the steps where she had descended, a narrow table was set between the benches to allow passengers sitting opposite each other to engage in a game of cards, to play at checkers or chess, and offer a place to rest their mugs of tea. The benches were covered in red velvet cushions. The walls were painted in a duck blue with gilded piping framing the windows, and these were dressed with curtains in red-and-gold patterned damask tied back with heavy gold braid, affording the passengers a view.

The deckhouse was also snugly warm, with a coal-burning brass heater in one corner, its brass pipe flue piercing through the painted ceiling, and there were tapestry carpets under foot. At the far end was a long curtain stretching from ceiling to floor in the same fabric as the windows, and it was at this long curtain Colonel Müller paused and rapped his knuckles on the painted wood paneling to announce his presence. He was called behind the curtain and held it aside to allow Selina to enter before him.

But Selina's gaze had not come down from the ceiling. It was painted, too, with a blue sky strewn with fluffy clouds inhabited by winged cherubs. It was such a fanciful piece, much in keeping with the rest of the decoration, that she was sure this barge had never been used in any utilitarian way but as some wealthy gentleman's pleasure craft. She was still on this thought when she came out of her reverie to find the Colonel patiently holding aside the curtain, and she quickly stepped behind the curtain, and again was met with the unexpected.

She found herself in what appeared to be a gentleman's dressing room. The space was fitted out with an array of campaign furniture, from fold-out camp bed that was made up with a down-filled coverlet and pillows, to a collapsible polished mahogany toilette stand with patterned porcelain shaving bowl. This stood in a corner by a caned mahogany chair which had a dark velvet frock coat draped over its back. In the opposite corner were a number of travelling trunks, one stacked upon the other, and by the head of the camp bed was a folding campaign table which had upon it an opened stationery *nécessaire*, the fold-out green felt writing surface strewn with the implements necessary for the sealing of letters with wax, of which there was a bundle neatly stacked by the capped silver inkwell.

Selina took all this in with one sweep, but failed to notice Alec standing by the window where his valet was threading a silver stickpin into the folds of his cravat, because her gaze remained fixed on the shaving bowl. It was full of soapy water, with an ivory-handled open razor propped over its rim. For some inexplicable reason the sight of these everyday but most personal of gentleman's accoutrements made her throat constrict. She turned her head into her shoulder, face flushed with heat as her thoughts flooded with images of making love with Alec in a Parisian bed. Suddenly her fur-lined black wool cape was too heavy and too hot.

"Thank you for bringing Mrs. Jamison-Lewis to me, Colonel," Alec said, coming away from the window, where he had been staring out at the view across the canal. He was still in his shirt sleeves over which was a fine black wool sleeveless waistcoat which matched his breeches, black curls neatly dressed and plaited and tied with a white satin bow. He picked up the bundle of letters and held them out to the soldier, continuing in German, "This is the last of them. All the souls needing safe passage to Holland are now accounted for. I assume there was little difficulty in returning their confiscated property?"

"No difficulty, Herr Baron," Colonel Müller replied evenly and with a small bow. "The Customs officials here in Emden are exceptional record keepers. Everything has been accounted for, except perhaps for foodstuffs, which went into the collective stores to help feed the extra mouths of having a garrison quartered here for the winter months."

"Their small contribution to the war effort then," Alec said, tossing aside the towel which he had used to pat dry his shaven skin. He was momentarily distracted by his valet who scurried about collecting up discarded towel and shaving apron, before tidying away razors, toothbrush, and tooth chalk, and all this while juggling the shaving bowl without spilling a drop of the soapy water over the lip. "I don't expect to see you for several hours, Mr. Jeffries," he said firmly in English. "Find yourself a corner to curl up in and get some sleep."

"I don't need—"

"Yes. You do," Alec said stridently. "Now go." He waited for Hadrian Jeffries to leave by the back steps, then addressed the Colonel, again in German. "I require a private word with Mrs. Jamison-Lewis. In the meantime, the other passengers may board, but fix one of your men at the curtain. We are not to be disturbed, failing a full-scale attack by opposition forces. And when you deem the convoy and your soldiers ready, you may order our departure."

He gave the Colonel a brief nod of dismissal and the soldier saluted and left, letting the folds of the damask curtain drop back against the wall, effectively shutting out the world.

It was the first time Selina and Alec had been alone in months.

Inexplicably, she was suddenly shy in his company with no idea of what to say. This was despite nights spent pacing before the fireplace in her dressing room, rehearsing the exact words she would say to him when this moment arrived. Now her tongue seemed unable to help her lips, and with no satisfactory outlet, her head ached with all the thoughts she wanted to put into words building up behind her eyes, or so it seemed to Selina.

It did not help that Alec remained by the table silently watching her, fiddling with the intaglio ring, turning it this way and that on his long finger, which surely underscored that here, in this place, in this foreign country, he was first and foremost the Herr Baron—a foreign title bestowed upon him and kept secret from everyone in his life who mattered, and with no satisfactory explanation given to her or anyone else how this circumstance arose. Thus he still had as much explaining to do as she did, possibly more.

When he caught her glance at the ring and frown he slipped it off and set it aside on the green felt blotter, without taking his gaze from her. He then put out his hand and it was enough to draw her further into the room, and to place her hand in his. Yet, she still could not find the right words, though she was able to find her tongue and blurted out in a rush,

"I've disturbed you!"

"Not at all, Mrs. Jamison-Lewis."

The use of her married name snapped her out of her self-consciousness, which was Alec's intent. He suppressed a smile when she unwittingly sighed and rolled her eyes.

"Oh, when will you stop calling me by that *hateful* name?" she complained.

He pulled a face of unconcern and lifted a shoulder, knowing this would further infuriate her, adding as casually as he could manage, "Today. If you wish it."

Her gloved hand in his flinched and she pouted.

"I do wish it! I wish it *very* much!"

Her pout almost undid him. She was quick to rile. He put this down to her youth. She was after all, just four-and-twenty, eleven years his junior. And then there was her marriage to a wife-beater; a quarter of her life spent with a monster had left scars, physical and mental, and a mistrust of others, even with loved ones, and even of him who loved her. But he had been absent and preferred to remain in ignorance of her marriage for those years of abuse, so it was only natural she resented him for that, even if she had yet to acknowledge this to herself. He believed time and patience would pull them through this. Time for her, patience for him.

"Then it will be done—tonight," he said evenly, features perfectly composed, but with a twinkle in his blue eyes.

Selina had no idea what he was talking about. His even tone and her curiosity took all the fight out of her. "Tonight? What will be done?"

"I will tell you. But first we need to talk, and before I fall asleep."

Selina frowned, her petulance evaporating with concern for him.

"Yes. Yes, you do need sleep. I can see it in your eyes—the-the tiredness. Perhaps it would be best if you slept first and we talked afterwards...?" she suggested.

When he nodded but made no reply, seemingly wholly absorbed in her gloved hand in his, she swallowed hard. He had turned over her hand and was nudging back the soft leather from the mitten covering her forearm to expose the bare skin at her wrist. He then raised her hand and gently pressed his lips there, and she spoke in a whisper, oblivious to her words, distracted by the pressure of his mouth on her warm skin,

"I dare say you've been up all night sorting through those petitions so the men waiting down by the tall ships are able to leave this place unhindered?"

"Yes," he replied with the ghost of a laugh, looking up into her dark eyes before kissing her wrist a second time and saying gently, "And all that time I was writing and signing notes of free passage, I was waiting for dusk to bring you to me. All so we could talk."

"Yes, talk," she added, slightly breathless and giddy. "We must talk because... because..."

She lost her train of thought completely as he slowly stripped off her glove, peeling back the kid leather, revealing the soft chinchilla lining and exposing first her wrist, then the soft pad at the base of her thumb, then the undulation of her palm, and finally inching the glove all the way to her fingertips, giving the task his undivided attention. He could very well have been stripping her bare, such was the evocative nature in which he divested her of her glove. She stared at his bowed head of blue-black curls pulled back off his forehead, and then down the thin line of his long boney nose to his mouth; it was all she could do to stop herself from fainting. And all he had done was kiss her wrist and remove one glove! Mustering all her self-control she said more severely than she intended,

"It is most important that we talk!"

"Yes," he said evenly. Still holding her glove, he told her to put up her chin so he could undo the silver button and clasp of her cape. "It's much too warm in such a confined space for gloves and a cape, as fetching as they are. Perhaps you would care to sit to have this talk?"

He turned away to drape the cape over the back of the caned mahogany campaign chair beside his frock coat. He next dropped the glove on the seat, putting out his hand for its twin, which Selina roughly pulled from her fingers and gave him. He then sat on the edge of the camp bed, hands on his knees and a nod at the space beside him.

"Do you wish to speak first?"

Selina sat where directed and they faced each other.

"Thank you. Yes. Though you will have to forgive me because it is all a bit muddled in my head. I've been waiting an age to tell you this."

"Please, take your time. We are not expected at Aurich until nightfall, though I hope we are fed and watered along the way."

Selina nodded, the frown between her brows indication enough his attempt at levity had fallen flat, such was her preoccupation. So he said nothing further and patiently waited.

How was she to start this confession—for that was what it was. What precisely did she want to say? she wondered, lips pressed together, dry in the mouth, and brushing aside her desire that he pull her into his embrace and give her a proper kiss. But she did not move, keeping her hands in the lap of her quilted cotton petticoats, back straight and body twisted to face him sitting next to her.

That he was regarding her with something other than tiredness in his blue eyes was disconcerting. There was a gleam—or was it a twinkle?—that reminded her of times past, such as the first time he had told her he loved her, wanted to marry her, and would be hers and hers alone. Or when they had first made love in the Grove and he again declared he loved her. But this was different. This was arrogance. Or was it confidence? Or both? It was a knowing-and-getting-what-he-wanted sort of look. For a moment she wondered if it was the Herr Baron and not Alec Halsey who sat across from her, but quickly dismissed this. Instinct told her that it was Alec, the man she loved, and that if ever there was a time to unburden herself, this was it, and he would listen and not judge her.

And because that kiss to her wrist and the look in his blue eyes had the power to make her thoughts whirl and her heart race, she just burst into explanation, rattling on, hardly knowing what she was saying but knowing her thoughts were leading her to a subject that had not been broached between them since they had parted in Bath, when he had not permitted her to explain herself or her actions. And as she spoke the gleam in his eye intensified, and his features softened, so that a smile hovered and played upon his lips that left Selina uncertain whether he was smiling in understanding, or smiling at her as if she were talking complete drivel. She had no idea what he was thinking, but what she did know was that he was listening, and listening intently. At that moment in time, there could have been cannon fire and soldiers engaged in sticking bayonets into each other on both sides of the canal, and he would not have heard any of it, just the sound of her voice. And so she allowed herself to confess to him what she had confessed to no other. And she knew that by this confession, she was laying her soul bare, that there was no turning back—her future was wholly in his hands.

"You are owed an explanation," she said. "About the accusations leveled at my head in Bath by the odious Lady Rutherglen. They came as a shock to you. I saw it in your face, and in your subsequent manner toward me spoke volumes about your distress. I now realize had I confided in you when you first came to me in Paris, and not allowed my-my *selfishness* to convince me otherwise—that all explanations could wait for another day because I wanted your visit to be a joyous one—then this predicament we now find ourselves in would not have occurred.

"You would not have learned about my miscarriage from others, but from me. And yes, I denied you the right to grieve the loss of our baby with me, which I know was wrong. And I am deeply sorry and-and *remorseful* that I took that decision. But I did so because at that moment in time I did not want to grieve. I wanted us to be happy in Paris. I wanted to feel all those things lovers feel when they are free to love and live and finally be together unencumbered. If I had told you about the loss of our child... how could we have spent a carefree week burdened with such news? And it would have been there, a big black cloud, the entire time of your visit."

"You did not perhaps feel the necessity to have someone—me— take some of the burden of grief from you?" he asked gently.

She shook her head. "No. I am perfectly capable—well, I thought I was perfectly capable—of shouldering such grief on my own. I did not want you to be troubled—"

"Oh, my darling, you know I—"

"Please! Please reserve judgment until after you have heard me out! Thank you," she added when he nodded and closed his mouth. "I have given my wretched behavior a great deal of thought since Bath. I wondered why I could not bring myself to tell you, to involve you. But it has always been thus for me since I married and you went away. To-to deal with-with *situations* and *consequences* on my own. I do not blame you for this. You must never think that."

She gave a crooked smile and a little sigh, adding, "The blame for my-my *unthinking* heartlessness I lay at the feet of my odious husband. When I was first married off to J-L, I quickly realized that I could not allow myself to feel—to feel *anything*. Bruises heal and disappear, and one can accept rape within marriage if one allows oneself to believe it is a husband's right to take from a wife what is his, however unwilling she may be. It is the law after all. I should have been a biddable wife. I was not. I dealt with his visits to my bed by taking my mind some place far away. In that way it was not I who was being abused, it was another.

"The wonder of it is that I did not shrivel and die inside. But had I allowed myself to-to *feel*, had I allowed my heart to absorb all that wretchedness, I would have killed myself, or killed J-L—or both of us, just to be set free. So I did the only thing I could: I hardened my heart. It became as stone. It was better that way, to have no proper feelings at all. It was the only way I survived six years of such vile maltreatment. I became numb to everything, and life was bearable. And that became the most important thing for me: That life be *bearable...*"

She looked up from her hands, where her gaze had been focused and smiled at him, but without really seeing him. If she had she would have noticed that his eyes were full of tears.

"But... For my life to be bearable, there had to be no children of the marriage. I could harden my own heart, look after myself, but how could I shield a child from such a monster? To have allowed myself to have J-L's child would have been my undoing. And so I took precautions. You don't need to know the details, or where I procured such substances and methods. But I did. And I do not regret using them to stop conception. I am guilty as charged by Lady Rutherglen. I also lied to protect myself. From time to time I would announce a pregnancy, just to have some respite from J-L's visits. But I could only maintain such a subterfuge for a few months.

And then I would, sadly for others, miscarry. And then the cycle of abuse would start all over again..."

She shrugged and bit her lower lip in thought as she stared across at the view from the undraped window, mind's eye filled with pictures of an abusive marriage she had fought hard to suppress. But this confessional would be the last time she ever need bare her soul about this chapter in her life. After she was done, she would move forward with her life, with Alec. Of that she was determined.

She was brought back to the present, that she was a passenger in a watercraft, and they had finally begun their journey east, when the trekschuit bumped up against the side of the wharf as it was unmoored and was maneuvered away out into canal, pulled along by two heavy horses out of view. She couldn't be happier to again be on the move. That the journey meant leaving behind the protection of Emden's fortified walls to venture out into the open of enemy territory and danger was unimportant, because this journey would bring them one step closer to Emily and Cosmo, and setting them free. Seeing the grenadiers in formation march along the tow path was some comfort. The soldiers would remain beside the trekschuiten until the barges passed beyond the three locks and under the four bridges to leave the town behind, and then they would march forward, past the horses, to provide a first line of defense for the convoy, while a similar company brought up the rear.

Alec, too, was momentarily distracted by the movement of the trekschuit, the sound of voices on the other side of the curtain raised in excitement that the journey was finally underway, and by the activity outside the window. But he knew progress would be slow and tedious and it would be an hour before the convoy of barges reached the outskirts and final lock, before leaving the town behind. Besides, he preferred to watch Selina in her distraction, gaze on her lovely profile and the apricot curls which sprang from the edges of a little lace-edged cap under a peaked velvet bonnet, tied with a lopsided bow under her chin.

And while he patiently waited for her distraction to end and for her to continue with her confessional, he quickly dabbed at his moist eyes with a white linen handkerchief. He then squared his neck and shoulders, as if preparing to take on more weight from her confession that already had the power to cause his back to stoop. It was just as well, for when she finally looked away from the view it was to meet his gaze openly, and her dark eyes were all desolation.

"Excuse me. I-I am glad we are finally on our way... I—There is no painless way to tell you... But you already know I miscarried... It was unthinkable to me I would find myself pregnant just months after J-L's death," she continued. "My first thought was that I was carrying his monster, and I was appalled. But there was another possibility. A much happier possibility and one I dared to hope might be the right one. That the baby was-was—yours. That I conceived when we were reconciled in the Grove. And then—And then I miscarried in Paris."

She put out a hand to him and smiled sadly when he took it in a firm clasp and rested their entwined hands on his knee. "I thought about telling you. But decided I did not need to, that I could best deal with the loss, and you need never know. And, selfishly, what I wanted more than anything was to spend our time in Paris making love. And had I told you, not only would we have spent that week with a big black cloud hanging over us, I would've had to confess everything to you. This meant telling you the physician's depressing prognosis: That I would never have another child. He believed the miscarriage had left me barren..."

When she felt Alec's hand give an involuntary flinch and his jaw clenched shut to stop himself from interrupting her, she quickly added,

"I realize now that the physician's opinion is just that, an opinion. He couldn't know for a certainty I had been left barren, and so Aunt

Olivia assured me. She was most strident that I should allow you to make up your own mind as to whether you wish to marry me, regardless of the physician's diagnosis. And she is right, I did allow myself to be persuaded by others as to what was best for *you*. Only you know what is best for you—for us, and our future, and I am—I am—I am truly s-sorry to have caused you pain and heartache, but you see it is because my heart—"

Alec could listen and be still no longer. Not now the tears were streaming down her face.

"Darling! Sweetheart! My dearest girl! For pity's sake, you must stop torturing yourself with—"

"Please! Please, do not interrupt! I must tell you the rest. *I must.* It is the most important part—the thing I *most* want to tell you."

When he let go of her hands and sat back, pressed his lips together and nodded, she smiled through her tears and quickly wiped dry her cheeks with the back of a trembling hand before saying quietly but firmly,

"I told you I had to harden my heart upon marriage to make my life bearable. But what I had not comprehended was that because it remained that way for six excruciating years, it has taken some little while for me to recover my-my *natural* way of feeling, and to-to—*soften* my heart to its natural state, to how it was before I became the Honorable Mrs. George Jamison-Lewis. For me to be able to trust and love again as I had before my marriage, for me to allow another—you—into my life again, became almost insurmountable."

She touched his close-shaven cheek and smiled into his blue eyes. "But I-I desperately want you in my life. I love you with my whole heart such as it is, damaged or no. But it is flesh and blood again and beats as it did when I was eighteen and met you for the first time, the handsomest but certainly the most unsuitable bachelor in all London." She giggled when he pulled an exaggerated face. "My parents, Cobham, my friends, they all lectured me against you, but I knew, *I knew* in my beating heart that you were the one. I have never wavered from that conviction. I wish I were that eighteen-year-old girl again. I know I can be, given time. For my heart is no longer stone. It beats strong and true, and only for you." She added with a shy smile, "I would very much like you to ask me again to be your wife, and I will give you the answer you—*we*—both want to hear..."

For what seemed like minutes but was less than one, Alec held her gaze and said nothing. He then slowly untied the silk bow of her bonnet, carefully removed it from her coiffure and set it aside. She blinked, searching his face for his thoughts. But his focus raked over her from sprung curls to her slightly parted lips before locking on her dark eyes. He smiled and drew her closer, so close she caught the masculine scent of him mingled with the bergamot, pepper, and soap of his freshly-shaved skin, and she caught her breath.

"And my heart beats strong and true, only and always for you," he repeated and raised her hand to kiss her fingers, then her palm, and then rested her hand in his on his knee. Smiling into her damp eyes he asked, "Will you consent to be my wife, here, today, from this day forward, Selina Margaret Olivia Vesey?"

The breath in Selina's throat turned to a sob at his use of her maiden name, and the last six years washed away from her. She felt as giddy as she had when he had first asked her this same life-altering question just after her eighteenth birthday. She nodded and smiled and gave a little tearful laugh. "Yes! Yes, I will! I want that more than anything. So yes, here. Today. This hour if you can arrange it!"

He felt a huge relief and gave a bark of laughter. "In an hour? I wish with all *my* heart it could be so arranged! But it *will* be today. That I promise."

With that assurance he gently cupped her face in his warm hands, turned his chin, and kissed her with great tenderness and deliberation. And when she yielded, when her mouth opened under his and her hands found anchorage in the billowing folds of his white cotton shirt sleeves, she gave a little whimper of need mixed with contentment. It was all the signal he needed to be ardent. And so they gave themselves up to a long luxurious kiss which was as loving as it was passionate, leaving no doubt as to the depth of their feelings and intentions.

# Sixteen

"**T**EA!" ALEC STATED WHEN THEY CAME UP FOR AIR. Selina smiled shyly and nodded. And when he smiled back, thumb caressing her flushed cheek, she dropped her gaze and her chin, flustered and still shaken from her confession, his declaration, her acceptance, and finally, their kiss. He understood. He too was overwhelmed with what had just occurred. So he endeavored to put her at ease by introducing the mundane. Making a cup of tea would serve to settle them both, and hopefully provide a little respite for their emotions before he launched into his own confession.

He rose off the camp bed, and gently kissed her forehead before turning away to rummage in the corner where the trunks were stacked. He lifted down a small leather trunk and placed it on the camp bed where he had been sitting. It was a *nécessaire de voyage* left to him by his mother, and inside was everything needed for the making and taking of tea: A decorated French porcelain tea service, a candle warmer to keep the tea in the matching porcelain pot warm, and a porcelain canister filled with his preferred blend of green tea. He cleared a space on his campaign table and began unpacking the *nécessaire*, saying as casually as he was able,

"All we need now is hot water, and some of Elsa's delicious ginger biscuits from the barge kitchen..."

"I'll have Evans send for them," Selina offered, suitably diverted from her introspection.

"Yes, ask Evans," Alec said with a smile over his shoulder, before continuing on with setting out the tea things, allowing her time to regain her equilibrium, just as he was doing.

She quickly fussed with her hair, repositioned a number of pins to catch up a stray curl, and hoped her face was not so flushed with color that it would betray her feelings, so that her lady's maid would beg the question, and worry more than she already did over her mistress's fragile emotional state. But the presence of others in the deckhouse, whom she could hear in conversation on the other side of the curtain, would be enough to preclude any but the most commonplace talk.

So she slipped behind the curtain into the main cabin, and Alec went to the window. He shrugged on his dark woolen frock coat over his waistcoat and shirt sleeves as best he could without the assistance of his valet, and gazed on the picturesque view.

Tall Dutch gabled houses lining the canal were bathed in a cool morning light as the sun's rays struggled through a heavy winter sky. The trekschuit was leaving the darkness behind as it moved slowly east towards the fortified walls, and the locks that would take them out of the town and into the frozen wilderness beyond. This would be his last look at Emden, of that he was convinced. Then again, he had had the same convincing thought ten years ago, and here he was in a place he never thought to return to in his lifetime. He shook his head at fate. So much for last looks! And so much for fate.

Now he must prepare himself to confess all to Selina about why he had been lured back to Midanich, and by whom. Just as Selina had laid bare her soul, he would do the same; she deserved the same courtesy and respect from him. They could not begin their married life under a black cloud; the same black cloud of doubt and deceit that had haunted Selina in Paris was now, metaphorically, well and truly hanging over his head.

Yet, despite the daunting task of confession ahead of him, his overriding emotion was one of complete happiness. He was filled with a sense of contentment he had not experienced in a very long time. Selina's consent to his proposal finally meant they could plan their future together. And he would marry her that very day, the Reverend Shrivington Shirley pronouncing them man and wife aboard the trekschuit, once they had docked at Aurich.

He just hoped Selina returned with hot water for the tea soon, so he had some chance of remaining awake for the next hour. The camp bed was becoming increasingly inviting, but he stayed by the window. He knew that if he lay down, even for a few minutes, he would be instantly asleep; he was that tired after a entire night awake. For a handful of seconds he envied Hadrian Jeffries curled up in his corner. And then the curtain was pulled back by the soldier on duty, and there was his betrothed. Her smile instantly vanished his tiredness, and he returned her smile with one of his own.

Behind her was a young man wearing a kitchen apron over his uniform carrying a large kettle of steaming water. He set the kettle on a trivet on the table, saluted and took his leave, the curtain coming down again, as the soldier on duty returned to his post guarding the Herr Baron.

"It seems your every wish is anticipated; the water was already on the boil," Selina told him.

"Surely not *every* wish," he said with a mock scowl, noticing her hands were behind her back but pretending not to. "Where are the Herr Baron's preferred biscuits?"

"I have them here," she answered with a mischievous smile, revealing a blue-and-white ceramic jar but which she kept hugged to her bodice. "You may have one when you answer me a simple question."

He chuckled.

"Is this is how you intend to have your husband bend to your will? By threatening to deny him Elsa's delicious ginger biscuits?"

She pouted, and he saw the hesitancy in her dark eyes. "It is not a threat," she said quietly and put the jar on the table beside the tea things and retreated to sit on the camp bed. She watched him pour hot water over the tea leaves in the bottom of the pretty patterned teapot. "Who is Elsa?"

"Elsa?"

"You said "Elsa's delicious ginger biscuits". Twice. Mr. Luytens' daughter's name is Hilda. I assumed she was the one who baked the ginger biscuits we had yesterday."

"She did. From a recipe passed down from mother to daughter."

"You call Hilda's mother Elsa? Not Mrs. Luytens? You must know her very well."

Alec's hand holding the kettle full of hot water paused in mid air. It was not only the nature of the question that surprised him but her tone. He heard the uncertainty, and he knew why. He set the kettle back on the table and faced her.

"Knew her, Selina," he replied quietly. "And not in the biblical sense."

"I wasn't implying—"

"Yes. You were." When Selina made no further protest, mouth set in a prim line, and held his gaze, he added patiently, "You did not meet her because she and the rest of her children are in Holland. With the harbor reopened, it is hoped they will be able to cross back home. And I have not seen her or her children in ten years. The last time I was here, in fact. She, along with her husband, helped me escape, and for that I am eternally grateful." He gave a lopsided grin. "My darling, the biscuits are generally known as 'Elsa's ginger biscuits'. The recipe was passed from a forebear who also bore the name Elsa."

Selina's dark eyes went round and her lips parted with surprise. And at his continued smile of understanding her face flooded with color and she felt foolish.

"I apologize," she said bluntly. "I did not mean to cast aspersions on the woman's character. It's just that... knowing something of your past... having heard the stories of your time on the Continent... Even while I was married, I could not help but overhear the gossip—No! That's not strictly true. I *wanted* to overhear it." She looked up at him, her eyes reflecting her uncertainty, "Any news shared about you was better than none."

"You were married. I was not," he replied evenly, remaining by the tea things, waiting for the tea to steep. "That seemed an end to any possibility of us being together. Thus I could not afford to think about what could have been between us. I decided to live my life. But far away from London, and you. Yes. I had many affairs. I will not lie to you about that, now, or ever. But most of that gossip, the salacious tidbits you would have overheard, concerned events in my life that occurred well before I met you." He gave a lopsided grin. "To point out fact, those scandalous events happened here, in Midanich, when I was much younger and a lot less wise. When I was, for want of no better description, an arrogant womanizing idiot."

When Selina sat up and looked at him as if he had two heads, he laughed and shook his head, strangely comforted that she did not believe him capable of arrogance or idiocy or, hopefully, womanizing. But this did not stop the heat of embarrassment flooding his thin cheeks at what he was about to confess to her, and no other.

"It was this arrogance and idiocy, not to mention my complete disregard for the consequences in satisfying my lust, that has our dearest friends locked up, and has brought me back to a place to which I vowed never to return. It has also put all I hold dear in this world—you, and my dearest friends and family—in danger."

He turned away to pour out the tea into the tea cups, giving her a moment to digest what he had said. He placed one of Elsa's ginger biscuits on the saucer beside the teacup and handed it to her. He then rummaged in a crate of provisions he'd had his valet bring aboard, and found what he was looking for: Emden rock candy.

"Unfortunately, we used most of the cane sugar on the voyage, and what was left was confiscated by Customs. I've asked it be returned to *The Caroline* for Olivia and Uncle Plant to use. So we must resort to the local rock candy. But I prefer my tea unsweetened, and we seem not to have any cream..."

He tipped a small quantity of the rock candy which had been broken up into useable lumps, into a silver dish, set the silver tongs atop the small mound, and put this beside Selina on the camp bed. When she ignored it, he was not surprised. He was sure her attention was very much on his past, and that she was waiting for him to offer her further explanation of his startling confession, particularly as he had blamed his past behavior for Emily's and Cosmo's incarceration. He sipped at his tea and gave himself a moment to enjoy the flavor on his tongue and the warmth of the liquid as it slid down his throat, and to fortify himself before saying in his measured tone,

"Before I plunge headlong into how a past salacious affair got us in the perilous predicament we find ourselves in, I want to apologize to you for my behavior in Bath. My reaction to your news of a miscarriage was less than gentlemanly. My uncle was right. I was selfish and unthinking. It will never happen again. But," he added with a gentle smile, placing his tea cup on its saucer, "should we find ourselves suffering a similar sad state of affairs again, I will be there to share the grief with you—always. Though I have high hopes that when you do conceive—and you will—you, my darling, will have to endure the ordeal of a full term pregnancy and labor."

"Oh, I admit that after being an eavesdropper on Miranda in labor, I am far from reconciled to the pangs of childbirth." She gave a little shudder but then smiled over her teacup. "Yet Miranda tells me all the unpleasantness is instantly forgotten when the baby is placed in a mother's arms. And after holding baby Thomas... Well, he is quite the most perfect baby, is he not?"

"Yes. But you were never reconciled to travel, either," he added, to bring her back to the present. He would've liked nothing better than to continue to discuss the merits of the Duchess of Cleveley's newborn, but his yet-to-be-made confession was weighing heavily on his mind, and he now just wanted to get it over with, dreading her reaction, yet so tired even that was becoming secondary to his need for sleep. "Yet, here you are in a boat on a canal, hundreds of miles from home. And the journey is not that unpleasant, is it?"

"I abhor the unrelenting roll of sea waves, but have decided I quite like this form of watercraft. And perhaps would even consent to a barge trip through the English countryside, if you were so inclined to join me. It is rather restful, and will no doubt put you to sleep in less than the click of my fingers." She sipped at her tea again, remembered it was without sweetness and quickly dropped in a little piece of rock candy, stirred it and while waiting for it to dissolve, nibbled on the ginger biscuit. "These truly are delicious... Forgive me. I've been rambling, and here you were about tell me all about your—arrogant womanizing idiocy...?"

Alec lost his smile and Selina saw by the change in his expression that the moment for playful banter was over. So she suitably schooled her features and braced herself for whatever revelations he was about to confide in her. And yet he still managed to shock her.

"I hope you will take into account that when I took up the post of secretary to Sir Gilbert to the Court of Midanich, I was younger than you are now. Men are ever boys if they can get away with it, and none more so than young vigorous males with too much time on their hands, and plenty of opportunity for sport, in all its forms. So my immaturity does play a part in why I was idiotic enough to think I could get away with my behavior without consequences. Come to think on it, I did not think about consequences! Coming here was not the posting I wanted. And, it appeared, it was not a post wanted by anyone else in the Foreign Department either. Thus I was more than a little petulant to be stuck with it. My first impressions of the place were much like yours and Aunt Olivia's upon sailing through the Ems estuary. Vast stretches of marshland on both sides, flat and about as interesting as a piece of blank paper! Ah, but in summer, the country transforms itself. Even here, in this flat wilderness, there is color and an abundance of wildlife—lots of waterfowl and swans, and sheep are grazed over the grasslands. But it is in the south and towards Hanover, where there is real beauty. Dense forests full of deer, quaint little villages all neatly arranged, and castles—more correctly *schloss*—that are distinctive as they are charming...

"Forgive me," he added with a huff of laughter, mentally shaking himself. "What started out as a confession has turned into a geography lesson! Suffice that I became enamored of the country and its people, in particular Friedeburg Palace, the Margrave's summer residence, where the Court spends most of the year, and thus, so did Sir Gilbert and I. The palace is distinctly Continental, inside and out, and with plenty of entertainments and distractions for a junior secretary of an embassy who had too much time on his hands."

He paused, expecting Selina to make some quip about the type of distractions that would interest a vigorous male in his early twenties. When she did not, features remaining schooled in polite enquiry, he continued soberly,

"It was at Friedeburg I first met the Margrave's eldest son and heir, Prince Ernst. I don't recall precisely the catalyst for our friendship. I think it was at the fencing academy. We are the same age and he liked that I was honest and just as competitive. He sought me out. He was interested in learning to speak English, because of the close connection between his neighboring state, Hanover, and England. It fascinated him that an Elector of Hanover had become King of England. I suppose he fancied he could do likewise if called upon to do so!

"I became his English tutor, and whenever we were together he insisted we converse in English as much as possible. Within six months, he was fluent. Which came as no surprise because he expected me to be in his company almost daily. There were those at court, in particular the Court Chamberlain, who disapproved of Margrave Leopold's heir spending his time with the lowly junior secretary of the English ambassador. And there was Sir Gilbert, who flatly forbade me to associate with the Prince. His was a prejudice born of Ernst's condition, which he considered a manifestation of a deeper malady—"

"Condition?"

"The Prince is unable to grow hair, facial or otherwise. Apparently his grandfather was afflicted in the same way, and he was the one who introduced the edict that all gentlemen at court must always be clean-shaven."

"But as the wearing of wigs and having clean-shaven chins are the fashion for the vast majority of men, his condition cannot have raised an eyebrow," reasoned Selina. "As for a deeper malady... Surely that was mere prejudice on Sir Gilbert's part?"

"Yes. It was. Sir Gilbert could not have known then that Ernst was possessed of demons, but those demons had nothing to do with his lack of hair; well, at least I think that to be the case. In truth, I was secretly pleased Sir Gilbert had stepped in to end the association. I was beginning to be smothered by the Prince's friendship. My every move was watched and reported to the Prince. I could not speak to another, male or female, without Ernst questioning me as to my relationship, real or imagined, with that person. I explained to the Prince I could no longer spend so much time in his company, that I had to return to my duties for the English Ambassador. I foolishly told him Sir Gilbert had barred me from his company. Within a fortnight, Sir Gilbert was advised to leave court. When he refused, he was thrown out of the country. In hindsight, I realized it was the excuse Ernst was looking for to get rid of Sir Gilbert, so nothing and no one stood in the way of our—of our—*friendship*.

"I traveled north to Castle Herzfeld as part of the Prince's retinue, when he went there as head of the army to review the troops. I could hardly refuse such an honor. Very few foreigners visit Castle Herzfeld, the military headquarters and training facility for the Margrave's extensive army. And it was while I was a guest at the Castle that I encountered the other side of Ernst—a dark, troubling side—not present at Friedeburg..." Alec frowned, cleared his throat of emotion and continued. "I noticed the change come over him before we'd ridden under the Castle's portcullis. He was moody. He became preoccupied. He was short with his men. He would not engage in conversation with me, or others. One of his officers confided that it was always like this whenever they returned to the Castle. He said not to concern myself, that in a day or two Ernst would be his old self again.

"I was at the Castle for three weeks and Ernst remained withdrawn. There were days and nights when I did not see him at all. And then there was the odd day when he was the Ernst I knew from Friedeburg. Upon those occasions, he would throw lavish banquets and demand to be entertained. His retinue were expected to be lively and witty and forget their master's morose episodes. They did their best to fall in with his wishes. No one denied the Margrave's son what he wanted. I, too, did my best. Then, one night in the final week of my stay, everything changed...

"I woke in the middle of the night to find I was no longer under the coverlet, and that I was not alone. Someone was—touching me. It was not the sort of contact made in an effort to instantly wake the sleeper from slumber. It was far more—intimate. It was the sort of pleasurable caress employed by a lover to arouse... In my half waking state I saw in the orange glow of the fire a stranger in a night chemise, with fair hair that fell unrestrained to the mattress, kneeling on the bed beside me. There was something familiar about them but I could not recall where we had met before. But my brain was not really thinking at all—Selina!" he said abruptly in an altogether different voice, meeting her gaze. "You must remember, I was no saint in those days. A beautiful woman invites herself into my bed, who am I to turn her away? I have willingly participated in such nights with no questions asked. But this time... There was something decidedly—*odd*... And yet I permitted her to seduce me..." He gave a huff of embarrassment. "I didn't care that I'd been tied to the bed. I thought it all part of the adventure—"

Selina shuddered. "Tied to the-the bed? *Adventure*? 'Odd' is an understatement! But I see from your blush," she added perceptively, "that being tied up was the least odd thing about this particular—*encounter*."

"Yes. You are correct," he answered meekly, cleared his throat with a sip of tea and continued. "When I... When she... To be blunt: When I was spent I asked to be untied so I could return the-the favor. But she did not reply, and for the longest time lay still beside me, so long, in fact, that I fell back to sleep—"

Selina blinked. Sometimes—no, not sometimes, *often*—she found men unfathomable.

"You fell asleep? You *slept*, still tied up? Truly?"

Alec looked sheepish. "Yes. It was the middle of the night and I was tired."

"Well, you would be, wouldn't you?" Selina stated mordantly. "Having to lie there and allow a complete stranger to pleasure you would make any man tired!"

"I'm not making this up. It is what happened. But if you'd rather I didn't tell—"

"Yes, I would rather you didn't!" Selina retorted, back straight, hands in her lap cradling the tea cup. "What your twenty-three-year-old self got up to between the sheets, how many females you permitted to pleasure you, is none of my business. I only hope that you weren't completely self-absorbed. Though..." She cocked her head at him and smiled knowingly. "You've always been wonderfully assiduous to my needs, so I presume you've been an attentive lover since the early stages of your bed-hopping adventures."

"Selina, this—*encounter*—is not what you think it. It started out as a piece of pleasurable fun, but manifested into something truly repellant... I told you I felt I was being smothered by Prince Ernst's friendship; that he was possessed of demons of which I was unaware; that his moods changed dramatically for the worse once inside Herzfeld Castle. All of that manifested itself that particular night when he and his sister, the Princess Joanna, came to my bedchamber—"

"Prince Ernst and his sister *both* visited your bedchamber?" When Alec nodded she huffed. "Why of a sudden does that not surprise me?"

"You have every right to think men barbarians who prey upon females for their own enjoyment, to do with them as they wish, regardless of their wishes, and often in spite of them, after your appalling experiences of the marriage bed married to J-L," he said quietly. "But there are rare instances when it is the male who is preyed upon..."

*Preyed upon*? She blanched. *He had been preyed upon*? Her immediate reaction was one of disbelief. She had never considered the reverse of her situation. And she knew better than any other that such sexual encounters had nothing to do with the giving and receiving of pleasure and everything to do with power, humiliation, and domination. Oh yes, when she thought of it in those terms, she could readily believe what he had just tried to confess but left unsaid. It broke her heart the love of her life, who was such a gentle man, who had only ever treated her and her carnal needs with the utmost reverence, had been so defiled, that she wanted to weep. But she did not cry. For his sake, she must not. She was sure if she did his confession would end there and then. She instinctively knew she had to allow him to confess all, for only then would he be able to put this episode to rest and be at peace.

So she allowed the silence between them to stretch before looking up into his eyes. What she saw reflected there made her repentant, and wish she had held her tongue and her petty jealousy. She swallowed, leaned forward and touched his knee.

"Forgive me," she said gently. "I know you have good reason for telling me, not to goad me, or to make me feel gauche. This confession has taken a great deal of courage. So please, do tell me. I promise I will be more circumspect."

He nodded, covered her hand with his, and continued.

"I admit to being a willing participant in the first encounter. But when I was awoken a second time, I not only found myself still tied to the bed, the woman who had seduced me was no longer there. A wholly different being had taken her place. And looking into the eyes of this-this creature, I knew I'd been tied up for any number of reasons but that pleasure was not one of them! Excuse me. I need fresh air."

He strode up the back steps and wrenched open the door. A gust of icy air rushed in and filled the warm space behind the curtain, and he breathed deeply. Even after all these years, the memory of that night had the power to make him nauseated.

Selina felt the cold on her bare neck, and heard voices beyond, but she did not turn about or move from the camp bed. She remained tight-lipped with both hands still hard about her tea cup on its saucer in her lap. And then the door was closed on the cold and the activity beyond, and Alec came back into the room, but not to her. He stood by the window.

She could see he was oblivious to the activity beyond the glass, where the locals, bundled up in layers of clothing to ward off the cold, had left the warmth of their hearths to huddle in the doorways of their cottages to watch the procession of barges float by, accompanied by enough soldiers to do battle with a small army. Observing the everyday continue on outside the window helped calm her.

"You somehow blame yourself. That you must have given the Prince some indication that your friendship was something more than it was," she heard herself say with a calmness that belied an inner turmoil in fighting to keep her feelings of outrage in check. "I blamed myself for being a bad wife. But what happened to you is not your fault, as it was not mine. You did not say it, but perhaps you should. You were raped, Alec. And that is nothing for which you should feel shame, but you do..."

He winced at the word, but he did not deny it. How could he? She had spoken the simple truth, yet he had been too ill at ease, too ashamed to say so. Not only because of a sense of emasculation, but because he had not wanted to belittle what she had suffered at the hands of a violent, sadistic husband. She had endured years of abuse. His was one such brutal encounter. And the physical pain upon that occasion, was as nothing to what was to come...

He put aside her teacup and saucer, took hold of her hands, and looked into her dark eyes.

"My darling, you are the only person in my life who could understand—will ever understand—the unspeakable predicament in which I found myself. I was the object of an unhealthy obsession, and this—*episode*—was the beginning of the end of my peace of mind. I knew I had to get out of the country. If I'd been less the arrogant, womanizing idiot, I'd have taken the first ship to set sail out of Herzfeld harbor. As it is, I did something you will think not only stupid, but arrogant in the extreme."

Selina's eyes opened wide and she caught her breath.

"How did you escape this horrid place? What did you do?"

"Escaping the Castle was easy. I simply rode out the next morning without taking my leave of Prince Ernst, and returned to Friedeburg. I had no idea what I could do, or what I wanted to do about such a vile episode. I just needed to put distance between me and that place, and those two. And I was utterly determined to expunge all recollection of that night from my memory. So I did the only thing at the time I thought would help..."

When he hesitated she anticipated any number of ways he might wipe away such a unspeakable experience, except the one he confessed to her. When he did, she sat bolt upright, stunned.

"I plunged headlong into a torrid affair with a high-ranking married lady of the court."

"*Torrid?*"

"Yes. It was torrid and it was tawdry," Alec stated bluntly. "And in a perverted way, it restored my manliness, which had been severely compromised, or so I thought, after the vileness perpetrated against me by Ernst and his sister. Whatever demons were driving me, I hoped the affair would be discovered by her husband and the court. And of course, meeting in a public space such as the palace gardens not only meant that discovery was highly likely, it added to the spice of the affair. But it also aided in my lover's destruction, for which we both paid dearly."

"Spice?" Selina's head was throbbing with every revelation, but she managed to say with tongue firmly planted in cheek, "I trust that rutting this lady helped resurrect your manly self-esteem?"

So much for circumspection! But she had a right to her petulant sarcasm, given his unpardonable conduct. But he was too tired to explain that any unfettered young man of three-and-twenty, offered the opportunity to make love to a beautiful woman on a daily basis, would take it without a second thought; it was not his brain which was making the decisions. And in his case, he had a point to prove. Instead he said patiently,

"Darling, this was many years before I met and fell in love with you. I told you that as a young man I was an arrogant, womanizing idiot. And believe me, I paid the price for my stupidity and my unbridled lust, and so did she. Unbeknownst to us, our—um—*assignations* were being closely watched. The Margrave was duly informed of his wife's adultery. Yes. I was—as you so indelicately but rightly put it—rutting the Countess Rosine, the much younger second wife of the Margrave Leopold."

"Of all the females with whom you could choose to restore your manliness you chose the Margrave's *wife?*" Far from taking offense, Selina's shoulders shook with laughter. She pressed her fingers to her mouth to stop herself from giggling, and when she could speak blurted out, "Dear God, you were an arrogant, womanizing idiot, weren't you?"

He blushed scarlet.

"Lest you think me the only arrogant idiot to fornicate with the Margrave's wife," he continued bluntly, "the Countess Rosine had taken other lovers, and with her husband's knowledge. It was not the affair which upset him, but its intensity and the total disregard for discretion, which was my fault entirely. Margrave Leopold did not want a public scandal, but that's what he got when the enemies of the Countess decided to act while he was still away from court.

"Ernst returned from Herzfeld before his father returned from his hunting lodge. He was informed by the Court Chamberlain that the Countess Rosine's behavior had overstepped the boundaries of moral decency and something had to be done. It was a very tactical move. The Court Chamberlain loathed the Countess Rosine, and so did Prince Ernst. They had been plotting to oust her for years. The public uncovering of our affair was their opportunity to rid themselves of what they considered the Countess's undue influence on the Margrave. Ernst assembled his father's trusted advisors, and a retinue of his own supporters, and with the Court Chamberlain went for a stroll in the gardens. No one but they knew the purpose of that walk out in the sunshine. So when this entourage stumbled upon us in the—er—act, their shock was very real."

Selina could not help herself. "How could you both have been so witless? Was there no indication of what was to befall you? Did she not realize she had enemies, or did she not care? And you should have been more discreet, for her sake, if for no other!"

Alec's voice was tight with shame. "Believe me, my love. They are all questions I posed to myself over and over while I was a prisoner in Castle Herzfeld's dungeon. But most of all I asked myself how I could have been so unwittingly naïve to have involved myself in the family machinations of the House of Herzfeld. I knew Ernst was not fond of his stepmother, but had no idea he saw his half-brother Viktor as a threat to his inheritance. He was convinced the Countess was plotting to have him disinherited in favor of his younger brother. Later I remembered that during the course of our English conversations, he was keen on the personal histories of our Hanoverian Kings. He was particularly impressed how our first King George had his wife Sophia Dorothea of Celle banished and incarcerated for her supposed adultery, and that she was never permitted to see her children again, or become Queen of England."

"What happened to her, and to you? Did the despicable Ernst succeed?"

Alec sighed. If he was not already beyond sleep from staying up all night, the burden of this confessional was sapping the last vestiges of any vigor left to him. Over-tiredness clipped his usually mellow voice.

"Yes. The very public nature in which the Countess's adultery was revealed to the Court, that she had the temerity to take a foreigner as her lover, and a man much younger than the Margrave, brought even greater shame on the House of Herzfeld. For the honor of the family and to restore respect to the Margravate, Leopold had no alternative but to do as the Court Chamberlain and Ernst demanded. The Countess Rosine and her young son were banished to her family home, the *Schloss* Rosine, and were commanded, just like Sophia Dorothea of Celle, to there remain, for their natural lives. Her son, Viktor, was stripped of his titles, but not, thank God, his legitimacy, and he was at least permitted to stay with his mother. He was only eleven years old."

"This little boy is the Prince Viktor who has declared war against the new Margrave and himself the rightful successor to his father, Margrave Leopold?"

"The very one."

Selina was up off the camp bed in a swish of her quilted petticoats. No longer able to sit still and in need of stretching her legs she paced the small space between Alec's campaign chair and the barge's low window, before finally coming to stand before him.

"Have you thought that if not for your affair with his mother, this civil war may never have happened? That you are the catalyst for why Viktor is at war with his brother? He wants to regain his birthright, and the only way to do so is to wrest it from Ernst! Oh, Alec!"

She did not add "how could you?" but she might as well have, such was the expression writ large on her beautiful face. Her reaction did not come as a surprise. He knew Selina, like himself, had a deep-seated sense of justice. So of course she would champion Viktor, the innocent party in this sordid tale. Naturally she would also identify with the little boy, betrayed by his mother and by him, his mother's lover, both of whom did not think through the consequences of their actions, and also by his own father, who punished him to punish his mother's infidelity.

Alec caught at her fingers and kissed the back of her hand, before looking up at her and saying resignedly, "The whole episode was certainly a low point in my life. Second only to being rejected as a suitable husband by your parents, and seeing you married off to

Jamison-Lewis. And as you now know the sordid details of my brutalization at Castle Herzfeld, you can understand why I couldn't care less about being discovered and disgraced. Men can recover from such tawdry scandals; some revel in the notoriety such an affair brings them. I did. For all of about five minutes. And then I realized what it meant for the Countess and her son. Regardless that she was a willing participant in our affair and knew the risks, she did not deserve such a public humiliation. And Viktor did not deserve to be punished for the sins of his mother. That I was the catalyst for this catastrophe was almost my undoing. And I was resigned to the punishment I received."

"What happened to you?" she asked gently, caressing his square jaw with the back of her hand. "What did they do to punish you, my love?"

He drew her to sit on his lap, hands about her waist, and she put her arm about his shoulder and snuggled in.

"I returned to Castle Herzfeld, this time not as a guest, but as Ernst's prisoner. To rot in the dungeons forever, as far as he was concerned. You see, the Court Chamberlain did not tell him the identity of the Countess Rosine's lover. He withheld that information deliberately, so that when Ernst came upon the Countess in the gardens, the shock of discovering the identity of her lover would be acute. And it was. I was already the object of an unhealthy obsession for Ernst and his sister, so to discover me fornicating with the one woman they hated above all others, was the ultimate betrayal. They were demented with rage and determined to punish me, and badly."

"But again you managed to escape, not only the dungeon this time, but Midanich. How?"

A rap on the wood paneling on the other side of the curtain, left Selina's question unanswered, though she was one breath away from telling the intruder to go away. At the very least she wanted to ignore them, such was her need to hear the rest of Alec's confession. But when the rap came again, and more insistent than before, her manners dictated otherwise, and she reluctantly got up off Alec's lap. She brushed down the fall of her petticoats as Alec slipped the intaglio ring back on his finger and called for the visitor to enter.

Colonel Müller stepped into the private space and bowed and apologized for the intrusion.

"What is it, Colonel?" Alec asked in French, so that Selina would understand the run of conversation. "Has Madame Jamison-Lewis managed to keep me in conversation long enough that time it has sped by and we have arrived at Aurich?"

"No, M'sieur Baron. Unfortunately, there are many hours to the journey yet. I have come to inform you that we have left the protection of the city walls and are now out in open country. We must be ever vigilant. I have advised the passengers of this barge, and the next, to remain within the cabin at all times, unless absolutely necessary. One cannot be too careful, with rebels military and civilian reportedly seen in this vicinity just last week. But do not concern yourself, Madame," he added with a short bow to Selina. "My men will guard these trekschuiten and your lives with their own."

"I believe you, Colonel," Alec stated with a smile. "Thank you. Now if you will both excuse me, I do believe I need to lie down before I fall, and have a few hours' rest. We shall talk again very soon, Mrs. Jamison-Lewis."

The Colonel bowed, and as he held the curtain up for Selina to pass out of the Herr Baron's private room before him, Selina had no choice but to curtsey and take her leave. It was only when she was on the other side of the curtain with the other passengers that she realized for all the revelatory nature of their conversation, he had not told her the one thing everyone, from his valet to his uncle, wanted to know: How he had become the Herr Baron of Aurich. Given what she now knew, she was more baffled than ever.

# Seventeen

ALEC SLEPT, DEEPLY AND UNTROUBLED, FOR MANY hours. He was exhausted, the peacefulness of his sleep aided by having purged his soul to Selina, and by the gentle rocking motion of the barge as it was pulled slowly along the canal. And when he did dream, he dreamt of Cosmo and happier times.

AND WHILE ALEC DREAMT OF COSMO, HIS BEST FRIEND WAS dreaming of him. But his dreams were the stuff of nightmares. He woke with a start and sat up in bed, bathed in sweat, hands covering his face, fingers plying at his skin, frantically trying to remove the scold's bridle that was clamped over his head. And while he struggled with the iron cage, his tongue, thick and heavy and dry, could not move, so he could not cry out for help. The more he panicked the tighter the bridle became until he was gasping for breath, fingers slippery and cold, head hot, the bridle bit protruding into his mouth pressing down so hard on his tongue that he gagged. But as hard as he tried to find the latch, as much as his fingers clawed at the metal cage, he could not remove the torture device Alec had forced him to wear.

It took him a full minute before he realized it was his own hands covering his face and mouth, and not an iron muzzle designed as a public humiliation for women who scolded their husbands. And

Alec was not there, had never been there in his little room, and with every day that passed now, since attending the Margrave's dinner, he very much doubted he would ever see his friend alive again.

Knowing he was not wearing a scold's bridle brought a huge relief, but with this also came tears of frustration and fear. Not for himself, but for Emily and her companion Mrs. Carlisle. He lay back down amongst the tangle of sheets and hugged his pillow, filled with relief and recalling into his mind's eye the Margrave's dinner. That had happened three days ago and was the first time he had been outside his room in a month.

The dinner was in the castle's oak-paneled banqueting hall, with its gilded beamed ceiling, gigantic central stone fireplace where lolled five faithful wolfhounds, and walls lined with all manner of medieval weaponry and portraits of past margraves in their military finery. Higher up, above the small gallery where a string quartet played out of sight, were the preserved heads of exotic beasts—elephants, bears, lions, antelope, rhinoceros, zebra, deer, wild boar—trophies of hunting parties, here in Midanich, and further afield in far-flung outposts of the Holy Roman Empire. The Margrave, his military commanders, closest male companions, and courtiers, sat at three long tables that lined all but one of the walls. Wives, daughters, and mistresses were not permitted at such dinners; all the servants, too, were male.

They ate off gold plate and drank from crystal goblets, as if it were a summer's day and food was plentiful. Not, as the Court Chamberlain, seated farthest from his master, had counseled, in moderation for a long winter, and with a mind to the fact that the Castle was under siege.

Behind the tall-backed heavy chairs of the diners, the armed soldiers of the Margrave's personal guard stood to attention. Their leader, Captain Westover, had pride of place behind the Margrave's throne-like chair, with an ever-vigilant eye on those present, and not, like everyone else, on a scatter of carpets in the large void central to the room, where a troupe of travelling circus performers were entertaining. Illustrious host and diners were finding diversion in their antics, but were also bored by them, as the troupe had performed three nights in a row, and their routines were becoming as stale as yesterday's bread.

Into this clamor and bright candlelight, wrists bound in front of him, Sir Cosmo was escorted. Unused to the loud conversation, laughter, shouts from the entertainers as they tumbled about, and the applause from their audience, Cosmo shut his eyes tight and did his best to fight the panic welling up within him. It had been such a long time since he had been amongst such a din that he wondered how he had ever survived the busy streets of Westminster and Paris. When he was taken by the elbow and marched to the center of the room he kept his head lowered, not because he had been ordered to do so, but because he was close to fainting.

The circus troupe scattered out of the way to allow for this newest and most intriguing form of entertainment. It was the sudden quiet and hushed conversation that had Sir Cosmo lifting his chin and blinking into the light. And when his surroundings came into focus he found himself standing only feet from the central table and its central figure, seated on a high-back chair and dressed in a dazzling frock coat of gold and silver thread. But it was not so much the magnificence of his attire which astonished Sir Cosmo, but the gentleman himself. He rightly presumed this to be the Margrave Ernst who had visited him in his room but whom he had not been permitted to look in the eye, and so had admired his thigh-high polished boots. From what his valet had confided about the Margrave's inability to grow hair, and thus suffered from *the unspoken truth*, he was prepared to find him strange, perhaps hideous to look upon. Nothing was further from the truth.

The Margrave Ernst's looks were in marked contrast to the fleshy, bushy-browed and heavy-jowled men sitting about him. He was fine-featured, with high cheekbones and a broad forehead. His eyebrows were pencil-thin. His large blue eyes were framed by blackened eyelashes and his rosebud mouth still carried the remnants of red lip paint. And if this were not enough to set him apart from his fellows, he was possessed of a peaches-and-cream complexion, lightly dusted with powder, which reminded Cosmo of his cousin Selina. And framing this beautiful face, for it was more beautiful than it was handsome, was a full wig of blond ringlets that fell to his shoulders and was threaded with silk ribbons and decorated with diamond clasps.

As if to convince himself here was a man and not a female parading about as a man, Cosmo glanced at the Margrave's hands, for surely this would give away his sex if nothing else visible could. If he possessed the prominent Adam's apple of a man, this was not on show, covered as it always was by the fine linen and lace of a cravat. But the hands of men were generally larger, the fingernails flatter, and the palms squarer than those possessed by a female. But again Cosmo was surprised, and confused. Ernst's hands were long, the fingers tapered and elegant, and as they were covered in jewels and the soft lace ruffles that fell from his wrists, it was difficult to decide on the sex of such smooth white hands.

Sir Cosmo dared to stare openly at the Margrave, and Ernst stared back, as did all the men sitting around the three tables. It did not take Cosmo many minutes to realize that he was now providing the diners with their evening diversion. He was being appraised as if he were the latest zoological exhibition at the Tower Zoo, and all because of his beard and long hair. And when two of the courtiers sought permission to approach the prisoner, Margrave Ernst waved a languid hand in consent. A smile curved his lovely mouth, and his blue eyes never left Cosmo's gaze for a moment.

Sir Cosmo forced himself not to flinch when the two courtiers dared to gingerly touch his beard, rubbing the short hair between thumb and forefinger and confirming to the assembled company when they returned to their seats that the prisoner's beard was indeed as coarse as a man's chest hair.

Cosmo did not understand the German tongue but whatever was said started up some heated discussion amongst the assembled company, though at no time did the Margrave add his voice. He took up his goblet and sipped, but his eyes remained on the prisoner. What could Cosmo do but remain silent and compliant? He had long given up the notion he would ever receive the consideration and standing a gentleman of his own country should be accorded, and would only ever be just another prisoner of war, and treated accordingly in this God-forsaken principality

So when the Margrave ordered the silk-covered rope to be removed from his wrists, and the prisoner be given a chair to sit upon across the table from him, it was only natural Sir Cosmo was wary. He hesitated to sit where directed until grabbed by the upper arm and pushed onto the chair by a soldier who then took up a position at his back. A plate was put in front of him and an empty goblet found and filled with wine. Servants were directed to bring across the platters of food, but when they were offered, Sir Cosmo waved them aside. The smell of such rich sauces and the look of large cuts of broiled meats churned his stomach. His usual prison diet was broth and bread, cheese, pickled herring with cabbage mash, and a sliver of meat once a week. So he was certain any other foodstuffs would not suit his delicate stomach and would make him instantly ill. But he did drink from the goblet, and the wine, his first in months, was liquid delight to his palate.

"You cannot believe, after all this time, your friend is still coming to save you, Sir Cosmo Mahon?"

Cosmo managed to set the goblet on the table with a steady hand, despite his surprise at being addressed in English. But his surprise was not the nobleman's ability to speak his tongue; he already knew that. It was the timbre of the voice. It was smooth, rich, and deep.

He'd forgotten that. Not a female in male clothing, then.

"Yes, Your Highness. I do."

The Margrave screwed up his mouth at such certainty.

"I do not think so," he said sullenly. "Why would he? He is a fugitive in my country. He knows the consequences that await him once he puts a boot into this castle."

"Nevertheless, he will come, Your Highness. And you must know he will, or I would not still be your captive."

The Margrave chuckled, but he was not amused. "What a fool you are, Sir Cosmo Mahon! You do not even know what happened to your friend the last time he was here, do you?"

"No, I do not, Your Highness."

"I had him tortured."

Sir Cosmo flinched on the word, but he did not reply.

"You do not believe me?"

Sir Cosmo thought of the severed heads on pikes along the battlements, and the fact he had been locked up in a tiny room for almost two months with no company but the soldiers who guarded him. And the time he'd had his head shoved in a bucket of ice water and almost drowned, all to make him compliant. Oh, yes, he could readily believe this ruler capable of having another tortured.

"Yes, Your Highness, I believe you."

"I do not see why he would choose you to be his best friend," the Margrave complained, sitting back in his chair and staring over his goblet at his hostage. "There is nothing about you that is appealing. You are ordinary. Your nose is unremarkable. Your eyes are too small. Your features will never be immortalized in stone. And with that mange covering your face you look like an ape-man. You're certainly not worth Alec Halsey's attention."

"Excuse me, Your Highness, but you mistake me for a woman. I am Alec Halsey's friend, not his lover."

"Lover?" The Margrave pulled a face. "Too true. I cannot imagine you would interest him as a lover." He leaned forward and asked in a confidential tone, as one friend to another, eyes suddenly bright, "Tell me: Does he take many lovers? Keep a mistress? Taken an Englishwoman to wife? Are there children? Bastards, perhaps? Or does he still prefer to mount other men's wives?"

"They are questions I cannot answer, Your Highness."

"Of course you can," the Margrave continued in that same confidential tone that was supposed to engender trust but which made Sir Cosmo's feel as if his skin crawled with ants. "You are his best friend. Best friends know these things about each other. Best friends confide in one another. And as his best friend you would know all this, and more."

"And even if I did know, I could not tell you, Your Highness," Sir Cosmo apologized.

The Margrave waved a bejeweled hand dismissing such honorable intentions. The soldiers behind Sir Cosmo's chair mistook this for a signal he was done with talking to the prisoner and grabbed Sir Cosmo by both arms and hauled him out of the chair.

"Sit him down! Sit him down, you fools!" the Margrave screeched in German and shot up out of his chair so fast he over-set his goblet. The wine splashed across the table. Everyone seated broke off their conversations and rose up as one. Margrave Ernst waggled a long bejeweled finger at the last guard in the line along the wall. "You! Yes, you! Come here and stand behind the prisoner. You two, get out of my sight!" He looked over his shoulder at his captain of the guard, who was setting the chair to rights. "Westover! Tell me why you are my captain when you allow imbeciles to guard me! No! Do not answer. But those two are dismissed. Take their uniforms and put them to work in the casements hauling filth!"

He flicked out the skirts of his gold and silver thread frock coat and sat again, and so did everyone else.

"You cannot tell me because you do not know," he asked Sir

Cosmo in English, and as if his outburst had not occurred. "Or because you are a stubborn fool. Which is it?"

"Neither, Your Highness," Sir Cosmo replied politely. "It is because best friends do not break confidences."

"Ugh! Have it your way then! You are as closed-mouthed as your female companion is a conversational rattle pate!"

"Emily?" Sir Cosmo hissed the name, and his sudden movement in the chair had the soldier's hand hard on his shoulder lest he decide to leap up. "Is—is Miss Mahon well? Is she being accorded every respect and convenience? May I know how she goes on, Your Highness?"

"Oh! Oh! Now you come alive! Well if you want a report on your female companion you had best be more forthcoming with answers to my questions." The Margrave lifted his penciled brows. "If you are very good, I may let you see her..."

"Thank you, Your Highness."

Margrave Ernst smiled mischievously. He looked about at his dinner guests and addressed them in their own tongue. "See how this hairy ape becomes animated when I make mention of his female companion! What beasts these English are! It is as well they have been kept in separate cages or we'd be expecting our first hairy infant, to be sure!"

There was a moment's silence and then one of the guests let out a forced hard laugh, and the others joined in, nudging one another and egging each other on to laugh harder at their ruler's weak bon mot. Baron Haderslev tried to catch Captain Westover's eye as he mentally rolled his eyes, but the Captain of the Guard was preoccupied with his own thoughts.

The Captain of the Guard was thinking that the son would never measure up to the father as a man, or as a ruler. Margrave Leopold had been an excellent ruler, a brave soldier, and a just and able administrator. And while his son Ernst was a fierce and brave soldier, capable of leading men into battle, he was not the administrator or the honorable head of state Leopold had been. There were many whispers about Ernst's fitness to be ruler and the increasing amount of time he spent visiting with his soft-brained sister the Princess Joanna. But none of this was enough to depose a Margrave who came from a long line of Herzfeld princes who ruled through the grace of God. Westover had sworn an oath of allegiance to Ernst, as he had to Margrave Leopold, and he would honor that oath until the last breath left his body.

And while Westover was convinced it was God's will Ernst was Margrave, Baron Haderslev, who had served the old Margrave, and was now an old man himself, was wondering how many more hours, days, weeks, perhaps months, he would need to endure listening to Ernst's inanities before his half-brother Viktor stormed the Castle and took the throne for himself. It was not that he particularly supported Viktor's claims to the throne. After all, he was the product of a morganatic marriage, and thus could not legally inherit. But the more time Haderslev spent in Ernst's company, the more he was all for throwing out the legalities in preference for a ruler who was sane, and not under the influence of a sister who had been locked up since her fifteenth birthday. When Leopold was alive he had controlled Ernst, and he had certainly kept Joanna under lock and key...

Perhaps winter would allow for the nobles to get up the courage to stage a coup. But Haderslev knew this would be impossible without the support or the capitulation of the doggedly loyal captain and his household guards.

"Haderslev! Haderslev! Are you daydreaming?"

It was the Margrave, and Baron Haderslev quickly banished his treasonous thoughts and stood.

"Where is this ape's female companion? Have her fetched!" Ernst turned to Sir Cosmo with a dazzling smile and continued in English. "While your companion is being fetched, perhaps now you will tell me more about our friend...?" When Sir Cosmo nodded he sighed his satisfaction and steepled his fingers, elbows on the table, and asked, "Tell me about his mistress, or his wife, or both. My sister is desirous of knowing with whom he fornicates, thus making a mockery of his vows to her, as her husband."

Sir Cosmo was certain he had heard correctly but wondered if in his translation into English, the Margrave had muddled his words. So politely corrected him.

"I beg your pardon, Your Highness, but Alec Halsey is not married, and never has been."

"Ha! Then you do not know him at all, and cannot possibly be his best friend if he did not confide that he is indeed married, very much so, to my sister the Princess Joanna. They were married here in the Castle, with my father and the Court Chamberlain as witnesses to the union. Is that not so, Baron?"

He repeated in German to the Court Chamberlain what he had just said to the prisoner, and Sir Cosmo turned to look at the Baron, who bowed and nodded in confirmation of his ruler's assertion. Sir Cosmo looked about at the diners, and as not one appeared surprised and continued on with their eating and drinking, he turned back to Ernst and said quietly,

"If that is indeed the case, Your Highness, then yes, you are quite correct. He did not confide this in me, or, for that matter, any one else in England."

The Margrave looked smug but then his mouth fell into a frown.

"I will tell you then what he did not tell you. My father ennobled him the morning of the ceremony—for we could not allow a commoner to marry into the family—and then they were married here, in the castle chapel. And what did he do? How did he treat us? He abandoned my poor sister. He fled in the night, leaving my sister heartbroken. She remains heartbroken. Such callous treatment of a bride—*my sister*—is beyond forgiveness. And yet, *she* would forgive him and have him back as her husband, I know it, were he to offer up his apologies to her upon his return. Ha! What do you think of your best friend now, Sir Cosmo Mahon?"

Sir Cosmo was at a loss as to how to respond. He was still trying to comprehend the astounding news that Alec had married the Margrave's sister and then abandoned her. His friend would never be so offhand about such a life-altering decision, or so cruel as to marry and then abandon his bride—he was too much the gentleman. That is, unless he'd been forced into such a union. That seemed within the realms of fantasy, until Cosmo remembered where he was, and who he was with, and how he had been locked up for more than two months, waiting for Alec to rescue him. Never again would he dismiss out of hand something that he considered could only be from the quill of an author of fairy tales. He was living one now, and it was becoming more peculiar by the day.

And sitting before this beautiful man with his blond ringlets, surrounded by his court of soldiers and sycophants, stuffing themselves as if food were in plentiful supply, Cosmo realized two things: He himself had not gone mad—he was as sane as the day he was arrested in the antechamber. Secondly, and more alarmingly, the Margrave was most definitely mentally deficient, particularly where Alec was concerned. Trust his friend to become the object of an infatuation! But it wasn't only the sister who was obsessed. It was more than a decade since Alec had been to this country, and in the company of this nobleman, and yet the Margrave spoke as if it were only yesterday. Time had moved on for everyone, it seemed, except for Margrave Ernst.

"Come forward! Come forward!" the Margrave was saying to the newest guest to the banquet hall, which drew Cosmo out of his introspection and turning in his chair in expectation of seeing Emily. "Here is your companion, Sir Cosmo! As you see, she has been well looked-after, and is being accorded every civility due her position as the granddaughter of an English duchess. Come closer, my dear! Come closer!"

Sir Cosmo's smile froze and his heart missed a beat at this reunion.

This poor creature could not possibly be Emily! She was being led into the room on a length of chain attached to the manacles on her wrists, but it was at her head that he stared in horror, for it was enclosed in an iron-ribbed cage. He knew what it was. It was a scold's bridle, and he had seen one on display at the Tower. It was said to have belonged to some long-ago lord and used for the subjugation of wives who were thought by their husbands to be scolds. He had been told that the barbarous contraption was still in use in parts of Scotland and on the Continent. He had never seen anything so hideously medieval and could not believe such a torture device had ever seen the light of day. But here was one now, in Midanich, very much in use.

The creature stared out from behind the iron frame, large dark eyes wide with fright and looking about her. But when she saw Sir Cosmo, her gaze became fixed and her eyes filled with tears of recognition. In response, Sir Cosmo burst into tears and covered his face with his sleeve to stifle his sobs and quickly dashed the tears away.

"Ah! Our hairy ape is overjoyed to see his mate!" the Margrave announced with applause, which was quickly followed up by applause around the tables.

Without permission and not a thought for his surroundings, Sir Cosmo strode forward and held the woman's hands. He stared down at her, trying to recognize in the terrified expression any semblance of his Emily. She blinked up at him and stared hard, as if wanting his undivided attention, and when he nodded in recognition, she smiled. He saw that the contraption protruded into her mouth and held down her tongue so that she could not speak. And although she could not say it in words, he knew what she was trying to tell him, and he knew who she was. This was not Emily; he'd known that from the first, staring into her eyes, which were dark, not blue. But until this poor creature smiled, he was unsure as to her identity. It was Mrs. Carlisle, Emily's companion, and she had somehow taken Emily's place. He could have wept, for her, and for joy, that it was not Emily being tortured in this detestable way. And with a huge relief for Emily came guilt and concern for her companion.

"You see that she is well-fed and healthy, but as she would not keep her mouth shut," the Margrave complained, "my sister found a way to stop her talking altogether."

"Surely five minutes wearing such a contraption would have been time enough for her to have learned her lesson, Your Highness?" Sir Cosmo asked quietly, fighting hard to mask his emotion.

"That is for my sister to decide. But do you not want to embrace your friend, Sir Cosmo? I am sure she will not bite!" He grinned at his own bon mot and then repeated it in German to his courtiers, who again laughed, but this time with genuine good humor. "Embrace! Do not be afraid! Embrace I tell you!" he demanded of the couple in English. "I want to see my ape and my caged bird embrace!"

Sir Cosmo slowly took Mrs. Carlisle in his arms and held her against him. She leaned into his shoulder. And there they stood for several seconds, oblivious to their surroundings and how they presented to the world, reveling in the gentle touch of another human being. The Margrave was up on his heels applauding, and so, too, were the other diners, as if this were the best night's entertainment they had ever witnessed, as if this couple were the main attraction of a freak show.

When Mrs. Carlisle began to sob, Sir Cosmo whispered in her ear, "Be good. Do as you're told. Have hope. Lord Halsey will save us both. I promise you." He pulled back so he could see her face clearly. "Tell me: Is she safe?"

Mrs. Carlisle nodded.

"Is she in the castle?"

Mrs. Carlisle shook her head.

"She escaped?"

Mrs. Carlisle shook her head and opened her eyes wide.

Sir Cosmo's eyes also widened in hope and he breathed in swiftly. "She escaped before you were brought to the castle?"

This time Mrs. Carlisle smiled. She was forced to step away when her minder pulled on the chain about her wrists. But Sir Cosmo went after her, caught up her hands and kissed them, adding breathlessly, tears streaming down his cheeks, "God bless you, dear lady. Thank you. Thank you with all my heart."

THE MARGRAVE HAD TIRED OF SIR COSMO'S COMPANY, AND that of his fellows, and he signaled for the diners to leave him, calling for Baron Haderslev to attend him.

"You, too, Westover." He made a gesture towards Sir Cosmo and said to them in their native tongue, "Have that disgusting mange removed from his face. I don't care how you do it. Either he allows his valet to shave him, or have your men tie him down and remove it anyway you care to, Westover. Understand me?"

"Yes, Your Highness. It will be done at once."

"And get him to keep it off. You know the law."

"Yes, Your Highness."

"We can't have the Princess Joanna getting any notions about this fool. He is no Alec Halsey by a long pole. She must never see him again—"

"She's *visited* the prisoner?" It was Baron Haderslev. His incredulousness was mistaken for shock.

"*No*, Haderslev," the Margrave groaned with annoyance. "Where are your wits?"

"Apologies, Highness," the Court Chamberlain muttered, hoping he hadn't given himself away. "Of course the Princess would not be interested in this ape of a man."

"No, she would not. And it is as well I do not permit the wives, sisters, daughters, any female at my banquets. For surely the sight of my friend's friend would be too shocking a sight for them, too, as it would be for my sister."

The Margrave turned on a heel to leave when he had a sudden thought. He turned to stare at his prisoner dispassionately as Sir Cosmo was being escorted from the hall.

"By my calculation Halsey has just under two weeks to show himself before his hairy best friend and that chirping female are due to breathe their last. Yes?"

"Yes, Your Highness. Eleven days to be precise."

"Good. If Halsey is not here by then, slit their throats. Two fewer mouths to feed should keep Cook off your back."

# Eighteen

ALEC WAS STARTLED AWAKE BY AN EXPLOSIVE discharge of a musket close to the trekschuit.

The convoy was under attack.

He scrambled up off the camp bed and peered cautiously out the window, back up against the wood paneling, head turned, neck craning so that only his profile was to the glass. The muted light of a winter's day was beginning to darken into night, and a thick fog clung to the swampy marshland beyond the towpath, which was eerily deserted. And yet the unmistakable pop-popping of gunfire continued, outside and overhead.

He reasoned the soldiers had to be on the far side of the barge, using it for cover as they fired over the roofline into the fog. Those returning fire were using the fog to their advantage. Between each volley of shots orders were barked out as muskets were re-loaded. The gunfire continued. There was a cry of surprise. The thud of something heavy hitting the roof over Alec's head had him momentarily looking up, expecting a soldier to come crashing through the ceiling. More orders were barked out. More gunfire.

Alec wondered what was happening on the other side of the curtain; if Selina was safe; if the passengers had managed to find cover. From where he was, flat up against the wall, to get to the curtain would mean crossing in front of the window and thus be in full view, if for the briefest of moments, which was not the most sensible course of action in a battle. So he edged back, out of sight, intending to go round the camp bed and, if need be, crawl across to the curtain. The sound of boots scrambling along the deck of the barge, followed by the back door banging open froze him to the spot.

It was Hadrian Jeffries.

Wide-eyed and wild-haired, his sealskin overcoat flapping about his booted ankles, the valet scuttled down the few shallow steps and immediately launched himself at Alec. Grabbing his master by the embroidered skirts of his frock coat, he yanked him backwards, took hold of him as if he meant to resist, and flung him to the floor, scattering campaign furniture as Alec's shoulder hit the boards hard. He then threw himself across his master as a human shield and ordered him to be still.

"For God's sake, Jeffries! I'm not—"

Alec did not get to finish the sentence. He was cut off by a deafening crack as wood splintered and glass exploded. Slivers of paneling and tiny glass shards blew across the room and rained down upon master and servant, a lead shot ripping through the deckhouse and exiting through the opposite wall.

There was a moment's awed silence as both men listened for further fire, but as the fighting seemed to have moved on down the canal, Hadrian Jeffries picked himself up and offered his hand to Alec to help him to stand.

"Sorry, sir. No time to explain," the valet apologized, breathing still short and dusting himself off. "I saw you at the window and—

"Please. No need," Alec stated, the shock also making his breathing shallow. He saw in the afternoon light that now poured through the large hole in the side of the deckhouse that the sleeves of his frock coat glinted with broken glass, and he began to gingerly shrug himself out of the garment, Hadrian Jeffries coming to his assistance. "Thank you, Hadrian. Not for this," he said with a huff of laughter as he was stripped out of the frock coat, relieved to have survived such a close encounter with a musket ball. "But for bruising my shoulder! What's going on out there?"

"We'd just docked at the Aurich lock—"

"We're at Aurich *already*?"

"Yes, sir. You slept the entire journey."

"Good—Lord. I must've been tired."

"Yes, sir. Not sure who's firing out there. There's some confusion. What with the fog, and the light fading, no one is certain who's doing what. Some of the soldiers were sent across the marshes toward the town, and that's when the first shots were heard. They came running back and took cover behind the barges. Looks like we've been ambushed by the rebels, who were waiting for us."

At the sudden sound of a half a dozen men shouting and scuffling, as if the barge were about to be stormed, both men looked towards the hole in the wall that allowed not only light but the freezing afternoon air to circulate in the small private space that had once been snugly warm. Soldiers rushed past the shattered window, and then it was quiet again for a few moments. Long enough for Alec to ask,

"Where are the other passengers? Mrs. Jamison-Lewis?"

"Herr Luytens and the Reverend Shirley were playing at cards last time I looked in on them. But Mrs. Jamison-Lewis, her lady-in-waiting, and the deaf girl had all gone for a walk along the towpath about half an hour ago."

Alec's face went white.

"You mean she's *out there*—in *this*?"

"Yes, sir—"

"Good God, *no*."

"—somewhere further down the towpath, walking back from the direction we'd come," Hadrian Jeffries explained hurriedly, following Alec who had flung back the curtain and was striding into the other section of the deckhouse. "Two soldiers went with them, so I'm sure Mrs. Jamison-Lewis and her companions are out of the line of fire—"

"Are you indeed?!" Alec stated tersely. "Who the devil had the stupidity to let her—them—leave the protection of the barge, when it's known the marshes are crawling with rebels? Where's Müller?" he demanded, taking a quick glance about the deserted space. He spied two crouching figures under the table. "Who's there? Is that you Luytens? Shirley?"

"Get down, my lord! Get down!" the Reverend Shirley wailed in a thin voice. "We are under attack! We are—"

Alec ignored the cowering figures and was about to cross to the other door when it was kicked open and the door frame filled with people, shouting, crying, issuing orders, and all trying to get into the safety of the cabin.

"Make way! Make way!"

A soldier came lightly down the steps to the table and swept it clear with the arc of his arm, sending cups, plates, playing cards, clay pipes, and newspapers hurtling to the floor. The ensuing commotion had Jacob Luytens and the Reverend Shirley scrambling out from their hiding place, wondering what was happening, a hand over their heads to avoid being hit, and tripping over smashed plates and cups.

The soldier who had cleared the table was followed down the steps by Jacob Luytens' brother-in-law, Horst Visser, who had a limp Selina in his arms. Behind them came Evans, being supported at the elbow by the barge captain, then the Reverend Shirley's granddaughter, who, upon spying her grandfather, rushed over and began frantically signing to him. Following up the rear, another soldier, who stayed by the steps, musket poised.

Alec was blind to everything and everyone but Selina.

The hood of her red wool cloak had fallen back off her apricot curls which were in wild disorder about her deathly pale face. The rest of this outer garment was so outrageously askew that it fell off her shoulders, muddied hem trailing on the floor, as Horst Visser laid her gently on the table, Evans quick to place her mistress's enormous fur muff under Selina's head.

There were calls for a physician. Someone. Anyone with medical knowledge. One of the officers, perhaps?

Alec wasn't listening.

What had happened? Everyone spoke at once. Soldiers. Rebels. Fog too thick to see. The convoy had lost at least six soldiers. One of the barge horses had been killed in the cross fire. Who knew how many rebels were dead or dying out in the marshes. All of them, it was hoped.

Alec heard none of it.

Smelling salts. Bandages. A medical kit. Someone fetch wine, sweet tea, anything to help revive the beauty. Was the kitchen still functioning in the other barge? Who would go? The soldier who had cleared the table volunteered.

Alec distinguished individual words but still they made no sense. He stared across at Selina lying motionless on the table, and his feet would not obey his brain to go to her. He saw that the front of her gown was splattered with mud, or was that blood? The hook and eyes of her stays had been ripped from their stitching, and the many soft cotton quilted layers that made up the garment had peeled apart like the leaves of an open book. And in the center of this tufted cotton mess, a gaping hole that exposed a large glistening red mass that moved with the rise and fall of her exposed breasts.

*Jesu*—*was that her heart?* With such an injury there could be no chance of survival. *What the bloody hell use was a physician? Or bandages or cup of sweet tea? Why were they talking drivel when the love of his life was dying on the table before them?*

He had to do something, anything, but stand there, gawping.

He came to life, shoved aside the small crowd, growling at them to stand back from the table and leave Selina to him. He grabbed up her fingers, pressed his lips to the back of her gloved hand, and went down on bended knee beside the table. He placed a cool hand to her forehead and stared at her pale face, disbelieving.

"Dear God, please, *please* let her live," he prayed aloud, her limp hand pressed to his forehead. "Don't let this happen. Our life together has yet to begin..."

"My lord, she—" Evans began, but then pressed her lips firmly together when her mistress rallied at the sound of his lordship's voice.

Selina's eyelids fluttered and she slowly turned her head on the muff and opened her eyes. Seeing Alec, she sighed and smiled.

"Oh, you're safe. Good. I think I fainted when—never mind. Is Janet safe? The girl?"

"I'm here, m'lady," Evans answered instantly from the other side of the table. She took hold of Selina's free hand and managed to say evenly. "I'm safe. So is the girl. We all are." She looked across at Alec, who had risen to his feet and had a shaking hand to his mouth, too overcome to speak, staring down at Selina as if she had come back from the dead. "My lord, one of soldiers with us was hit—killed," she explained, and when Alec tore his gaze from Selina to look at her, a nod for her to continue, she said, "The blood on her gown and mine is his. He'd bent to scoop up her hair ribbon which had come loose in the strong breeze and fallen by the canal edge. He never did get to return it. The lead shot passed right through the back of the poor boy's skull, and then straight across the front of my lady's bodice. You see, she was standing side on, otherwise the lead shot would have gone through her too. It was the narrowest of escapes, thanks be to God. I think the jewelry helped—The jewels may have stopped the lead shot doing any real damage..."

"Jewels?" Alec repeated, uncomprehendingly.

"The ransom... Olivia's jewelry," Selina added, struggling to sit up.

And when Alec mechanically helped her to be upright she thanked him, adding. "I don't remember fainting. It must have been when the lead shot whizzed past... Alec, I'm cold."

He did not at first hear her statement. He was staring hard at the glistening red mass nestled on her left breast, and trying to make sense of what he'd just been told and what he was looking at. *Olivia's jewelry? Ransom? What had that to do with this?* And then the shock fell away, and with clarity of mind came clear vision. On closer inspection, and now that she was upright, he saw that the red mass had shifted, and that it was not a living thing at all. It was a ruby necklace spilling forth from a slit in a pocket within the damaged bodice. And that wasn't the only piece of jewelry hidden amongst the cotton layers of her corset. The loop of a string of pearls was poking through from a slit, and there was the glint of something golden in there, too. If he wasn't very much mistaken, Selina's corset held a treasure trove of his godmother's best jewels.

His sigh of relief was audible, and so was his intake of anger at the naïve duplicity of the two most important women in his life. How could Selina and Olivia do this to him? But he quickly quelled his feelings. What mattered was Selina's welfare. Something about her being cold finally registered, and it was then he realized that she was practically naked from throat to waist. He took a swift glance around at their audience and one word from him had them turn away to look anywhere but at the table. He fixed on his valet.

"Jeffries, go through and shake the bed free of glass, and tidy up. Take Herr Visser. Between the two of you, you should be able to shift the stack of trunks up against the hole in the wall. That at least will help keep the frigid air out until the window can be boarded up. You," he added to the guard by the shallow steps. "Find out what's going on. And find your captain. Reverend? I trust your granddaughter is not injured, though I do not doubt she must be in shock at what she has just witnessed?"

"Sophie will be fine directly, my lord," the Reverend Shirley replied, slightly distracted that his granddaughter kept tugging on his upturned cuff, insisting that he tell his lordship what she had witnessed while outside on the towpath. He signed to her, and they had a short conversation before he said aloud to Alec, "When you have a moment, at your earliest convenience, I need a word with your lordship. Of course, once Mrs. Jamison-Lewis is settled... It is of some importance, not unconnected with the tragic incident that saw the young soldier lose his life."

"Yes, yes, of course," Alec replied, somewhat distracted himself, watching Evans adjust Selina's cloak so that it now covered her irreparably damaged bodice and corset. "Are you all right?" he asked the lady's maid. "There is blood on your petticoats... You are not injured?"

"Oh no, my lord. I think I told you, it's the young soldier's blood," Evans replied, coming around to his side of the table. "I was standing on the other side of him when—He wasn't much more than a boy, my lord," she added, and then promptly burst into tears. But she quickly made a recover. "Forgive me. It must be the shock. That poor soldier...the near miss...I will be fine directly."

Alec put an arm about her shaking shoulders, just as Jeffries poked his head around the curtain and gave a nod, the signal the room was as ready as it ever would be. Horst Visser held the curtain aside and waited.

"I'm going to carry your mistress through to my camp bed," he said quietly to Evans. "She needs a change of clothes. I'll have her trunk fetched. And once she's settled, and you've both had a cup of tea, please empty that bodice of its contents. I have a strongbox. I suspect you'll both feel better to be unburdened of such weight, and responsibility."

Evans sighed her relief. "Yes, my lord. We will! And I must tell your lordship," she continued, following behind Alec as he carried

Selina through to his camp bed and gently set her down, "and I'm sorry for my disloyalty, m'lady, but I was very much against Her Grace's perilous scheme from the off. I knew no good could come of it. There was the danger, of course, but my main concern was that the wearing of such a heavy bodice day in and day out would be laborious and had a detrimental affect on m'lady's health."

Selina gaped at her. "Evans! You never said a word!"

"I doubt that would have stopped you," Alec muttered. And when she blushed guiltily, he gave her a chuck under the chin, to show he was no longer angry with the elaborate ruse she and the Duchess had effected.

"But now, on this day," Evans continued ignoring her mistress, and addressing Alec exclusively. "I am very glad she was carrying all those jewels in her bodice, my lord, because if she hadn't she might not now be with us, nor might your ba—"

"Janet! *Enough*," Selina cut in before Evans could ruin her surprise, something she would share with Alec after they were married; it was to be her wedding present to him. "The shock has made you run on at the mouth. I am shaken but perfectly well—*all of me* is well."

"Yes, of course you are," Alec stated stridently, not because he didn't enter into Evans' feelings, but so their thoughts would not plunge into melancholy and recrimination given what they had just been through. And because he was intent on lightening the mood, he failed to pick up on either woman's inference, but winked down at Selina and said to Evans with a lop-sided grin, though his tone was grim, "Don't you worry, Janet. There'll be no more harebrained scheming—well, not without my knowledge—once I make your mistress Marchioness Halsey, of that you can be assured!"

"I'm very glad to hear you say so, my lord," Janet Evans answered primly, and with a mental grin of satisfaction turned away for fear his lordship would see her blush at his use of her Christian name.

Selina pouted, settling deeper under the folds of her fur-lined red

woolen cape. It had nothing to do with the winter wind whistling
through the destroyed window that now had a stack of trunks in
front of it, but with an unease at being caught out by Alec, in carrying
a king's ransom upon her person, and keeping him in ignorance.

"Schemes?" she said petulantly, to hide her guilt. "Harebrained?
Alec! How can you say so when—" And then she suddenly realized
the absurdity in worrying over such a petty detail when she had come
close to losing her life in the crossfire of battle. She was so very glad
to be alive. She laughed and caught at Alec's fingers when he put up
his brows in mock disapproval, and teased him. "I suspect making
me your marchioness is a ploy just to get me to call you 'my lord'!"

"Oh, how did you find me out?" He chuckled and dropped a
kiss on her forehead, saying teasingly so only she could hear, "But
I expect to earn the declaration, one way or another... Hear that?"
he added as he straightened, and put a finger to his lips for them
to remain silent.

Both women listened and heard nothing. They looked at each
other and then at Alec for further explanation

"The fighting, it's stopped."

All three wondered for how long.

IT HAD BEEN AN HOUR SINCE THE LAST SHOT WAS FIRED. IT
was now dark, the sky as dark as a coal pit. A heavy fog blanketed the
ground, blocking a night sky that Alec knew in summer was awash
with twinkling stars and a bright moon. The winter weather soup
was so dense nothing beyond the towpath was visible. Somewhere
close by was the fortified township of Aurich. Built atop a man-made
mound against flooding, and protected from invasion by a high
wall, the town itself had a lovely church, its spire seen for miles and
providing a landmark for travelers and farmers alike. There was also
a town square, and extensive gardens where fruit trees blossomed
in Spring, and to Aurich was where farmers brought their cattle to

market. Alec knew it well, that and the fact he was Baron Aurich; how could he forget such a place?

He had left Selina to change in the privacy of his chamber, ordered the rest of the passengers to remain within the deckhouse, and seen to it that they were supplied with hot water for tea, and more coal for the ceramic heater. He had then thrown his fur-lined cape over his wool frock coat, pressed his tricorne low on his brow, and slipped on his gloves, leaving the safety of the trekschuit in search of Captain Müller. Hadrian Jeffries and one of Müller's aides-de-camp went with him, the soldier carrying a lantern to light the way.

Soldiers patrolled the tow path the length of the convoy, and at either end of this section of path those soldiers not on duty had set up tents, a fire providing light, and heat to boil water. The jagers had tethered their work horses and the horses that would pull the sledges the following day, and set up their own camp, their charges fed and watered, and blankets secured across their backs to ward off the chill night air.

Alec walked amongst the three camps and spoke to the soldiers and jagers alike, and listened to their stories of the afternoon's battle with the rebels. He discovered that seven soldiers had lost their lives defending the trekschuit and two of the horses had been put down after being badly wounded in the crossfire. He was surprised to learn that the rebels had managed to break through the line, and ransacked one of the trekschuiten of its supplies. When he asked what was taken, the replies were vague: A couple of crates and a few sacks. And when he made the observation that he found it interesting the rebels had targeted one barge in particular, and not all five, no one could posit an explanation. So he was not surprised that when he asked the whereabouts of Colonel Müller, the men could not tell him that either.

It did not go unnoticed by him, that with each question the soldiers became increasingly nervous, one infantryman in particular was agitated enough to respectfully advise Alec that it would be best if the Herr Baron returned to his trekschuit; in a fog where it was hard to see the nose on the end of your face, the rebels could be anywhere, and were possibly listening to the conversation. Which was why no one wanted to be forthcoming with information. He didn't doubt they would consider capturing the Herr Baron a prize indeed. To which one of his fellows told him to *shut it*.

An argument between this infantryman and another ensued, but it was not conducted in German, but in the Midanichian dialect, which meant these men at least were from around this area, not from the south of the country. It was assumed Alec and his valet would not understand, and thus the men were relaxed and uninhibited in their comments. Alec gave no indication he understood them as he wished the men a good night and had the soldier with the lantern take him across to inspect the convoy of barges.

Out of earshot, Hadrian Jeffries said quietly in English at Alec's back, "Did you understand what they were arguing about, sir?"

"Yes. Did you?"

"No. But they weren't speaking in German, but in some dialect I'd heard before at the Emden docks amongst the wharf workers. It makes you wonder if we've wandered into the camp of the enemy, if you get my meaning."

Alec was grim about the mouth. "Yes. That they chose to argue in the local dialect was telling enough. We'll keep this to ourselves for now. No point upsetting the others..."

When they were standing before the barge which had interested the rebels, Alec ordered the soldier to hold up his lantern so they could see their way on board. He was standing on the deck with his valet, watching the soldier cast his lantern to see beyond their own toes, and if it was possible to go below, when he continued their conversation in English.

"The men back there mentioned muskets and gunpowder. You

were on the docks supervising our luggage and supplies while the barges were being loaded... Do you remember seeing crates of muskets and barrels of gunpowder being brought on board?"

"No, sir. If I had, I'd have remembered, and how many barrels, too!"

Alec smiled. "Yes, I thought you would. Of course, carrying a stock of armaments and powder is not out of the ordinary for soldiers crossing into territory known to be occupied by rebel soldiers. However, a barge loaded up with muskets, and barrels of gunpowder enough for a small army would suggest contraband—"

"For the rebels?"

"That was my first and only thought, particularly as this barge was the only one the rebels were interested in." Alec lowered his head to accommodate his hat as he went down the steps into the cabin. He had the soldier shed light across the open door. There was a bolt and a large ring for a padlock. But neither the door or the bolt had suffered any damage. "Not a forced entry then..."

With Hadrian Jeffries at his back he followed the soldier about the interior of the cabin with lantern held high and poked into corners and areas as ordered. The floor was awash with a fine layer of dust, possibly spilled gunpowder, and in that dust were boot prints and scrapes of something heavy being dragged from one side of the deckhouse to the other. But for a few textile bales up against the far wall, the cabin had been cleared of its entire cargo. There was also, surprisingly, a scattering of feathers and bird droppings from a duck, or was it a goose? Alec scooped up one of the feathers.

"How exceedingly interesting," he said without surprise, inspecting the feather. "A pigeon's feather, Jeffries. Any ideas as to why the rebels would want to abscond with a crate of pigeons?"

"For pie?" the valet replied, not at all convinced. "There were a number of animals and birds brought on board with the sacks of foodstuffs."

275

"Loaded onto this barge? I would have supposed that any produce required by the cook would be stowed in the barge housing the kitchen?"

"Yes. Yes. You're right, sir," Jeffries replied with a far away look, remembering in his mind's eye the events of that morning, when the barges were loaded up with their cargo. "Come to think back on it, sir, the animals and foodstuffs *were* loaded onto the second barge, the one with the kitchen. I was occupied making certain the inventory of our trunks and campaign furniture was placed in the first barge, that I didn't take much notice what was going on with the other barges. But I do remember now that the cargo for this barge was handled solely by the soldiers. They wouldn't let the wharf workers near the boxes; they were guarded at all times. Sorry, sir. I should have taken more notice."

"Why should you? You were exhausted after being up all night assisting me with those letters of passage for the travelers wanting to return to Holland, and there was nothing unusual in soldiers guarding cargo. The military have control of everything and everyone. Let's return to our barge and some warmth. Not even this cape can keep out the arctic temperatures for long."

Alec indicated to the soldier to lead the way back up on deck.

"But why were there pigeons in here with the gunpowder and muskets?" Hadrian Jeffries asked, following at Alec's back. "Doesn't that seem an odd assortment?"

"Not if they are the very things you want to take," Alec replied calmly. "It makes sense to have everything in the one place—on the one barge. And the rebels were particular about what they wanted. They could have ransacked all the barges, taken food, taken hostages, taken coin and jewels, and our sacks of coal. All highly-prized booty. And yet all they took, they took from this barge and no other. Only those couple of bales were left behind."

"They probably would have taken those too, if they'd had the time!" the valet scoffed.

"Oh, but they did have the time," Alec stated confidently. "I believe they had all the time in the world. There is no spillage, nothing to show they were in a hurry to get the goods and run. The lock wasn't broken or the door forced open. If they'd been in a hurry, surely they would have fumbled, stumbled, dropped a sack or two? Broken a crate? The bird droppings and feathers indicate nervous birds, nothing more. Given the noise of gunfire, that is no surprise. But I am very sure they were handled with care. And as nothing of value was left behind, in here or outside, or on the deck or towpath, I'd say they were given every assistance—"

"—by Colonel Müller's men?" Hadrian Jeffries practically hissed.

"No names, Jeffries," Alec said smoothly, continuing to converse in English, and confidently waving the soldier on when he glanced over his shoulder at the mention of his colonel by name. "We don't want to alert our uniformed friends we are onto them."

"Are we onto them, sir?"

Alec paused at the base of the shallow steps leading up on deck, and turned to face his valet. As the soldier had gone up ahead of them, they were left in pitch darkness.

"I have no way of knowing if all or some of the soldiers guarding this convoy are involved, or indeed, if their colonel is, also," Alec said quietly into the darkness. "Though, given the ease in which this barge was cleared of its contents..."

"You think the battle was staged for our benefit—well, for your benefit, sir?" the valet asked in surprise, a glance up the steps to the pool of light.

"Or for the benefit of those few soldiers loyal to the Margrave, and so as not to cast suspicion a particular way until this cargo was secured behind rebel lines, yes. Come, we had best disembark before suspicions are raised as to our particular interest in this barge. Watch your head," Alec advised as he ducked, a hand to his tricorne, to go back up the shallow steps into the cold night air.

"Sir! But why the pigeons?" Jeffries asked, pausing on the steps. "I presume they are not being used for pie?"

Alec turned to look down into his valet's face, suddenly illuminated by candlelight as the soldier peered down into the void, lantern swinging.

"No. Not for pie," Alec said with a smile. "They are too valuable and important to end up baked in pastry. Have you ever heard of the pigeon post, Hadrian?"

"Letter carriers? Yes. There are dovecotes all over Holland for the purpose."

"And here. Emden's principal dovecot is in the loft of the Customs House. Did you notice the popholes and landing platforms under the roofline?"

"You think the pigeons that were in this barge were stolen from the Custom's House? Why?"

"Any town under siege needs a way to communicate with the outside world, efficiently and fast. Men could be sent on horseback or on foot, by ship, or in our case by trekschuit, but all are slow and dangerous. They have to cross enemy territory, or in the case of a ship, outmaneuver those pirates at the entrance to the Ems estuary. A note is much more likely to reach its destination, and more quickly, if sent by carrier pigeon. Take away a town's communication and they are further isolated, and another step closer to surrender."

"That's crafty. Removing those pigeons from their dovecote would take some planning. So to my reckoning this was no ambush but a planned military operation, of which the good colonel would need to have knowledge. Unless he was ambushed himself and taken away by the rebels, because he isn't here, is he, and—"

"All questions we can ask Colonel Müller," Alec said in German as he emerged onto the deck to find the officer in question waiting for him. "Ah! Colonel. We were just wondering as to your whereabouts, and if you survived the rebel attack. And here you are, none the worse for the ordeal. And I see you've changed your stripes, too..."

The valet understood what his master had said in German, just did not comprehend what he meant by it, or his suddenly buoyant tone, until he came up the steps onto the deck and into the candlelight from the lantern. And there was Colonel Müller, and behind him half a dozen soldiers. All had their swords drawn and all were pointing the tips menacingly in Alec's direction.

# _Nineteen_

"VERY DROLL, HERR BARON," COLONEL MÜLLER replied to Alec's less-than-subtle quip that he had changed his stripes, and thus sides in the civil war, though he did not refute the assertion. He signaled for his men to put away their swords. "We will return to your barge, Herr Baron, where it is warm, and where you can be protected from the _elements_."

He signaled for Alec go before him and follow the soldier with the lantern, and with Hadrian Jeffries at his master's back, followed them off the barge. On the towpath the soldiers formed a guard around master and servant.

"I would advise you and your man not to attempt anything foolish for the remainder of our journey or—"

"That is hardly necessary advice, Colonel," Alec stated wearily.

"—it will not be you who suffers for your recalcitrance, but those dear to you. Understood?"

"Understood, Colonel. But again, unnecessary."

"It's General Müller of Prince Viktor's own regiment."

Alec made him a grandiloquent bow. "I stand corrected. Accept my apologies, and my congratulations. Though I suspect you have been a general in the prince's army from the start of the civil war...?"

General Müller's only acknowledgment of this assertion was to give a small nod. He was about to march the Herr Baron to his cabin, when one of his men approached, saluted and came forward to whisper a piece of urgent news. There was a terse exchange between the soldier and his superior, and then the soldier went away with his instructions, disappearing into the thick fog from whence he had appeared. Müller sent the guard with the two prisoners on ahead, and half an hour elapsed before he came down the shallow steps into the warmth of Alec's cabin.

ALEC WAS STANDING IN THAT PART OF THE DECKHOUSE WHICH had been curtained off for his private use. The damask curtain used for this purpose had been torn down, and thus the space was no longer private, and two soldiers stood guard at either entrance to the trekschuit. He was inspecting the damage to the pair of stays—or as Selina had called them *jumps*—caused by the stray bullet which had killed the soldier who had gallantly tried to retrieve her ribbon. The bullet had sliced through the front of the material, shaving off the outer layers as a nutmeg grater finely shaves the outer skin off the nut, just barely touching the quilting but enough to burst the stitching and cause the cotton to pop out, irreparably damaging the garment. By his dispassionate reckoning, had the bullet's trajectory been a mere inch higher it would have entered Selina's breast.

He quickly put aside that horrifying thought and inspected the garment's construction, and was all admiration for the ingenuity of its design in concealing its precious cargo. The padded quilting along with the intricately stitched pockets helped smooth out the contents so that when worn the jumps looked no different to any other female undergarment, except that the hook and eyes drew the two sides together across the breasts... Finding his thoughts wandering again to the unimaginable, he put the jumps aside on the camp bed and looked about for the strong box he had left for Selina to deposit the jewelry into for safekeeping. And that's when he saw General Müller. He had been so absorbed in his inspection he had not heard the soldier enter the cabin.

Müller stripped off his leather gloves and put them in the crown of his tricorne which he then handed to a subordinate saying with a nod at the pair of stays on the bed, "A close call..."

Alec had no wish to discuss Selina's undergarments with this man—with any man. And when Müller picked up the garment and examined it, fingers prodding deep in the little hidden pockets, to convince himself all its hidden treasures had been found, Alec felt his face glow hot with embarrassment and an unreasonable anger.

"An ingenious method of hiding a King's ransom," Müller mused, continuing to poke about in the soft cotton layers. "Your idea?"

"No," Alec replied brusquely, itching to snatch the stays away.

"I did not think so. You are too chivalrous to put a lady's life in danger. Still," Müller continued, turning the garment over, "if the jewels and coin had not been concealed in that way, and provided a layer of protection, there may have been a very different outcome..."

Alec had crossed to the window by the table and was looking out on the view, anywhere but at the soldier as he continued to manhandle Selina's corset. He wondered if Müller was deliberately goading him, wanting him to do something he regretted. He told himself to remain calm, that he was being irrational. It was only a pair of stays—Yet, they belonged to Selina... He counted to ten, before he found his voice. All he could manage was a curt "yes".

"You would not know this, but one of the rubies was chipped by the ball that killed Sergeant Schmitt," Müller told him. He finally dropped the stays on the bed, and joined Alec by the window. "Though there is surprisingly little blood on the stays given his head—"

Alec cut him off.

"I would prefer not to discuss this further. Your soldier lost his life as a casualty of war, and that is regrettable. For his sake, I hope he was killed instantly."

"He was."

"Good. Perhaps you can also tell me how Mrs. Jamison-Lewis fares? I left to give her some privacy to change her garments, and expected to find her—and the rest of the passengers—upon my return."

"Mrs. Jamison-Lewis and the others are being held on another barge, one that is warm, and are being fed and attended to with all the care that can be offered them, given the circumstances."

"I am pleased to hear it, General. I did not think you an unreasonable man. Perhaps you would now be good enough to take me to join them."

"You and I will have dinner here," General Müller stated, and signaled to the two soldiers hovering nearby to go about setting the table with cutlery, plate, and goblets. "You'll be pleased to know that the females of your party are all holding up well after the regrettable incident on the towpath. The Reverend's granddaughter was distraught and required a draught of laudanum. One of my aides is also a physician. He offered to examine Mrs. Jamison-Lewis—Please, Herr Baron, do not be alarmed," Müller added, raising his hand in a gesture of conciliation when Alec clenched his fists. "She is perfectly well. She refused but did accept some liniment for the bruising to her knee—"

"Bruising?"

"Her lady's maid said she collapsed with shock when the soldier died before her and—"

"She did not tell me—" Alec began then stopped himself.

"Mrs. Jamison-Lewis means a great deal to you, Herr Baron, yes?"

"Yes. We are engaged to be married."

General Müller bowed his head. "Accept my felicitations. And my thanks for being truthful."

"I have no reason to hide that information from you. I believe I am a good judge of character, and thus I have every confidence you will accord us the respect that our circumstance deserves."

Müller indicated the bench on the other side of the set table. "Please, won't you join me? You must be ravenously hungry since you have not eaten since first light."

Alec sat where directed and slid the linen napkin across his lap. "Not as hungry as you. Making sure those musket crates, gunpowder kegs, not to mention the crate of pigeons, were spirited away behind Aurich's walls, must have given you quite the appetite."

Müller smiled for the first time since returning from the township. He flicked out the skirts of his uniform frock coat and sat across from Alec, then signaled to his hovering subordinates to begin serving dinner.

"Beef stew and some fresh bread, courtesy of the citizens of Aurich, and for their Herr Baron."

"No pigeon pie on the menu...?" When this made the soldier shake his head with a smile, Alec added, as he took up his soup spoon, "My guess would be those birds are worth more than the muskets and gunpowder combined...?"

"Very true, Lord Halsey. May I call you by your English title? The coronet of marquess better befits you than that of Baron Aurich. Although, you have been most useful to me, and to His Highness, as the Herr Baron. But first, let us eat! We have all night to talk, do we not?"

"As you wish, General," Alec replied congenially, the aroma of the hot broth making him realize that he was indeed hungry, and it would not do to try and negotiate his freedom, and those of his fellow passengers, on an empty stomach.

The men ate their stew in silence, both relishing its warmth and taste. When Alec was offered the loaf of fresh bread, it was gratefully taken, and he pulled off a chunk, dipping the fluffy white bread into in the rich liquid heavy with onions and spices. With a second helping ladled into their bowls, Alec asked conversationally,

"Would you mind telling me why a high-ranking officer in the Margrave's army turned traitor and joined the rebels?"

"I am no traitor, Lord Halsey," Müller replied just as calmly, sopping up gravy with a hunk of bread in much the same manner as Alec had done. He ate it before speaking. "I am a loyal officer of the Midanichian army who served his sovereign Margrave Leopold during the Seven Years' War, and with distinction. I am still loyal to my sovereign and to my country. It's just that I do not recognize his eldest son as fit to rule."

"Not fit to rule? But surely you do not deny Prince Ernst proved himself in battle to be a great soldier?"

"That I do not, but great soldiers do not necessarily make good and just rulers in peace time, as I am sure you are aware. As a loyal soldier, my words are treasonous, but as my actions have gone far beyond words, it hardly matters what I say now. All I care about is the future of my country, and that it be ruled by a just and sane man."

Alec set down his soup spoon and let the hovering soldier take his empty bowl away and replace it with a clean plate and cutlery. Covered dishes of eel and herring, and one of carrots and potatoes, were put in the center of the table, and serving spoons set beside them. The diners were to help themselves. Alec waited for General Müller to finish his stew. When the soldier looked up, he held his gaze and said quietly,

"You do not believe Prince Ernst to be just or sane...?"

Müller did not hesitate in his reply.

"I do not, Lord Halsey. My tongue is free to finally speak my thoughts, here, at Aurich, surrounded by my fellow soldiers of the rebel army. You were at one time intimately acquainted with the Prince and his family. You were ennobled by the Margrave Leopold. The intaglio ring you wear is testament to that. But you are intelligent and astute and have lived outside Midanich for a decade. Would you have returned here of your own free will with Prince Ernst as Margrave? I think not. You are here only because you were forced to it, in a bid to rescue your English friends."

LUCINDA BRANT

Alec was surprised. "You have known about my mission all along, or is it something you have only recently learned?"

"The British Consul made me aware of your reasons for returning to Midanich; Luytens was never to be trusted."

"My government and I have been aware of Luytens' long history of sitting on the wall until one side or the other proved more to his advantage." Alec frowned on a sudden thought. "You used the past tense when mentioning the British Consul. Is there something else I should know about him, other than his lack of principles?"

"He and his brother-in-law have been dealt with accordingly," Müller stated bluntly. "That is all I will say for now. As for your friends imprisoned in the Castle, whether they are still alive is a moot point," he added, almost apologetically. "Nevertheless, you are determined to go to them. I admire such determination, though I think your venture doomed from the outset precisely because the Prince is mentally unbalanced. By returning to this country you are either exceedingly brave or touched with madness yourself. Which would explain a great deal to me. But... I believe the former. And thus I salute your courage, even if I believe your quest, as I said, is doomed."

"We shall have to agree to disagree, because I believe—I *must* believe—I will be able to free my friends. They are locked up for no other reason than their association with me. If you would indulge me: How did you reach the conclusion the Prince Ernst is of unsound mind? When I was last in this country he was capable of hiding his mental difficulties from the majority of his courtiers, with the help of his inner circle, and his father in particular."

General Müller elaborated.

"I was, for a time, part of that inner circle, serving as his aide-de-camp on a number of campaigns. Call it gut instinct. But there were times when I felt as if I were serving two completely different men, such was the volatility of his mind. This became more apparent at Castle Herzfeld in the months before Margrave Leopold's death.

286

The Prince withdrew into himself, and stayed in his apartments. More and more he came under the influence of his sister, until it was obvious to those closest to him that his decisions were being made by her. He does not want to be ruled by her, but he is too weak to go against her wishes. Even the Margrave Leopold, in his final weeks, was too feeble in mind and body to resist her demands."

"And yet knowing his eldest son was not of sound mind, he still made Ernst his successor. There was a time, when I was at court, when it was hoped Leopold would overlook Ernst in favor of his son by the Countess Rosine."

General Müller was genuinely surprised. "Ernst is the son of a Bavarian Princess. Prince Viktor's mother, the Countess Rosine, is a commoner, and as such, any children of the marriage were excluded from the succession. Midanich is not the only Germanic state that enforces such medieval inheritance laws on its rulers."

"And yet you and others have turned traitor and fight to put the son of a commoner in his brother's place?"

"Yes. It is the only sane option left to us if we wish to take our nation out of the Middle Ages and see it survive into the next century. With Ernst on the throne, we are likely to be invaded time and again by Holland or Prussia. And there is every possibility we could be subsumed into your king's Hanoverian electorate. That cannot be allowed to happen. But it will if Ernst remains Margrave."

Alec sipped wine from his goblet and returned the conversation to the occupants of Herzfeld Castle, asking as casually as he was able, though he was certain he knew the answer, "While aide-de-camp, did you ever meet the Princess Joanna?"

Müller shook his head.

"You were not curious?" asked Alec.

"Curious, yes. But not enough to attempt to get past her minders. I am not telling you anything you do not know when I say she has been under constant guard since her teens. And as her servants live in fear of having their tongues cut out if they dare mention her name, least of all speak about her to others, very little has ever been reported about her. It is a long-held belief, whispered in court circles, she became weak-brained after a bout of measles. I for one do not believe it—"

"You do not? Why?"

"Measles had nothing to do it. She was born mad." General Müller stared unblinkingly over the rim of his goblet. "Like her mother before her. Though that cannot be confirmed because she died in childbed after the birth of her twins. But you would know better than anyone, save her father and her brother, what the Princess Joanna is truly like. You married her. Unless that marriage document you showed me, along with your ennoblement, are forgeries? I think not."

"They are not forgeries. And as we are all for plain speaking, and my association with that family can no longer influence the outcome of events here in Aurich, I can tell you that the union was forced upon me—"

General Müller gave a shout of laughter so loud one of his subordinates standing to attention by the door took two paces forward, thinking his commander had perhaps been attacked with the cutlery, or at the very least been insulted by his dinner guest and had wine splashed in his face. But when he saw the General was genuinely amused, he quickly stepped back, red-faced and not an eye on his fellows who were all smirking under their breath at his impetuosity.

"My dear Lord Halsey!" the General gasped, napkin dabbing at a watery eye. "If I thought anything else, I'd have had no hesitation in putting you up against a wall and shot a long time ago! But please, go on," he continued, wiping the smile from his face and becoming serious. "I will not interrupt again. I can see that recalling such an episode still affects you, and I apologize for my levity. But how you came to be married to such a creature intrigues me."

Alec nodded, cleared his throat and continued.

"While I was locked up in Herzfeld's dungeons, Leopold gave me one of two choices, and as I wished to live, marrying the Princess was the only option. Of course, the union is not legal, regardless of my *coerced* participation in the ceremony. As an Englishman and a Protestant I cannot be married in the Catholic Church. But all Leopold cared about was that the Princess believed I was bound to her forever. I think he held out hope that marriage to me would somehow temper her troubled mind, and allow her to find some peace.

"As for my ennoblement...that is legal. Conferred upon me by the Margrave before the ceremony. Again, it was not something I wanted, but Leopold would not marry his daughter to a commoner." It was Alec's turn to smile and shake his head. "He was quite the old autocrat. He knew very well his child was not of sound mind, but that did not stop him making certain the groom was worthy of his offspring. And yet his second wife was a commoner—"

"The Countess Rosine is a commoner, yes, but she is not in the common way. Is she, Lord Halsey?"

Alec held his gaze, hiding his surprise at the edge to the soldier's voice—as if Müller would be personally affronted if Alec disagreed with him. And if he agreed, surely that would give him away as knowing the Countess better than he ought? He soon realized the remark was rhetorical when the soldier replenished their goblets and the General went back to eating what he had spooned onto his plate.

"You say it only remained for the Princess to believe that her marriage to you was a legal union," the General said after a few minutes of silence between them. "But what of the Prince? Did he also believe it?"

Alec rested his fork on the edge of the plate and met the soldier's gaze openly.

"Prince Ernst championed the union, but it was only the Princess Joanna, her father, myself, and Leopold's chaplain who attended the ceremony. Does that answer your question?"

The soldier did not break eye contact, as if he was weighing up Alec's words. Finally he blinked and nodded and went back to eating. When his plate was clean, he said,

"Thank you for your honestly, Lord Halsey. Would you now do me the courtesy of telling me how you managed to escape—"

"The marriage? The castle? Or both?"

Müller was again amused. "Both. But I am sure you have realized before now that what I am most interested in is how you escaped the castle. But by all means, while we finish our dinner, entertain me with an account of your escape from the clutches of your mad bride!"

"If you will first do me the courtesy of explaining how you think I've been useful to you and Prince Viktor in my capacity as the Herr Baron."

"Very well. In return you will reveal to me how you managed to break out of an impenetrable castle, a feat attempted many times in its history, but never successfully—until you. Your escape is so miraculous that it has entered the folklore of our country; the soldiers stationed at the castle have many times tried to replicate your daring flight, but to no avail." Müller held out his goblet to Alec. "It is agreed?"

Alec touched his goblet to Müller's and both drank up. "Agreed."

General Müller pushed his plate aside and settled back against the bench's backboard, fingers lightly about the stem of his goblet.

"I will tell you, Lord Halsey of England, Baron Aurich of Midanich," he began. "I was never more glad than the day you arrived at Emden's port. I knew you were on your way. One of the fishing fleet came early with the news *The Caroline* had been captured, so we were waiting for you. With your arrival came hope and a plan. Without you, I would not now be sitting here enjoying this meal, and the rebel force that holds Aurich would only have had a week's worth of food to sustain them through the winter. Most of the barrels of gunpowder were filled with maize and other foodstuffs. The muskets will arm the farmers further afield who are vulnerable to attack from Ernst's soldiers. And without their messenger pigeons, Emden is effectively cut off from all communications with Castle Herzfeld, the Margrave's military headquarters, and their roost. It is now only a matter of when, not how, we shall take Emden, the jewel in the west of Midanich's crown. With the fall of Emden, comes the fall of Ernst's tenure as Margrave. And we have you to thank."

"Me?" Alec was doubtful. "You give the Herr Baron too much credit. All I did was disembark and show the Herzfeld intaglio; that was an act of self preservation, and protecting my fellow passengers, nothing more."

"I will not allow you to be so self-effacing!" the General said, slapping his palm on the table to underscore his point. "By showing yourself in that manner, you had no way of knowing how you would be received. Emden could have been controlled by rebel forces, and you taken into custody, locked up as a prize to be ransomed for concessions from the Margrave, should the war not go the rebels' way. Yet you bravely strutted yourself as the Herr Baron, and as luck would have it the town was controlled by the Margrave's troops, and citizens loyal to the House of Herzfeld."

"Such as yourself?"

"Yes, such as myself, until such time as I could act in the interests of Prince Viktor," Müller explained. "Which is why I was only too willing to fall in with your plans. My display of fealty before the troops and Emden's Customs officials was just that, and helped dispel any rumor I might be a rebel spy."

"Which you were."

Müller nodded and drank up, sticking out his goblet to have it refilled by an attendant soldier who stood close by. He waved for the attendant to refill Alec's goblet, too, but when this was declined he said with a shrug,

"Moderation in most things, eh, Lord Halsey?! I approve, and I approve of you." The General sat forward, goblet nestled in the crook of his crossed arms. "Through force of personality you brought order to a town on the brink of rebellion. Do you realize that? Had you not arrived when you did, then set in place what you did, blood would have flowed in the canals, make no mistake!"

Alec was skeptical. "You think so?"

"I not only think it, I know it! For I was the one about to give the order to the rebels within the town to take up arms. And then you appeared and gave us our miracle. Your second in fact."

Alec pulled a face and laughed off his embarrassment at such effusive praise. "Are you sure you should be drinking, General? I think the wine has befuddled your thoughts."

Müller shook his head. "No. No. You are too modest. But then that is the problem with modest men, they do not fully appreciate their strengths, and often see these as a weakness, which of course they are not. And as I am not so modest, I can tell you now, that while you thought yourself in control of the situation in Emden as the Herr Baron, I was controlling you."

"I may be modest, Herr General, but I am not dull witted," Alec quipped. "You were very willing to fall in with my orders, no questions asked. That in itself was a highly suspicious circumstance."

"Agreed. But make no mistake. Had your orders not been to my liking and helped the rebel cause, there would have been a very different outcome. You certainly would not be sitting here enjoying dinner at my table. I used your sense of justice, of fairness, of doing what is right, to my advantage. I allowed you to be the Herr Baron, to carry out your good deeds, to have the port open and those merchants and their families who had been stranded in Emden due to the civil war, to return home to Holland, or wherever it was they were travelling to and from. I am a reasonable man. His Highness is a reasonable man. Our cause is reasonable. We do not want any unnecessary bloodshed. This country and its people have suffered enough through the Seven Years' War, and the wars before that.

Indeed, your country drove out the French occupying forces and then used Emden for its own purposes.

"I could not open the port. Only a direct order from the Margrave could do such a thing. And then you arrived, the Margrave's brother-in-law, a member of the House of Herzfeld, and it was a simple thing to convince my subordinates, and the town councillors that your word was the word of the Margrave. Having the port opened was a priority for the rebel cause, and in the end, you did that for us, too."

"I gather then that the petition-waving display outside Luytens' house the night before our departure was staged by your good self?"

Müller shrugged a shoulder. "I wish I could say yes. For it would have been a brilliant ploy, but no. In essence it was a spontaneous demonstration, begun by your English priest and his deaf granddaughter. But it caught on, like a grass fire at the height of summer. And then, yes, we helped to fan the flames of dissent."

"I presume then that Prince Viktor has gathered forces on the other side of the Ems, who were just waiting the opportunity for the port to be opened, to cross and take Emden?"

The General's eyes shone.

"Precisely! A large contingent awaits at Delfzijl. They are dressed as civilians and will enter the port in the ships that you permitted to leave with the citizens bound for Holland. The soldiers will infiltrate the town, distribute arms, and when the time is right, rise up. And while Emden surrenders or burns, ships will be sailing around to Herzfeld, ships carrying cannon, weapons, men, and food supplies for the rebel army stationed just outside the Castle. All that remains is for your good self to show us the way into the castle, and then justice will be served—on Ernst and his supporters at court."

Alec nodded, but he had only heard the first half of what the General had been saying because with the revelation that some of the ships leaving Emden's port were headed north around to Herzfeld, he had a sickening presentiment.

"Müller, tell me you kept your word and allowed my godmother and uncle to leave on *The Caroline* and disembark at Delfzijl."

When the General hesitated and shot a look at the two soldiers closest to him, and they came forward, hands to the hilt of their swords, as if expecting the Herr Baron to react with violence, Alec had his answer without a word spoken. He threw up his hands, feeling foolish and furious with himself for believing Müller would honor his promise. But of course, why would he set free the two people, who, with Selina, Alec loved most in the world, when they could be much more useful as a means of keeping him compliant?

"You came to a country in conflict," Müller stated. "You and the members of your party were aware from the outset of the dangers. *The Caroline*, its crew and passengers, are on their way to Herzfeld, along with a number of smaller ships. A veritable rebel flotilla. No harm will come to your uncle, the Duchess, and the English Ambassador, as long as you are cooperative—"

"No harm? You have put them in harm's way by turning their schooner into a warship! You cannot offer me such assurances with any degree of confidence, so it is pointless to try!"

Alec was done with talking, and with keeping company with this soldier. He needed to see Selina, to make certain she was all right after her ordeal, and to make certain the other passengers were being treated well. He had lost all faith in leaving the welfare of those for whom he felt responsible in the hands of others, particularly those with a political agenda.

"If you would allow me to see the other passengers, to satisfy myself they are safe and do not need for anything before we bed down for the night, I would be most grateful, Herr General," Alec said at his most formal, napkin put aside on the table, and rising up, a signal dinner conversation was at an end.

General Müller also set aside his napkin. He stood with a sigh. He had enjoyed the dinner and Alec's company. In fact, he admired the man, and wished they could have been friends, though he knew under present circumstances, that was unlikely. Lord Halsey, the Herr Baron, or whatever he wished to call himself, was too honorable, too bound by what was right, rather than what was expedient and necessary. And as such he would judge him, Müller, by his actions rather than the circumstances which had brought them about. And thus Müller considered him weak, and he had no time to offer up explanations. He gave Alec the response that was necessary rather than what was right or just.

"I cannot allow that, Lord Halsey. You will remain here, under guard, until it is time to leave. Which will be at first light. I will send you your valet when it is time to dress, and to pack you a small portmanteau for the journey. Regrettably, the sledges cannot accommodate your lovely traveling possessions, so they must remain here. I will give the order for them to be distributed amongst the men, and put to good use. Though you will be relieved that I have found room on the cargo sledge for the mechanical table. There are some spoils of war worth keeping, and His Highness will appreciate such a generous gift from your English government."

Alec stared out the window; there was no point in commenting, and so Müller made him a formal bow and turned to leave. And then something on the camp bed caught his eye.

"You did not enquire about the jewels and coin found hidden in Mrs. Jamison-Lewis's ingeniously made bodice."

"I presumed they, too, are spoils of war."

Müller smiled thinly. "Yes, they are. And your strong box is now under guard, and all the pieces accounted for." When Alec looked puzzled, Müller added, "You have the deaf girl to thank. She may not hear, but she does have sharp eyes. She saw Horst Visser steal several pieces of jewelry which had spilled from the corset to the ground when Mrs. Jamison-Lewis was struck. She rightly alerted her grandfather, who rightly told me. When Horst Visser could not be found, I sent a search party. The fool was captured walking back towards Emden with his booty, and has been dealt with."

Alec could well imagine how, so did not ask, but Müller told him anyway, and managed to surprise and shock him, too.

"There is no place for looters in time of war—at any time. You saw what happened to that imbecile who tried to steal a sack of coal at the wharf. He was made a necessary example of. There is also no place for traitors. Luytens betrayed you. He offered me the mechanical table, which is why I know of its existence. He also offered to split the jewelry and coin with me. He says you had no idea about such a ransom, and that it was his idea, and not something Prince Ernst demanded in return for the lives of your friends. Yes, I thought that would surprise you. It did me. What won't surprise you is that I consider a selfish duplicitous wretch with no beliefs worse than a thief. But I am not cruel by nature. I assure you that their deaths were quick and painless."

"Not painless for their families!"

"They should have thought of nothing but their families *before* they committed treason and theft. Now you must excuse me, there is much to do before our departure."

"I have a request, Herr General."

Müller paused at the steps leading up to the deck and waited.

"I wish to get married—tonight."

# Twenty

MÜLLER CAME BACK INTO THE CABIN, SURPRISE WRIT large on his features. He wondered if he had heard Alec correctly, but when the Englishman just looked at him, he grinned.

"What a romantic you are!"

"The English priest on board has agreed to marry us," Alec told him.

"But—are you not already married to the Princess Joanna?"

"No. I explained that to you," Alec said with great patience. "That marriage ceremony was a ruse on the part of the Margrave to keep his daughter compliant."

"Does the lovely Mrs. Jamison-Lewis know about your earlier marriage—Ah! You have yet to tell her. Thus the urgency in marrying her without delay. You intend to tell your bride *after* you are married that you *were* married? Is that any way to begin married life?"

"Aurich has a fine church in which the Reverend Shirley can conduct the ceremony," Alec continued, ignoring the General's tongue-in-cheek question.

"These are indeed uncertain times. But you have my assurance you are more valuable alive than to be put up against a wall and shot, if that is your concern."

"I gave Mrs. Jamison-Lewis my word we would be married tonight."

"Then I will break the disappointing news to her. The town is under siege conditions and is now off limits, even to me. Our little collection of barges, and my soldiers who guard us, are on their own. Perhaps His Highness will grant your oh-so-romantic request before he passes sentence on you for your part in the Margrave's war?"

"My part? I had no part. I am here on a diplomatic mission to negotiate the release of my friends, nothing more," Alec argued. "And you said yourself, my actions at Emden have helped, not hindered Prince Viktor's bid for the margravate.'"

"I have no doubt that will be taken into consideration by His Highness," agreed the General. "Though, regrettably, the moment you stretched out your hand to me wearing the Herzfeld intaglio you became very much a part of this civil war." The General bowed politely. "But it is not for me to pass judgment, that is for His Highness. Tomorrow you will have the opportunity to put your case to him. For now, I suggest you get some rest. You will be woken before the dawn, and we leave at sunrise."

Alec followed the General across to the steps. He could not keep the anxiousness from his voice. "We are journeying to Herzfeld as planned?"

"Eventually. But not immediately."

"I *must* travel to the Castle. If I'm not there on time, my friends—"

"Lord Halsey, it is best that you come to terms with your altered situation," General Müller replied from the steps, two soldiers with their bayonets crossed at the mouth of the stairwell keeping Alec from following. "Your travel plans are unimportant. What matters is winning this war. Your fate now rests with His Highness Prince Viktor, not Prince Ernst. As for your English friends locked up in the Castle..." Müller stuck out his bottom lip and pulled a face of unconcern. "For all anyone knows, they are already dead."

"I won't believe that. Ever!"

"You may believe what you like. But you had best prepare yourself. Prayer is now the only recourse left to you—and to them. Good night."

ALEC SPENT A RESTLESS NIGHT AND WAS WOKEN WHEN IT seemed he had just managed to fall into a deep sleep. It was Hadrian Jeffries, and it was still dark outside. His valet had set out a change of clothing, but apologized for not being able to shave him. On the orders of General Müller all gentleman were forbidden to be shaved.

"As one of the soldiers explained it to me, sir, officers in the rebel army have put aside their razors and taken to growing facial hair as a gesture of support and solidarity for their leader Prince Viktor, who wears mustaches in defiance of the Court edict banning facial hair."

Alec rolled his eyes and bit back a retort about wondering if the Prince was old enough to grow pubic hair, least of all a set of mustaches. Thus dressing was accomplished in silence until Jeffries was buckling the straps of Alec's over-the-knee leather boots, and Alec said,

"I don't see my sword. I presume it's been confiscated along with my razors?"

"Yes, sir. One of General Müller's aides has it," Jeffries replied, helping Alec shrug into his seal-skin coat. He handed him his gloves. "Something about you publically presenting it to the Prince as a gesture of the defeat of the Margrave's armies...?"

Alec suppressed the desire to roll his eyes again, and explained while putting on his gloves,

"Offering up one's sword to the leader of an opposing force is indeed the usual grand gesture of capitulation. But as I am neither a commander of an opposing army, nor will it see Prince Ernst's troops surrender and Prince Viktor become Margrave, it is a hollow gesture at best. My guess is that Müller hopes such a theatrical display will serve to bolster confidence amongst Prince Viktor's men. Just as his callous treatment of Luytens and Horst Visser will serve to instill fear in the local people to refrain from looting, even in the bleakest of winters and circumstances, or face being shot—Sorry, did you know?"

"Yes, sir. No need to apologize. Müller's aide-de-camp made the announcement at supper last night after the absence of Herr Luytens and Horst Visser was remarked upon by the Reverend Shirley. Callous, if you ask me."

"He made this announcement with the ladies present?"

"Yes, sir. Sorry, sir. He did," Jeffries replied and instinctively winced when Alec swore under his breath.

"The Reverend's granddaughter, too?"

"Yes, sir. But the grandfather kept from her the exact nature of what had happened to the two men. That's what I overheard Mrs. Jamison-Lewis tell her lady-in-waiting when she asked if the girl understood what the soldier had said. I suspect the Reverend told her an untruth."

"I hope you are right."

"We were then suitably distracted by the comings and goings of the soldiers with our belongings. We were made to choose what to take with us; it had to fit in one portmanteau, which kept everyone occupied for most of the evening, and our minds off our situation."

Alec dared to smile. "No doubt Mrs. Jamison-Lewis railed against the General's high-handedness?"

Hadrian Jeffries looked up from pressing down on the lid of the leather trunk he had packed to bursting with as much of Alec's belongings as he could stuff inside.

"Yes, sir, she did."

"And he took his verbal punishment with good grace?"

"Yes, sir."

Alec came across to help his valet close the trunk.

"Good. That would have made her feel better. Our travelling companions need to be reassured, and if not that, then diverted from our present predicament." Alec let go of the trunk's lid, now the locks were secured, but he did not move away from his valet, saying quietly, "Hadrian, I won't lie to you. Given General Müller's barbaric treatment of Luytens and Visser, I have no idea what sort of reception we'll receive from Prince Viktor. But regardless of what happens to me, I will plead with the Prince for the freedom of the rest of my party. I cannot see him being unreasonable, not if he wants my help to storm Herzfeld Castle...

"I want you to look after Mrs. Jamison-Lewis and her lady's maid. *The Caroline* is due to dock at Herzfeld port, and I will request that you all be taken there, and given safe passage, even if it's just across the strait to Denmark. You'll at least be out of harm's way."

"What about you, sir? Surely, you'll be able to come with us?"

"My priority is to rescue Sir Cosmo and Miss St. Neots. I hope to do that when Prince Viktor invades the castle, with my help. So you see why I am asking you to look after Mrs. Jamison-Lewis and Mrs. Evans?"

"I won't fail you—or them, sir."

Alec stuck out his gloved hand, and when his valet gladly and firmly gripped it, he held the young man's hand a little longer.

"Thank you, Hadrian. I am indebted to you. I sincerely mean that."

Hadrian nodded, a little overcome and forced a smile. "I wouldn't have missed accompanying you for the world, my lord."

Alec stepped back as the cabin door opened and two soldiers entered.

"I hope to hear you say that again when we are safely far out to sea on our return voyage. But what I need you to do now," he continued in English, knowing the soldiers did not understand, and watching them take up his trunk and depart with it, "is to keep up

301

the pretense that we are not the least intimidated or anxious about the situation we now find ourselves in. I don't want the others in our party panicked or worried. We must make believe that everything is as it should be, and enjoy the sledge ride with all the enthusiasm as if we were off to a Thames ice fair. Do you think you can do that?"

"To be truthful, sir," Hadrian Jeffries confessed, following Alec up and out onto the deck, "I won't need to pretend. I've never been in a sledge so I'm looking forward to it."

They disembarked from the trekschuit and crossed the towpath, Alec wishing he shared his valet's excitement as he surveyed the activity for their departure by dawn's early light. But weighing on his mind was the fact that time was running out for Cosmo and Emily. He was now only two days' ride from the Castle, but in his present predicament he was no closer than had he remained in Emden.

BEYOND THE TOWPATH, IN AN ICE-COVERED FIELD, SOLDIERS patrolled in long coats and heavy boots, a watchful eye on the small group of passengers wrapped in fur coats and hats, chins buried deep in warm mufflers as they huddled together waiting to be directed into the sledges. Lined up side by side, each sledge was harnessed to two magnificent Frisian heavy horses. Standing around fifteen hands, with powerful quarters, a noble head and pitch black hair, the breed was indigenous to Midanich and, with the country's well-trained soldiers, a much prized export.

The wooden carriage of each sledge was affixed with two smooth polished running boards that allowed the sledge to glide effortlessly and quickly over icy terrain. The interior was large enough to carry two passengers and a small amount of personal luggage, a domed canopy of leather stretched over cane providing shelter from the harsh winds and sleet. But being open to the elements facing forward, each carriage had the luxury of a brass foot warmer and its occupants were provided with a bear skin rug to snuggle up under. There was no such protection for the driver who sat in front of them on a wooden seat.

One sledge had no such canopy. It was piled with the passengers' luggage, and the large wooden crate holding the mechanical gaming table. Soldiers were putting the last of the trunks aboard under supervision of an officer, and had a tarpaulin and ropes ready to secure the cargo for the journey. A number of other officers were already on horseback, General Müller amongst them.

Alec looked further afield, across the bleak, flat landscape to the township atop its man-made mound, its people and rebel soldiers safely behind its heavily-fortified walls. The cluster of red brick buildings were shrouded in morning fog, and thrusting through this low cloud, the spire of Aurich's church.

The church brought his thoughts back to Selina, and he looked for her, just as the order was given for the passengers to climb up into their assigned sledges. He caught sight of the Reverend Shirley with his granddaughter being directed to the third sledge, and was relieved Müller was not leaving them behind in Aurich. He wondered what had prompted the General to bring the vicar and the girl along on their journey, for surely their presence was more a hindrance than a help. Perhaps they were to be used as hostages, too? He saw Evans being assisted by a soldier into the second sledge, and Hadrian Jeffries was then escorted over to sit up beside her.

It was then he heard his name, turned and saw Selina waving a gloved hand from the first sledge. He waved back. She was already aboard and rugged up under the bear skin. He joined her under the sledge's domed roof, snuggling in beside her out of the cold, a soldier tucking them in securely, and putting up the foot rail, and with a nod to the driver the sledge was ready.

Alec was quick to search out Selina's gloved hand under the rug and hold fast, as if needing anchorage, as if he feared she would somehow be taken from him if he let her go. Looking into her delicately flushed face, and large dark eyes, he was momentarily overcome with emotion, and did not know what to say to her: About their predicament; about the execution of Herr Luytens and his brother-in-law; that he thanked God she was alive and well, and looked no worse for the ordeal after being caught up in the crossfire between rebels and soldiers loyal to the Margrave; because he loved her so very much and would not know how to go on without her. His blue eyes must have told her everything she needed to know of his thoughts, for she smiled in understanding and leaned in to first kiss his stubbled cheek, and then his mouth, before nestling in, head on his shoulder.

It was then that General Müller reined in alongside their sledge on a magnificent black Frisian steed that was well over fifteen hands, and whose mane of glossy black hair had been braided and set with ribbons. Here was a much-prized animal, and a proud rider.

"Enjoy the journey, Lord Halsey," Müller said, addressing Alec in German. "All going well, and we encounter no resistance along the way, there'll be a change of horses in two hours at Wittmund. And then there is another two hours of travel before we reach our destination. Plenty of time to admire the winter landscape, spend a last few private hours with your sweetheart, and contemplate the future, such as it is." He glanced at Selina, adding with a grin and a wink, before tipping his fur hat to her and swinging his mount away to give the order for the convoy to move out, "You see, I, too, am a romantic."

Alec did not believe him. His grip on Selina's hand tightened.

THE FIRST HALF OF THE JOURNEY BY SLEDGE WAS SPENT TRAVeling east, into a rising sun that was hidden behind low hanging gray clouds. The fog still clung low as they approached the village of Wittmund. The General was right in his calculations. Two hours of travel through a flat landscape of frozen marshes and abandoned peat bog farming lands, without encountering a single soul, living or dead. It was as if nothing and nobody inhabited this part of the world. But with the village in sight, there were a few isolated farmhouses close to the road on the outskirts of the township. Their inhabitants pulled back a curtain from a single window, or cracked open a door to the icy winds, to catch a glimpse of the travelling party, in particular the sledges pulled by magnificent black Frisian horses, and their wealthy occupants in fur hats and snuggled under bear skin rugs. But those same doors were instantly shut and bolted again when the convoy, protected front and rear by armed soldiers on horseback, sped past without a look right or left.

There was little to show for the civil war in this remote northeastern area of Midanich. Alec reasoned that perhaps there was nothing worth fighting for in such a desolate patch of marshland, with few inhabitants, and little to pilfer beyond the livestock kept indoors at this time of year. But as the horses slowed on approaching the town, it was apparent that Wittmund had not been spared from the conflict. A windmill on the edge of town had damaged sails, and there was evidence of a clash between opposing forces in the shattered and splintered wood of the shutters and the white-washed walls full of lead shot. Most telling of all were the fresh mounds of ice-covered earth. Unmarked graves. Alec countered at least twenty mounds as the sledges slowly glided into town. He wondered which brother's forces these simple farmers regarded as their enemy.

MÜLLER SENT A SCOUTING PARTY ON AHEAD, TO DISCOVER IF there were any hostile forces. But the place appeared deserted, its residents and their livestock locked and bolted behind closed doors, to keep out the winter, and a war abandoned until the spring thaws. The sledges were driven to an inn at the far end of the village, and here Müller and his men dismounted, the General and two of his aides-de-camp disappearing inside the inn, while the rest of his force protected the sledges.

An hour later, with the horses and the passengers of the sledges watered and rested, the convoy set off again. During their stop, the women were separated from the men and taken into the inn first, all under escort. They were able to use the facilities, such as they were, offered hot tea or beer, and then escorted back to their respective vehicles, with no opportunity or time for conversation. Given it was bitterly cold and the inn was little better than a hovel, this suited everyone. It even provided a moment of light relief, when Alec returned from the inn to find Selina nestled under the bear skin still wearing the same expression of utter disgust on her beautiful face that she had tried unsuccessfully to hide when she emerged from the inn.

"Don't tell me. Let me guess what you found most frightful back there," he said, climbing up beside her and throwing the heavy rug across his lap, and then tucking them both in. "Was it the all-pervasive odor of animal excrement mingled with the root vegetable stew, or was it the lack of adequate—um—amenities?"

"You mean their second-best bucket?"

"Second best?"

"Surely they keep their best for their animal feed?"

At that, Alec chuckled.

Selina smiled, liking his laugh. She pulled her gloved hand out from under the rug and showed him a small empty porcelain container shaped like a sauce boat, decorated with a floral pattern and fine gold leaf, before quickly returning it to its hiding spot under the seat beside her shargren covered *nécessaire de voyage*.

"I may hate travel," she grumbled, cheeks flushed, not so much from the cold, but from her impulsive action in showing him such a deeply personal item. "But I do know *how* to travel. Men's needs are so easily accommodated—*in every respect*."

Far from taking offence, Alec grinned, and kissed her temple.

"How true, my darling. But females are far more ingenious in overcoming obstacles."

"Not all obstacles," she replied cryptically, and sighed her relief when the horses set to and their journey continued, hoping she need not explain herself.

She had shown him her *bourdaloue* in the hopes of diverting him. She did not want to tell him that while the primitive conditions found inside the inn had startled and revolted her, and no doubt the pungent odors had increased her discomfort, the nausea she was experiencing was in truth morning sickness. She had had the same queasiness when she woke that morning, and that had had nothing to do with odors—vegetable, animal, or otherwise. Evans reaction was to be overjoyed, telling her that morning sickness was a good thing, that the baby was thriving, and in the next breath saying she couldn't wait for her to inform his lordship because then they would have to be married without delay—and that the Reverend Shirley, with the Bishop of London's authority, was qualified to perform the ceremony. Selina was too ill to argue, other than to say Evans's dearest wish would no doubt be granted.

But glancing at Alec's handsome profile, as the village of Wittmund was left behind and the convoy began the journey south— the sun appearing from behind the clouds told her so—she decided he had enough to worry him without her condition adding to his burden. Regardless of how happy she knew her news would make him, she could not be so selfish. They were in a hostile country, one where men were dying for their convictions; one young soldier before her very eyes. And while she had done her best to block that harrowing image from her mind, it had still left her shaken. As had the violent deaths of Luytens and his brother-in-law. But most of all, she thought of Cosmo and Emily, still held prisoner in a castle which also harbored the mad sister of its ruler. Yes, her happy news could wait—for now. Particularly as they had no idea what fate awaited them all at their final destination.

So she snuggled in to Alec, smiling when he put his arm around her and drew her closer to make her more comfortable. She watched contentedly as the bleak countryside was left behind, the landscape transforming from endless plains of frozen fields without a house or tree in sight, to one where winter trees lined either side of the road, their black leafless branches covered in snow reaching out to one another across the narrow divide. There were hamlets of tidy red-bricked houses, large windmills by frozen canals, snowy fallow fields, all quaint and picturesque and with none of the damage that comes with war. It was as if war had never touched a clod of earth in this part of Midanich.

No one was more surprised than Selina when she woke late afternoon, with the convoy slowly moving across a bridge spanning a wide canal. On the other side of this bridge was an ornate gatehouse with double gates of black-and-gold painted ironwork thrown open for the visitors. Two soldiers, muskets over a shoulder, stood to attention in front of a sentry box on either side of the gates. They saluted General Müller as he passed through as the head of the convoy.

When Selina stirred and sat up, Alec removed his arm that had been holding her against him, and sat up too. Both took in the scenery of dense forest lining the canal as their sledge glided across the bridge. Looking past their driver to see what was up ahead proved more difficult, but soon the horses turned left into a quadrangle, bordered on two sides by a collection of long, low-set, two-story buildings of red brick, and at the far end, a large complex of stables. Beyond the stables were more buildings, set against the backdrop of dense forest, and appeared to be the officers' barracks, which faced an encampment of many canvas tents occupied by the regular foot soldiers. There was also the usual weapon stockpile of cannons and cannon balls associated with a large military force. Soldiers were busily engaged in all manner of activities, and to Alec looked to be readying themselves to go into battle, and soon.

And while Alec was occupied observing the military encampment, Selina's attention was focused in the opposite direction, across a second bridge and another set of ornate double gates, but these were closed and guarded.

The bridge crossed a moat which widened out into a small lake which surrounded its island castle.

This ornately decorated island castle was what Selina supposed a castle in a folktale would resemble. But it was not its size, for the building itself, with windows that ran all the way down to the water line, was no larger than any substantial red brick Queen Anne manor house back in England. It was its various components, mostly seen on the Continent, that set it apart from the English castles and houses: The very steep pitch to the mansard roof of slate, covered in a light dusting of snow; the large circular turret with its four levels of windows; and at its apex a bell-shaped slate roof with gilded motifs that had set into it a large ornate clock, that no doubt chimed the hours. Off to one side of this decorative turret was the main entrance, which had double doors framed by a carved entrance over-mantle of marble which looked to be something plucked from a Greek temple. The marble pediment was fashioned with classical figures, and atop it sat two gargoyles leering down at those who came to the front door. Most of all, this fanciful castle looked to be floating on the partly-frozen lake, for the red brickwork disappeared below the water line.

It was so quaint, so enchanting and inviting, that for several moments it was not only Selina but the rest of the sledge passengers who stared unblinking at the whimsical *schloss* and forgot their sorry predicament. That is, until a company of soldiers under command of their captain was marched up from the encampment to attend to the officers and their mounts, uncouple the sledge harnesses, unload luggage, assist the passengers to firm ground, and to take orders from General Müller.

The General dismounted, and after handing over the reins and giving orders to his subordinate, went over to Alec, who was helping Selina alight from the sledge.

He made the couple a short formal bow. "Welcome to *Schloss* Rosine—"

"Rosine?" Alec turned a frown on the General. "This is the Countess Rosine's home?"

Müller watched Alec carefully, a glance at Selina. "Yes, Lord Halsey. It is. Her ancestral home, and the boyhood home of Prince Viktor, and the home of—my wife."

Alec's frown deepened, finding the General's sentence ambiguous. He could not help asking, "Your wife?" Adding, because he didn't want to appear rude or completely dim-witted, "Then we are only about an hour's ride from Castle Herzfeld?"

"Correct."

"Why did we not travel due east from Aurich, rather than head north to Wittmund before turning south? Surely the road as well as the route is more direct that way?"

Müller was impressed with Alec's knowledge of his country's geography. "It is. But the largest force of Prince Ernst's troops are occupying Friedeburg, believing His Highness and the rebel force are garrisoned at the palace until the winter thaw, which they are not. They are here."

"Here? Prince Viktor and the majority of his troops are here, at *Schloss* Rosine?" Alec was surprised. But observing the number of soldiers and their preparations at the encampment beyond the stables, he knew General Müller was telling the truth.

"Yes. And with your help, we will take the castle and end this war before the winter truly sets in. Now you must both excuse me," he said in German before turning to Selina with a bow and addressing her in fluent French.

"*Bienvenue au Château de Rosine, Mme Jamison-Lewis.* I hope you were able to have a pleasant journey. At least by sledge it was uneventful. This collection of buildings you see behind us is not only the unofficial headquarters of the army, but of Prince Viktor's court. As such, there are comfortable quarters for the various court officials, foreign dignitaries, and nobles and their families loyal to our cause. Thus I am certain you will find the accommodation acceptable, and the company congenial. Most of the nobles do speak French. And I hope that while you are with us, you will think of yourself as an honored guest of His Highness Prince Viktor, and of my wife, his mother, the Comtesse Rosine. Please excuse me if I now leave you in some haste. I have not seen my wife or stepson in months."

Alec and Selina silently watched the General make his bow, turn and stride off toward the castle, and such was their shock to discover this soldier was none other than the husband of Alec's former lover of all those years ago, the Countess Rosine, morganatic wife and widow of Margrave Leopold, that were a feather to hand and they poked with it, the couple would have been knocked off their feet.

And that was the least surprising revelation awaiting them within the *Schloss* Rosine.

# Twenty-one

MID-MORNING THE FOLLOWING DAY, A CARRIAGE TOOK Alec and Selina the short distance to the castle, even though it was a few minutes' walk across the bridge. Another carriage followed, sent to take up their personal servants, what luggage they had been permitted to bring with them from Aurich, and the specially-crated mechanical gaming table.

Passing two sentries at the main entrance, and ushered inside by a court official in livery, they were met in the sparse entrance vestibule by an earnest young nobleman of middling height with a wide jaw and a mustache so luxuriantly bushy Selina could not help staring at his hairy upper lip, expecting it to spring to life and scurry away. She was so awe-struck she was deaf to his welcoming speech, first made in French for her benefit. He told the couple that on the orders of the Countess Rosine, they had been assigned an apartment within the chateau, adding as a confidential aside that this had taken some administrative juggling because the castle's accommodations were full to overflowing now that the Rebel Court had taken up residence.

Hadrian Jeffries, Janet Evans, and the luggage were then sent off with a hovering liveried servant, and the Court Chamberlain turned on a polished heel and asked Alec and Selina to follow him. The

Court and the Countess were awaiting them in the Mars Reception Gallery on the first floor.

Selina heard only one word in five, such was her preoccupation with the young nobleman's mustache, and she quickly unfurled her fan and fluttered it close to her face to hide a spreading smile. The bushy mustache provided some light relief after the traumatic events of the previous few days. That is, until she latched on to the Court Chamberlain's announcement they were about to be presented to a room full of courtiers, chief among these the Countess Rosine.

The prospect of coming face-to-face with Alec's lover from his days at Friedeburg Palace set her heart racing. She had never met one of his lovers, nor wanted to. While married to George Jamison-Lewis she had heard whisperings of Alec's exploits abroad, for he was quite notorious. But what happened at Continental courts was a world away from English Society and her world. Never in her wildest imaginings had she conjured up this scenario: Here she was on the Continent, at a foreign court, and about to make her curtsey to her betrothed's ex-lover. She did not know whether to weep or laugh, and thus she chose the latter.

"Do you think all the men at this court are wearing a stoat under their noses?" she teasingly asked Alec, picking up a handful of her velvet and silk quilted petticoats, as soon as the Court Chamberlain turned on a heel and had the couple follow him up the flight of stairs.

"Regrettably, yes!" was Alec's clipped response, keeping his gaze on the earnest young nobleman's back.

"Are you now growing one, too?" she taunted, though she knew well enough he'd again been refused his razors, and thus his valet had not been able to shave him. His cheeks and chin were decidedly unshaven and had the beginnings of a beard. She supposed if she'd been refused her tortoiseshell hair brushes and Evans' assistance to arrange her curls, she'd be ill-tempered, too. But she also knew he, like she, must be apprehensive at this audience with the Countess

Rosine. Good, she thought. So he should be. So she goaded him further. "I would like to kiss a man with a mustache, just once. To see what it feels like. I'm sure it must tickle, and I will squirm and giggle. Will you oblige me?"

"No! But any number of young men here would be only too willing!"

When there was a long silence, Alec halted on the top step, turned and stared down at her, barely aware of his trite response to her playful banter. His thoughts had been preoccupied with wondering how they would be received, not only by Prince Viktor, but more importantly by the Countess Rosine. When, on the trekschuit, he had confessed his sordid past to Selina, she had declared that if not for his affair with Prince Viktor's mother, the civil war may never have happened; there was more than a grain of truth in that, and it niggled. So, did the Countess blame him for what had happened to her and her son in the aftermath of their affair? Was she out for revenge, as was Prince Ernst? Would mother and son help or hinder his quest to rescue Cosmo and Emily? But most of all he wanted to protect Selina from any unpleasantness which might arise from this reunion and, frustratingly, knew he could not. Hence his uncharacteristic irritability.

His unblinking stare made Selina say with a sigh of regret, "Ah, my love, I wish you'd said yes..."

Alec saw the playful light in her dark eyes fade, as did her smile, when she dropped her gaze to the closed sticks of her fan, and knew his unfeeling remark had wounded her. So instead of following the Court Chamberlain across the passageway to a set of double doors where two soldiers in immaculate ceremonial uniforms stood as sentries, he pulled her into an alcove, and into his arms.

"Forgive me," he said, kissing her forehead. "My apprehension is unwarranted. I know that whatever happens in that room, we will always have each other. No one and nothing means more to me than you. It has always been thus since your eighteenth birthday. You must know that, surely?"

She nodded and smiled up at him. "And what happened in your past, will remain there, if you let it. It is how you conduct your life today, and in the future that matters to me—should matter *to us*. So if we enter that room with that in mind, I know you will be able to deal with and overcome whatever these people demand of you... Agreed?"

He kissed her gently on the mouth. "Agreed..." Then stepped back and playfully pinched her chin with a smile. "But I draw the line at growing a mustache. That I won't agree to!" He took hold of her gloved hand, and as he led her out of the alcove he gave it a little squeeze. "My nose is long enough without drawing further attention to it!"

"Oh, but I like your boney nose very much," she responded and laughed when he huffed.

But her smile was instantly swallowed up looking past him to the double doors, which had been thrown open. Bright light, the low hum of conversation and warmth, beckoned.

ENTERING THE MARS RECEPTION GALLERY, THEY WERE instantly enveloped in a curtain of warm air. A large blue-and-white ceramic tiled heater in a far corner was responsible for the summer's day temperature, and explained why those in attendance were able to wear their best silk gowns and spangled frock coats without the need for heavy velvets, furs, cloaks and muffs. The four chandeliers, and the floor-to-ceiling mirrors along one wall which reflected the candlelight and the light from the windows opposite helped to banish winter from this audience chamber.

There were at least a hundred people in attendance. All were positioned at the French windows with their view out across the partially-frozen lake to the military encampment, observing the soldiers of Prince Viktor's rebel army being drilled on a parade ground that was covered in the crunch and crackle of thick frost.

At first glance, these courtiers were no different to those ladies and gentlemen Alec had seen time and again at the various courts across Europe. Always dressed to impress in their best silks, pomaded wigs, heeled shoes, and enveloped in a heady scent, flirtation and intrigue occupied their day. There was lots of teasing, laughing, and witty observations made, about the weather, a matron's outfit here, a gentleman's paunch over there, and the boredom of being at court, when it was anything but tedious. And always with an undercurrent of cynicism, and need—of wanting to be noticed, and greed—of expecting to benefit from the effort. Such was court life.

But while the courtiers who came away from the windows in groups appeared like those at any European court—the ladies fluttering fans across their square-cut necklines; the gentlemen showing a fine leg encased in a white silk stocking, snuffbox in hand—they were decidedly different in temperament. There was no sly looks or puckering of mouths as their eyes swept over the new arrivals. Their gazes were steady, their talk low and serious in tone. And Alec supposed that perhaps this was to be expected, given war was on their doorstep and not hundreds of miles away.

In a piece of well-rehearsed theater, the courtiers silently took up their positions either side of a dais which had upon it a single over-large chair—a throne. With its padded cushions of blue velvet trimmed in gold braid, and a high wooden back that reached almost to the ornate ceiling and was carved and painted with the coat of arms of the House of Herzfeld, its purpose here was clear.

Only the Margrave of Midanich was permitted to sit on this ceremonial representation of his power, and this throne had been wrenched up out of the glittering audience chamber at Friedeburg Palace. Here at the *Schloss* Rosine it was a potent symbol of support for an alternative Margrave, recognized by the assembled nobles, the hundreds of troops marching up and down the parade ground outside, and, Alec guessed, by thousands of their countrymen out in the towns and hamlets across the country, as one Prince Viktor Fredrick Leopold Rosine Herzfeld.

And just as Alec and Selina were wondering where the occupant of this elaborate throne could be, out from behind the crowd stepped a woman in black velvet and white silk, with luxuriant dark hair and bright eyes. She was not in the first flush of youth, but she was beautiful, and glowed with vitality. Facing them, her wide panniers disguised her condition. It was only when she placed a hand on her rounded belly under her breasts that it became obvious. The Countess Rosine, widow of Margrave Leopold, and now wife of General Müller, was heavily pregnant.

The Countess walked a little way up the center of the room and stopped and waited for Selina and Alec to come to her. It did not take a court usher to announce her presence, or the crowd parting, the ladies curtseying and the gentlemen bowing as one, for Selina to know who she was. It was her smile and the light in her eyes when she looked upon Alec that told her here was his ex-lover, and, contrary to her fears and his, she was very pleased to see him.

Alec bowed and Selina curtseyed, and when the Countess Rosine put out a plump hand for Alec to take, he kissed her fingers. He then stepped away, but not before Selina caught the private smile exchanged between the pair. The years peeled back for the couple, and for one moment it was as if the Countess and the English diplomat were again the young lovers in the grotto. The moment came and went in a blink, but the smile lingered. It was a smile that recognized a past shared, and yet there was no animosity and no regret, only one of lasting affection. It fascinated Selina. But what surprised her more was that she was not jealous of this woman. Her overwhelming feeling was one of relief, that with this smile she knew the Countess still cared for Alec, and thus she would never do him any harm. Everything would be all right. They would be protected here at *Schloss* Rosine, if for no other reason than the Countess cherished the past she had shared with Alec.

So when the Countess orchestrated time alone to talk with him, Selina accepted the ruse and went off on the arm of one of the courtiers, to sip mulled wine and to look at the portraits of Rosine ancestors gracing the walls between the full-length mirrors.

The Countess Rosine spoke over her shoulder and immediately liveried servants appeared with trays of refreshment for the assembled courtiers. She waved away the tray, gaze never leaving Alec, though she did take a moment to look at Selina as she strolled off with the Court Chamberlain.

She had seen from first glance the Englishwoman was very pretty, her hair an enviable mass of vibrant light copper curls that would do as they pleased no matter how many pins were applied. She saw, too, that she was young, possibly a decade younger than her ex-lover, thus much younger than she, and around the same age as her son. With a twinge of envy, she returned her gaze to Alec, rested a hand on her belly, and offered him her arm. They would take a stroll up the gallery, so they could be alone and not overheard.

At the far end of the room by a window, the Countess turned her back on the view and faced Alec. They spoke in German, her native language.

"At the risk of sounding trite, a great deal has happened in the ten years since we last saw each other."

Alec smiled.

"Not trite, Your Highness. But an understatement."

"Call me Helena."

Alec lost his smile. "That would not be—*politic*, would it—Helena?"

She laughed behind her fan. "No, it would not!" She lowered her fan and lifted her lashes to look into his eyes. "But there was a time when politics was the last matter on your mind…"

He lifted an eyebrow. "That was hardly my fault."

"I cannot believe you have returned. So many times did I think of writing to you—but... What to say? How to explain..." She shrugged, smiled and sighed without knowing it. "Men age beautifully. Well, some men do. You have. But you always were the handsomest of men, even when you were much younger and so-so—virile. I dare say that about you has not changed." When he blushed crimson she laughed harder. "Ah! Yes! That I did forget. You English are so self-effacing. It is delightful!"

Alec rubbed the stubble on his cheek and muttered through his embarrassment, "I don't feel particularly *delightful*. The journey and the reason I am here have taken their toll."

"Yes. I imagine they have," the Countess said seriously, all humor extinguished. "Our country has been in and out of a war since before you escaped to England. And this war, the war which will end all wars, has been particularly brutal. But before I speak of that, before my son, and my husband, return at any moment from reviewing our troops, I wanted these few minutes with you alone to apologize for what I put you through—"

"Apologize? To-to *me*? What you put me through?" Alec repeated, incredulous. "Your Highness—Helena—you have nothing to apologize for, surely?"

"Yes. I do. If not for me you would not have been thrown in Herzfeld's dungeon and been forced to endure—*Verdammt*! I promised myself I would not be teary, and here I am weeping within seconds of my confessional. It must be this wretched pregnancy."

Alec caught up her hand and kissed it swiftly, and said with a sad smile. "If anyone is to apologize I must. And now I'm the one being trite. If not for my lust-fueled recklessness you and your son would not have been banished and—"

"That is simply not true. No! It is true, but it was not your recklessness that got us banished," the Countess confessed. She sniffed back her tears. An indulgent gleam came into her eye and she smiled crookedly. She fluttered her fan. "It was *my* recklessness. And that was intentional. Oh, I very much wanted you as my lover, from my first sighting of you. Leopold knew this, and he indulged me as he always did. But this time it was different, because you were different. For the first time when taking a lover I allowed my feelings to get the better of me. Now *that*, Leopold did not like at all. He was an *understanding* older husband, but he could also be a jealous one. But because he wanted our son, and me, to be safe, and he knew my plan would work, he let our affair continue."

"Plan?"

"Yes, plan. My plan to have myself and my son banished from court."

"You *wanted* to be banished?"

It was news to Alec and his surprise ripened the color under her cosmetics. She had hoped that after all these years he might have figured it out for himself and she would not need to explain her calculated subterfuge, but she had not counted on—or perhaps she had just forgotten over the years—that this man lived by a code of honor and expected his friends to do likewise. It seemed it had never entered his thoughts that he had been duped by her and the Margrave Leopold. He had taken their passionate affair at face value: A couple so in lust with each other that satisfying their physical appetites was paramount to everything and everyone else in their lives. There was a grain of truth in that, of course, but he would never have betrayed her. There was no ulterior motive in his actions, just pure lust and enjoyment, and for her that had been a powerful aphrodisiac, and she had been flattered. But aside from enjoying him carnally, she had other reasons for engaging him in a very public affair which became a court scandal, and so she told him.

"Yes. I wanted to be banished. More importantly, I wanted Viktor to be sent away with me. I knew that if I did not get my son away from court, away from Ernst, he would be in great danger. Leopold knew this also. But I could not simply leave court and come here to live with our little boy. That would only make Ernst suspicious, and he would think I was plotting against him. Leopold and I had to make him believe he was the one who had instigated our banishment, and with Leopold's blessing. He had to be convinced his father was furious with me, that he no longer cared, and that he was intent on punishing me through our son."

"And so you used Ernst's friendship—or put more correctly, his obsession—with me, as the catalyst for your banishment?"

"Yes," she confessed guiltily.

"Well that at least answers the question and tempers my hubris, as to why you singled me out, when you could easily have had the pick of any man at court," Alec stated with a huff of annoyance at such duplicity, to think he'd been a pawn in the high-stakes game between the Countess and Leopold on the one side, and Ernst on the other. But he could not be angry for long. He smiled down at her, and bowed. "I am all admiration for your ingenuity."

"Do not think for a moment any man would do. I very much wanted you for my lover, make no mistake. From the first moment I saw you in the corridors of Friedeburg. You were so-so—"

"—gullible?"

"—manly, and young."

"Yes. Which made me gullible, Your Highness. No matter. I don't regret our affair, just the outcome, particularly for myself. Though now that I know our discovery in the grotto was precisely as you had planned it, and you achieved your objective in having yourself and your son banished here, I can finally absolve myself of a decade of guilt."

The Countess looked stricken. "You have been feeling guilty for that long? No!"

"No. Just the occasional twinge now and again. Perhaps, if I'd known I was your lusty pawn, I'd have been more circumspect and not felt the need to purge my soul as easily as I did."

She saw him glance down the room and fix momentarily on Selina who with the Court Chamberlain stood before a portrait of Ivan, General Count Rosine, the Countess's grandfather. A number of nobles fluent in French had joined them in conversation.

The Countess itched to ask him about his titian-haired beauty, but first she needed to make him understand why she had shamelessly used him, and then done nothing to save him from Ernst and torture in the Herzfeld Castle. If she was truthful with herself, it was she who had a decade of guilt weighing on her shoulders, which she now wished to unfetter with a confession.

"You and I know of what Ernst is capable. I could not afford to take the chance that upon Leopold's death he would turn on my son, seeing him as a rival for his throne."

"But isn't that precisely what has happened?" Alec quipped.

"It was a self-fulfilling prophecy, and you know it!" the Countess retorted.

Alec bowed his head. "Forgive me. Yes, I do know that. And I do not blame you for wanting to spirit Viktor away. He was much better off growing up here, away from the Court: Out of sight, and thus out of mind, to Ernst."

The Countess nodded, relieved he understood. Unconsciously, she rubbed her belly with a soothing hand when she felt the baby move. "Yes. He was able to have a childhood, and be tutored and groomed for the position he would one day inherit."

"Inherit?" Alec was surprised. "I thought Viktor excluded from the succession because of his birth?"

"He was, and it would have stayed that way but for two reasons. I will tell you the second reason first. In the last years of his life, Leopold had a change of heart and mind," explained the Countess. "You will understand immediately when you see my son. He is the image of his father, and grandfather. A true Herzfeld. For Leopold that was a strong incentive to recognize Viktor in the succession."

"What ruler would not want a son in his image to succeed him?" Alec stated. "Particularly a man with Leopold's arrogance and bearing. He must have thanked God daily, and you, for providing him with at least one son who not only looked like him, but who was in full possession of his faculties!"

"Yes. I see that you do understand," the Countess replied with relief, oblivious to the hint of irony in his tone. "But for the longest time Leopold did not want to admit that his children by his first wife were not sane, that they were in fact as mad as their mother. Leopold had married the princess and impregnated her before it became obvious she was insane. It helped that she also suffered from a condition which meant she lacked body hair, because that *unspoken truth* became the reason used why she kept to her rooms. So when Joanna began to exhibit the same symptoms as her mother, Leopold used the *unspoken truth* as an excuse to lock her away, too. At first, as you know, Ernst's bouts of insanity always occurred at Herzfeld, when he was with Joanna. But after the-the *hell* you were put through at the castle, these are not revelations to you, are they?"

"No, they are not," Alec stated quietly. He had no wish to relive those moments, nor did he want to discuss them with her, so he asked, "Leopold died at Herzfeld, and not at Friedeburg?"

"Leopold went to Herzfeld to review the troops, and to present Ernst with the Midanich Minotaur, the country's highest military honor. I went with him. He had not been in the best of health for several months, but he was determined to confront Ernst. He had been receiving reports, secret reports, from within the castle that Ernst was relying more and more on Joanna to tell him what to do. But the situation was far worse than we thought possible. Seeing his son in that state... Leopold's health deteriorated further..."

The Countess gave a little shiver at the memory. "In retrospect it was an idiotic thing to do. Leopold walked into a trap. He, a follower of the teachings of Machiavelli, had not counted on factions within the court with their own political agendas. They wanted Ernst to succeed because he could be manipulated to their will, whereas Viktor was an unknown quantity. And there are those within Leopold's own council who would not hear of a commoner—Viktor—succeeding to the Margravate, regardless of Ernst's instability of mind." She met Alec's gaze. "We suspect that Leopold did not meet a natural end. That he was—that he was first poisoned and then, near the end, *smothered*."

"Good Lord! Murdered?" When the Countess nodded Alec frowned. "I'm sorry. I had no idea."

"Not many do. It would not serve our purpose to make that fact known. It would be seen as a lame attempt by Viktor to discredit Ernst. Ernst is Margrave for the present. To the conservative majority, to the clergy, and to the soldiers of his personal bodyguard, he is Margrave because his succession was ordained by God. Even when Viktor wins this war, which he will, if we want a continuing peace, he must still win over Ernst's supporters. To do that, Ernst must fall on his own sword. That is where you are instrumental."

"Me?" Alec was startled. "What can I possibly offer—"

"Why do you think Ernst has your friend locked up? Why does he demand you plead for his release in person?" She squeezed Alec's forearm through the velvet sleeve of his frock coat and opened wide her eyes. "Because *she* wants to see you. He does what *she* wants. And *she* wants you; she has always wanted *you*. You are the only one who can separate Ernst from Joanna, who can lure her out of the shadows, and when you do... No one wants a Margrave who is insane, no matter how loyal they were in the past. General Müller believes this is our chance; so does my son."

Alec was not only startled by this, he was incredulous. It made him sound harsh and disbelieving.

"They both know the truth about Joanna? You told them what I confided in you? And they *believe* you?

"Of course. If one can accept that Leopold's children by his first wife have madness in their veins then it is not difficult to believe the rest, is it? And that is why we—the three of us—believe you will succeed, where others have failed, and died for their efforts. By our reckoning, just seeing you returned to her, for that is what she will think, will be enough for Joanna to throw caution to the four winds. The only man you need to convince is Captain Westover, captain of the Margrave's personal bodyguard. He may already suspect, but like others before him, like General Müller, he may be unable to reconcile what he is witness to, and what his reason tells him cannot be the truth, though it is! Thus Joanna must manifest before Westover's eyes."

"I think I preferred the role of lusty pawn to sacrificial pawn!" Alec retorted, though he did not argue against the plan. After all, he had every intention of fronting up to the castle, and confronting Ernst, to have his friends released. If in the process, he managed to lure Joanna from her shadowy world, and expose Ernst for what he truly was, then he would oblige Viktor and his General. "But I will only do as you ask, if your son assures me my friends will be rescued and unharmed."

The Countess kissed his cheek impulsively, overjoyed. "Thank you. I told Henrik you would not fail us. I do not blame him for his initial skepticism, but now that he has met you and spent time in your company he is willing to concede that I was right to put my trust in you all along."

Alec knew to whom she was referring, but asked anyway, hoping she would confide in him about her marriage. "Henrik?"

"My husband. General Müller. He knows all about us. I thought it only fair to tell him."

Alec's brows contracted over his long nose. "Only fair? When did you tell him?"

The Countess shrugged and said matter-of-factly, "He has known about you since I first tumbled into bed with him five years ago. But we were only married two months ago." She put a hand to her round belly. "I could not hide this baby for much longer, and so I had to dispense with the required period of mourning for Leopold." She smiled up at Alec. "I am a reformed woman since meeting my stern Henrik. He warned me that he would not tolerate unfaithfulness, and if I dared look at another man he would put me over his knee and spank me! Imagine! Never mind what he would do to my lover. How could I not fall in love with such a man?" She moved closer, and pressed her open fan to Alec's chest, confiding, "But of course I could not let him be complacent. So I promised to be good, except if you ever walked back into my life. Yes! I did. But I never dreamed in a hundred dreams you would return here. That wounded him a little—"

"*Wounded him?*" Alec huffed. "I am all sympathy for your General. That was most cruel of you, Helena. The wonder to me is, he did not put me up against a wall and have me shot the first time we met."

"That is because he is like you. He has scruples and morals, and will not act without good reason to do so. You have nothing to worry about. He tells me he likes you."

"I'm glad to hear it. I like him, too, despite not being enamored of how he dispenses justice, even if there is a war on."

"He is a soldier. He does what has to be done. He is also fiercely loyal to my son, and believes he is the future for our country. Which makes me love him all the more. Ah! And here they are now!" she announced with a smile, turning as the double doors opened and the usher stepped forth to announce His Highness the Prince Viktor, and the most noble General Baron Müller. "Come!" the Countess commanded of Alec, putting her arm through his. "Let me introduce you to the other wonderful men in my life."

THE PRINCE WAS A TALL, LEAN YOUNG MAN WITH SANDY-RED shoulder-length hair and a matching mustache. He had bright blue eyes, and his mother's fine cheekbones. But in every other respect he was the image of what Alec supposed his father Leopold must have looked like when a handsome young man of two-and-twenty. The resemblance was marked enough for Alec to show surprise, and the Countess Rosine to press his arm in acknowledgment.

Dressed in a military uniform of blue and gold, with orders pinned to his left breast and a sash of crimson across his right shoulder, from which dangled a military cross at his hip, the Prince strode into the assembly chamber and immediately searched out his mother. With his chin up, and a gloved hand on the ornate hilt of his sword, there was an aura of command about him, of knowing his place at the apex of his society and everyone else knowing it too. He expected absolute loyalty and received it. And yet, there was an easy-going energy about his person, and such a passion for life, that everyone who came within his orbit was infected with the same enthusiasm. And this was why the men and women in the room surged forward and surrounded their chosen ruler, with applause and smiles.

Alec had last seen Prince Viktor when he was a thin-shouldered boy of eleven. He remembered their last day together vividly, because they had been sailing the boy's model ship in one of the many ornamental lakes in the gardens at Friedeburg palace. Stripped to their shirt sleeves, they had removed their shoes and stockings, rolled their silk breeches up over their knees, and were wading in water that lapped at the boy's hips. The Countess had been most annoyed and sat with her ladies-in-waiting around her on the grassy bank, pouting and telling Alec he and her son would surely suffer a misadventure, at the very least contract a fever from such foolishness. Alec and the young prince had ignored her. It was a hot sunny day, and Alec knew by the boy's grin he was happy and grateful for any excuse to be out of his restrictive court frock coat. Alec was unsure how it started, but soon he and Viktor were splashing each other, ignoring the Countess as she stamped her foot at their tomfoolery, until they were soaked through to the skin, the model sailing ship forgotten.

And now here was the boy grown into a tall young man who had started a civil war and who would, everything going according to plan, and with God's blessing, soon be the ruler of his country. He was now tall enough to look Alec in the eye, and did so when Alec straightened from a formal bow. What he did next surprised Alec into speechlessness, the first time in a very long while he was lost for words. But it sent the courtiers, who now formed a ring around Prince Victor, General Müller, the Countess, and Alec, into a frenzy of applause.

Prince Viktor stepped forward and embraced Alec as one does a long-lost favored uncle, then held his hand in a firm clasp, eyes wet and bright.

"It is very good to see you again, Herr Baron. I wish it were in better circumstances, but perhaps if my country were at peace, I would not have had this opportunity at all to thank you—"

"Your-Your Highness, I-I need no—"

"Please. Allow me to thank you. You did my mother and me a great service all those years ago." Viktor smiled at the Countess. "I had the most wonderful childhood growing up here, and she tells me that was in no small part due to your sacrifices on our behalf. So, please, you will accept with good grace my thanks, and allow me to formally endorse the honor that was bestowed upon you by my father. General Müller has told me what you did for our citizens in Emden, and for that alone I would again make you Baron Aurich." He looked at Alec's hand and frowned. "But you do not wear the ring? You still have it I trust?"

"Yes, Your Highness," Alec replied and dug deep in a frock coat pocket and handed the Prince the little velvet box. "Ready to return to its rightful owner."

"You, Herr Baron, are its rightful owner," Viktor stated, and removed the intaglio from its box and slipped it back on the ring finger of Alec's right hand. "Here is where it belongs, for your lifetime." He pressed Alec's hand before letting it go and stepping back with a small bow and a smile. He then turned and surveyed the circle of courtiers and announced Alec's title, the expectation in his tone and look that they make their bow and curtsey to the Baron Aurich, which they duly did. Satisfied, he then made an announcement to the assembled company which not only drew another round of applause but was punctuated with gasps of excitement mixed with trepidation, "The day after tomorrow I ride with General Müller, Baron Aurich, and our troops for Herzfeld. We will take the castle and end this war so that our people can finally live in peace. No more will we bow down to tyrants and foreign powers. Midanich will reclaim its rightful place within the Holy Roman Empire."

He put up a hand, in acknowledgment of the applause, and to have the courtiers be quiet and listen. And when he had their full attention he motioned for Alec to step forward, then spoke over a shoulder to General Müller, who replied at the Prince's ear, gaze directed at Selina who was in the circle beside the Court Chamberlain. The Prince immediately stepped over to Selina and with a bow offered her his crooked arm. He then brought her to stand beside Alec, the couple exchanging the merest of glances, both self-conscious to be the center of such attention.

"Today we will not think of the war! Today is for celebration," the Prince continued. "Today my good friend the Baron Aurich is to be married, and we shall have a feast and dance and make merry into the night!"

When the courtiers erupted into loud applause, Selina looked at Alec enquiringly, for she had not understood a word. The Prince had spoken in German.

Alec leaned in to speak to her, to be heard over the din

"This is to be the last day for the rest of our lives you will ever be addressed as Mrs. Jamison-Lewis."

Selina blinked up at Alec's grinning countenance, unsure of his meaning, so he told her, and she gasped, and smiled, and said with a note of wonder,

"We are to be married—*here*?"

He nodded and put out his hand to her. She took it, tears glistening on her lashes.

"My only regret," he continued, kissing her hand, which elicited more applause, "is that our family—my uncle, your aunt, Cosmo, and Emily—are not here to share the day with us."

Selina nodded her agreement just as the Prince turned away from his mother and General Müller, to address her and Alec in French.

"General Müller informs me you have brought me a gift from your King George of England. With your permission I will unveil it at your wedding breakfast, for I am told it will provide entertainment for the entire court. I, too, have a gift for you both. But this gift cannot wait until your wedding." He smiled and lifted his brows with a conspiratorial twinkle. "I am certain you, in particular, Madame Jamison-Lewis, will appreciate its comfort and support before and during the ceremony. And my mother says it is most cruel of me to deny you both. And so let us not wait a moment longer!"

He made a gesture to his Court Chamberlain who in turn made motions to two liveried footmen, who stepped up to the ring of courtiers and broke the line, ushering ladies and gentlemen left and right, to make way for the Court Chamberlain who came into the center of the ring to make an announcement. Selina and Alec looked at one another and then with expectation as the double doors to the audience chamber were thrown open. Given no indication of what their wedding gift might be, they were open to all sorts of possibilities, except one.

The gift was not an object or an animal, but a person. It was Emily.

She had never looked lovelier or happier and was smiling from ear to ear. After a curtsey to the room, and then to Prince Viktor and the Countess Rosine, she swept up to Selina and Alec in a froth of printed cotton and quilted petticoats and threw her arms around Selina.

"Oh! I'm so happy you've finally come!" she announced, a look over at Alec, who was staring at her as if she were an apparition. "I've missed you both dreadfully. Isn't this the most magical place?"

Such was Selina's shock her knees buckled, she slid out of Emily's embrace, and crumpled to the floor in a dead faint.

# Twenty-two

**T**WO HOURS HAD PASSED SINCE SELINA'S EMBARRASSING faint before the entire rebel court at the shock of seeing Emily. Alec had caught her before she hit the parquetry, and she had woken in his arms, assuring him she was well, but wondering if Emily was a specter. And there was her fair-haired cousin, down beside her on the floor and holding her hand. So many questions rushed up into her throat, and she saw that Alec was just as shocked and confused, and brim full of questions. But they were surrounded by courtiers, and she was not permitted to move until the court physician gave her permission to do so.

She was then helped into a sedan chair and two burly chairmen took her up and carried her to rooms within the turret, Emily following along beside the chairmen.

Alec was not permitted to go with her. Bride and groom must remain apart until the ceremony. Assurances from the court physician Selina was unharmed and would make a full recovery, and from Selina herself, and he allowed himself to be led away by Prince Viktor and General Müller and several of the male courtiers. The Prince said he had matters to discuss with Alec regarding the storming of his half-brother's stronghold, and General Müller added his voice, saying he wanted Alec to tell them all about how he had managed to escape the dungeons of Castle Herzfeld all those years ago.

In the Turret apartment, Selina was attended on by half a dozen of the Countess's maids, and Evans, who flitted about the rooms humming to herself, overjoyed her mistress was to finally marry Lord Halsey; Selina suspected had she nothing to wear but a flour sack to the ceremony, her lady's maid would have been just as content. As it was, all she did have to wear was a day gown of velvet with quilted petticoats, both crushed almost beyond repair, having been stuffed into the one portmanteau allowed them for the journey by sledge. Not the most lavish or the prettiest ensemble to be married in. But Selina did not care. She was finally marrying Alec, and Emily was unharmed.

She was still dazed thinking about it as she sat on a chaise longue by the warmth of the fireplace, fresh from her bath with a silk banyan over her underpinnings and a wool blanket across her knees, and listening to Emily chattering away about her time at *Schloss* Rosine. Her cousin was safe and well, and seemingly untouched. Most surprisingly of all, she seemed oblivious to the danger, death and deprivation that existed, caused by the civil war beyond the well-guarded walls of this sanctuary.

Selina could think of a few words to describe their situation and the wintery landscape, not to mention the harrowing last couple of weeks, but Emily's choice of the words *magical* and *enchanting* were not amongst the ones that sprang to her mind. But she would not disabuse her young cousin. Nor open her eyes to what was going on beyond this peaceful haven protected by the presence of hundreds of soldiers. They all needed their spirits lifted, and what better way to do so than with a wedding celebration. She had always imagined her wedding to Alec would be a joyous occasion, but never dreamed it would take place on foreign soil in the midst of a war. But she was determined today and tonight would be a celebration of everything that was good in their lives. Emily's happy state of mind would go a long way to helping them achieve this.

Yet, Selina could not quell her curiosity. She just had to know how Emily came to be at *Schloss* Rosine and not at Herzfeld Castle with Cosmo. She was sure Alec would ask at the earliest opportunity, wedding breakfast not withstanding.

"Oh, that's simple, but complicated to explain," Emily said matter-of-factly, not at all perturbed. "And I will try my best not to make a muddle of it all." She settled herself against the tapestry cushions on the window seat. "When we arrived at Herzfeld's port, Cosmo went off to the castle with Herr Luy—Luytens? Yes, Herr Luytens, the British Consul. Mrs. Carlisle and I were left aboard ship. Cosmo wouldn't hear of us accompanying him. He said he would be absent for only a few hours. He and Herr Luytens needed to deliver a piece of officious diplomatic correspondence. And it did look officious, too, in its red leather folio with gold lettering. I think it was from the King... And while he was away, Mrs. Carlisle and I were to prepare ourselves for the onward journey across the strait to Denmark.

"Cosmo said the passage was all arranged. And the ship was in the harbor. He even pointed it out to us. So we waited, and waited, and *waited*. But it was the morning of the next day when we decided to disembark with our luggage, and Cosmo's bags, and take them and ourselves to the dock in readiness for the short trip by barge out to our new ship. And it was while we were on the dock waiting with our portmanteaux that we were witness to the most extraordinary sight."

Emily leaned in, eyes wide.

"Soldiers! Too many soldiers to count! They swarmed over the docks like ants, and were just as quiet as ants, too. And just like ants, they disappeared into cracks and crannies before our eyes, because one minute they were there, and the next—gone! They hid themselves below deck on board the ships, and in the darkness of the warehouses. It was seeing these soldiers that decided Mrs. Carlisle that we, too, should hide. She said that if she was not very much mistaken, we were about to be caught up in a skirmish between two opposing forces. And never a truer word was spoken! It truly was the most exciting fun, Selina!"

She giggled behind her fan at a remembrance; Selina transfixed that her young cousin could be so cavalier about the obvious danger she and her companion had faced at that moment. But she remained mute and let her cousin continue.

"So we hid behind some fat bales. They were full of textiles, or cotton, or was it wool? No matter, they were large but we could still see what was occurring along the docks through the space between the bales. More soldiers arrived, but these men marched in formation, with muskets over their shoulders, and a captain barking out orders. Of course we had no idea what was said because it was all in German. These soldiers boarded only one ship, the ship we had sailed in on with Cosmo. While the soldiers who had swarmed over the docks like ants and were in hiding—and who I later discovered were in fact Prince Viktor's men—remained in their hiding places.

"It was only when the soldiers searching the ship started marching up and down the docks, questioning the men going about their work, overturning crates and pushing bales aside, that Mrs. Carlisle was certain they were looking, not for the soldiers in hiding, but for us. For why else would they search just one ship, the one we had sailed in on, and not any of the others? She had a feeling *in her waters*—those were her exact words—something was very wrong. Especially when Cosmo had still not returned. Now, thinking back on it," she mused with wonderment, the first time it had occurred to her, "I fear Mrs. Carlisle sacrificed herself so that I could escape..." She looked across at Selina and smiled hesitantly. "Those men in the castle will treat her, a lady's companion, with the respect due her, won't they, Selina? They will treat her just as well as they have treated me here, at *Schloss* Rosine, won't they? They ought to... I'm sure they will... And if she were to get into any difficulty, I know

Cosmo would come to her rescue and make certain they accorded her every respect. Is that not so?"

Selina returned her smile, and tried to sound reassuring. Though she did not believe a word of what she said. She was amazed at how effortlessly she could give such a hollow response that did indeed offer her cousin reassurance, because she did not have the heart to tell her what she truly feared may have happened to Cosmo and Mrs. Carlisle.

"I know—we both know—if Cosmo is in a position to do so, he will do everything in his power to protect Mrs. Carlisle. He will see to it she is provided with every comfort and consideration... So, as I am to understand it, Mrs. Carlisle gave herself up to these soldiers, and they remained none the wiser they had left you behind?"

Emily nodded eagerly.

"Yes! That is precisely the case. She identified herself to these soldiers as me, and why would they have reason not to believe she was speaking the truth? And so they left the port with her almost immediately. That's when the other soldiers came out of hiding, and, to my very great surprise, with the Countess. It was she they had been protecting all along. We had completely overlooked seeing her amongst their number when they had first come onto the dock because she was wearing a hooded cloak and was surrounded by a group of soldiers. It was spying her that decided me to show myself."

"To show yourself to these other soldiers, the ones who had swarmed over the dock like ants and gone into hiding, and who had the Countess in custody?" Selina repeated, trying to keep clear in her mind Emily's convoluted story.

"Yes. But she wasn't in custody. Those soldiers had helped her flee the castle where she was being held prisoner. And when I saw an officer—who turned out to be General Müller—stride up to her, take her in his arms and kiss her, he so pleased to see her, and she him, I knew I could seek their assistance." She gave a deep sigh of contentment and stared out across the opulent interior, reliving the moment in her mind's eye. "Seeing them reunited is possibly the most romantic scene I have ever witnessed! Better than any theater performance."

"How very romantic," Selina conceded. "But why did you believe they would provide you with assistance?"

Again Emily laughed behind her fan.

"Oh, Selina, don't be a silly! You of all people must know why. Because couples who are in love cannot be evil, can they? Being in love makes people happy, and they want everyone around them to share in their happiness, and be just as happy. I could see General Müller and the Countess Rosine were very much in love, and so happy to see each other that they would look upon my plight favorably. And they have cared for me, very well. Shall I make you a dish of tea?"

"Yes. Yes, you are right," Selina acknowledged quietly, in awe of Emily's naïve insight. "And yes, a dish of tea would be welcome. Thank you, dearest."

She watched Emily hop off the window seat and shake out her quilted petticoats as two maids wheeled the tea trolley to the chaise, curtsied and departed, leaving Emily in charge of the tea things. She tried to keep her voice neutral when asking lightly,

"And so you came here to *Schloss* Rosine in company with General Müller and the Countess Rosine, and it was here you were introduced to His Highness the Prince...?"

"Oh, no. We—Viktor—His Highness—we were introduced on the outskirts of Herzfeld. He was waiting to escort his mother here, to their home," Emily explained, fiddling with the tea things. She had a sudden thought and looked up from the silver teapot, blue eyes wide. "Do you know your wedding ceremony will be the second one I have attended in as many months, and in the very chapel you and Alec will exchange vows. General Müller and the Countess Rosine were married almost immediately we arrived here from Herzfeld. And just like you and Alec, they spent their wedding night here, in the Turret apartments. It was a hurried and rather secretive affair because the General was due to journey to Emden at the head of his regiment as part of the Margrave's army, the very next day. And because..." Emily dropped her lashes as her cheeks ripened with the heat of embarrassment and spoke quietly as she continued on with arranging the cups and plates. "Because the Countess was some five months with child, and they were unsure when or if the General would return."

"Then it was important they married when they did, so he could go off to fight knowing he had a wife and child to come home to. It is ironic, but it is in times of conflict that life—what is most important to us—is brought into sharp relief."

Emily handed Selina a cup of tea and set the sugar bowl and milk jug before her on the low table.

"I'm so very happy you and Alec are finally to marry, and this afternoon. It is what you have both wanted for such a long time, and now, it is to be! I just hope... I hope that with this war, with everything that is happening around us, we all manage to survive... Oh! Selina! Oh! I am so very glad you and Alec found me!"

Selina set aside her tea cup on its saucer and opened wide her arms, to gather up Emily, who for the first time allowed her carefree façade to drop and could not stop her tears. Emily fell into her embrace, and there stayed curled up beside her cousin on the chaise, Selina's cool hand to her fair hair. Until Emily finally sat up and asked fearfully,

"Do you think—Do you *believe* Cosmo and Mrs. Carlisle are still—*alive*?"

"Yes! Of course I do!" Selina replied instantly, for she believed it. "Just as Alec and I always knew we would find you alive and well. So, too, we will find Cosmo. I am certain of it." She smiled and tried to sound cheerful. "And I am very sure he will be looking after Mrs. Carlisle, too."

"But if they are still inside that castle..." Emily swallowed. "I have heard a little about that place, enough for me to be very glad I am here, and not there, even though His Highness and the Countess have been at pains not to mention it. I know Alec was captive there for a time, and that he managed to escape the dungeons, which I am told is a miracle in itself. And anyone who speaks of Herzfeld does so with the greatest unease."

Selina faced Emily and took hold of her hand. "I have every faith that Alec and the Prince and whatever forces they take with them to Herzfeld will rescue Cosmo and Mrs. Carlisle, and bring them to safety. I must believe that, and so must you. Now let us not dwell in a sad place anymore today," she added, forcing a bright smile. "I am finally marrying the man I love this afternoon, much to Evans' delight—and who cannot stop humming her excitement at the prospect of seeing me Lady Halsey—and you, my dearest, will be there beside me as my attendant. Not to mention there is to be a wonderful wedding breakfast. So we have everything to be happy about and we can at least give our men riding into danger tomorrow an afternoon and evening they will never forget, agreed?"

Emily nodded eagerly.

"No doubt they are at this very minute thinking of little else but enjoying an afternoon of fine food and drink, though I am very sure Alec is so nervous at the prospect of going up before the Reverend Shirley in front of an entire foreign court of nobles, that he is thinking of nothing at all. Now, we must drink our tea and make ourselves ready. But first, why don't you show me the gown you have chosen to wear."

Despite Selina's confident pronouncement, which instantly lifted Emily's spirits, she did not believe her own words. The men would not be thinking of weddings and celebrations at all, but would be rightly preoccupied with the campaign to infiltrate and take Herzfeld Castle. And she was right.

～    ～    ～

"I DO NOT UNDERSTAND... THAT CANNOT BE TRUE!"

It was General Müller. And he was incredulous, and thus angry. He was standing on the opposite side of the wide table, that had spread out across its surface a detailed map of Herzfeld Castle and its fortifications, knuckles leaning on the table but gaze firmly on Alec.

The General, Alec, and Prince Viktor were the only occupants in the cabinet room, with its view of the parade ground. Medieval weaponry adorned one wall, another was covered in floor-to-ceiling pigeon-holed slots which held rolled parchments of maps, old and new, of Midanich and surrounding electorates. Central to the room was the great map table.

The Prince's generals and advisors had been dismissed. The excuse given was that the hour for the wedding ceremony was fast approaching and the groom should have some time alone with his male attendants to gather his thoughts and his mettle. Truth told, Alec needed no encouragement. He couldn't wait to be up before the Reverend with Selina, but what he had to confide to the Prince and Müller had everything to do with their military assault on Herzfeld, planned for the morrow, and thus was for their ears only.

The Prince, who had been biting his thumb in concentration and peering at the map, eyes tracing the outline of the star castle's northwestern walls that ran parallel to the shoreline, glanced up at General Müller's outburst. He said quietly,

"Alec Halsey does not lie, Herr General."

Müller immediately came out of his angry abstraction and muttered an apology, which Alec accepted with good grace, but just as quietly. When the silence stretched, the Prince took his gaze and his concentration from the map and looked from his mother's husband to her former lover, smiled to himself and crossed his arms in their shirt sleeves across the front of his gold-threaded silk waistcoat, with no thought to the meticulous dressing by his valet, and the delicate gold thread embroidery. A matching frock coat, just as dazzling, was draped over one of the high-back chairs, and beside the chair stood the Prince's valet, ready to attend to this article, and anything else required of him to ensure his royal master was at his sartorial best for the wedding. Also in the room was Hadrian Jeffries, standing to attention just three chairs along, and with similar charge over Alec's frock coat and a small velvet box containing two gold wedding bands, and with his ears very wide open to the conversation. That the valets were privy to a very private conversation between a Prince, a General, and a foreign nobleman was not even considered worthy of notice by the former; they were, after all, lackeys. Yet, more than once, Alec glanced over at Hadrian to see if he was paying attention. He did so now, before shifting his gaze to the Prince when addressed by him.

"Please, Herr Baron, would you repeat what you just said, and then elaborate further. I admit to being astounded, though I do not disbelieve you."

"Of course, Highness," Alec replied evenly. He cleared his throat, removed his eyeglasses, and repeated what he had not told a living soul since escaping Midanich ten years ago. "I did not escape from the dungeons at Herzfeld. By force, magic, or any other means at my disposal. There are only two ways of leaving that—*place*. One is death. The other is to be set free. Fortunately for me, the latter applied, and it was Leopold who came to my rescue. And it was Leopold who put it about that I had orchestrated my own escape through cunning and derring-do."

"Why?" Müller asked, still skeptical. "Why perpetuate the myth that you escaped? Why allow this myth, that a foreigner was able to find an escape from a dungeon that for a century at least was supposedly—and now we discover quite rightly—inescapable?"

"I can only think it gave false hope to the families of those who had loved ones interned within its gruesome walls, that they had some chance of escape, which they did not," Alec replied without hesitation. "It was a cruel hope, but hope nonetheless. But that was not Leopold's reason for doing so. He needed a plausible explanation, one Ernst and Joanna would accept, for my escape. One that did not implicate him, or the Countess."

"And why would Margrave Leopold go to so much trouble on your behalf, Herr Baron?" General Müller asked, though he had a good idea he knew the answer. Still, he wanted to hear Alec Halsey say it.

When Alec hesitated to respond, Prince Viktor did so for him, because he sensed Alec was embarrassed to state the truth in his company, and that he did not wish to elicit the ire of the General. It had everything to do with the Countess Rosine. But his mother had never kept anything from him. He knew all about her affairs and her open marriage with his elderly father. And he knew that Alec Halsey, when a young English diplomat, had been his mother's lover and that he had made her happy; just as he knew General Müller loved his mother, and made her happy now. But he also sensed that the General was just that little bit, though quite needlessly, jealous of the history this handsome Englishman shared with the Countess.

"Because my mother asked it of my father, Henrik," the Prince stated quietly. "But you knew this, as you do everything about the Countess and the Herr Baron. Just as you are aware that was all in the past and will remain there. The Herr Baron is marrying the woman he loves in less than two hours' time, and the woman *you* love, my mother, will give birth to your son in less than a month; God willing in a country finally at peace."

Alec was all admiration for this young man's self-possession, and he knew at that moment without reservation that in Prince Viktor, the people of this small margravate on the outer reaches of the Holy Roman Empire had a worthy successor to his father, the Margrave

Leopold. General Müller knew it too, had known for months, if not years, and he was suitably contrite.

"Forgive me, Highness," General Müller agreed, a bow of his head to the young prince. Then, in a gesture of conciliation he bowed his head to Alec. "Please accept my apology, Herr Baron. You have only ever been fair and reasonable. And I have been unjustly envious... I will not again doubt you, or your story. Please continue, Herr Baron."

Alec inclined his head and did as requested.

"The myth about my escape stuck because no one dared question Leopold. If he said that was what happened, that was that. All that mattered to him, though, was that Ernst believed it. And if Ernst believed it, then so, too, would Joanna."

"Everyone did believe it, Herr Baron," General Müller stated. "Your escape from Herzfeld became the stuff of legend, and you a hero in the eyes of many, particularly the disaffected amongst our people who were sick of our country being a thoroughfare for foreign powers and who had rallied against what they saw as the Margrave's capitulation to foreign interests."

"A metaphor, if you will, of the impossible overcoming the probable. Alec Halsey was Midanich, the Herzfeld Castle dungeon the yoke of foreign invasion, his escape, a miracle which we all craved."

"Just so, Highness," Müller agreed with a rare grin. "So how did you did manage to escape the castle, Herr Baron?"

"Leopold came to the dungeons to see me," Alec explained, unable to stop a heightened color to his lean cheeks. All this talk of legends and heroes did not sit comfortably with him. "He had with him one of his personal attendants in heavy disguise. We swapped places, this attendant and I, and I left with Leopold, in this disguise. He led me through the warren of casements to an iron grate. This he unlocked and showed me a set of stairs leading down to the drains deep below the casements. He then gave me directions, a taper, and the documents I presented to you, Herr General."

Alec put his glasses back on to look closely at the map, and put a finger to a point along the northwestern shoreline.

"Here. That is why I mentioned this wall that faces the ocean. At low tide the entrance to the drain is visible, but few see it, as you would be required to be in a boat on the ocean at that particular time of day. While the mouth to the tunnel is not above a crouching man's height, once inside, it opens up so that even the tallest man can easily walk its length. And it is wide enough that a party of twenty men would not feel cramped. At low tide the sluices remain in the center channel, leaving the side paths dry. With adequate tapers, your soldiers would have no trouble navigating the drain right through to the iron grill. This you cannot miss, for there is a stair."

"You propose that I take a force into this drain and penetrate the castle in this way?" General Müller asked.

"No. I will lead the force into the drain," Prince Viktor stated, attention back on the map.

He ran his finger diagonally across the detailed outline of the castle from the northwest outer wall, and the General and Alec followed. His finger went through the center of the palace buildings and on out across the moat, and then out across the southeastern defensive wall, to the small township of Herzfeld. Here he stopped and tapped at the small cluster of buildings.

"Our soldiers overran the town some weeks ago, before the snow, and are now bivouacked here, with cannon and muskets, awaiting orders." He looked at Alec and then at Müller. "We should have a contingent of men, no more than a hundred, made ready to storm the castle, but only after you are granted access. And once inside and in a position to do so, we will open the front gates and simply let them in." He chuckled. "We shall take a leaf out of my father's book, and create our own myth of how fewer than a hundred soldiers stormed Herzfeld and brought us victory, and the war to an end."

Alec understood at once. "The victory will be stage-managed. It will occur only after you have secured the castle from Ernst. A bloodless coup if you will."

"Precisely. That is what must happen. Enough brotherly blood has been shed, and I want this war over with before winter truly sets in, and men on both sides of the conflict begin to freeze to death in their respective encampments. General Müller will front up at the castle gates with several of his men and you as his hostage. Ernst has no idea his colonel is a traitor to his cause, so no one will be suspicious and he will gain instant admittance. And while you are brought before Ernst, the men with you will quietly slip away to the casements, and open the grate to allow me and my men entry into the castle. Once the soldiers with me are secure throughout the palace, and castle grounds, I will find you, be assured of that. What is required then, is for the Captain of the Guard to capitulate. When he does, the entire palace guard will do so, and with Ernst left defenseless—he must and will surrender."

"How do you intend to get Westover to do so, Highness?" General Müller asked. "All our intelligence suggests he is a doggedly loyal captain of the guard to Ernst, as he was for Margrave Leopold."

Prince Viktor glanced at Alec and said, "If the Herr Baron plays his part well, Westover will have no choice but to surrender. His eyes will be well and truly opened."

General Müller's brows lifted in surprise. Yet he knew to what the Prince alluded. He addressed Alec. "You think you can do what no one else has yet managed to do? Bring the Princess Joanna out of the shadows while there is an audience?"

Alec gave a lop-sided grin and said flippantly, "I have wrought a miracle before, by escaping the inescapable, so why not again?"

"Ha! By the use of conjury?"

"If one is to bring forth the devil from the shadows, yes."

"I have never... I have never *seen* Joanna," the Prince admitted soberly. "I have only Müller's word for it—and yours, Herr Baron. I believe you both, and so does my mother. But you will forgive me if I voice my skepticism. I still find it difficult to believe the truth of her existence, of what she truly is. Can you understand why?"

"Perfectly," both men said in unison and, surprised, inclined their heads to one another with a smile.

"I believe Leopold knew almost from their cradle his twins were out of the ordinary," Alec said quietly. "And as they grew older and closer it became impossible for him to separate them, to do anything about their singular attachment to each other. And then, when Joanna became ill... By then it was too late. By then all your father could do was hope that with time, Ernst might be able to shake her influence, at least enough to govern. But then... Ernst's obsession with me, and Joanna's jealousy of our friendship... It clearly showed Leopold that Ernst was never going to be cured."

"But Margrave Leopold was stubborn, Highness," General Müller said, agreeing with Alec, addressing the Prince. "He refused to acknowledge he had spawned such a creature. He woke every morning believing that today was the day Ernst had finally banished Joanna. It did not matter that his Court Chamberlain and Ernst's closest friend—me—told him differently. It did not matter that the evidence was there before his eyes when he went to visit Joanna's apartments and saw his daughter for himself. She dressed in all her magnificence, surrounded by her mute attendants, slaves trapped in her apartments with her. She would be entertaining—torturing— some poor sot of a male, brought to her by Ernst to be used as her plaything, and who would be dead by morning, because the truth could not out. Those men did not matter, their deaths an unconcern, because they were found amongst the lower orders and their disappearance was of concern to no one."

The General took a breath and forced himself to be calmer. Neither the Prince nor Alec interrupted, though they shared a glance, which surely indicated they both realized Müller was speaking from personal experience—he had witnessed it all. It was as if he read their minds, or caught their glance, because he confirmed their suspicions, saying quietly,

"There were only two instances when Joanna allowed herself to be persuaded by Ernst to show herself outside her apartments. Once, with me. Fortunately, I had already had my suspicions and so did not react, and more fortunately, a fire had broken out in rooms not far from Ernst's apartment, and she was forced back into the shadows when attendants burst through the door to alert the Prince of the danger." He looked at Alec then. "The second occurrence was with you, Herr Baron. But she was far more cunning with you—"

"Yes. Very," Alec interrupted. "I do not think it serves our purpose now for me to relive that most unpleasant episode, Herr General. Your Highness."

Both men agreed and said no more about it. The General adding,

"But what you propose once we enter the castle and are brought before Ernst—of coaxing Joanna out of the shadows—that will not only be unpleasant for you, but dangerous, Herr Baron."

"Equally so for you, Herr General. And for His Highness," Alec replied quietly. "And we agreed, it is the only way to open Captain Westover's eyes to the truth. So we will carry out the plan as intended, and succeed. We all have too much to live for."

The Prince clapped Alec's shoulder and squeezed it affectionately. "That is very true, my friend! And so, on that note, let us finish our toilettes and make our way to the chapel! I for one am looking forward to an afternoon and night of festivities and frivolity!"

"There are two matters that remain unresolved, Highness," Alec apologized. "Firstly, and most importantly, is rescuing my good friend Sir Cosmo Mahon, his servant, and a Mrs. Carlisle, Miss St. Neots' companion. They have now been held against their will for almost three months. God knows what state they are in, if indeed they are—" Alec swallowed hard and cleared his throat before continuing. "—if indeed they are still alive…"

"We have not had any reports to the contrary, Herr Baron," General Müller told him gently. "And we have agents within the walls of Herzfeld Palace who have smuggled out many reports since the death of the Margrave, and I can assure you none have mentioned the death of any Englishman, or any foreign captive."

Alec nodded. "Thank you, Herr General. That is reassuring. I trust then that you, Highness, will have your men locate and rescue him and those others mentioned, and keep them safe while the castle is made secure by your men?"

"Yes, Herr Baron. Of course. Fraulein St. Neots has so often spoken to me of her cousin Sir Cosmo Mahon, that I feel I know him already. You can be assured I will make it a priority to discover his whereabouts." The Prince glanced at his general and added, "What Müller did not add, but I think you should be made aware, is that your dear friend, while he is still alive, he has not been treated—well. You must prepare yourself that he may not be—*himself.*"

Alec was startled. "He's been tortured?"

The Prince closed his mouth and nodded.

Alec wiped a hand across his mouth and breathed in deeply. "Thank you for telling me."

"The second matter…?" the Prince prompted.

"I am aware a flotilla has set sail from Emden and is due in Herzfeld harbor any day," Alec stated. "My godmother—Fraulein St. Neot's grandmother, and my uncle are aboard *The Caroline.* So, too, is the English special envoy to Midanich, Sir Gilbert Parsons. I want a boat sent to intercept the ship and my family removed, along with any other civilians, and taken out of harm's way. Your Highness, this is not negotiable. They are to be removed or I do not go to the castle tomorrow, but to the docks, to row myself if necessary, to save them."

General Müller and the Prince exchanged a look. It was the General who spoke.

"I regret that members of your family have been caught up in this war, Herr Baron. But I do not regret requisitioning *The Caroline* for our purposes. As you know, I have removed the pigeon post, and thus communication with Emden is cut off, and so Prince Ernst will be unaware that town has been overrun and taken by rebel forces. More importantly, he will have no knowledge that a flotilla is headed this way, with cannon and men should they be required. And so the cannon facing out to sea at Herzfeld will not have been primed in readiness, and the grenadiers ready for such an eventuality—"

"You do not know that. For all we do know, the flotilla has already been spotted off the coast and the cannon made ready."

"But even if ships are spotted," the General replied patiently. "They will be flying the English ensign and so not seen as hostile. Herzfeld Castle will not know that these so-called English ships carry cannon and soldiers from Emden.

"If all goes according to our plans, Herr Baron, there will be no need for the ships—*The Caroline* specifically—to engage with the castle. The castle will be ours, and there will be peace declared, there and at the docks, where I have soldiers in readiness. One of the ships with cannon aboard has been told to fire a number of warning shots near the castle, but only once the majority of the flotilla has sailed into the harbor. *The Caroline* will simply anchor in the harbor, its cargo, men and equipment disembarked all in good time, and safely."

Alec was not to be placated. "I concede that what you say will in all probability happen. But as it cannot be guaranteed, I want your word that a boat will be sent out to *The Caroline*, and the civilians removed and brought safely to shore, and kept safe, until such time as we are reunited."

When the Prince and the General did not immediately jump

into the silence to agree to Alec's demand, assistance came from an unexpected quarter.

"Lord Halsey! Herr Baron! I volunteer. Allow me to collect Her Grace and Mr. Halsey and such persons who need to be disembarked from *The Caroline.*"

It was Hadrian Jeffries. He stepped forward when all three nobleman at the map table turned to stare at him. Alec was the only one not to be startled into speechlessness to hear a servant speak—and a foreign one at that—without first being addressed, and who spoke acceptable German.

"You would do that, Jeffries?"

The valet nodded, nervousness creeping into his voice to now be stared at as if there were visible food stains down the front of his waistcoat. And none stared harder than the Prince's own valet, who was a gentleman in his own right.

"Yes, my lord. Someone should go who is known to Her Grace and Mr. Halsey," Hadrian Jeffries explained, reverting to English. "To my mind, they will be apprehensive enough having been kidnapped and taken against their will out to sea, and not, as they had expected, to be set down in Holland and safety." He did not allow his gaze to wander to General Müller, the architect of the Duchess's and the old man's distress. "They are unlikely to want to disembark into a boat if requested to do so by persons equally foreign to them. But if I was to be in that boat, and able to deliver a short missive from your lordship, then I believe they would gladly come with me, and to any destination of your choosing."

"Thank you, Hadrian," Alec said with a smile. "You have relieved me of a great anxiety. If I can get the Prince to agree, I would be most grateful to you—"

"That is an idea most excellent!" the Prince announced, also in English. When Alec and his valet now stared at him, stunned, he laughed. "My English it is not good, but I understand better than

I speak." He leaned into Alec and winked. "But please you not to tell Miss St. Neots. We enjoying to converse in French. So! It will be arranged," he continued in his native tongue, including Hadrian Jeffries in his conversation. "Your valet will travel with us tomorrow. I will send a small party of soldiers with him to the dock, and they will take a boat out to *The Caroline*, collect all who are required to be collected, and return with them here, to safety. Agreed?"

Alec bowed to the Prince. "Agreed... And thank you."

The Prince clapped his hands then rubbed them together. "Good! And now we must hurry and dress, or your bride she will be at the altar before you, and that would never do. We do not want her and the congregation thinking you are a reluctant groom, now, do we, Herr Baron?"

Alec could think of nothing that was further from the truth.

# Twenty-three

ALEC WAS BEING WOKEN FROM A DEEP SLEEP. HE DIDN'T want to wake up. He was exhausted. He was sure he had just set his head upon the pillow five minutes before. With his eyes still closed, he drew the coverlet up to his chin. He then put out a hand across the bed, felt warm flesh beside him and smiled. He remembered now why he was so tired. He shifted his naked body under the covers to curl himself around Selina's naked warmth. Her curves were glorious. He snuggled in, face buried in her mussed curls, which smelled of lilies, and with a big grin splitting his face fell into a sound sleep.

He was shaken awake again.

A voice hissed in his ear that it was time.

Oh God, must he? What time was it precisely? Why had he agreed to it? Surely, on this of all mornings, the morning after his wedding night, he should be allowed the deep sleep required after lust and love are celebrated with vigorous gusto until satiated. He needed a few more hours with his wife cradled in his arms, just to savor that fact alone. His wife. Selina was his wife. He was her husband. Selina and he were now married and that fact had the power to make him pause in wonder if indeed the events of the previous afternoon and evening had actually happened.

They had been brought before the English parson—the Reverend Samuel Shrivington Shirley—and exchanged vows in front of upwards of a hundred foreign nobles dressed in their best silks, furs, and velvets. A royal Prince in a golden ensemble and a golden mustache to match stood beside him as best man, and half a dozen highly-decorated mustachioed Generals in all their medals and gold braid finery stood to attention at his back. He had then led Selina out of the chapel into the crisp air of a sunny winter's day to the deafening sound of a musket salute, and cannon fire. They had walked the snow-covered quadrangle, back across the fairy bridge that spanned the frozen moat, lined from chapel to banqueting hall with soldiers in full regalia and standing to attention. Sophie Shirley as flower girl, with Emily on the arm of Prince Viktor following, both carrying a bouquet of silk flowers. The Countess Rosine, refusing a sedan chair and wanting to be part of the procession, leaned on her husband's arm and followed at a sedate pace, her advanced pregnancy making her take deliberate steps in the snow. And trailing this little wedding party, the nobles of the foreign court, who had patiently sat through a service conducted first in English and then in German for their benefit, and who were now wanting an evening of wine, song, and entertainments that went with the celebration of a noble marriage.

Alec could not remember if he ate what was put before him or not. He must have. Plates came and went. Crystal glasses were filled, emptied, and refilled; he had no idea how much he drank, if anything. He was just so happy. He couldn't remember when he had been happier. His happiness, and he was sure the exuberance with which the revels were entered into by everyone in the room, were more acute because of what was to come the following day. Most of the men present would be setting off for Herzfeld Castle before dawn, all with their particular tasks to perform, all hoping that by the setting of the sun, the castle would be in rebel hands, Margrave

Ernst usurped by his brother, and Prince Viktor acknowledged by one and all as the new Margrave of Midanich.

For now, though, all anyone cared about was eating, drinking and having a good time. To that end, once the speeches were over with, Prince Viktor called for his gift from the English King to be brought out and uncrated in the middle of the room. He then asked the groom if he would do the honors of unveiling this most extraordinary present. Alec agreed and asked Emily to offer him her assistance in demonstrating the gaming table to His Highness and assembled guests. Selina had squeezed his hand in understanding, tears in her eyes at the gesture, for the last time this marvel of mechanical engineering had been demonstrated, Cosmo had been with them, and it was he who had proudly shown the mechanism to Emily. Having Emily occupied throughout the demonstration would surely divert her attention and not let her dwell on Cosmo and his situation, which was uppermost in all their minds.

The crate was duly brought to the banqueting hall by four liveried footmen, who carefully placed it upon the parquetry flooring. Those seated at the back of the room stood for a better view, while others craned their necks from behind fluttering fans, and quizzing glasses to gaze at this gift. All were intrigued. But when the crate was unlocked and a polished wooden box extracted, none were impressed. Next, out came four turned, polished wooden legs, and these were carefully screwed into place, which allowed for the box to be elevated and become a table. But again it was nothing special.

Yet, the Prince was all wide-eyed excitement, perched on the edge of his spindle-legged chair, in anticipation of what would happen next. That Emily was giggling behind her fan and hunching her shoulders, elevated the Prince's excitement to breath-holding level.

With the turn of the first leaf, Alec and Emily had the attention of every person within the banquet hall. They had never seen the like before. This gaming table, which could be packed away in a nondescript crate and taken anywhere, was made up of many polished wooden leaves, which could be turned like the pages of a book that, when laid out flat, revealed a different playing surface with each turn. First there was a table of inlaid felt that allowed for the playing of all card games. With the next turn of a leaf, a surface inlaid with leather was revealed, for the writing of letters. Not only that, but with one finger, Emily lifted a corner of the inlaid leather to reveal an easel that when set up allowed for a book to be propped and read without needing to be held by the person sitting at the table.

While Emily turned the leaves, Alec provided a commentary, in German, then in French, and finally in English, which in itself was a marvel to those present. And with each turn of the wooden leaves, more and more of the guests moved their chairs closer, or brazenly walked up to the table to stand behind Alec and Emily to take a closer look at this mechanical marvel.

Of course the most startling revelations were left to last, as Emily turned over a leaf to create a table that had in its center a chess board and to each side of the inlaid wood, she rolled away lids to reveal two hidden drawers where the chess pieces were kept. But not only chess pieces but backgammon pieces.

Alec explained how the drawers worked. Emily put the pieces upon the chessboard and Alec invited the Prince to come forward to take a closer look at this most marvelous invention. The Prince duly stepped forward, the delight writ large on his handsome features. He was so taken with his gift from the English King he could hardly contain himself. He wanted two chairs drawn up to the table so he and Alec could play at a game of chess.

But would not His Highness prefer a game of backgammon? asked Emily as she put away the chess pieces without his permission. He nodded. Of course! But he did not see a surface on which to play at backgammon. Emily then invited the Prince to push on a particular part of the board with one of his fingers, but to be very careful he did so gently, so as not to startle those present.

He did as requested and as he did so, he felt the surface of the table give way. Such was his surprise that he leapt back, fearing the table was about to collapse. It did not. The opposite occurred. A section of the table rose up out of nowhere and opened out as if by magic into a backgammon board. The Prince not only took another step back in astonishment, he then rushed up to the table to assure himself it was not a trick of sorts.

He was so taken, so excited, that with Emily's help he folded the backgammon board away again, all for the pleasure and excitement of watching it pop up again as if by magic.

The court applauded. The Prince invited his courtiers to come forward and inspect the table for themselves, and such was the intense interest that the Prince forgot there was to be dancing. Until his mother reminded him, then excused herself for the rest of the evening. The baby was being particularly active, and she needed to rest. Before the General escorted her away, she kissed the groom's cheek, then the bride's, wished them happy and a long life together. And with a twinkle in her eye ordered her son to let the happy couple retire for the evening well before the dancing was over; they could make more pleasant use of the limited time they had together before Alec was to join the Prince, his General, and the army marching on Herzfeld on the morrow.

That brought Alec out of his half-sleeping reverie. Blinking in the semi-darkness, he sat up on an elbow and pulled his long black curls out of his eyes. The velvet curtain on his side of the bed had been drawn back and tied off, giving him a view into the room. It was illuminated by a candelabra on the table, and the orange glow from the fireplace. Two lackeys were pouring scented water into a hipbath before the hearth. A third lackey was setting the room to rights, while his valet rummaged about, picking up various items of discarded clothing—clothing strewn across the bedchamber. So, too, was half the bedding. Part of the night they had slept—no, they had *not* slept—in front of the fireplace. His gaze darted to the window seat, to the scatter of cushions; they'd not slept there either. He fell back on the pillows with a grin and stared up at the pleated canopy for all of five seconds, supremely happy. Resisting the urge to kiss his wife so as not to wake her, and resigned to the inevitable, he threw back the coverlet with a sigh and fairly leapt out of bed. He meant to cross to the hipbath, just seven paces away, but was confronted with Evans, standing directly in front of him holding a tea tray.

He was naked and she had frozen.

"Good morning, Evans," he said conversationally, casually took the tea tray from her fixed grip, placed it on the bedside table, then stepped past her and went to his bath.

"Good-Good mor-morning, my lord," Janet Evans finally squeaked in a dry throat, still frozen, but better educated than she thought she would ever be about her dearest Selina's lord and master.

HADRIAN JEFFRIES WAS SECURING THE BUCKLES OF ALEC'S knee-high jockey boots when Selina came through to the dressing room, wearing the coverlet like a Roman Senator, mass of mussed curls tumbling about her shoulders like an apricot cloud, and carrying a cup of tea.

Alec looked up from watching his valet and smiled. "Good morning, my lady."

"Good morning, my lord." She held out the cup of tea with a shy smile. "Evans thought you might like some tea before you set off."

Alec took the teacup. "How thoughtful of her."

"Evans also thought it would be a good idea if I told you my news now, before your departure. She said it will give you something to think about other than what you must confront in that horrid castle. That it will give you the strength required if you are called upon to surmount the insurmountable."

"Then it is best we heed Evans' advice; she has never let you down yet."

When Selina nodded but did not continue, he realized that whatever it was she wished to tell him, she wished to do so in private. Hadrian Jeffries did not need to be told. He thought so too, and he rose up from his haunches, and with a short bow to Alec, and not a glance at her ladyship, was about to excuse himself. But Alec addressed him directly, Selina going to the window, drawn by the noise of departure down in the cobbled courtyard outside the turret—the movement of wheels and horses hooves and men's boots on the cobbles, of barks of command, and conversation.

"Tell His Highness I'm only a few minutes behind you." He stuck out his hand and when his valet gripped it said, "Be careful. Keep your head down. Don't play the hero. I need you alive. Her Grace and my uncle need you alive. Don't let Parsons bully you. You are in charge of my family's safety. If for any reason you deem the situation too dangerous, it probably is. So find shelter, keep yourself and them safe, and wait for reinforcements. General Müller's men will find you, eventually."

"Yes, sir. I will. I won't let you down."

Alec smiled. "Of course you won't. Thank you."

"Sir! Forgive me. There is one last task I forgot to perform, and I must." Jeffries went to a darkened corner to retrieve a sheathed sword and leather sword belt. They belonged to Alec, confiscated at Wittmund by General Müller. Jeffries now returned them with a small bow. "With the General's compliments, my lord."

Selina waited until the valet had helped secure the belt and sword under Alec's frock coat then departed, before she came away from the window. She had been watching the soldiers make ready in the semi-darkness under the orange glow of dozens of tapers; officers mounted on their magnificent Frisians in all their military finery; wagons loaded with supplies, and a dozen or more lackeys running in and out between these vehicles, horses, and soldiers, attending to last-minute requests. All brought a sense of the enormity of what lay ahead, for these men, and for Alec, and what the outcome of this day would mean for them all. Herzfeld was only an hour away. By sunrise, they would be in the thick of the fighting, ready to die for their cause. She was certain those left behind with her at the *Schloss*—the women, old men, children, and the infirm—would hear the roar of the fighting and each deafening cannon blast, and live every heart-stopping moment with them.

Was it any wonder she wanted the day over with before it had even begun?

Alec met her halfway across the room and took her in his arms. He kissed her forehead, then leaned his against hers for a moment, and they stood silent, enjoying the moment of stillness. But the activity and noise below soon intruded, and both were gripped with a sense of urgency. For Selina there was no other way to say what was on her mind, so she just came out with it.

"I'm pregnant."

Alec chuckled, disbelieving. "That was quick! Is this the best ploy Evans could manage to have me stay?"

Selina took a step away, pulling the coverlet closer, and looked up into his blue eyes. There was no amusement in her dark eyes or in her tone.

"No. It's the truth. I conceived in Paris, when you came to stay. We've not made love since—until last night." She smiled hesitantly when he continued to stare at her, dazed and mute. "We think—Evans and I, and I am sure a physician will confirm my calculation, I am so very good at figures, as you know—the baby is due mid summer. So plenty of time yet to find our way back home, to Delvin. Your son should be born at the estate, don't you think? I'm not telling you this to make you stay with me. I-I want you to rescue Cosmo, and bring him, my aunt, and your uncle—well, he's my uncle now, too, whether he likes it or not—back here to be reunited with Emily and me. We can then make the announcement together, about our marriage, and about the-the baby. Evans and I just thought you should know that whatever awaits you at Herzfeld, whatever unpleasantness you are forced to face, you have us—your wife and child who love you—waiting for you."

She smiled through her tears and swallowed in a dry throat when Alec, too overcome to speak, dropped to his knees and hugged her, face buried in the coverlet. A hand to his black curls, she gently held him against her, and let the tears stream down her face.

This was how a lackey found the couple, sent by the Prince to hurry the Baron Aurich along. The sun, such as it was, would show itself on the horizon in the next hour. The weather being favorable, there would be a cloudless sky, and they would march with the sun directly in their eyes. The servant took one look into the silent dressing room and retreated as quietly as he had entered it, reporting that the Baron was on his way. What he had witnessed between the couple was no man's business but their own, not even that of his future Margrave; but it was a memory he would keep for the rest of his days.

⁓     ⁓     ⁓

EVERYTHING WENT ACCORDING TO THE PLAN DISCUSSED AND agreed over Prince Viktor's map table. In fact, it was so perfectly executed a clean-shaven General Müller (he could not enter the castle with his mustache for surely that would give the game away) with Alec as his hostage, dared to glance at one another in surprise when one of the heavily-studded doors in the portcullis was slowly cracked open, and they, with four of the General's most skilled assassins, were granted entry into Castle Herzfeld.

WHILE GENERAL MÜLLER'S PARTY WERE BEING ESCORTED BY members of the Margrave's personal bodyguard across an eerily deserted quadrangle with only a ginger cat as witness, Prince Viktor and upwards of forty soldiers were stealthily making their way along the sandy shore at the base of the castle's northwestern battlement, an imposing red brick wall that was some ten feet thick and which rose thirty feet into the air. The North Sea had retreated enough at low tide to provide a wide strip of wet sandy beach, and there, where Alec had advised the Prince, was the hole in the wall—the mouth of the sluice drain, no taller than a man when crouching, from which Alec had escaped a decade earlier. As unassuming and ineffectual as this drain mouth appeared, it was the Achilles heel for a fortification deemed impenetrable and which had only ever been successfully breached once, and that a hundred years earlier.

And just as Alec described, once inside the drain, and with their tapers lit, the passage was easily if uncomfortably navigable. With Prince Viktor leading, the soldiers quickly scurried through this section of the drain, either side of a deep channel which carried all manner of waste away from the castle at high tide. They then scrambled up a set of shallow spiral steps, and found themselves in a much larger tunnel that allowed them to stand tall. They were now in the casements which were a series of interconnected tunnels and rooms that ran under the battlements and under the main palace building. This particular tunnel led straight to the dungeon. They found the heavy iron grill, bolted as predicted.

Here the air might be less dank but it was unbearably fetid. Alec had failed to mention, and was something he had probably deliberately forgotten—the Prince understood why—the indescribable and overpowering stench. Dipping the tapers to cast light at their boot heels, the Prince and his men found themselves ankle-deep in human excrement, and the bones and rotted flesh of recently mutilated victims of torture.

More than one soldier turned and heaved and splashed the contents of his stomach across the tunnel walls. Soldiers scrambled to quickly rearrange their stocks and mufflers to cover their mustachioed noses, to help block the overpowering smells. The Prince ordered tapers to be set upright, and his men to keep their gaze heavenward, to remain quiet and ready. All did their best to ignore the stench under their feet, listening for signs of life above, and waited silently, if impatiently, for their comrades to find them, to slide the bolt and lift the grate.

ALEC WAS ESCORTED ACROSS THE CASTLE GROUNDS BETWEEN the shoulders of two of General Müller's men. General Müller walked ahead, and in front of him were two of the Margrave Ernst's unsuspecting personal bodyguards, who led the way. Just as the party turned down a corridor inside the main palace building, two of Müller's soldiers marching behind Alec, quietly dropped back and slunk away to disappear in the shadows. In their place, one of the soldiers at Alec's side fell back, and the General took his place beside Alec. The ruse worked. When the bodyguards came to a halt at a set of ornate bronze and walnut double doors, where two guards stood either side of two liveried footmen, these escorts were none the wiser two of Müller's men were now loose in the castle.

The assassins made their way down into the casements, to the dungeons, one to search out the cells, looking for Sir Cosmo, the other in search of a particular heavy iron grate. This iron grill was only ever opened by lackeys required to dispose of bodily waste and of the bodies of torture victims, or prisoners who had died in their cells, by natural means or foul. They were supposed to cart the remains through the tunnel as far as the sluice drain, and there offload the bodies and the body parts into the channel, knowing that when the tide rose, the sea would rush in and take away these hapless victims to an unmarked watery grave. In practice, the lackeys saw no point in exerting themselves, and often opened the grill and tipped the contents of their buckets directly into the tunnel. Only when the stench became overpowering and noxious fumes wafted up through the grill did they bother to shift the human waste and detritus further along the tunnel to the drain.

And so when one of Müller's assassins marched up to a lackey and barked out the order that the air was far too putrid to breathe and the tunnel needed clearing, the lackey dozing in a dark corner outside the cells, immediately jumped to life, went off and returned with a set of long keys. The assassin followed, the heavy grate was found, the shackle unlocked, the bolt drawn back, and the grate lifted. For his effort, the lackey had his throat cut. Prince Viktor and his men silently scrambled into the dungeon, and the lackey's lifeless form was tossed down the hole, and the grate replaced. But it was not bolted.

THE CASTLE'S EXPANSIVE AUDIENCE CHAMBER WAS NOISY AND crowded with noblemen gathered for the Margrave's morning audience. Courtiers were clustered in conversation, liveried footmen moved amongst the crumpled velvets and tatty furs, with trays laden with foodstuffs for the Margrave's table. Blank-faced soldiers of the Margrave's personal guard stood to attention at the entrance doors and lined a wall hung with an enormous tapestry proclaiming in woven detail the glorious military history of Midanich.

The Captain of the Guard stood silent and grim-faced by his ruler's high-back chair, ever vigilant. The daily whisperings of discontent were growing louder as the food stores became ever more depleted. Last week an assassination plot had been uncovered. The week before that, a councilor was discovered bribing soldiers to allow him and his wife and son to flee the castle under cover of darkness. Reports received confirmed that Prince Viktor's rebels had taken the town of Herzfeld and now controlled the entire south of the country. With no word from Emden—there had not been a pigeon post in the past sennight—it was assumed that the merchant town had also fallen to the rebels. and if not the rebels, then foreign troops in alliance with Prince Viktor.

And if this wasn't enough to try the resources and patience of Captain Westover, the most loyal of the Margrave's servants, there was the disturbing fact that His Highness was spending more and more time away from his duties and his court closeted with his sister in her apartments—apartments which were forbidden to Westover, and which remained off-limits to all but the Prince and Princess, and her retinue of mute servants. This made Westover's prime objective—to protect the Margrave's person at all times—nigh on impossible upon these occasions.

Baron Haderslev was of the opinion that come the spring thaw, Ernst's tenure as Margrave would meet with a brutal end when the castle was forced to surrender to Prince Viktor. But Captain Westover had taken an oath to serve and protect his Margrave, and had done just that under Margrave Leopold, and would do so for his legitimate heir, Ernst, and protect him and his sister with his life. Westover was doggedly loyal and a believer in the divine right of kings—that God had ordained Prince Ernst to rule after his father, and thus only God could remove him. And so he told the Court Chamberlain. He would uphold Ernst's right to rule for as long as there was breath in his body, and breath in the bodies of his men, who to a man were loyal to him.

WITH HEART THUMPING, BUT ANGULAR FEATURES DEVOID OF his thoughts, Alec's gaze swept the audience chamber from painted and gilded ceiling down to the long gallery opposite the tapestry wall, where the women of the court were permitted to view proceedings from behind latticed screens, and out across to the far end of the chamber where, upon a dais, the Margrave sat in state on an enormous ebony chair, or behind a table at meal times. He remembered it all as if it were only yesterday when, as a fresh-faced under-secretary, he had accompanied Sir Gilbert Parsons as part of the English delegation. And just as the chamber had been then, it was now crowded with noblemen going about their business. Which surprised Alec, given the castle was under siege conditions. But nothing was as it seemed, and none more so than on this day.

As Alec, General Müller, and their escort shouldered through the crowd, heads turning with interest to see why they were being ordered to make way, they were caught off-guard by the acrid stench of the great unwashed. Sour body odor, disheveled clothes, inexpertly powdered wigs which looked tired and in need of grooming, were glaring indicators none of these men had been outside the castle walls in months. And with the turn in the weather and the war now on their doorstep, nothing and no one had entered the castle either.

But Viktor did not want unnecessary bloodshed, or troops on either side to die for little gain. Usurp Ernst's position as Margrave in a peaceful coup and the country could again be at peace. But to do so, he needed the Margrave's household guard to stand down, and he was confident the nobles loyal to Ernst would then bow down to him without a fight.

Noting the haunted expressions on the gaunt faces of these reeking noblemen, and their furtive glances, Alec was confident that whatever loyalty these men had shown Ernst upon his elevation to the Margravate it had been all but eroded since Leopold's death. They might talk amongst themselves, wear their best velvets, however in need of good laundering, and pretend that all was normality within Ernst's dominion, but it was obvious they remained in the chamber under sufferance and fear; when the time came, Alec was certain Viktor would have no trouble in gaining the allegiance of the heads of the first families of Midanich.

Colonel Müller (for here in the Castle he was no General), however, looked neither left nor right at the noblemen surrounding him, and strode on with purpose, ignoring the sourness which assailed his nostrils, and keeping his heavy chin elevated above his linen stock. He had a gloved hand to the hilt of his rapier, and secured under his cloak, and under his arm, was the casket of jewelry belonging to Olivia, Duchess of Romney-St. Neots, which Alec planned to use to coax the Princess Joanna out from the shadows.

Müller was ready for any eventuality, and when Prince Viktor thought the time right to show himself in this chamber, would defend his stepson with his life; so, too, this Englishman beside him. So he was put on the alert when into his path stepped the Court Chamberlain. Baron Haderslev dismissed the liveried footman with a wave, and with a quick glance at Alec which told him he had no idea who he was, said through his teeth,

"This is not the best time, Colonel!"

"Good to be back, Herr Baron," Müller replied loudly and evenly. "As you can see for yourself at long last, I had a safe journey from Emden, despite the icy roads, fog as thick as your mother's cabbage soup, and barbarian rebels lurking in every hovel from here to Wittmund!"

Up ahead there was a yelp, someone let out a bark of laughter, and then in response the noblemen laughed too, the half-hearted laughter rippling back amongst the crowd, who had no idea what or who was fueling their amusement, but it was best to laugh so as not to be singled out.

Müller's brows drew over his large nose and his gaze darted toward the dais, but his view was blocked by the crowd surging forward shoulder to shoulder, in curiosity and trepidation.

"What's going on?" Müller asked in an altogether different voice.

"'Tis madness. *Madness*," Haderslev hissed, a glance over his shoulder, which told Alec he feared being overheard, and thus feared such disloyalty would uncover him a traitor. "You should have stayed in Emden until someth—"

"Take us to His Highness, Haderslev. This here is Alec Halsey—the Baron Aurich."

Baron Haderslev staggered back a pace, as if struck. He could hardly believe it. He put a gloved hand to his chest, as if he had a sudden pain in the heart. He stared at Alec with wide eyes, terrified, and finally in recognition. "My God! It *is* you! You came!? I never thought—" He glanced at Müller. "We never thought you would!"

Alec saw the glance and understood instantly. "Why wouldn't I? Your master is holding my best friend hostage. But perhaps that was just a ploy—telling Ernst I would come for Cosmo, even when you thought I wouldn't—to suit a much grander plan?"

The latter part of the sentence was directed at General Müller, who confessed evenly, "Yes. To keep the Margrave occupied until such time as we could convince Westover to capitulate, or we found a way to infiltrate the castle, whichever happened first. Of course," he added with a wry smile at Alec, "the Countess never wavered in her conviction that you would indeed heed the call and come to plead for your friend's release."

"That you allowed Ernst to use my best friend as his plaything, all to further your own ends, I will never forgive," Alec stated with suppressed anger. "I understand why you did so—for the greater good. But it doesn't make me in charity with what you did. And now, here we all are!" he added bitterly, and then addressed the Court Chamberlain. "I presume Westover is as intractable as ever or you'd have let Müller know differently by now?"

"Unfortunately, that is so, Herr Baron," Haderslev apologized. "Westover is determinedly loyal."

Alec threw back the front of his gray woolen cloak over a shoulder and stripped off his gloves, suddenly uncomfortably warm in this crowded stinking room.

"Then there is nothing for it. Westover needs his eyes opened. And at once. But first, you'd best have this chamber cleared out. She'll never show herself before an audience." He jerked his head at the lattice screens of the gallery "You will have a ringside seat from over there. Make certain Westover does too. There'll not be a repeat performance." He stuck out his hand to Müller. "I'll take the casket now." When he had the jewelry box in hand and Haderslev had yet to move, he waved a hand at him. "Lead the way, Herr Baron. Time is of the essence, if you want to avoid a bloody struggle."

Haderslev hesitated, brows raised at General Müller to offer further explanation. When he did not, he swiveled on a heel, and with the sweep of an arm, and a bark of command, ordered those in front of him to make way.

Müller and Alec followed, without another glance at one another. They discovered, just as Prince Viktor and his men had discovered minutes earlier, that Sir Cosmo Mahon was not being held captive in the Castle dungeons after all.

SIR COSMO AND HIS VALET MATTHIAS WERE ONLY A FEW FEET away, standing before the dais, with heads bowed. So they could not make a run for it, not that that was likely, given they barely had the energy to stand and the room was full of soldiers, two of the Margrave's bodyguards stood to attention behind them. Both men were resigned. They had been prisoners just a handful of days shy of three months. It felt like three years. Sir Cosmo's soiled clothes no longer fitted, his stockings which had once been white were grey and full of ladders. His hair was not only matted but also infested with lice, and he carried the sores of malnutrition. But neither had stubble; their cheeks and chin were clean shaven.

The only thing keeping Sir Cosmo on his feet was Matthias, who was supporting him at the elbow. And the only thing keeping Matthias from shaking with despair was that the soldier at his back was his friend Hansen, and Hansen had promised, when the time came, to end their lives as quickly and as painlessly as possible. He had shown Matthias the dagger he kept in his boot, and assured him he always kept the blade hair-splittingly sharp.

The Margrave was eating his breakfast, and to amuse himself and his courtiers he had offered his prisoners a last meal. He wanted them to eat up, to enjoy the moment. But as neither man was the least interested in the plate of stewed fruit and nuts placed at the scuffed toes of their shoes, and merely stared down at the floor, unmoved and unappreciative, Ernst grew increasingly angry to be so defied. He threw the odd nut at them to elicit a response, which sent his courtiers laughing, but the two men were too drained of hope to even react to this puerile torment. He was about to give the order for the Englishmen to finally be taken away, to the dungeons, and there to rot, when the crowd parted down its center.

Coming towards him was the only man who mattered.

Ernst was so disbelieving he broke off mid-sentence, the two prisoners no longer of interest or given another thought. He dropped his fork and stared open-mouthed, and with an expression of one who is witness to a specter. He never thought this day would come, despite wishing and praying for it every day since Alec Halsey's escape ten years ago.

His first thought was a vain one. He was not properly attired for such an occasion. He should have been wearing his best frock coat, the one with gold spangles. And his best boots, the black leather and silk pair with covered buttons that went all the way up over his knee. And his wig wasn't elaborate enough. He'd not paid attention to his face. He was without rouge and powder and his eyebrows had not been penciled in since the day before. That he was not looking his sartorial best for this reunion made him irritable and petulant. His second thought was that he should be feeling furious, murderously so, that the man had the supreme audacity to stride up to him as if it were only yesterday they had been sitting back, boot heels up on a footstool, enjoying a good port and a laugh. But he didn't feel anger, he felt apprehensive. He didn't want his sister to find out about Alec Halsey's return, not until he was ready to tell her; she would monopolize his time; and hadn't he told her time and again that Alec Halsey was first and foremost *his* friend?

When Captain Westover stepped forward and spoke at his ear something about the Court Chamberlain clearing the chamber of courtiers, Ernst waved him away impatiently without taking his eyes from Alec. He wouldn't allow anything or anyone to spoil this moment.

"Yes! Yes! Get them out. Get them *all* out of here. And send that lot away, too!" Ernst demanded waving a lace ruffled hand at the row of guards standing to attention along the tapestry-covered wall. "You leave also!"

As Ernst made no mention of the two prisoners, they were ignored, along with the guards standing behind them. But then Hansen muttered to his fellow guard that if he wished to earn merit points with their captain and the Court Chamberlain why didn't he help shift those nobles dragging their feet to take their leave; he, Hansen would keep an eye on the prisoners. And so off went this second guard, much to the satisfaction of Hansen, who then gave Matthias a friendly nudge in the back and said in his ear,

"Take your master's elbow. We're going to slip away. Move slowly, and keep your eyes down."

And as Hansen shuffled Sir Cosmo and his valet slowly towards the gallery and to safety, his fellow guards were herding the courtiers out through the double doors; the noblemen couldn't get out of the chamber quick enough. Baron Haderslev, with General Müller and Alec beside him, approached the dais and the Margrave. They had barely straightened out of a respectful low bow, when Ernst suddenly came to life. He leaped up, sending his high-back chair to the floor with a clatter, and stabbed a finger in the air at all three men, shouting at his captain of the guard,

"Westover! Arrest him! Arrest that traitor! Arrest Baron Haderslev!"

# Twenty-four

APTAIN WESTOVER HESITATED. HE DIDN'T BELIEVE for a moment the Court Chamberlain was a traitor. That small hesitation was all the time Alec needed to step right up to the dais, set the small jewelry casket in front of Ernst, and put his hands flat on the table. He then leaned into him and spoke in a voice that had all jaws in the room swinging.

"Haderslev isn't a traitor, and you know it, Ernst," Alec admonished mildly, as one does a small child. "You're just being bad-tempered for its own sake because you never thought to see me again. But here I am! Returned! Aren't you pleased to see an old friend?"

Ernst's bottom lip quivered. He was instantly reprimanded. He pointed at Haderslev.

"*He* said you wouldn't come! *He* said we'd never see you again!"

Alec came around to his side of the table, propped a buttock on an edge and casually swung a booted leg.

"But here I am! Just because the Baron said I wouldn't come, doesn't mean he's a traitor, does it?" Alec cajoled. He jerked his head towards the others in the chamber. "Send them away," he said softly. "Then we can talk... Just you and me... It's been too long, and I'm certain you have so much to tell me..."

371

Ernst hovered in indecision. He glanced over at the main entrance as the last of the noblemen were being herded out and the large bronze inlaid doors closed on their backs. The guards were now also on the other side of the doors. He then looked at Baron Haderslev who was wringing his hands, and beside him he recognized Colonel Müller. He thought he'd sent him to Emden... And over by the gallery were the two English prisoners, and a guard. What were they still doing here? He didn't want any of them here now; he just wanted to speak with Alec, who had come all this way from England to see him—No! He'd come to collect his English friend! Why should he pretend otherwise? Why should he listen to him? But Alec had not once looked over at the Englishmen. It was as if they were not there at all. Alec had kept his eyes on him and him alone.

He wanted—no he *needed*—to be alone with him, to talk with him. Just the two of them. He was so lonely now Papa was gone... And he had to talk with him before Joanna got wind of his return, because she'd be there in a trice, and monopolize Alec's time as she always did, and he'd never get another word in... She was becoming more and more demanding, and he was running out of excuses to keep her locked up. He hated not being in control... He was the Margrave... No one had a right to tell him what to do. No one.

And then Westover came over and set his chair to rights, and spoiled his mental musings. And when the Captain continued to hover by his shoulder, it irritated him beyond measure. As much as the Captain's presence had been a comfort, there when he needed him, like an old favorite toy, for some inexplicable reason now, at this moment, with Alec Halsey smiling down at him, asking to be alone with him, he didn't want Westover or anyone else near him. He just wanted to be with Alec; just like the old days. Just like it was before Joanna got it into her head it was somehow *his* fault Alec had abandoned her. Well, she wasn't the only one who'd been abandoned!

"Get out, Westover! Take them with you! I don't want any of you—"

"Highness, I cannot leave you! I must stay—"

"Get out! Get out!" Ernst screeched.

"But Highness, he has a sword—"

"—and I'll use it on *you* if you don't leave us!"

"Highness, I must and will protect you!"

"Then protect me from over there somewhere! Just get out of my face! And if you send word of this to my sister, it'll be your head on a pike! Understand me!? Not a word to her!"

Westover blinked. "Not a word, Highness. Not without your permission!"

"Come, Captain," General Müller said quietly at Westover's shoulder. "Let us repair to the gallery."

Alec unbuckled his sword and held it out. "Here. Take it."

"There. You can't have any objection now he's unarmed," Baron Haderslev said at Westover's ear. "If you stand just inside the entrance you can still see what's going on through the lattice. You'll be only two strides away."

Westover capitulated. He glanced at Alec, who remained inert beside the Margrave, then bowed deeply and turned on a heel. General Müller went on ahead of him. He had seen the two prisoners with their guard slip into the gallery, and he now went after them, found them making for the door cut into the paneling and demanded they stay where they were.

Instantly, Hansen stepped in front of Sir Cosmo and Matthias, shielding them, drawing his sword as he did so.

"I am taking these two innocent men to safety! That, or you will have to cut me down where I stand! I've had enough of His Highness's particular brand of justice!"

"Wait! Stay!" General Müller demanded in a loud whisper, a look over his shoulder and a gloved hand raised. His sword remained in its scabbard. When Hansen remained where he was, he asked, "Who are these two men?"

"They are Englishmen. A lord and his servant."

"Sir Cosmo Mahon?" asked Müller with surprise, taking in the disheveled dirty state of both prisoners. When Hansen nodded but said no more, he added, "You'll be safer with me. Trust me. Events are about to overtake the Margrave."

Hansen hesitated in indecision, weighing up whether this was a ploy to get him to put away his sword, before having them all arrested. It was Sir Cosmo who decided him. The Englishman's knees buckled and he collapsed. Matthias caught his master, and Hansen, still with his sword drawn had only one hand free so was unable to help. In two strides, Müller pushed past the guard and had Sir Cosmo by the other elbow. He helped Matthias sit him down, back up against the paneling, before rising up to face Hansen.

He put out his hand to the guard, who immediately sheathed his sword, and took it.

"Prince Viktor could use a soldier like you, Herr—?"

"Hansen Bootsman, Herr Colonel!" said the body guard, coming to attention. He could not hide his grin. "Yes, he could, Herr Colonel!"

"It's General Müller. But we'll worry about the formalities later. For now, look after these men with your life. When this is over, we'll discuss your career prospects."

Müller returned to stand with Baron Haderslev who was at Captain Westover's shoulder.

The Captain of the Guard peered at Müller with a frown. "What is the meaning of this, Colonel? What is going on—"

"Don't look at me! Turn about and watch!" Müller hissed. "Watch and *listen*."

All three men peered through the lattice screen, listening, disbelieving their own eyes and ears.

~ ~ ~

Alec waited until he was alone with Ernst in the cavernous audience chamber before moving to close the gap between them. Having Alec in such close proximity, Ernst cowered. But he did not move away. His bottom lip set to trembling again and tears filled his eyes. He quickly blinked these away because he had to be certain his long-lost friend was still there, that this wasn't a bad dream. Instinctively, he put out a hand and almost had his fingers to Alec's cheek, when Alec took hold of his hand and held it in a firm clasp.

"Now that I am holding your hand," Alec said with a friendly smile, "do you believe I am truly here with you?"

Ernst nodded and sniffed, but then tugged his hand free and said crossly, though there was no heat in his voice, "You didn't come here to see me. You came to save your hairy English friend. You were almost too late, too! He's practically dead already, so not much use anymore as a friend, is he? I should still have him killed, just to teach you a lesson for leaving us—for leaving *me*."

"I cannot believe you meant to kill him, all to have your revenge on me?" Alec lied.

He had forced himself not to look at Cosmo, though he had been aware of him and his valet, and the guard standing over them both. He assumed Müller had taken them away to some place safe, and he would take care of Cosmo, be reunited with him, once he had this creature and its monster locked away for all time. For now he could not afford to think of anyone or anything but the fine-boned nobleman whose hand he held. He smiled down on him with such a lovely smile he was sure Ernst was fast believing the lie he had come all this way just for the pleasure of his company, English friend and the war be damned.

"I hope you brought me a gift worthy of a Margrave?" Ernst said peevishly. "I'm Margrave now, don't y'know!"

"Yes. I do know. And yes, I did bring you a gift."

Alec opened the casket and tipped its contents onto the table by the candelabra. Out spilled strings of pearls, gold rings, brooches, diamond-encrusted shoe buckles, and gold earrings dripping with precious stones. There were pieces set with diamonds, emeralds, rubies, and sapphires. There was even a large handful of single gems, and then there was the ruby necklace Alec had mistaken for Selina's heart when she had been struck down in the crossfire at Aurich.

Ernst's eyes lit up with unconcealed avarice and he let his fingers caress the precious pile. He picked up a shoe buckle, then found a particular diamond ring, dropped the shoe buckle atop the pile and slipped the ring on a slender finger. He held out his hand to admire it.

When Alec slowly guided Ernst's hand into the candlelight and gently turned his lace covered wrist so that the diamond's facets winked, General Müller, Baron Haderslev, and Captain Westover moved closer to the lattice screen so that their noses were almost poking through the holes in the woodwork, all just as mesmerized as Ernst. And when Alec moved closer to Ernst, their chests a mere button width apart, General Müller and Baron Haderslev held their breath.

Alec looked down into Ernst's delicate features framed by an overabundance of blond ringlets, the wig falling in fat curls to the shoulders, and at the bright blue eyes that blinked up at him with something akin to adoration, and he forced himself to continue on with the subterfuge. He knew his next move could very well decide Cosmo's fate, and his. So while his voice might be soft and pliable, every fiber, every sinew of his being was taut. It was as if his boots were nailed to the parquetry. His jaw was clenched and his hands were in fists; those behind the lattice screen saw this, but Ernst did not.

376

"It's a beautiful ring, isn't it," he murmured near Ernst's ear. "A beautiful ring for a beautiful woman. It will fit Joanna's finger perfectly. But will she like it, do you think? Is it worthy of your sister? Look at it closely and tell me what you think, Ernst. Tell me if the ring is worthy of a princess..."

Ernst stared at the diamond ring, at the way the light caught in the many facets. How it winked in the candlelight and drew in the surrounding colors. Light and color swirled before him. And when his hand moved out of the light, as if by magic, for he was certain it had a mind of its own, his gaze remained riveted to the diamond. And all the while he listened to Alec's voice near his ear. The deep dulcet tones washed over him like the warm water of his bath, and when his hand drew level with Alec's chin, his gaze slid effortlessly from the diamond to Alec's face, to the dark stubble that dotted the square chin, up to the curve of his lovely mouth, then up further to the angular lines of his cheekbones. His friend's face was thinner. Older. There were creases at the corners of his eyes. Eyes that were blue, but much darker than his own. Had his hair always been so thick? He knew that when it was not caught up in a ribbon it fell in waves past his shoulders. He'd forgotten just how blue-black was his friend's hair. Joanna had always been covetous of such hair...

"You've not shaved... Everyone must shave..." Ernst managed to mutter. "It's the law..."

"No. Not shaved," Alec repeated in a low, soothing voice. "That's how she prefers me. She likes it when I wear my hair out, down my back... She likes my cologne, too. It's sandalwood with a hint of pepper... Do you remember it?... Do you remember how it makes you feel... How I make you feel...?"

Ernst fell deeper under the spell of Alec's caressing tone. He swayed as he breathed in the scent of him... It had been such a long time since he'd smelled anything so-so—*manly*. It brought to the fore memories of a time long ago, of carefree days spent in the company of his English friend. The days of the summer at Friedeburg Palace spent swimming in the lake, fencing at the academy, hunting in the forests, flirting in the corridors and at balls with the daughters of the court nobles. He was able to forget for a time this dark place, and the demands of his twin. Alec had helped him forget, and to gain a new-found confidence in himself. He dared to think that he might just be able to exist without Joanna telling him what to do; without Joanna at all. Such was his confidence that he invited Alec to Herzfeld Castle when it was time for him to return to his duties with the Midanich army. With Alec by his side, he would have the confidence and strength to stand up to Joanna, to stand up for what he wanted in life, and not what she told him he wanted.

He should have known better. He should have realized that as soon as Joanna saw his English friend, she would want him all to herself. If only she had allowed him this one friend, things would have turned out very differently. But Joanna had a way of making him believe that what she wanted was what he wanted too. And with Alec Halsey that was indeed true. She convinced him they could share him. Twins shared everything, even those they loved. Did they not share Papa? And they had always shared their lovers. What was the point of love, of enjoying being loved if it could not be shared with the one you loved most in the world? And she loved her brother more than she loved anyone or anything. Surely he felt the same about her? She could not live if he did not love her as much as she loved him. He could not be so cruel as to keep the handsome Englishman to himself. Ernst capitulated. He always did. But this time he refused to be relegated to spectator. They would share the Englishman in all things and every way or he would not let her into his bedchamber. She had agreed, and he couldn't have been happier.

But then the Englishman had escaped them, and while he blamed Joanna, Joanna blamed him. So he was reluctant to want to share him, now he was back. He did not even want his sister to know Alec Halsey had returned. He wanted to keep it a secret from her for as long as possible. But he knew that for wishful thinking. His sister had an overwhelming desire to have her revenge on the Englishman for abandoning them. Even after all these years, and when she was at her lowest, when she railed against their father and him for keeping her locked away when he had promised upon their father's death to set her free, it was Alec Halsey she blamed for her past and present ills. If he had stayed. If he had been a proper husband. If he had loved her as she loved him. If Ernst was more a man and less a milksop. If she had been a firstborn son and not a daughter, she and not Ernst would be ruler of Midanich. If only she weren't consigned to living in the shadows. If only she could show herself to him, here in this room, now. If. If. If. If. *If...*

"WHAT ARE YOU DOING HERE?" JOANNA SPAT UP AT ALEC. "I wish you'd never come back! I wish you'd drowned! Died of exposure. Been stabbed, mutilated—anything but be here now!"

"Ah! There you are," Alec murmured with satisfaction. "It is good to see you, too, Highness. And to know you missed me so *very* much."

"Missed you? *Missed you*? I've not given you a thought since the day you left!"

"Come now. You can do better than that," Alec chided playfully, holding her hand and circling her slowly, moving them closer to the lattice screen, positioning them both so that those who watched on saw and heard every word. "Truth told, you've thought of little else but me. Weaving your web and waiting in the shadows; waiting the opportunity to strike back. Poor Cosmo. He had no idea what he'd walked into coming here."

"More fool *he*. If he was ignorant of the pain you caused us, that's your fault. His suffering is *all* your fault."

"Yes," Alec said sadly, and drew her closer.

His words and his touch cooled her anger and she willingly

closed the gap between them. Her gaze searched his face, mouth quivering in anticipation that he would kiss her, he must, but her words belied her thoughts and her actions.

"I so *hate* you."

"Yes, you must," he murmured caressingly, dipping his head, moving his mouth close to hers. "You are a monster and a vile wretch, and yet for all that you have suffered in your own way, and for that I am sorry. I am here to end your suffering. Do you understand me, Highness?"

"Call me Joanna," she pleaded, finally putting her arms up about his neck and pressing herself against him. "It's Joanna. It's *always* been Joanna."

His mouth hovered so teasingly close she felt his breath on her lips. Her nostrils quivered, drinking in the peppery scent of him, and all she wanted, desperately wanted, was to take him in her mouth.

"Then, *Joanna*, do with me as you please... That is what you want, isn't it?" When she nodded mutely, gaze riveted to his, he smiled. "Then I am yours to command..."

Unable to resist a moment longer, she pulled him down and put her mouth to his.

He closed his eyes, let his mind go blank, and accepted the inevitable. Where there was no choice, there was contentment. It had to be this way—to set Cosmo free, to set himself free of the past, to give Ernst peace and free him of the monster who ruled him, and through him, Midanich. Thus he allowed himself to succumb to the fantasy, to be caught up in the moment, to make this kiss every bit as passionate and all consuming as if they were truly lovers. Joanna had to believe it, and she did.

She melted against him, the kiss everything she had dreamed it would be, as it had been ten years ago, when she had gone to Alec's room, seduced him, forced herself on him, and made Ernst part of it all. And for abandoning her she had been intent on punishing him and anyone he cared for. But now, with this kiss, all the fight, all the hate, all the torment, and all the artifice, drained away.

"*A-A WOMAN? GOTT IM HIMMEL! A WOMAN!*"

It was Captain Westover, and the words hissed from him watching the couple exchange a passionate kiss. He staggered back from the lattice screen, disbelieving, breath ragged, as if he'd been winded. He was confused; livid; betrayed. And he was having none of it. He hadn't spent the past five years as Captain of the Household Guard, protecting Margrave Leopold and the Herzfeld royal family to be duped by a female—no matter how noble her lineage, and she Leopold's daughter. She wasn't entitled to rule. It was forbidden. And it was against nature for a woman to parade about society, rule a country, dressed and acting like a man! Ordering men about as if she were one of them. How could he have been so blind? Why hadn't he worked it out for himself!? He stared at Haderslev and Müller, wild-eyed and shaking.

The General took him by the upper arm and pushed him further down the gallery so as not to be overhead by the couple. His voice was not much above a whisper and his words were rasped out, laced with shock at what he, too, had just witnessed. Never in all his days would he have thought to see the creature manifest in the blaze of candlelight before his eyes. He was all admiration for Alec Halsey's skill in teasing the monster from her shadowy lair.

"Now you've seen it with your own eyes, Westover, and heard what was said, you surely understand now why Prince Ernst is unfit to continue as Margrave."

*Understand*? Westover understood all right! He now understood why Ernst was unable to grow facial hair; why beards and mustaches had been outlawed. It had nothing to do with an *unspoken truth* but because as a woman this so-called Ernst was incapable of growing

facial hair in the first place! No wonder he had a pretty nose, large
blue eyes, and wore long blond wigs tied up with ribbons. He even
tittered and gossiped like a woman, too. He now understood why
*Ernst* surrounded himself with a cadre of fops and whey-faced fools,
all so that he—*she*—did not appear so emasculated. That explained
why he'd never married, never once looked twice at a female, even
when they practically threw themselves at him, all for the chance
to become Margravina. He now understood why Leopold on his
deathbed had bemoaned that if his line were to continue on after
him, it would be through Prince Viktor, the son born to a commoner.

And there was only one explanation for what he had just
witnessed. Westover addressed Baron Haderslev, who had followed
the General and Captain further into the gallery.

"She's insane, yes?"

The Baron nodded and sniffed. There were tears in his eyes. He
could not bring himself to speak.

Westover whipped out his sword, the blade quivering in his
shaking hand. "Good. I know what to do now."

"Wait! Stop!" Haderslev pleaded, and would have gone after him,
but was restrained by General Müller who used his own sword to
keep the Baron inert.

"Let him be, Baron," the General purred. "Let him do what
should've been done a long time ago."

"He's going to kill him," whimpered the Baron.

General Müller smiled crookedly.

"I heartily hope so. It will save me the trouble."

It was over before Alec knew what had happened.

Joanna moaned, went limp, and slumped against his chest. He
caught her to him before she slipped out of his arms to the floor,
and cradled her, unaware she had been fatally stabbed in the back,
and through the heart.

But he knew something was terribly wrong when she did not respond to his voice, or touch. Her head rolled back, eyelids fluttering, and the blond wig slipped to one side. It was then he saw the large spreading stain, and the blood to the front of the saffron waistcoat, and knew she was dead.

He looked up, coming out of the mental fog that had enveloped him since the Princess Joanna had shown herself, and saw Captain Westover, face flushed with fury, bloodied sword in hand. The soldier wiped the blade clean between his gloved fingers and contemptuously flicked the blood off, and it sprayed across the floor. But he did not sheathe his sword. He stared at Alec with sneering contempt and took a step towards him.

Alec wondered if he was to be Westover's next victim. He was still dazed by what he had just put himself through to open wide Westover's eyes to the truth. He had expected the Captain to react, but not with murderous intent. And then Westover spoke, and Alec realized the soldier, despite what he had just witnessed and the conversation he had overheard, was still none the wiser to the larger truth. But that really should not have surprised him. For even with the facts laid bare, it was surely beyond the comprehension of most to appreciate precisely the nature and shape of the monster they were dealing with.

After placing the dead Margrave gently on the floor, Alec calmly faced Westover, a glance over at the gallery when Baron Haderslev and General Müller emerged. The Court Chamberlain scurried across and dropped to his knees beside the Margrave's body and let out such a wail that it set the hairs up on the back of Alec's neck. The old man was prostrate with grief, and threw himself across the body and sobbed.

"Not like this. Never like this," the Court Chamberlain cried, sitting up on his knees.

He set to adjusting the Margrave's blond wig so that it better framed his delicate face, then straightened out the frock coat, smoothing the creases, as if it mattered. He then took the Margrave's arms and carefully placed them across his chest, so his dead master appeared merely at rest. And all the while he cried and muttered to himself. Finally, he kissed the Margrave's forehead before sitting back on his haunches with head bowed to pray.

It was harrowing to watch his ministrations and Westover was in no mood to witness such fawning grief. He ordered the Baron to get up off his knees and join Alec and General Müller. But when Haderslev swayed and his stockinged knee slipped out from under him, Alec went forward and helped him up.

Through his tears, the Baron looked up at Alec who was supporting him by the arm. "Ernst was a good, sweet boy who never meant anyone harm, but—"

"—he was weak, and infected with his mad sister's evil," Müller interrupted, unsympathetic. "Joanna was a she-devil. She killed her father and was slowly killing her brother."

"Baron, you know better than anyone, that Ernst was dominated and tormented by his sister almost from the cradle," Alec said. "Even in death she never left him. Now, at least, with his own demise, he can finally be free of her, and at peace."

Haderslev nodded. "Yes. Yes. Finally. Ironic is it not that it took death to separate them..."

Alec raised an eyebrow. "Ironic? Herr Baron, believe me, that is the least ironic detail about this tragic state of affairs."

Westover waved his sword menacingly.

"Get over here! I want answers before I have you all locked up!"

"Westover, your Margrave is dead," Müller stated calmly. "And you killed him. The only person who is to be locked up is you, if you don't come to your senses and realize what is happening around you!"

"Müller, where is Sir Cosmo? Is he safe?" Alec interrupted, a glance over at the gallery.

"He's behind the screen being protected by a brute of guard. Have no fear. He is safe."

"I must go to him—" Alec began and was stopped when Westover's rapier poked the folds of his cravat.

"You're not going anywhere," Westover stated.

"There are three men behind that screen, and at least two of them require assistance—"

"No one is to move until I have answers," Westover growled, pacing before the three men, wild-eyed and wondering at his next move. "One shout from me and this chamber will be filled with my guards." He pointed his rapier at the corpse and addressed them all. "How long have you known about her, eh?"

"There is no *her*, Westover," Müller answered with an impatient sigh when Alec and Haderslev remained silent. "That is the body of Prince Ernst, Margrave of Midanich. And you killed him."

"Killed *him*?! That's a woman!" Westover pointed his rapier at Alec but addressed General Müller. "The way she looked at him— kissed him—spoke to him—What do you take me for? He'd not kiss a man like that, even with a musket barrel to his head! Ha! You think me completely without wits? I know what's going on here. That isn't Prince Ernst, but his mad sister Joanna parading about as our Margrave!"

"How perceptive of you, Captain," Alec replied calmly, though he could not keep the heat out of his face when he said, "I did indeed share a passionate moment with the Princess Joanna. She has always harbored an irrational affection for me. We had hoped that if I could *entice* her out of the shadows your eyes would be opened to the precise nature of the—er—*relationship* between Prince Ernst and his sister."

"Relationship? I don't care about that! All that matters is that dead body does not belong to Prince Ernst. It is a woman dressed as a man. And I did not take an oath to serve and protect a mad woman! Tell me what's she's done with her brother, or what you've done with him, or so help me, I will have you all tortured until you do!"

"But, Herr Captain, I assure you, that is the body of Prince Ernst," Baron Haderslev replied sadly. "The Princess Joanna died when she was fifteen and is buried in the family crypt in the casements. She was mad almost from her cradle, though it took many years for Margrave Leopold and her women to realize just how mad. It was when she became a woman that it truly manifested itself in the most base ways. She became a whore, allowing her guards, her servants, any man who took her fancy, to mount her. She even tried to seduce her own father. Monster! And she used her whore's ways to seduce and control Ernst. Disgusting foul creature! It was a godsend when she contracted measles and died at fifteen."

"Ballocks! Everyone from the pot scrubber to you as Court Chamberlain, Haderslev, knows the Princess Joanna was a prisoner, and very much alive! She has guards, she has servants, and her father and her brother made regular visits to her chambers. What I don't know, and what you are going to tell me, is when the switch was made, when His Highness died, or when he was killed, and you allowed her to take his place!"

"As neat as that theory is, Westover," Müller stated. "It is not the truth. I wish to God it were. It would be so much easier to get the facts through your thick skull to your brain! All you need do is accept the Prince Ernst was as mad as his sister—well, since her death, most certainly."

"What he says is true, Westover," Baron Haderslev assured him. "Despite Princess Joanna's insanity and her whoring ways, Prince Ernst was devastated by her loss. He did not know how to go on without her. We—Margrave Leopold and I—hoped that with time, Ernst would make a recover. That with Princess Joanna's death he would finally see he was free of her. And for the longest time, particularly when he was at Friedeburg Palace, Prince Ernst appeared to make a full recovery. What we did not know then, but which became apparent only after some years, was that when Ernst returned here, here to the castle, it was to spend time with his twin. In truth, he had refused to believe she was gone. He thus kept her alive. And the more time he spent here, in her rooms, the more his mind was taken over by her, until he—he—when he was in her rooms, he *became* her." The Baron shook his head sadly and appealed to Alec. "That is how it was, was it not, Herr Baron?"

"Yes," Alec replied quietly. "Yes, that is precisely how it was..."

"If you need convincing," Müller stated irreverently to Westover, "pull down his breeches and take a look at his cock for yourself!"

Westover had no time to take up Müller's offer. A great deafening boom shook the audience chamber. There was second boom. And then another.

"Dear God! What is happening?" exclaimed the Baron, grabbing Alec's sleeve.

General Müller knew the sound of ship's cannon when he heard it. The sound of cannon fire meant the rebel flotilla had arrived safely in harbor, a ship remaining out to sea as planned firing warning shots near the castle.

"Hear that, Westover?" the General said smugly and laughed. "That is the sound of victory!"

It was indeed cannon fire. And all four men quickly took shelter in the gallery. But the cannon fire had ceased, replaced by the shouts and grunts of men in close combat and the steady rumble of boots as more soldiers filled the corridors beyond the double doors. Finally, with the audience chamber doors being pounded by the combined efforts of half a dozen rebel soldiers, the locks gave and the doors sprang wide with a great whoosh and slammed against the oak-paneled walls. A cheer went up. Soldiers poured into the space, swords drawn, ready to do battle with any and every soldier who opposed them. And leading this final charge was a golden-haired young man with a golden mustache.

To the amazement of Prince Viktor and his victorious rebel soldiers the chamber was empty but for the lifeless body of his half-brother, Prince Ernst Leopold Herzfeld, fifteenth Margrave of Midanich.

RUNNING FOR COVER, ALEC BROKE AWAY AND JOINED THE three silent figures at the far end of the gallery. A wide-shouldered soldier stood protectively over two men slumped up against the wall with their legs drawn up to their chins, one silently staring at the floorboards, while the other stared at his companion. A nod to the soldier, and Alec went down on his haunches beside them. When Matthias went to scramble up, Alec put a hand on his arm and shook his head, and so the valet remained beside his master.

Alec took in the state of the men's soiled garments, matted hair, and the way their clothes hung off their limbs, and he swallowed back his shock and guilt at what his best friend and his valet had endured as prisoners of Prince Ernst. This man sitting before him looked like a beggar from any European city backstreet, so unlike in form was he from the Sir Cosmo Mahon he knew: The fastidious dresser who was particularly vain about his long soft fingers with their buffed nails. So it was at the state of his friend's hands, at the ragged nails, and covered in filth and sores, that was the breaking point for Alec. He finally lost mastery over his emotions, put his face in his hands and silently sobbed. But he quickly dried his eyes on the back of a sleeve and pulled himself together enough to put a hand on Cosmo's shoulder and to say gently,

"Cosmo? Cosmo, my dear fellow. It's Alec. I've come to take you home."

It was Matthias who responded when Sir Cosmo did not.

"You'll have to forgive him, my lord—Yes, I do know who you

are—He's been like this for the past sennight. Just staring into nothingness, and not saying a word. Before that he'd been the bravest man alive, always looking forward to this moment, when you'd come for him..." The valet, too, then lost his nerve and burst into tears, tears of joy to think their lives had been spared, and they had been rescued. He sniffed back tears. "Forgive me, my lord. I didn't mean to cry like a babe. It's just—we're so happy to see you. Aren't we, sir?" he said, addressing Sir Cosmo. "Aren't we overjoyed to have Lord Halsey here with us. To finally come for us..."

Alec tried again to get through to Cosmo. He gently took his friend's face between his hands, lifting it up so that their eyes were level. He looked into Cosmo's vacant stare with a smile. "Emily can't wait to see you, Cosmo. So too Selina. They are both waiting for you. You want to see Emily and Selina, don't you?"

Cosmo blinked and when he focused on Alec's blue eyes, Alec withdrew his hands.

"Emily?" he said wonderingly. "Emily is-is *safe*?"

Alec nodded. "Yes. Emily is safe. And she is very well indeed."

"And-and Selina?"

"Yes. Both. They are but an hour's journey from here. I am going to take you to them."

"And Matthias and Hansen. They must come too."

"Of course."

"Me Hansen!" stuck in the wide-shouldered soldier. "I speak English. I come, too."

"But poor Mrs. Carlisle can't come with us."

When Cosmo's shoulders began to shake, Alec realized he was crying, so looked to Matthias for an explanation. The valet swallowed hard and found his voice.

"Mrs. Carlisle is dead, my lord. We don't know how it happened. Hansen says she threw herself from a window—"

"Dear God, that poor woman..." Alec muttered.

"We won't tell Emily," Cosmo said to Matthias. "Emily must not know, Matthias!"

"No, sir," Matthias replied gently. "We won't tell her. Will we, my lord?" he added looking to Alec.

"Of course not. Emily will not be told how she died, that I promise," Alec agreed, still in shock to think the woman who had bravely taken Emily's place to allow her charge to flee to safety was dead.

"We get out now!" Hansen stated, indicating the door cut into the paneling. "Get out before we caught! Come!"

"I don't think that's necessary," Alec stated in German, a look over his shoulder when a spontaneous cheer went up amongst the soldiers on the other side of the latticed screen. He saw General Muller with Westover in custody, and Haderslev following behind, leave the gallery. Such was his preoccupation with events in the audience chamber, that he was slow to respond to his name, until he realized just who was asking after him.

"Alec? Alec? Is that you?" Cosmo asked with genuine surprise, seeing his best friend as if for the first time. "Alec! Alec! It *is* you! You did come!"

"Yes! Yes, dearest friend, it is me!" Alec responded with a tearful grin, adding with a self-deprecating smile, "Sorry it took me a bit longer to get here than I'd hoped. Not the easiest place for travel, is it? Boats, barges, and a bumpy old sledge ride!"

"Not to worry. You're here now. And that's the main thing, isn't it?" Cosmo said in something of his old manner, and gave his valet a dig in the ribs with his elbow. "See. Told you. Told you he'd come. Told you Alec would never give up on us."

The valet and Alec exchanged a look, Matthias saying with a sigh, "Yes, sir. You did indeed. How many shillings do I owe you?"

"About a year's wages, but not to worry, Alec will pay your blunt, won't you?"

"Yes. Gladly. And for looking after you, twice that and more!" Cosmo squeezed Alec's arm. "Alec. My dear, dear fellow, I can't tell you how happy—how *exceedingly* happy—I am to see you!"

"The feeling is entirely mutual, my dearest, bravest friend."

Both men cried in each other's arms, grateful to be alive, to have found each other again, and to know the future was all before them. They stayed that way until Cosmo broke away with a start, whispering fearfully,

"What's that?"

Cheering and three Hip Hip Hoorays! filled the audience chamber.

"Nothing for us to worry about," Alec assured him, giving Cosmo's hand a reassuring squeeze. "The people of Midanich are celebrating the dawning of a new day. And we shall, too." He stood and put out his hand to help his best friend to his feet. "Come on. Let's go home..."

# Epilogue

"WILL HE MAKE A RECOVER, DO YOU THINK?"

"Yes. With time—and care. I'm taking him down to Delvin with us. The country air, good food, and eventually a baby to keep him diverted as doting godfather—all these things will help."

The Duchess of Romney-St. Neots squeezed Alec's arm a little too tightly as they strolled the Mars Reception Gallery used by the noble inhabitants of the *Schloss* Rosine for daily exercise during the winter months. This night being Twelfth Night, the room was ablaze with light, and all the guests had assembled for an evening of fun and games.

"I still haven't forgiven you for marrying Selina without your uncle and me present!"

"We can have another ceremony when we return to London, if you wish it—"

"No. I'm just teasing you, my boy," the Duchess replied and was suddenly teary. "I cannot tell you how-how—*happy* you and Selina have made me—all of us! To think you are to be a father in the summer... a long-held wish finally realized."

"For us both, my dear Olivia. Though I still find myself wondering at odd times if it is truly real."

Both looked over at Selina, who was seated at a long table, which had at its center a beautifully-painted *Cavagnole* board. At the table with her were Cosmo, Emily, Plantagenet Halsey, Sir Gilbert Parsons, and a number of the nobles from the court. Margrave Viktor was acting as banker and held the silk bag containing the green-dyed ivory beads, and this he shook from time to time and made an elaborate show of extracting a bead. This never failed to elicit a laugh from players and audience alike.

"Why do they play it? It's such a boring game!" the Duchess said dismissively. "But they all seem to be enjoying it as if it is the most entertaining thing they have ever experienced in their lives. I suppose the Christmas season lends itself to revels, and though I wish I was back in London, it is quite magical here, now that the war is at an end and we can sleep peacefully in our beds."

"After the events of the past six months, even a boring game of *Cavagnole* is welcomed with enthusiasm. They are just happy to be alive, Olivia. We all are." He added to goad her, "You're just jaded because the most exciting episode of your life happened aboard *The Caroline*, sailing into Herzfeld port with a shipload of rebel soldiers, and my uncle threatening every last one of them not to harm a hair on your lovely head!"

The Duchess's mouth set in a prim line, ready to refute this. But then she smiled to herself, remembering that particular episode on board ship when the French frigate closest *The Caroline* opened fire on the castle. She had leapt into the old man's arms with the first explosive boom, and there stayed; Alec was right. Nevertheless, she squared her shoulders and lied. "Rot! I'll only be too glad to see the back of the wretched man and set sail for Copenhagen."

"You still mean to take Emily to see her mother?"

"Yes. I've come this far. Besides, I don't have a choice. Emily wants to see her. And truth be told, I've not seen my daughter in years. Besides, it will put distance between her and Viktor."

"He's halfway to falling in love with her, too."

"I know! What a muddle. The last thing I want on this earth is for her to be a Margravina. God help us if that happens."

Alec shrugged. "Midanich is lovely in the spring... and Friedeburg Palace delightful..."

"Don't encourage her—or him! Time and distance will put paid to this little winter romance, of that I'm convinced."

"Or make it stronger..." Alec countered. "Time. Distance. Age. None of that matters when one is in love, does it? Oh, and I'm sorry to disappoint you, but nothing I have said to him can dissuade him. Uncle tells me he is duty-bound to accompany you and Emily to Copenhagen—"

"What?!"

"—so he can make certain you both are returned home in time for the birth of our child," Alec ended smoothly, a glance down at his godmother and a private smile when he detected the flush to her cheeks. "He doesn't want to miss that, or the christening. Like you, he was most disappointed to have missed our marriage ceremony."

"I won't have him! Managing man," the Duchess grumbled. Though her annoyance was directed at herself for being secretly elated at Plantagenet Halsey's chivalry. To deflect attention away from herself she focused her gaze on Sir Gilbert and complained, "I cannot believe you're allowing that toad to take the credit for the trade deal with Midanich. Parsons doesn't deserve such praise, nor does Cobham. But you do. You were the one who negotiated the terms with the new Margrave." She glanced up slyly at her godson. "If you put yourself forward, I am certain it would get you that ambassadorship...?"

Alec let out a bark of laughter that got him the attention of half the room.

"Ha! I wondered when you'd bring that up! Your persistence alone is deserving of a medal. No, my dear Olivia. In fact, a thousand times no. I am going to be perfectly content rusticating at Delvin."

"I don't believe you!"

"What don't you believe, aunt? What little lies has Lord Halsey been spinning?" Selina demanded, sweeping up to them and attaching herself to her husband's velvet sleeve. She looked up at him lovingly. "Not that I think you capable of lying, my lord... I won, by the way." She held up a velvet pouch full of gold coins. "Enough to buy my own village, it would seem. Though I shall donate the lot to the soldiers' benevolent fund."

"An excellent notion, my love. I shall match the sum. Your aunt does not believe me when I say I am happy to rusticate at Delvin for the foreseeable future."

"Oh, until the babe is born, to be sure," Selina agreed, then showed her husband a marked lack of loyalty by confiding in her aunt, "Truthfully, I have grave doubts he'll last out the full term. I foresee we will be in London well before Easter."

"Selina! You wretch! I am looking forward to doing nothing more than sitting on the terrace with Cosmo, surveying my sheep."

"Surveying your sheep? Oh dear, that does sound rather dreary, my boy," Olivia agreed, and exchanged a giggle with her niece.

"I rest my case," Selina quipped, laughed, and when Alec pulled a face, kissed his cheek.

Before he could make a suitable retort there was a commotion at the double doors, and those present in the room who were seated stood to welcome the newest member of Margrave Viktor's family, his three-week-old half-brother, Carl Philip Rosine Müller, created Count Emden the day of his birth, the day Castle Herzfeld was stormed. He was being carried by his proud father, the Countess Rosine at his side. They came up to Alec and Selina, family and guests crowding in to have a peek at the sleeping infant.

"We have a favor to ask of you, Herr Baron," the Countess Rosine said, a glance up at her husband, who smiled down at her. "We would be honored if you would be our son's godfather."

"You must say yes!" Prince Viktor stuck in, coming to stand on Alec's other side and gripping his shoulder. "Of course he says yes!"

"If that is your wish, yes," Alec agreed. He looked from General Müller to the Countess. "You are certain?"

"Certain!? There is no question. My half-brother must have the Baron Aurich as his godfather. Is that not so, Herr General?"

"Yes. It is what we both want," General Müller agreed. "Regardless of my stepson's wishes."

"Then it is settled. And to celebrate this most auspicious of occasions, we shall have dancing," Viktor announced.

Everyone applauded, and servants were quick to clear the center of the room of card tables, chairs, and footstools. The musicians, who had been playing quietly in the background, now tuned their instruments and organized their sheet music for a set of country dances. The nobles chose their partners, Viktor taking out his mother for the first set, and Emily quick to partner up with Cosmo, who was at first a little reluctant to be involved, until Emily whispered in his ear something that made him laugh and shake his head and consent.

"I think Cosmo is going to be all right, Selina." Alec smiled, watching his best friend lead Emily to join the line of dancers. "It may take months to put the fat back on him, but it was his mind that had me most worried... But I think he will mend, with our help."

Selina put her arm through his and snuggled in. "Yes. I think you will, too."

He frowned and looked down at her. "You think me in need of mending?"

Selina's dark eyes sparkled. "Not mending. But being all right. Being yourself again. Others obviously think you are all right because you have that sort of face—"

"Sort of face...?"

"—that makes new parents want you as godfather for their

infants. You do realize this is the second time you've been made a godfather in less than six months!? First Cleveley's infant, Thomas, and now little Carl Philip. I'd say that shows you have the sort of face that reflects what's inside here," she said, placing her hand on his black velvet and silver brocade waistcoat, over his heart. "You engender confidence, compassion, loyalty, honor, love... What more could a parent want from a godfather for their infant?"

Alec caught Selina to him and kissed her, not caring they were in a public room full of people. "My dear Lady Halsey, and I thought you'd fallen in love with me because of my looks; your brother Talgarth calls me Apollo..."

Selina pressed herself against him. "Yes, but now that I have you all to myself—forever—it's what you have in your heart that matters most, and that's why you'll be all right, too." She rallied, saying cheekily, "But it is because you are the person you are, that I don't believe for a moment you will be happy counting your sheep. I'll wager the first letter that comes your way asking for your help, or seeking your advice, it will be 'Farewell Kent, and how may I help you, London?!' But this time it will be different—"

"—because you will be there right beside me in the carriage, helping too."

"Yes," she said softly, and kissed him again, placing his hand to her belly. "We both will..."

*— The End —.*

...until the Halsey family's next adventure in *Deadly Kin*.

Made in the USA
San Bernardino, CA
01 April 2018